Katie Agnew was b...... in E.......
spent her childhoo....................
English at Aberdeen....................
at City University i....................
features writer on 1....................
written articles, celeb....................
many magazines a....................
*Evening Standard, Co................. and the
Daily Mail.* She worked as features editor on *Marie
Claire* magazine before becoming a full-time author.
Katie now lives in Bath with her husband, John
Latimer and their daughter, Olivia. Her first novel,
Drop Dead Gorgeous, is also published by Corgi Books.

Acclaim for *Drop Dead Gorgeous*:

'This début novel has got it all – sex, scandal and
celebrity' *Sun*

'Read this for a flash of celeb glamour without the
hangover' *Cosmopolitan* (Book of the Month)

'There's drugs, sex, rock 'n' roll and heartbreaking
tragedy – and we loved every single juicy word of it!'
19 magazine

'Irresistible fun' *Woman's Own*

'A fantastic, powerhouse description of life in the fast
lane' *Irish Tatler*

'A deliciously funny insight into the world of celebrity
. . . the egos, the backstabbing and the heartbreak. She
writes with searing honesty' Liz Jones

www.booksattransworld.co.uk

Also by Katie Agnew

DROP DEAD GORGEOUS

and published by Corgi Books

BEFORE WE
WERE THIRTY

Katie Agnew

CORGI BOOKS

BEFORE WE WERE THIRTY
A CORGI BOOK: 0 552 14977 2

First publication in Great Britain

PRINTING HISTORY
Corgi edition published 2004

1 3 5 7 9 10 8 6 4 2

Copyright © Katie Agnew 2004

The right of Katie Agnew to be identified as the author of this
work has been asserted in accordance with sections 77 and 78 of
the Copyright Designs and Patents Act 1988.

All the characters in this book are fictitious,
and any resemblance to actual persons,
living or dead, is purely coincidental.

Condition of Sale
This book is sold subject to the condition that it shall not,
by way of trade or otherwise, be lent, re-sold, hired out or
otherwise circulated in any form of binding or cover other than
that in which it is published and without a similar condition
including this condition being imposed on the
subsequent purchaser.

Set in 10½/12pt Palatino
by Falcon Oast Graphic Art Ltd.

Corgi Books are published by Transworld Publishers,
61–63 Uxbridge Road, London W5 5SA,
a division of The Random House Group Ltd,
in Australia by Random House Australia (Pty) Ltd,
20 Alfred Street, Milsons Point, Sydney, NSW 2061, Australia,
in New Zealand by Random House New Zealand Ltd,
18 Poland Road, Glenfield, Auckland 10, New Zealand
and in South Africa by Random House (Pty) Ltd,
Endulini, 5a Jubilee Road, Parktown 2193, South Africa.

Printed and bound in Great Britain by
Cox & Wyman Ltd, Reading, Berkshire.

Papers used by Transworld Publishers are natural,
recyclable products made from wood grown in
sustainable forests. The manufacturing processes
conform to the environmental regulations
of the country of origin.

For John

Acknowledgements

Thanks to Diana and all the team at Transworld for believing in me and giving me this chance to 'live the dream'. To Lizzy, thanks for your constant support (especially when I almost lost my plot) and thank you, also, to everyone at Ed Victor for your help over the past couple of years. Thanks to my best school chums Wendy, Fiona and Clare for being there all those years ago when The Great Gatsby obsession began. Thanks to all my friends and especially to Jenny and Nancy for listening to me wittering on about this book. Shelley and Matt, thank you so much for taking us to Babington for 'research' and for your steam room story – much appreciated! To all the girls at Apple Tree Day Nursery, thank you so much for looking after Olivia and keeping her happy and safe while I work. And to Mum, Dad, Paddy, Heidi and Helen – thanks for taking her off my hands in times of crisis. To Olivia, thank you for being a good girl and not pressing the delete button when I was fifteen chapters in (I know you were tempted, darling). And finally, John, thanks for just being you and keeping me sane(ish). This one's for you, babe.

Chapter One

In the beginning

It started as a joke. A drunken, giggly, late after-noon joke during a loved-up weekend in Bath. It was the kind of spur-of-the-moment thing they did back then – before they were thirty – and neither of them thought for a moment about the con-sequences of such a silly little conversation, about how it would change the course of their lives for ever and how it might even drive them apart. Without the luxury of hindsight or the caution that comes with age, they jumped together off the highest cliff and waited to see where they would fall.

The way Rachel remembered it, it was all Simon's idea.

'I know, sweetheart,' he'd said, in the animated, enthusiastic way he'd had back then, when they were newlyweds. 'Let's look in that estate agent's over there. I bet we could get a great pad round here for the price of our flat.'

He was right. Simon was always right when it came to money. Wasn't he the one who'd bought an airy two-bedroomed mansion flat in Belsize Park just six months before the London housing market went berserk? And wasn't he the one responsible for the huge amount of equity they now had on paper, if not in the bank? And hadn't the clever boy gone and bought himself a little shoe box of an investment in Hoxton just before it became the most hip and happening address in London? He now rented it out to a trendy young photographer for over a grand a month. Yes, Simon was very clever when it came to all things financial. And Rachel? Well, according to Simon, Rachel was just very good at spending it. Predominantly on shoes.

A quick glance in the window of the estate agent's had showed that while they couldn't quite run to a Georgian townhouse, a four-bedroomed Victorian terrace with a 100-ft garden and views over the city could be theirs with some change left over.

'Wow!' Rachel had said, trying to focus through a fog of red wine. 'I could handle living there.'

'Or,' salivated Simon, pointing at a picture-perfect country cottage with roses round the door, 'we could do the whole rural idyll thing.'

'Oh, now that's gorgeous,' Rachel had said with gusto. 'Imagine living there.'

She'd read from the details in the window: ' "Grade II-listed, 200 years old, three double bedrooms, two reception rooms, study, kitchen/ breakfast room, many original features, including wooden beams and inglenook fireplaces – inglenook fireplaces! – Located in the heart of an

exclusive village in Wiltshire, six miles from Bath."
Six miles, that's nothing.'

'Ten minutes in the Land Rover, darling,' laughed Simon.

'Oh yes, we'd need a long wheel base,' agreed Rachel. 'And a black labrador, a couple of Barbours and some Hunter wellies.'

Simon had laughed at the thought of his chic and oh-so-fashionable little wife wearing countryside green rather than fashionista black. He shivered. It was October, and although Bath was basking in autumnal sunshine Simon was getting cold in his shirtsleeves.

'Shall we go and see the Roman baths now or do you fancy finding another pub?' he'd asked.

Rachel wrinkled her button nose. 'Pub?'

'Pub,' nodded Simon.

They had spent the rest of the afternoon snuggled up in a comfy booth, drinking whiskey and joking about their imaginary life as country bumpkins before staggering down to Bath Spa station and falling onto the last train to Paddington. It had been a lovely weekend.

The winter that followed was long, cold and dreary and had lasted well into April. As the rain drizzled constantly on their North London flat and Hampstead Heath turned into a mud bath, Simon and Rachel would often talk about the cottage in Wiltshire with the inglenook fireplaces and the roses round the door. It would be OK to be rained-in there, romantic even. How cosy to be curled up on the sofa, listening to the raindrops on the sash windows, watching the countryside turn green as spring arrived. But it was only a joke.

Sometimes on the Tube, on the way to her job as a fashion PR in Soho, Rachel would imagine cruising through the countryside in her 4x4, dog in the passenger seat and wellies in the back. She'd get so engrossed in her day dream that she'd forget about the elbows crushing her ribs and the smell of stale commuter on the Northern Line. Once she even missed her stop. But it was only a dream.

Work for Rachel was dull, dull, dull. Seven years earlier, after returning from her post-university year out (Thailand, India, Vietnam) she had accidentally fallen into a junior position in a small PR company through a friend of a friend of a friend. It had just been something to do in the short term to pay off her student loans while she decided what she really wanted to do with her life. Over the years, there had been promotions and pay rises, increased responsibility and even her own office, and then somehow, one day, it had become a career. But it wasn't her vocation. It was just something she did – rather brilliantly by all accounts – to help pay the bills.

In the meantime she'd met a dashing young advertising executive called Simon. He was the friend of a friend of a work colleague and he'd just come back to London after making his name in New York. They met at a party in Clapham and, although she'd been a bit merry by the time they actually exchanged numbers, Rachel thought he was the best-looking, most wonderful man she had ever met. Even Zoe, her cynical best friend,

12

admitted somewhat grudgingly that he was 'handsome in a well-bred, well-fed, Home Counties kind of way' and nice and kind because 'nothing bad had ever happened to him in his comfortable, middle-class existence'. Which was a vote of confidence of sorts. Rachel was certain that there were no chips on his broad shoulders or excess baggage on his muscular back. What you saw was what you got. And she liked what she saw a lot. Rachel had never felt as contented and relaxed as when she was with him.

'When I'm with Simon I feel as if I've found my "home",' she had gushed to Zoe.

'When I find a man with a luxury penthouse apartment overlooking the Thames then I'll know I've found *my* home,' Zoe had retorted.

If relationships were made or broken on public approval alone, then these two were in it for the long haul. His friends fancied hers and her friends flirted with his. Soon their two groups were permanently intertwined with various sub-relationships. Before long, Zoe started seeing Simon's best mate Anton, and the cosy twosome became an impenetrable foursome. Hell, even their parents approved. There were no silly games or infidelities in the early, uncertain stages of the relationship, and it made sense to everybody when Rachel moved into Simon's Belsize Park flat within six months of meeting him. Zoe might have complained more about losing her flatmate if Anton hadn't been moving in. When Simon proposed a year later, Rachel didn't even consider saying no. They married on a sunny Sunday in June in

Hampstead. The bride was raven-haired, tanned and petite, a vision in an ivory couture strapless dress (thanks to her enviable contacts in the fashion world). The men in the congregation secretly wished that they'd rodgered Rachel Rodgers before she'd become Rachel Travis. The single girls felt a pang of unrequited longing as Simon said 'I do' and his new mother-in-law said a little too loudly, 'Doesn't he look just like Cary Grant?'

Rachel was so delighted with her lot that she cried on and off all day without smudging her waterproof mascara. Simon thought he would explode with pride and couldn't wait to get his new wife into their hotel room that night so that he could rip her designer dress off and get his hands on her sexy little body. They honeymooned in the Maldives and returned to a flat full of state-of-the-art gadgets and tasteful soft furnishings, thanks to their Conran Shop wedding list. Life was good. For a while at least.

But about a year after the wedding Rachel became aware of a slight niggle of discontentment gnawing away at her perfect existence. She wasn't unhappy with her relationship. That was great. It was their London lifestyle that got her down. Life felt just a little bit boring and mundane.

'It's all too samey,' she'd explained to Zoe. 'Same office every day, same bars every night, same people, same tube journey, same flat . . .'

'Are you bored of us, babes?' Zoe had asked with a frown.

'No, no, no.' Rachel had backtracked, not wanting to hurt her friend's feelings. 'But maybe I'm a bit bored of London.'

Zoe had scoffed at that. 'What do they say? If you're bored of London, you're bored of life.' But then she'd never lived anywhere else and was fiercely loyal to her home city.

Rachel had spent her early childhood in leafy Surrey, making daisy chains in her parents' rambling garden and climbing trees in the surrounding fields. And although she'd left the relative peace and quiet of suburbia at a young age, she remembered those days with rose-tinted nostalgia. That's what she wanted for her kids, when she had them, not the noise and pollution of London. More and more, the city began to make her feel claustrophobic, and she craved wide open spaces. Being short didn't help. Sometimes, as she fought her way through the crowds on her way to Tottenham Court Road Tube station after work, Rachel was convinced she would be crushed to death by the seething masses. She wished she could see above their heads, beyond Centre Point, which loomed above her, and out to the world beyond. She felt as if the microcosm of her London existence was false and that while she fought for her personal space with a zillion other miserable commuters, real life was somehow going on beyond the M25.

Simon, being Simon, understood. He agreed that their long-term plan should be to leave London, have children and settle down somewhere less manic. In the meantime he provided his wife with short-term relief by whisking her out of London for little weekend breaks away from big-city living. And that's how they found themselves in Bath that autumn, full of whiskey and plans for the future.

* * *

As winter turned into spring, Rachel felt a stirring somewhere deep inside. It was a kind of squirmy, nauseous niggle.

'I feel weird,' she told Simon as she frantically de-iced the fridge with a bread knife. 'Kind of restless.'

'Shall we go away for the weekend then?' suggested Simon. They hadn't left London since they'd had a mini break in Prague in January. 'Where do you fancy?'

Rachel shrugged.

'How about Bath again. We could do some house hunting.'

Rachel put down the knife and looked up in excitement. 'Seriously?' she asked.

'Seriously,' nodded Simon. 'I've done my sums and, with both our salaries, the income from the Hoxton flat and last year's Christmas bonus, we can definitely stretch to a cottage in the country.'

'Just a lovely little something for the weekend,' mused Rachel happily.

'A house for the future,' Simon corrected her. 'Somewhere big enough for me, you and the rugby team of boys you're going to produce for me.'

'Oh, that sounds perfect,' said Rachel. 'Except we're having a chorus line of girlie girls, remember.'

She reached up to Simon, who was just over a foot taller, and snogged the face off him in sheer, unadulterated gratitude for the perfect life he'd given her. They celebrated with three bottles of red wine and a quick romp on the kitchen table. Then Rachel spent the night on the bathroom floor, sporadically throwing up into the toilet.

'You've turned into a lightweight,' said Simon the next morning as he kissed her clammy forehead goodbye. 'I'll call your office when I get to work and tell them you've got flu.'

'Thanks, darling,' croaked Rachel before crawling back to bed with the mother of all hangovers.

Rachel was still feeling sick three days later as they sat in a smart estate agency in central Bath. But she put the nausea down to the excitement of this, the ultimate shopping spree: buying a house.

George, the estate agent (or property executive as he liked to be known) had found three suitable properties in Bath's outlying villages. They jumped into his Mercedes and went on a magical mystery tour of the West Country. The former toll-house with rustic charm near Freshford was as delightful as George had promised, but there were only three bedrooms (one the size of an airing cupboard) and the ceilings were so low that Simon, at six foot two, had to stoop. It was almost big enough for a weekend bolthole, but it was never going to be a family home. What's more, the rain the night before had turned the driveway into a bog.

'Oh no, I've got mud all over my Jimmy Choos,' squealed Rachel.

It was a definite no no.

The second property, a charming double-fronted village house on the outskirts of Bradford-on-Avon, was much roomier, with four double bedrooms, a large kitchen with an Aga and a conveniently tarmacked drive. What's more it had been 'extensively upgraded by the current owners to provide a stylish family home'. But whatever way you looked at it, the house was on the main road to Trowbridge and shook every time a lorry drove by. It wasn't quite rural enough.

'I'd worry about the dog with that road,' said Rachel pensively.

'We haven't got a dog,' Simon reminded her.

'Yet,' said Rachel firmly. 'We haven't got a dog *yet*.'

On the way to the village of Combe (pronounced 'Coom', as George informed them), it started to rain again. But to Rachel the wet weather only added to the area's charm. In London, rain made her want to hibernate, but here it somehow brought the countryside to life. The fields and trees were so green that they dazzled her eyes and she had to put her Chanel shades on.

'Rachel,' Simon whispered loudly. 'It's pissing down. Take your sunglasses off. You're not on Bond Street now.'

'Oops,' giggled Rachel. 'I'm breaking the countryside code already.'

As George's Mercedes pulled into Chillyhill Lane, Rachel knew immediately that it was 'the one'. Just as she'd known Simon would be her future husband within five seconds of seeing his chiselled face, so she sensed that Ivy Cottage – 'a larger than average, characterful village home dating back to the 17th century in need of some updating' – would be hers.

'Wow! It's gorgeous,' she gushed, taking in the ivy-clad Cotswold-stone walls, leaded windows and roses round the door. Suddenly, Rachel had a vision of herself in a long, flowery skirt, carrying a gardening trug filled with roses. A dog trotted obediently at her ankles and an angelic toddler, who had walked straight out of a Baby Gap advert, played contentedly on the lawn. This, she was sure, was her future.

'Looks a bit dilapidated,' said Simon doubtfully, taking in the peeling paint work and cracked window panes. 'And God knows what damage that ivy's done to the brickwork.'

'The property is in need of some TLC,' George jumped in. 'But it's Grade II-listed and it has heaps of potential. Honestly, properties of this type very rarely come on the market. We only got the instruction yesterday and you're the third couple to have a look. Believe me, if you're interested you'll have to act quickly with this one.'

Rachel gave Simon a pleading look. She longed for this house.

'Let's have a look inside before you make an offer, sweetheart,' he said sensibly to his wife.

George had promised that the cottage was 'deceptively spacious' and for once the estate agent was telling the truth. The beamed ceilings were high enough for Simon to walk without stooping and all four bedrooms were of a reasonable size – even the attic room in the eaves was large enough to swing a good-sized cat. But Simon still had reservations.

'I can smell damp,' he explained to his starry-eyed wife, who was already perusing Farrow & Ball paint charts, mentally at least. 'And the bathroom's downstairs. There's no central heating and I really think we need somewhere with a second loo and a utility room.'

'The cottage offers flexible living accommodation,' insisted George. 'You could knock a few walls down to create a more open living space, move the bathroom upstairs perhaps, and if you look out here' – he kicked open the rotting French doors in the kitchen to reveal a deliciously overgrown cottage garden – 'you'll see that there are two outhouses attached to the main building which could be converted into a utility room and a second loo. All subject to planning permission, of course,' he mumbled quickly.

'Oh, he's so right,' enthused Rachel. 'It really is very versatile.'

'Now you're beginning to sound like an estate agent,' whispered Simon, out of George's earshot.

'Whatever,' said Rachel. 'Anyway, it's not going to be our full-time home yet, so it doesn't need to be perfect straight away. We'll be in London while the work's being done, so it won't get in our way, will it? Plus, it's twenty-five grand less than our budget.'

Rachel was already spending the extra money on Cath Kidston fabrics and Philippe Starck bathroom fittings.

'Our *maximum* budget, darling,' Simon reminded her. 'Just because we can spend it, doesn't mean we must spend it. I know that's a concept you find hard to grasp but—'

'But it means we can get a new kitchen, a new bathroom and have the garden done,' she continued enthusiastically. Rachel was a level-headed woman, but she did have a stubborn streak and her heels were already beginning to dig into the kitchen's flagstone floor.

'This garden is south facing, right?' called out Simon, stepping over brambles towards George, who was trying to locate the well promised on the property's particulars. 'So it gets good sunlight when it's not raining.'

'Oh yes,' promised George.

'But doesn't this hedge cast a shadow?'

George, Simon and Rachel looked up at the 20 foot beech hedge at the back of the garden.

'Oh no,' lied George.

'What's behind there?' asked Rachel, curiously. She could just make out the tip of a turret above the hedge.

'The Beeches,' said George with grave pomposity. 'Lord and Lady Lilywhite Smythe live there, so there's no need to worry about the neigh-bours. Fnar, fnar. Actually, this cottage and the one across the lane, Daisy Cottage, used to belong to the manor house – for the staff.'

'Don't they have staff any more?' asked Rachel.

'Oh yes, they still have a number of staff,' explained George, proud to be so knowledgeable about the local landed gentry. 'But they don't live in the village these days. They can't afford it.'

'Friends of yours, are they, the Lilywhite Smythes?' asked Simon mischievously, knowing full well that there was no way a jumped-up estate agent would hang out at The Beeches, even in his wildest dreams.

George shuffled his shiny loafers amongst the brambles sheepishly. 'No, I don't know them as such,' he admitted. 'But one does read about them in society magazines from time to time. Not that I read those magazines, you understand, it's my wife; she leaves them in the bathroom. Anyway, have I told you about the well. It's here somewhere.'

Over dinner that evening, Rachel and Simon discussed Ivy Cottage.

'Please can we buy it, Si?' pleaded Rachel. 'I really love it and I don't think I'll ever find a house like that again, and what if someone else puts in an offer first. Oh my God, I'd be gutted, but we could guzump them, couldn't we, and—'

'Sweetheart,' said Simon patiently. 'You've only spent half an hour of your life in the place, you can't be *that* emotionally attached to it.'

'Oh, please,' she continued. 'It spoke to me.'

'What, like those Gucci boots I bought you for Christmas? They spoke to you too and you've only worn them once,' Simon was teasing her, but affectionately. He didn't mind pandering to her shoe fetish. But he wasn't about to part with over a quarter of a million pounds on one of Rachel's whims.

'I do like it,' continued Simon. 'And the village itself is picture perfect – great pub, village shop, cricket pitch. Maybe I could start playing again in the summer,' he pondered. 'I played in the firsts at school, have I told you?'

'You might have mentioned it once or twice,' teased Rachel.

'OK, you win,' said Simon. 'I'll get Gavin over here to have a look and, provided he thinks it's

22

a sound investment, we'll put in an offer. Happy?'

'Ecstatic.' Rachel lifted her glass of Chianti in celebration.

Simon's younger brother was a newly qualified architect with skipfulls of enthusiasm and a million bright ideas. One phone call from his brother and he abandoned Notting Hill, jumped in his lime-green Beetle and zipped along the M4 to Bath.

'It's not exactly my cup of tea, Bro,' said Gavin as he took in the crumbling cottage. 'It's very pretty and all that, but I'm more of a loft-living kind of guy, you know what I mean?'

Rachel and Simon knew what he meant. Gavin was all baggy jeans hanging off his bum and trainers imported from Japan. He had his eyebrow pierced and several tattoos. Gav was only four years younger than Si, and the brothers were very alike physically, but their outlook on life, not to mention their dress sense, belonged to different generations entirely. Rachel secretly quite fancied her brother-in-law. He had a slightly dangerous edge that nice-guy Simon lacked. She guessed that Gavin probably did quite a lot of drugs and had very dirty sex with edgy young girls in the grubby toilets of east London nightclubs at four o'clock in the morning. Simon, on the other hand, drank quite a lot of champagne and made multi-million-pound advertising deals with Chanel-suited American women in expensive restaurants in Belgravia in the middle of the afternoon.

There was an inch of naked flesh visible directly above Gavin's low-slung jeans where his mis-shapen T-shirt didn't quite meet his boxer shorts.

Rachel suddenly realized she'd been staring at this taut, slightly hairy bit of skin for quite some time. Thankfully both brothers were too busy surveying the property to notice her letching. As Gavin ran his fingers through his Hoxton fin, Rachel sighed to herself gently with a shiver of never-to-be-requited longing.

'I'm more into modern industrial-style design than all this period business, man,' Gav spoke very slowly, as if permanently stoned. 'But you know what, Bro? I think I could do something with this.'

'Gavin,' said Simon bluntly. 'I don't want you to do anything with it. I just want your opinion on the building. Is it about to fall down? Will I get planning permission to move the bathroom? Should I knock down this wall? That sort of thing.'

'Oh.' Gavin looked disappointed. 'I could really have fused ancient with modern here. You know what I mean, man?'

Rachel and Simon didn't have a clue what he meant.

Their offer was accepted on Tuesday morning. Simon was in New York on business, so Rachel celebrated with Zoe and several Caipirinhas in Soho House.

'You'll have to become a member at Babington House,' advised Zoe.

'Babington House?' asked Rachel blankly.

Zoe looked at her friend as if she just got off the boat from deepest, darkest Peru.

'Duh. Soho House in the country. Haven't you heard of it? I went to a wedding there last summer, remember. Hilary and Jeremy? The designers.'

24

'Vaguely,' said Rachel.

'I wore that red, D&G dress,' prompted Zoe. 'Anton got trolleyed and tried to snog one of the bridesmaids. Oh, you must remember, I was traumatized for weeks.'

Rachel nodded. 'I remember now. Anton swears he wasn't trying to snog her he just got his bow tie caught in her tiara.'

'Yeah, whatever. Anyway,' continued Zoe. 'Babington was *way* cool. And it's near Bath somewhere, so you'll have to join. I mean, you won't want to go to the village pub, will you? It'll be full of old people in flat caps who smell of manure.'

Zoe was born and bred in Wandsworth. She didn't really *do* the country. Except for weddings, of course. Rachel and Zoe had been best friends since for ever. Or at least since 1984, when Rachel's parents bought the townhouse next to Zoe's parents on Wandsworth Common. Rachel had moved from a commuter town in Surrey, so was pretty 'out of things' in Zoe's opinion. Zoe made it her duty to transform her new neighbour into a cool, happening London chick and had been meddling in Rachel's affairs ever since. The only reason that Rachel had done her degree in Brighton was because Zoe had convinced her that 'Brighton really rocks – great clubs, gorgeous men, cool people'. She'd been right but, unfortunately, all the gorgeous men had been gay. Not that Rachel minded Zoe's meddling. Zoe was her best friend. She had a right to interfere. And anyway, Rachel's flair for fashion would never have blossomed had it not been for the gay men she'd met as a student.

Some people, Simon in particular, were baffled by Rachel and Zoe's friendship. It appeared to work like this – Rachel was a supportive, nurturing, ego-boosting friend to Zoe, while Zoe spent much of her time insulting Rachel with catty comments and hurtful digs. It had always been that way. But Rachel knew that, deep down, Zoe loved her. She was just prickly and defensive and scared of being hurt. Her dad had left when she was a baby and her mum had been too busy trying to scrape by to give any of her three children much attention. Over the years, Zoe had developed a hard shell and a permanent sneer to ward off the world. She was determined not to let anyone get too close. But Rachel was well aware that Zoe depended on their friendship. It had been the most stable, permanent relationship in her life.

'You're not going to move away properly, though, are you?' Zoe asked with a worried expression. 'I mean, I think you might get a bit bored.'

'God no,' lied Rachel. She hadn't plucked up the courage to tell Zoe her long-term plans. 'We'll just use it for weekends and holidays and stuff. There are four bedrooms, so we can all go down – you and Anton, me and Si, and anyone else who wants to tag along. The whole crew. Can you imagine? We can drink Pimms in the garden in summer and Baileys in front of a real fire at Christmas.'

'Thank God for that,' said Zoe. 'I had a horrible vision of you in one of those hideous Driza-Bone coats for a moment there. It was quite scary. Drink?'

Rachel said yes please, even though she was beginning to feel sick again.

* * *

Rachel rummaged in her handbag for the cigarettes she'd bought the night before. She awkwardly lit a cigarette on the gas hob, singeing her hair as she did so, and returned to the bathroom in a cloud of smoke. She paced the tiled floor impatiently, sneaking furtive glances at the offending white tube that mocked her from its perch on the side of the bath. Rachel willed the second line not to appear. She screwed her eyes up really tightly and prayed to any God that would listen.

'Please don't let me be pregnant. Please, please, please,' she pleaded.

The cigarette made her feel sick but she persevered. She needed something to do with her hands while she waited for the seconds to tick away on her watch face. Eventually, it was time. Rachel threw the fag into the sink and picked up the pregnancy test. It shook in her hand. Slowly, very slowly, she had a peek. There, as bold as the first, was a second blue line. She shut her eyes to make it disappear. Then she opened them and checked the box. She read the instructions very slowly and out loud, so as to be sure she'd got it right.

'If a second blue line appears then the test result is positive. Bollocks!'

Rachel tore open the second test from the box and tried to squeeze out another pee. She managed to produce a dribble. Then she redid the entire process: light cigarette, pace nervously, pray, quick peek, definite blue line, re-read the box, bollocks!

She burst into tears.

'I don't want to be pregnant,' she wailed to the

empty bathroom. 'I'm too young.' Rachel was almost 29. Yes, she'd always wanted children, sometime in the vague and distant future, but not now. Now was way too soon. Way too scary.

Rachel walked on shaky legs to the kitchen and poured herself a glass of red wine. It was an automatic response to any shock. She had gulped down half the glass before she realized she shouldn't be drinking in her condition, or smoking, or having any sort of irresponsible fun at all.

She poured the wine down the kitchen sink, slithered into a heap on the kitchen floor and stared numbly at the wall. It was at this exact moment that Simon chose to arrive home from New York.

'Rachel!' he bellowed from the front door. 'I'm home . . . What's that smell?'

Nobody ever smoked in their pristine flat – at Rachel's insistence – so no one could blame Simon for being a little taken aback by the cloud of smoke that hit him as he walked in. He found his wife, slouched on the kitchen floor with a shell-shocked expression on her face.

'Rachel, what's going on? You've been smoking? You don't smoke,' said Simon, scratching his head.

'I do,' pouted Rachel. 'Sometimes.'

'Yeah, but only when you're out with Zoe, totally legless and completely beyond rational thinking. You don't smoke in the middle of the day in our flat.'

Rachel shrugged. 'It was an emergency.'

'Rach, you thought Gavin should pay for the curtains to be dry-cleaned last time he smoked in this flat. You're being really weird. What's going on?'

'I'm pregnant,' she blurted out.

Simon's legs buckled slightly and, for a split second, he looked as though he'd been slapped around the face with a large fish.

'Pregnant,' he repeated as if the word were completely alien to him. 'What do you mean, pregnant?'

'It means,' replied Rachel solemnly, 'that in approximately eight months' time we're going to have a baby. What's more, in the months leading up to that monumental event, I'm going to get enormously fat, develop varicose veins and stretch marks.'

'But how?' Simon dropped his holdall on the kitchen floor and slithered down onto the floor next to his wife. 'How did you get pregnant?'

Rachel rolled her eyes. 'How do you think, Si? I haven't been abducted by aliens in the night, and no angels have visited me, proclaiming the arrival of the second messiah, so I assume it happened when you and I had sex at some point.'

'But we're always so careful,' he insisted. 'Since you stopped taking the pill we've always, *always* used condoms.'

They stared at each other blankly, both at a loss to recall the moment of conception, and then, simultaneously, the penny dropped.

'Zoe's birthday,' they announced in unison.

Five weeks earlier, Zoe had turned thirty and Anton had arranged a suitably glamorous celebration for his girlfriend's 'coming of old age' (as she put it). Anton worked for a City bank who owned, amongst many other status symbols, a rather ostentatious boat which was moored on the Thames in Chelsea. If an employee made the company enough money, he or she would be awarded with one night's free use of the vessel. Anton had recently made the deal of the decade, and so Zoe's party took place on the water. The boat had been decorated with balloons, streamers and banners, supplied with enough delicious canapés to feed a battalion of marines and laden with enough bottles of champagne to sink a battleship. The boat had been fully staffed and the dress code was 'glitzy and glam'.

Zoe did not disappoint her guests. She wore a silver satin dress, four-inch heels and a white feathered headdress in her peroxide blonde crop. Only Rachel had upstaged her – by accident, as always – in a scarlet floor-length gown, large gold hoop earrings and a rose in her jet-black hair. She'd looked like a gypsy queen, and when she'd stepped onto the boat behind Zoe, all eyes had been on the best friend rather than the birthday girl. This fact was not lost on Zoe. It never was. Zoe would spend hours carefully choosing her outfit, applying her mask of make-up and blow-drying her hair, while Rachel would just throw something on at the last minute, add a dollop of mascara and a smudge of lippie, run her hand through her hair and there she was, the belle of every ball. Zoe was attractive in a well-groomed way. She was not really a natural beauty but years of careful shopping, highlighting and working out had made the most of what nature had provided. Rachel, on the other hand, had been blessed with the kind of good looks that don't require make-up or good lighting. Rachel could stumble into bed at 2 a.m. and wake up five hours later with mascara smeared over her face and *still* look beautiful. It made Zoe want to spit.

The girls had drunk and shimmied, gossiped and giggled in the comfortable, if unconventional, manner they'd developed over almost two decades.

'You look gorgeous,' Rachel had said to Zoe. 'That dress is fabulous on you.'

'Thanks, babes,' Zoe had replied. 'Yours is nice too, but I think you should have got it in a bigger size. Have you put on weight?'

Rachel had glanced down at her almost flat stomach and shrugged.

'Maybe a little bit,' she'd replied cheerfully. 'But it's winter, and we all need a bit of extra padding in the cold weather.' Unlike Zoe, Rachel was not particularly vain.

Simon and Anton had propped up the bar and watched their women boogie. Simon had smiled happily at the scene, proud to be Rachel's husband, knowing full well that every man on the boat would have swapped his Christmas bonus to be in his Gucci loafers. Anton knew it too. And he knew how hard it was for Zoe to always be second best. He'd watched the girls over the years and he'd listened to Zoe's drunken rantings about how Rachel was so perfect and how she'd never come close. Zoe would never have said those things to Rachel, but she said them back home, in their flat, at the end of the night when she was drunk and tired and emotional.

31

He always told her she was wrong, but in a way he knew she was right. Facts were facts – Rachel was prettier in a conventional way, kinder, definitely, and probably easier to love. Zoë had always been more of a challenge but over time Anton had started to love her, jagged edges and all. Mind you, Rachel was very easy on the eye. He watched his girlfriend's best friend jiggle her curvy little body and sighed to himself. He'd never been tempted to touch, but he did like to look.

Rachel had beamed at Simon and Anton and shaken her butt to the music.

'She's quite a mover, Rachel,' Anton had mused. 'Puts Beyoncé to shame.'

'Zoe's not bad, either,' Simon had added charitably, without taking his eyes off his wife. Rachel was always the best dancer on any dance floor.

Zoe meanwhile, desperately tried to copy Rachel's moves, and was doing a moderately good job, but while Rachel laughed and tossed her long hair, enjoying the music, Zoe wore a studied frown of concentration. She'd glanced up just in time to catch Anton eyeing up Rachel and her cheeks burned with indignation. She knew he had a crush on her; it was embarrassingly obvious.

Every now and then Zoe would trip over her stilettos, blush and look over to the boys, to make sure they hadn't seen her mistake. But it was Simon, not Anton, she was trying to impress. Despite the fact that she constantly put him down to Rachel, Zoe adored Simon. Not in a platonic, best-mate's-husband kind of way, but in the Biblical sense. The fact was, she had seen him first. She'd been the one who'd had the nerve to approach him and start chatting. Rachel had just sat there, fluttering her obscenely long eyelashes and flicking her glossy hair. Zoe had done all the leg work, but it was Rachel's number he'd asked for at the end of the night. In time, Zoe had come to terms with the fact that Rachel had won the man, but Zoe was still determined to win the war. Eventually she'd settled for Anton, but the truth was that Zoe still loved Simon.

'Let's dance on the tables,' Rachel had proclaimed, pert buttocks jiggling.

The boat had lurched down the Thames and Zoe had tripped over Rachel's long dress.

'OK,' she'd said, uncertainly.

Rachel had hopped gracefully onto a table and started doing a faux pole dance. Zoe had clambered up after her and tried to join in, but her shoes were too high and the boat swayed too much and she'd had too much champagne to balance. As Rachel had danced, Zoe had fallen flat on her face on the grimy dance floor, and when she'd stood up her beautiful dress had been covered in beer stains and cigarette ash.

'Are you OK, darling?' Rachel had asked, jumping off the table to help her best friend. 'Shall I help you wash your dress in the loos?'

'No, I'm fine,' Zoe had snapped. 'Just leave me alone.' Before storming off towards the deck.

Anton had scurried after her, leaving Rachel and Simon alone.

'What have I done now?' Rachel had asked with a confused frown.

'You don't have to *do* anything, darling,' Simon had answered, shaking his head at Zoe's retreating back. 'She's just jealous of you.'

'Don't be silly,' Rachel had scoffed. 'That's nonsense.'

Simon watched as a drop of perspiration meandered its way down Rachel's neck, over her collar bone and then disappeared into her cleavage. His wife was so sexy that it was no wonder Zoe was jealous.

'You look extra hot tonight, Rach,' Simon had panted into her ear. 'I think I might need some fresh air to cool me off.'

Rachel had laughed and grabbed her husband's hand, leading him out into the cold winter night. It had been a clear, starry evening, and as the couple arrived on deck, the boat was just passing the London Eye.

'Isn't it beautiful,' Rachel had exclaimed. 'London looks best from the river.'

Simon and Rachel found a quiet spot at the back of the boat and leaned against a life boat. Simon's hand had found flesh under Rachel's dress and he sighed as he felt the velvety softness of her skin. Rachel giggled under his touch. She was drunk and giddy and excited.

'I haven't got a condom,' Simon had whispered.

Rachel had been taken off the pill a couple of months earlier after suffering from migraines.

'Never mind,' Rachel had shrugged. 'We can still be careful.'

But, of course, they hadn't been careful. Not nearly careful enough.

* * *

Rachel and Simon sat on the kitchen floor in shocked silence.

'A baby,' said Simon after a while. 'We're going to have a baby.'

'A real live, crying, breathing, pooing, puking baby,' Rachel added.

'It's what we wanted,' Simon reminded himself and Rachel, but he didn't sound convinced. 'It's just sooner than we'd planned.'

Rachel turned round and looked at her husband with huge, scared eyes. 'I'm not sure I'm ready,' she whispered.

Simon pulled her towards him and kissed the top of her head. 'We'll be OK,' he promised, uncertainly. 'It's just a bit of a shock, that's all. We'll be brilliant parents.'

'Do you think?' Rachel bit her wobbly bottom lip.

'I know it,' he replied, but he wasn't sure. He wasn't sure at all.

'Pregnant?' said Anton, incredulously, when Simon told him the news. 'Shit! That's a bit of a bombshell.'

'It is,' agreed Simon, sipping his beer and lounging comfortably on Anton and Zoe's leather couch. 'But we've kind of got our heads around it now and it'll be cool.'

'Aren't you scared, mate?' asked Anton. He peered at Simon over the top of his wire-rimmed glasses. 'I mean, getting hitched was a brave move, but babies, that's serious stuff. It's like, really grown-up.'

35

'I know.' Simon grinned. 'But it's about time we all started acting like adults.'

Anton shrugged. 'If you say so, Si,' he pondered. 'Fancy a game on the PlayStation?'

'Good idea,' enthused Simon like an overgrown ten-year-old. 'But I want to be James Bond.'

Zoe was struggling to take in the news of Rachel's pregnancy. The wedding had been difficult enough, with all the shopping for gorgeous dresses, planning dream honeymoons, organizing hen weekends in exclusive health spas and having to do the whole chief bridesmaid thing. Not to mention the fact that she was secretly in love with the groom. The 'Big Day' had been painful for Zoe. She'd walked up the aisle behind Rachel, taking in Simon's beaming face as he'd spotted his radiant bride-to-be. When he'd said, 'I do', she could tell he meant it right down to the tips of his toes and she'd stood there, next to the happy couple, trying to let go of the feelings she had for him, knowing they were wrong, but still wishing that she could be Mrs Travis. Meanwhile Anton, the best man, had been closely watching his girlfriend for signs of unrequited love. He'd long since suspected that Zoe had the hots for Simon and when he watched her face fall as the vows were said, he knew he was right.

When the wedding photos were printed, Rachel had noticed that both Zoe and Anton were wearing rather strained smiles. 'I think they must have fallen out and not wanted to tell us in case they ruined the day,' she'd said to Simon. 'Nah,' Simon had mocked. 'Zoe was probably just heartbroken that I was off the market and Anton, well, Anton always looks like that.' Rachel had laughed at her new husband.

And now Rachel and Simon were having a baby. It was the end of an era for them all. Zoe knew that the minute that little embryo had implanted itself in Rachel's womb, their friendship had changed for ever. Rachel would be far too busy with her own life from now on to continue pandering to Zoe's.

Oh, she'd put on a brave face, as Rachel had excitedly told her the news in the pub after work. Christ, she'd known something was up when Rach had ordered an orange juice. That was a revelation in itself. She'd tried really hard to bite her tongue and stop anything nasty escaping from her mouth. But it was difficult to just sit there and watch Rachel glow with excitement.

'Ugh!' she'd said. 'You'll get stretch marks and your boobs will sag. And I've heard that almost everybody does a poo when they give birth.'

Rachel had sat there for a moment with a horrified look on her face, and then she'd giggled and replied, 'Oh well, it's Simon who'll be at the end where all the action takes place. I won't be able to see a thing. And I plan on having so much pain relief that I won't be able to feel anything from the neck down.'

Rachel always took Zoe's insults so well. Never once had she said, 'Actually, Zoe, that was really out of line. Shut up.' It was all it would have taken to make Zoe stop, and the truth was that Zoe had been expecting a backlash for years. But Rachel understood the game. Zoe was insecure. She said nasty things to test Rachel's loyalty to her. If Rachel took it, as she always did, it meant that she really loved her. If she ever stood up for herself, it would mean game over and Zoe would be left alone, just as she always suspected she would be.

Zoe played the same game with Anton, but with less success. She had quickly learned that Anton wouldn't take any shit. If she put him down he would just say, 'Well go, if I'm not good enough for you. I'll survive.' And Zoe was sure he would. He was very smart and sociable and fun to have around. Plus he was a good-looking guy in a slightly nerdy way. He was a little too tall at six foot four, and a little too thin. But he had floppy black hair which he was always tossing out of his dark eyes in the cutest possible way, and underneath his crisp City-boy shirts was a torso so toned it made Zoe want to weep. Oh, he wasn't in Simon's league – Simon was Batman and Anton was Robin – but she was sure, deep down, that he was too good for her. She would lose him too. Eventually. In the meantime she continued pushing him away, testing him, waiting to see how much he'd take before he proved her right and walked away.

Zoe let herself into the flat and found Anton and Simon playing on the PlayStation. They had met up straight from work and both wore expensive suits and shiny Italian shoes. Anton's glasses made him look older and more responsible than he actually was. But the men were lying on their stomachs in front of the TV, kicking their legs excitedly behind them and punching each other playfully on the arm as they shot at each other on screen. Zoe could see quite clearly the little boys in thirty-something bodies on her living-room floor.

'Hello, love,' said Anton cheerfully. 'Good day?'

'It was OK,' replied Zoe flatly.

'Hi, Zoe,' called Simon without turning round.

She felt the usual pang of disappointment when Simon failed to notice her.

'Oh bollocks! You shot me in the nads,' exclaimed Anton.

'Game over,' said Simon cheerfully. 'I am victorious.'

The men sat up and faced Zoe.

'Has Rachel told you our news?' asked Simon excitedly. 'It's amazing, isn't it? I'm going to be a daddy.'

Zoe nodded. 'Congratulations,' she said coldly before disappearing into the bedroom and closing the door.

'What's up with her?' asked Simon.

Anton shrugged. 'Ignore her,' he said. 'She's being a right moody cow at the moment.'

'You must have done something wrong,' said Simon. 'She's huffing and you've got to guess why.'

'Probably.' Anton sighed. 'But I can't be bothered with all these games.'

'Maybe she wants you to propose,' suggested Simon.

Anton frowned. 'God, I hope not. I'm not getting married. Not now. Not to Zoe.'

'No?'

'No way. I've told you, I'm saving myself for Kylie.'

'Of course,' Simon remembered grinning. 'Zoe's just a filler until Ms Minogue is ready for you.'

'Exactly.'

Simon turned to Anton and looked serious for a moment. 'You shouldn't mess her around, though, if you're not serious. I know she's a bit...' he searched for the word.

'Of a nightmare?' suggested Anton.

'No, I was going to say touchy,' replied Simon. 'But, you know, I hear stuff from Rachel, and Zoe's not had an easy time of it. You mustn't string her along.'

'I'm not,' insisted Anton. 'Zoe and me, we're fine. I know I take the piss out of her moodiness sometimes, but I do like her – a lot. Christ, I probably even love the mardy mare. She's a great girl, she's got a lot going for her – she's sexy and funny and she gives the best blow job in the whole damn world, but I'm not sure she's "the one". I'm not her dream man either. That I *am* sure of.'

Simon scratched his head. He loved Rachel so much that he couldn't understand his best friend's so-so relationship. What was the point in hanging around if she wasn't 'the one'.

'Why do you stay with her?' he asked. 'If there's no future?'

'Because,' said Anton, flicking his hair out of his spectacles. 'She's an animal in bed.'

'Really?' asked Simon.

'Really,' confirmed Anton. 'Why do you think I'm always so knackered? She's a three-times-a-night girl, and the imagination she uses. Jesus! She's taught me positions the *Karma Sutra* didn't think of.

40

Must be all that yoga. Right, you ready to have your ass whipped, boy?'

The men turned back onto their stomachs and began a new game, but Simon couldn't concentrate. He kept thinking about Anton and Zoe's sex life. Why wasn't Rachel an animal in bed, he wondered. He thought best girlfriends shared everything, particularly sex tips.

Chapter Two

You're not from round here,
are you?

Harriet thought she would die of boredom if she had to stay at home a moment longer. Her father had refused to fund a shopping and sunbathing trip to LA (so unfair), none of her friends were in London at the moment, so she couldn't escape there, and even her mother wasn't at home in Chew Magna, having recently met a new (and much younger) man who had spirited her off to Florence to look at art galleries. Even her favourite horse, Monty, had abandoned her – off to Worcestershire on stud duties. How depressing, both her middle-aged mother and her pet were getting more action than she was. It was time for drastic measures. Phoning Bianca Mills was not something Harriet would normally consider, but she had to do *something*, and she needed somebody to do it with. Even if that somebody was a Glaswegian airhead with breasts the size of pumpkins and a brain the size of a pea.

'Oh hello Hattie,' sing-songed Bianca in her annoyingly cheery, high-pitched voice. 'What can I do you for?'

'I'm bored,' stated Harriet flatly. 'I want to go shopping in Bath and I need you to come with me.'

'Well, you see, Hattie, the thing is I've just promised the twins that I'd do some finger-painting with them.'

'Can't TJ do that?' snapped Harriet. 'I mean, it's not as if he's working or anything. He's been waiting for a new record deal since 1987, so it's unlikely "the call" will come this afternoon. I don't know why you two don't have a nanny anyway.'

'Oh come on now, we've been through this before, you know we believe in raising our children ourselves.'

'But you can get those little Eastern European girls so cheaply these days,' continued Harriet.

Bianca ignored her views on getting 'help' and said, 'Look, I'll just get these two started with their painting and then TJ can take over. Give me an hour, OK? Shall we take my new car?'

'If we must,' agreed Harriet ungratefully. 'But we'll look like a couple of footballer's wives. I shall have to wear a disguise.'

She was unable to drive herself, thanks to a nine-month ban for drink driving. In fact, it was fortunate for Harriet that the police hadn't thought to test her blood for anything else. She'd been under the influence of a lot more than alcohol on the afternoon in question. She'd only been arrested after someone reported seeing a silver Audi TT driving across Richmond Park, off road so to speak, and narrowly missing a herd of deer. Had it not been for the busybody who'd shopped her, she'd be able to drive herself into town without needing the taxi services of Bianca Mills and her ridiculously flashy tartmobile.

Fifty-five minutes and thirteen different outfits later, Harriet Lilywhite Smythe was impatiently pacing the sweeping driveway of The Beeches. Her handsome English pointer, Moriarty, paced obediently behind her. A screeching of brakes and a crunching of gravel hailed the arrival of Bianca Mills in her brand-new black Porsche. She did an emergency stop inches away from Harriet's toes and beamed a toothy smile. Harriet squeezed her tall frame into the passenger seat of the tiny sports car as Moriarty squeezed his long limbs into the back seat beside Bianca's Scottie dog, Jock. They growled half-heartedly at each other. The dogs had a similar relationship to their owners – they tolerated each other begrudgingly because, quite frankly, there was nobody else to hang out with in Combe, but there was no real love lost between the pair.

'Don't you just love the car?' asked Bianca enthusiastically.

'It reminds me of your husband,' said Harriet haughtily, taking in the bright-red leather interior.

Bianca cocked her head quizzically.

'The styling is a bit Eighties for my taste,' explained Harriet in her most patronizing tone.

'Oh,' said Bianca in a small voice.

Harriet firmly believed that Bianca's driving was worse when she was sober than Harriet's was when she was drunk. The Porsche skidded down the drive and pulled out onto Chillyhill Lane at breakneck speed, much to the disgust of a passing tractor. Bianca raced down the lane, chattering about her twins' relative successes and failures with potty training while Harriet stared out of the window and tried to ignore Bianca's witterings.

'And then Poppy put the potty on her head . . .'

'Stop!' shouted Harriet suddenly.

'Oh God, am I being a baby bore again?' blushed Bianca.

'No,' said Harriet. 'Well, yes, of course you are, but that's not what I mean. I mean stop as in stop the car.'

'Why?' asked Bianca, slamming on the brakes so dramatically that both dogs banged their noses on the seats in front.

'Because there are people moving into Ivy Cottage. Young people,' said Harriet with a glint in her eye.

'Young people? What, young as in under fifty?' asked Bianca in disbelief.

Harriet nodded. 'That's what it looked like.'

'Oh my God,' giggled Bianca, crunching the gears into reverse. 'How very exciting.'

'It's a bloody miracle,' added Harriet.

The Porsche reversed past Ivy Cottage at speed and then crawled very slowly back down the lane. Rachel and Simon looked up from their struggle with Alfie's cot and could see, quite clearly, the open mouths of two very glamorous young women.

'You're not from round 'ere, are you?' said Simon to Rachel in a lame local-yokel accent.

'Oi, don't make me laugh while I'm carrying a heavy load,' warned Rachel. 'I might prolapse.'

Harriet and Bianca watched their new neighbours for a moment.

'Damn it, they've got a brat,' huffed Harriet, spotting Alfie's buggy parked on the front path.

'Oh brilliant,' enthused Bianca. 'We could do with some more young mums round here.'

'He's quite handsome,' perked up Harriet, taking in Simon's square jaw. 'But she makes Vanessa Feltz look skinny. I wonder what he's doing with her.'

'She's not fat,' said Bianca gently.

'She's obese,' insisted Harriet.

'Don't be silly, Hattie. She's just had a baby,' cooed Bianca sympathetically as she spotted Rachel lifting two-month-old Alfie out of his pram. 'Oh, isn't he adorable?'

'I can't see,' snapped Harriet. 'He's completely smothered in blankets. Anyway, all babies look the same – their faces are all red and squashed. They always remind me of aging alcoholics.'

'No they don't. Anyway, the twins looked completely different when they were born. Lotte had this cute little dimple on her chin, just like TJ, and Poppy—'

'Yeah, whatever,' yawned Harriet. 'OK, bored with the new neighbours, let's go shopping now.'

The Porsche disappeared back down Chillyhill Lane in a cloud of dust.

'The natives don't look very friendly,' said Rachel nervously.

'Very pretty though.' Simon grinned.

'And rich,' added Rachel.

For the first time, Rachel wondered whether moving to Combe had been a good idea.

It was three weeks before Rachel met her two glamorous neighbours properly. She had spotted the flash black Porsche whizzing past her living-room window several times, but it was always going too fast to focus on the occupants. With Simon back in London during the week, Rachel spent her days breastfeeding Alfie, hour after hour, and watching the slow pace of village life unfold. She hadn't actually spoken to anybody, except the rosy-cheeked old lady in the village shop who kept her supplied with chocolate Hobnobs, but she did feel like an expert in the daily rituals of the inhabitants of Combe. Rachel had become a silent spy, perched at her window, quietly taking in her new surroundings and gradually falling into a pit of depression. She missed Simon, and his bear hugs in particular. She missed Zoe, although perhaps not her catty comments. She missed the buzz of London if not the pollution. She even missed her job – the one she used to loathe – but most of all she missed Rachel, the person she used to be before she was Alfie's mother.

Nine months of pregnancy had not prepared her for life as a new mum. She hadn't slept for more than two hours in the past two months without being dragged from her dreams by the penetrating screams of a hungry baby. Nobody had warned her that it would now take three hours to get out of the front door just to pop to the corner shop. By the time she'd changed Alfie's nappy, wrapped him up snugly, struggled with the preposterous three-wheel buggy that Simon had insisted on buying, packed the emergency baby bag full of nappies, wipes, clean clothes for Alfie, bibs, muslins and breast pads, Alfie would invariably decide he needed another breastfeed. The feed would take anything from twenty minutes to two hours and would always result in another nappy change being required before the whole process of trying to leave the house could begin again. It was little wonder Rachel hadn't ventured further than the village shop on foot and that she had only used her new car once for an ill-fated trip to Tesco in Trowbridge, which had culminated in tears – both Alfie's and Rachel's – in the frozen-food section.

It had all seemed like such a good idea: Rachel would work until the baby was born and then spend a couple of months in the flat in London coming to terms with motherhood before moving to Ivy Cottage permanently. After a few hiccups with the local planning department, the house had been fully renovated by local builders during the summer of the previous year and they'd been down there a few times for weekends with their friends. Everyone had agreed that Ivy Cottage would be a lovely place to raise a baby, especially now that it had a sparkly new bathroom and a kitchen diner. Only Zoe disapproved.

'I think you'll be bored shitless,' she'd warned Rachel. 'You'll wish you'd stayed in London, got a nanny and gone back to work.'

Rachel hadn't wanted to go back to work. She'd decided she wanted to be there for her baby's first smile, first word, first step. It wasn't as if her job had been her life or anything and she'd been sure she wouldn't miss it. Simon had had a promotion and they could afford to give up Rachel's salary. There wouldn't have been much of her wages left at the end of each month anyway if they'd chosen to pay the ridiculous costs of childcare in London. It had seemed a much better idea for Rachel to be a full-time mum and to put her career on hold for a while. Plus, Combe was a much better place to bring up a baby than North London, they were both sure of that.

Rachel had found being heavily pregnant in London a complete nightmare. She'd spent most of her time frantically protecting her growing bump from the elbows, umbrellas and briefcases that were constantly banged against her stomach on the jammed pavements of W1. The Tube had been worse. Even though it had been winter outside, the underground was always steaming with the hot, recycled breath of a zillion commuters. What's more, Rachel had discovered that a pre-term baby was like an internal hot-water bottle, and five minutes into her commute she'd be dripping with sweat. The journey to and from work became increasingly difficult the bigger she got, until it reached the point where she'd feel dizzy every time she stepped on a Northern Line train. And nobody would give up their seat. OK, very occasionally a rather frail pensioner would struggle from his or her seat and offer it to Rachel, who would always decline because their need was even greater than hers. But the able-bodied passengers would slouch down behind their *Evening Standard*s and pretend they couldn't see the enormous bump in their midst.

Rachel had been horrified to discover that the worst culprits were the immaculately dressed twentysomething women – the very type of person she'd been seven months before. They not only refused to give up their seats on the Tube, they also sneered at her when she had the cheek to browse in trendy shops and tutted when she got in their way as they rushed down Oxford Street towards their next appointment. Rachel had racked her brain, trying to remember whether she'd ever been that rude to a pregnant woman, but she honestly couldn't remember ever seeing one in London. They must have been there, of course, but pre-pregnancy Rachel had been blind to such things.

The no-seat situation had eventually come to a head one evening between Warren Street and Mornington Crescent, when Rachel was thirty-four weeks pregnant. She had always been too short to reach the overhead handles kindly provided by London Regional Transport for their taller commuters and, on this occasion, was desperately trying to hold onto a side bar instead. The problem was that there were two middle-aged businessmen in her way and she was having to stretch her arm behind their backs to reach. Her clammy fingertips were only just managing to cling on. Rachel was aware that her bump was gently nudging the back of one of these men, while her enormous backside was being shoved in the face of an elderly Indian gentleman behind her, but there was nothing she could do about it. Her cheeks had burned with humiliation. She'd felt wretched and vulnerable, unable to maintain even the slightest semblance of dignity or personal space. As the train trundled shakily out of Warren Street Station, Rachel's head had begun to swim and she'd started to see white lights before her eyes. The last thing she remembered before she fainted was the look of absolute horror on the businessman's face as the full force of her swollen body lurched in his direction. She'd come round in Mornington Crescent Station, lying on the filthy carriage floor, with a couple of concerned looking LRT employees peering down at her. She could hear the mumbled grumblings of her fellow passengers, complaining about the delay in their journeys home. Once it had become clear that Rachel was going to be OK, the train guard had actually had to ask everyone on board if they were willing to give up their seat. The elderly Indian gentleman had been the first to stand up. For the remainder of the ten-minute journey home, Rachel had fumed silently to herself, and when she'd eventually reached Belsize Park, she'd stood up on wobbly legs and said, 'Thanks, everyone. Thanks a lot. Just remember the next time you see a pregnant woman on the Tube that you were all bumps once.' They had remained hidden behind their newspapers, magazines and paperback books, pretending to be deaf and blind, just like they did when they were confronted by hungry Kosovan women begging for food for their children. After that, Simon had insisted that she got a cab to and from work.

After Alfie was born, things had got even worse. Rachel had quickly discovered that most Tube stations didn't have lifts for buggies, shops had steps not ramps, restaurants were cramped and smoky and bus drivers were too impatient to wait as she struggled to fold the pushchair and hold Alfie at the same time. More than once she was left abandoned at a bus stop, with the buggy collapsed on the pavement and Alfie screaming in her arms.

At first, Rachel had been a bit sceptical about Simon's idea of her moving down to the cottage in Combe with the baby. But by the time Alfie was eight weeks old she'd been desperate to get out of London and convinced that motherhood would be easier once she had some breathing space. Yes, she'd be a bit lonely, but she would soon make friends. Simon would work in London during the week and then join his family at the weekend. She'd be so busy going for bracing country walks, joining in with mother-and-baby groups and wandering around the beautiful, historic city of Bath that she wouldn't even notice her husband's absence. Or at least that was the theory. Reality involved a mountain of shitty nappies, baby puke on the new sofa, mounds of dirty washing spilling out of the newly converted utility room, mindless daytime television and no human contact for days on end. Rachel phoned Simon often, but he had a Rottweiler of a new secretary, ironically named Grace, who screened his calls viciously.

'Is it urgent, Mrs Travis? Because Mr Travis did insist that he shouldn't be disturbed,' Grace would bark down the phone from London.

'No, just let him know that I called,' Rachel would whimper. 'Again.'

Zoe did at least take Rachel's calls, but she was almost as useless as Simon.

'Is this important, Rach?' she would ask impatiently. 'Because I've got a lunch meeting at Momo's in twenty minutes and I need to do my face before I leave the office.'

'No, I'm just feeling a bit down,' Rachel would venture.

'Well, I did warn you,' Zoe replied. 'But now you're there, you might as well make the most of it. At least, you're not stuck in an office any more, eh? Go and pick some wild flowers or something rural like that. Or bake some scones. That's what mums do. Anyway, must run . . .'

'But Zoe, I really need to speak to you. I haven't got anyone here I can talk to and I miss our chats.'

'I know, babes,' Zoe had softened. 'It must be difficult, but I really haven't got time now. Listen, I'll call you tonight and I'll try to get down to see you soon, OK?'

'OK,' Rachel had conceded, but she couldn't help feeling that Zoe was being less than supportive, especially when she failed to call back that evening.

Despite the initial misgivings she'd had when she'd first discovered she was pregnant, Rachel had quickly come to terms with impending motherhood. She'd carried the twenty-week scan picture around in her wallet and spent hours of the working day gazing adoringly at the tadpole that would become her son. From the moment Simon had shouted, 'He's got black hair!' in the delivery room, Rachel had loved Alfie. And that love had grown into an all-consuming infatuation which obscured everything else – even Simon. It didn't matter how difficult the day-to-day routine of tending a new-born had become, Rachel loved Alfie with a passion that was so basic, so animalistic and so urgent that it scared the life out of her. When he was sleeping she would just sit and watch him, in awe of his perfection, but petrified that he would somehow be snatched away from her. She tormented herself with the 'When things go wrong' chapter of her baby manual and could recite the cot-death section word for word. So, Rachel would watch her son sleep and she would will his chest to keep rising and falling, rising and falling, because somewhere deep down she was terrified that she didn't deserve him, that she was a useless failure of a mother and that her punishment would be his death.

Rachel's dark mood wasn't helped by the lack of sunlight in Ivy Cottage. It was mid March – a year since they'd bought the house – and spring had arrived early. But while the rest of Combe basked in glorious sunshine, Rachel's new home remained gloomy. The garden, which had been lovingly restored to its former glory by an award-winning local garden designer and her team, was plunged into perpetual darkness by the imposing hedge belonging to The Beeches, and the front of the house was north facing and never felt the warmth of the sun.

Summer was on the other side of the street. As Rachel sat by the window she was tormented by the view of Rose Cottage opposite. The house was a mirror image of her own, except for the fact that it still had the original thatched roof and it baked in perpetual sunshine. Its occupants – a woman of about Rachel's age and her daughter – seemed to be similarly sunny in their disposition. Of all the villagers, it was this mother and child who interested Rachel the most. The woman was beautiful. She had wavy, blond hair that fell in a thick curtain to her waist; wide, cornflower-blue eyes; honey-coloured skin and curves that would make J-Lo cry. She dressed in long hippie skirts with bells and mirrors sewn on and low-cut smock tops in shades of fuchsia, raspberry and sky-blue. Her daughter looked about ten or eleven and was a carbon copy of her mother, flowing skirts and all. By Rachel's calculations, they had five cats. There was no father to be seen, and whenever Rachel watched them she was struck by how close the two seemed. There was a lot of laughter in Rose Cottage – Rachel could hear it through her open windows – and music, always music, wafting from across the street. Sometimes, in the evening, Rachel would catch sight of her neighbours dancing together in their candlelit sitting room, long skirts flowing to the sound of The Mamas and The Papas. Rachel would watch, enchanted. Their camaraderie would remind Rachel of how lonely she had become. How she longed to dance with Zoe like they used to do.

Rachel willed the weekdays away, living for Friday night when she would hear Simon's car pull into the drive. Then she would hold on to him for dear life, so relieved to have some adult company, and talk to him until his head hurt because she hadn't spoken to anyone but Alfie all week, and for all his good points, her son wasn't much of a conversationalist. Simon, meanwhile, longed for peace and quiet at the weekend after his hectic week at the office (and nights in the pub). He found himself getting mildly irritated by Alfie's crying and Rachel's witterings. Couldn't a man just get a little peace? And sex. Sex would be good. It had been four months since Rachel had let him any-where near her. He understood that she hadn't felt much like it at the end of the pregnancy – and to be honest, she'd got so big that it would have taken a structural engineer to plan the event – and he'd been patient since Alfie was born. Rachel was bound to feel tender at first, but it had been weeks now, months even, and his patience was running out.

'I don't feel sexy,' Rachel said one Friday night when Simon tentatively tried to make a move. 'You understand, don't you?'

Simon sighed, laid back against his pillow and shrugged his shoulders. Rachel knew that he didn't, so she tried her best to explain.

'I'm exhausted, Si. I get no sleep and I spend my entire time looking after Alfie. I feel as if I'm giving everything I've got to him . . .'

'. . . and there's nothing left for me,' concluded Simon petulantly.

Rachel could feel a ball of anger rise up from her stomach. She was shocked at how selfish Simon was being.

'Nothing left for you?' she asked incredulously. 'There's nothing left for me, for Christ's sake. I'm a walking, talking feeding machine. My nipples bleed and my tits leak. My stomach looks like a deflated balloon, my labia are permanently torn to shreds, my hair's falling out and I don't even have time for a shower most days. When I get to bed all I want to do is sleep. Understand?'

Simon nodded huffily.

'If you're that desperate, have a wank,' said Rachel as she slid under the duvet with her back to her husband.

The minute she closed her eyes, Alfie started to cry in his room next door. Rachel lay still for a moment, waiting to see if Simon would go to his son. He didn't.

'I'll get him then, shall I?' snapped Rachel, dragging herself out from the warmth of the duvet.

'Well, it's you he wants,' said Simon.

Rachel detected a jealous tinge to her husband's tone and she realized, suddenly, that Simon was struggling with fatherhood just as much as she was with motherhood.

The argument brewed quietly under the surface for the rest of the weekend. On Saturday they played at happy families and took Alfie for a walk along the river which flowed through the village. Rachel spent the next half-hour, perched on a log, uncomfortably breastfeeding the baby while Simon shuffled above them.

'Is he nearly finished yet?' he asked a little impatiently.

'I don't know,' replied Rachel.

'But he can't be hungry,' continued Simon. 'You only fed him an hour ago.'

'Well he is hungry, obviously,' said Rachel.

'You feed him too much,' concluded Simon.

Rachel raised an eyebrow. Simon was treading on dangerous ground.

'So what do you suggest I do when he cries for a feed?' she asked.

'Don't give in to him. He's got to learn who's boss.'

'Uh-huh, and you'd be the world's expert on breastfeeding, would you, Simon?'

'No, but I think this whole feeding-on-demand business is a bit much.'

'Right.' Rachel tried to remain calm as she nursed Alfie. 'So I should ignore everything the midwives tell me, should I?'

'No, but they were a bit New Agey, weren't they? All that natural-childbirth stuff you got into and antenatal yoga, not to mention those baby-massage classes you took Alfie to when he was about three days old.'

He snorted to himself in mild amusement.

'I'm sure we weren't pandered to as much when we were babies,' he mused.

'Things change,' explained Rachel patiently. 'New research is done all the time and almost all the books agree that feeding on demand is best for the baby.'

Simon rolled his eyes. He didn't *do* baby manuals. He thought that parenting should be instinctive.

'I don't need to be told how to be a good father by some aging earth mother' – Simon's take on Miriam Stoppard – 'or by an Antipodean Fascist in a nanny's uniform' – Simon's view of Gina Ford – he said, not for the first, second or third time.

'I know, Simon,' said Rachel suddenly. 'Why don't you take Alfie for a walk and I'll go home and have a lie-down. I mean, if he doesn't need to be fed then he doesn't need me around, does he? It'll give you two boys some time to bond.'

Rachel gently prized her finger between Alfie's sucking mouth and her nipple and broke off the feed. The baby looked at his mother in surprise and then with sheer, red-faced anger began to bawl for the boob that had been so cruelly snatched away.

'I'm sorry, little man,' she whispered to him. 'But Daddy says you've had enough.'

Rachel handed the crying baby to Simon, turned on her heel and stomped purposefully back towards the cottage in her new wellies.

'Rachel!' shouted Simon. 'Rachel! Come back!'

'You'll be fine,' replied Rachel. 'You don't need to be told how to be a good father, remember?'

Simon and Alfie arrived home ten minutes after Rachel. Alfie was still crying and Simon didn't look far from tears himself. The baby was naked from the waist down and Simon's jumper had a suspicious-looking mustard-coloured stain down the front.

'I'm sorry, Rach,' he said. 'I had no idea how difficult this baby business is.'

'Welcome to my world,' said Rachel drily, taking her son from his father and heading for the bathroom with a smug grin on her face. One nil, she thought.

The next day, the Travis family went on an outing to the Cotswolds. After a pleasant walk around Westonbirt Arboretum they stopped for lunch at a gastro pub. For once, Alfie gurgled happily in his car seat while his parents ate and talked. Rachel was keen to clear the air and she wanted to let Simon know that she still loved him, but there were problems that needed to be addressed.

'I love you, Si. More than ever,' said Rachel tentatively as she waited for her grilled trout to arrive. 'It's just difficult, adapting to the baby and the new house and everything.'

'I know, darling,' said Simon. 'It's a bit of a weird situation.'

'It's much more difficult than I thought it would be, having a baby,' ventured Rachel. 'I mean, I love Alfie to bits, I adore him. You know I do. And I'd murder anyone who harmed him, but it's just a bit . . .' she pondered as she chewed a mouthful of asparagus. '. . . bloody knackering,' she announced. 'Not to mention mind-numbingly dull.'

She smiled to show she was joking. Well, half joking.

'I'm sure it's normal to feel like that,' said Simon. 'You should find out about baby groups or something. I bet if you talked to other mums, you'd find out that they feel exactly the same.'

'You're right,' Rachel agreed. 'But I do think,' she continued, feeling brave, 'that you could help out more. I mean, I know you work hard and you're not here much of the time, but at the weekends you could do more with Alfie and give me a bit of a break.'

Simon stared down at the little man in his car seat and wished he didn't feel so useless. The truth was that since Alfie was born, Simon had felt completely shut out. He knew that Rachel was struggling emotionally, and she was obviously exhausted, but at least she'd taken to the practical side of parenting as if it was the most natural thing in the world, which, Simon supposed, it probably was. So why couldn't he manage it? While Rachel could change a nappy in her sleep and cuddle the baby while making a cup of coffee, he couldn't even hold his son properly. He felt awkward and clumsy, as if Alfie's head was about to fall off at any minute in the hands of his bumbling big father. And as for changing nappies, every time he tried, Alfie would pee everywhere. He'd had an eyeful of his son's urine only that morning and it had stung. And then there was the crying. While Rachel seemed to care hugely what was wrong with the baby every time he so much as whimpered, sometimes Simon just wished he would shut up. Did that make him a bad father? A terrible man? He wasn't sure.

But Simon was a proud man and he'd never been very good at admitting his weaknesses, so he said nothing to Rachel about the way he was feeling. Instead he just nodded and said, 'I'll try harder to be understanding and to help out, OK?'

'OK.' Rachel smiled. 'Thanks.'

When they got back to Ivy Cottage, Alfie was asleep in his car seat, so Rachel transferred him gently into his cot and looked forward to spending some quality time with Simon. If only she could prize him out from behind the Sunday papers.

'I'm going to sue the estate agent,' she announced from her perch at the window.

'Mmm hmm,' Simon responded lazily from

behind *The Sunday Times* financial pages. 'And why's that, darling?'

'Because he lied.'

She pressed her face hard against the leaded window and watched the glass steam up.

'That's what estate agents do for a living, darling,' replied Simon, half-heartedly. 'It's a well-known fact that they're the most odious creatures on the planet.'

'But he described this place as a sleepy little village – it's not sleeping, it's in a bloody coma.'

'Combe is idyllic,' said Simon patiently. 'It's perfect.'

From her window seat Rachel could see down their green and leafy front garden, across the lane, past Rose Cottage and over the manicured village green to the Fox and Hounds, a whitewashed, picture-perfect, thatched country pub. The beer garden was empty despite the spring sunshine. Nobody played cricket on the green and it had been two hours since any vehicle had driven down the lane – and then it had been those mad women in the flash sports car again. In fact, other than the Porsche girls, the odd tractor and the lorries on their way to the building site at the top of the hill, nobody ever came down Chillyhill Lane.

Rachel slithered off the window seat and padded over to her husband in stockinged soles. She snatched the paper from his grasp and dropped it messily on the polished wooden floor before dumping herself on his lap. Simon tried not to wince. His wife wasn't quite the waif she once had been.

'You look fed up, sweetie,' he said gently, stroking her cheek. 'I thought we were friends again.'

'We are, but,' Rachel pouted. She was almost thirty, but now, without any make-up on, Simon thought she could pass for eighteen. His wife was big-eyed and full-lipped and he always melted when she flashed him that look. Even now, as his thighs ached under her weight.

'You're never here.'

'I'm here now.'

Rachel glanced at her watch. 'Yeah, for another three hours and then you'll be off to London again and it'll just be me, Alfie and these four walls again.'

'I thought this is what you wanted,' said Simon, confused.

'I know. It was. It is. But . . . oh, I don't know.'

'You just need to get out and about a bit more. Keep busy. I'll leave you some money,' suggested Simon, eyeing the newspaper longingly. He didn't have much time to relax these days, what with his promotion, the commuting up and down the M4 and the baby. 'You could go into Bath tomorrow. Go mad in Baby Gap!'

'Oh hurrah,' said Rachel sarcastically.

'But you love shopping.' Simon was very confused now.

'Correction. I used to love shopping. Before I had to take a baby with me. When I was a size ten.'

'Why don't you buy yourself something nice, too?' suggested Simon. 'That'll cheer you up.'

'I'm sorry. I seem to have been abducted by aliens

63

and relocated in the 1950s.' Rachel's brown eyes flashed and he could sense another argument brewing. They seemed to jump out of nowhere these days. He'd be happily minding his own business when suddenly, wham! One of Rachel's outbursts would shatter the peace of their country idyll.

'What are you talking about?' asked Simon perplexed.

'You. Me. This place. My life.'

Rachel ran her fingers through her hair in frustration, discovering a lump of baby puke as she did so.

'Argh!' She struggled off Simon's lap, squashing his groin with her elbow on the way.

'Ouch,' moaned Simon.

Rachel carried on oblivious. 'I hate it. I hate this house and this village and this flab.' She grabbed the soft mound of her post-pregnancy tummy in both hands. 'And I hate me. I'm fat and I'm ugly and I'm bored and I'm boring and I'm miserable.'

'Have you spoken to the health visitor about post-natal depression yet?'

'I haven't got post-natal depression, Simon,' she shouted. 'I just haven't got a life any more. Anybody would be depressed in my position.'

Simon tried to be patient. 'Rachel,' he reminded her. 'You've got a gorgeous, perfect, amazing son; a detached, listed cottage; half an acre of garden; a brand-new car in the drive – practically unused – a husband who earns a decent salary; you don't need to work; you don't want for anything; you can spend your days wafting about, wandering along country lanes—'

'Is that what you think I do all day?' Rachel's face turned a scary shade of beetroot. 'Do you think I just waft around in my rural paradise. Alfie sleeps all day, I never have to change him, or stop him crying, or feed him, or wash his clothes, or your clothes, or iron babygrows or your fucking shirts—'

'Oh, here we go again.' Simon rolled his eyes. He'd tried to be reasonable, but Rachel was beyond reason when she got into one of these moods. 'Just let me know when you've finished ranting, will you?' He picked up the newspaper, smoothed out the pages and continued reading the financial section.

Rachel thought she would explode.

'I don't see you from Sunday night until Friday evening, I haven't got any friends round here, I can go for days without having an adult conversation, I can't leave the house without taking half of bloody Mothercare with me, I never have any time just for me, I might as well be a single mother.'

'Get a grip, Rachel,' muttered Simon. 'Most people fantasize about leaving work and spending more time at home. We'd all love to be in your shoes.'

Rachel wasn't wearing any shoes. Her feet were so puffy that none of her dainty little designer numbers fitted her any more and, anyway, she never left the house, so what was the point of her extensive footwear collection? She looked wildly around the room for a heavy implement with which to bash her sexist bastard husband's brain in. The shovel by the fireplace looked tempting, but she managed to restrain herself enough to merely kick the open newspaper in front of Simon's face instead. She missed his nose by a millimetre.

'I hate you!' she screamed.

'Rachel, what are you doing?' Simon was perplexed. 'You've gone loopy. What's wrong with you?'

'I'm going to leave you,' she announced, surprising herself that the thought had even entered her head.

'Don't be silly,' said Simon, half laughing at the preposterousness of the idea. 'We're happily married with a new baby. You're not going to walk out with our son.'

'Yes I am. He's my baby. He needs me. You can't be on your own with him for ten minutes. He doesn't even know who you are. You're just some bloke who visits every now and then.'

Simon was losing his patience. He had approximately two hours of his weekend left to enjoy and he didn't fancy spending it being abused by a ranting Rachel.

'Whatever you say, Rachel. You know where the door is,' he said. 'Just let me get a bit of peace, will you?'

'Exactly when did you turn into a pompous old freak?' she demanded.

'Probably around the same time you turned into a whingeing misery guts,' answered Simon without missing a beat.

Just then, the lights on the baby monitor began to flash red and the familiar wails of a hungry three-month-old began to fill the room. Rachel waited for a moment to see whether Simon would respond this time. He didn't.

'I'll get him again, shall I?' she snapped.

'He's hungry,' said Simon. 'And I didn't have tits the last time I looked.'

'Well maybe you should look a bit harder next time,' muttered Rachel as she left the room. Simon had piled on the pounds recently – too many business lunches and M&S ready meals – and Rachel had definitely noticed the beginning of man boobs when he was in the shower that morning.

'Are you calling me fat?' shouted Simon with an incredulous snort as Rachel climbed the stairs to the nursery. Simon had many good points, but modesty was not one of them. He was a sex god, a legend in his own living room, no one could possibly criticize his looks. Suddenly he was interested in what she had to say.

'Well you're not the fine figure of a man I married,' she called back, smiling to herself. Now he was listening to her. Her hand was on the nursery door.

'Yeah, but I probably weigh less than you do, lard arse,' he hollered.

The words hit Rachel like a ten-ton truck. They both knew that since Alfie came on the scene her weight was a taboo subject. The cruelty of what Simon had said knocked the wind out of her, and when Alfie looked up from his cot to greet Mummy, all he could see were her tears. She gently picked up the baby, sat on the rocking chair, unclipped the ugly nursing bra and watched Alfie clamp greedily onto her mammoth blue-veined breast. And then, as her son fed blissfully, she wept and wept for the girl she used to be and the woman she had become.

'You look dreadful,' announced Zoe as she wafted into Ivy Cottage carrying a Louis Vuitton holdall. 'And that top's not doing you any favours. I can see your stretchmarks.'

Rachel pulled awkwardly at the misshapen T-shirt she was wearing and tried to make it cover her lardy tummy.

'It's lovely to see you too, Zoe,' said Rachel sarcastically. She'd been looking forward to her best friend's midweek visit, but within thirty seconds of arriving Zoe had managed to make her feel completely wretched again. Once upon a time her best friend's insults had been water off Rachel's back, but these days they stung like an acid bath.

'Oh I'm sorry, babes,' Zoe apologized, putting down her holdall and giving her mate a hug. 'I just thought you would have sprung back into shape by now.'

Zoe took a step back and eyed her friend critically. 'It's weird,' she said with her white-blonde head on one side. 'You look like you, but as if someone's blown you up with a foot pump.' Zoe laughed at her own witty observation.

'The house is looking lovely, though,' she continued, wandering through the rooms.

Well, that was something at least. Rachel had scrubbed and cleaned until her knuckles bled in an attempt to appear suitably domestic goddess-like for her friend's visit.

'I can't believe how much work you guys have

had done. It was a shit hole last time I was here.'

Zoe threw herself onto the couch and rubbed her hands together. 'So,' she said with a look of expectation. 'What's the plan? What are we going to do with ourselves? It's not often I get two whole days off work, so you'd better have some exciting countryside pursuits lined up for me.'

'Um, not exactly,' said Rachel apologetically. 'It's difficult to do much with Alfie, you know, and he's having his lunchtime sleep at the moment, so—'

Rachel disappeared into the kitchen for a few moments and then reappeared carrying a bottle of champagne and a DVD, 'I thought we could just chill out here instead.'

Zoe pouted. 'Do we have to?' she whined. 'I thought we could at least go shopping in Bath or something. I want to get some Ugg Boots.'

'Some what?' asked Rachel.

'Ugg Boots,' Zoe looked at Rachel in horror. 'You must have heard of them, surely. I thought you were supposed to be a fashion queen. They are *the* boots to have this season. All the celebs are wearing them.'

'Oh right,' said Rachel, feeling small. She hadn't had much time to study *Vogue*'s fashion pages since Alfie was born. She did sometimes catch the fashion slots on daytime TV, but they weren't as cutting edge as Zoe. 'Can't you get these boots in London?' she persevered, dreading the thought of lugging Alfie and all his paraphernalia into town.

'Yeah,' scoffed Zoe. 'Of course I can, but I thought I might as well do something useful while I'm here.'

'What about just catching up with me and spending time with Alfie?' suggested Rachel.

Zoe looked as if the thought hadn't even crossed her mind. Eventually she shrugged. 'OK, I suppose we could do that. What film did you get out?'

Rachel grinned broadly. 'Our favourite,' she teased, hiding the DVD behind her back.

'Does it involve Keanu Reeves, Patrick Swayze and lots of naked, wet male flesh?' asked Zoe excitedly.

'Oh yes,' promised Rachel.

'*Point Break!*' squealed Zoe in delight. 'We haven't watched that since you were recovering from having your wisdom teeth out in 1999 and I threw a sickie to keep you company. We spent three whole days drooling over Keanu. Oh clever you, Rach.'

Miraculously, Alfie slept through the entire film and even allowed his mother to share a pizza in peace with her oldest friend.

'I'd love to shag a surfer,' drooled Zoe as the titles rolled. 'It's way up there on my to-do list.'

'Mmm, me too,' agreed Rachel.

'In fact,' continued Zoe. 'I'm sure I meant to do it before I was thirty, but I've missed that opportunity. You've got a few months left, Rach. Perhaps you should try and slot that into your diary for the summer.'

Rachel giggled. 'Yeah, Simon would love that. April: join a gym. May: take Alfie to playgroup. June: shag a surfer.'

'I don't think Anton would give a monkeys who I slept with,' said Zoe sadly.

'Don't be silly,' said Rachel. 'Anton loves you.'

Zoe shook her head. 'No, babes. He doesn't. It's all going a bit pear-shaped, to be honest. He's really distant at the moment and he refuses to talk about the future. You know, he won't even book a summer holiday with me. That's not a good sign, is it?'

'He might have his reasons,' suggested Rachel kindly. 'It's not necessarily about you. Something else might be bothering him – work or something.'

'No, Rach,' said Zoe with certainty. 'He's going to dump me. Soon. I can see it in his eyes. It's gone. He just doesn't think I'm all that any more. D'you know what I mean?'

'Well if that's the case, the guy's an idiot,' Rachel put her arm around Zoe's narrow shoulders and gave her a reassuring squeeze.

'So that's another thing I meant to do before I was thirty completely scuppered,' Zoe laughed sadly. Zoe had a habit of turning everything into a joke, especially her own feelings. 'Top of that list was "Get married". Second was "Have children". I'm not doing very well, am I?'

'You never wanted all that, did you?' asked Rachel, surprised. Zoe had always said she wasn't bothered about the whole husband-and-kids package.

'Of course I did,' scoffed Zoe.

'But you always said—' Rachel started.

'Oh, never mind what I said,' Zoe cut in. 'I lied. It's what I've always wanted – church, white frock, husband-to-be dressed up like a penguin. All the stuff my mum never had, I suppose.' Zoe's Mum had spent her days cleaning and her evenings serving pints in order to make ends meet. Zoe, meanwhile, found a ready-made family to adopt at Rachel's house and became part of the furniture next door.

'That's why I'm so jealous of you, you jammy bitch,' continued Zoe. 'You've got everything I ever wanted.'

Zoe grinned but her eyes were cold.

'Don't be silly,' scoffed Rachel. 'You don't want to be like me. You said yourself that I'm fat, so you definitely don't want my body. Simon's a bit on the dull side, in your opinion, so you wouldn't want him.'

Rachel continued without noticing Zoe's guilty blush.

'You love having lie-ins so you'd hate having a baby who woke you up in the middle of the night and, apart from all that, you come out in a cold sweat if you're out of London for more than a couple of days, so you'd never survive out here in deepest, darkest Wiltshire.'

Zoe knelt on the window seat and gazed at the view of the village.

'But it's so pretty here,' she said.

'Yeah, pretty boring.' Rachel laughed.

'Really?' asked Zoe.

'Really,' confirmed Rachel. 'Honestly, Zo, I'm struggling. Just like you said I would. There's nothing to do and nobody to do it with. I'm going out of my mind with boredom.'

'So come back to London,' said Zoe with a non-chalant shrug. 'There's nothing stopping you.'

'Oh yeah, Simon would love that.' Rachel sighed. 'He bought this house for me, spent months pouring over planning applications and architects plans, not to mention the fortune he spent on making this my dream home. He did all this for me. I can't throw that back in his face.'

'He'd understand,' said Zoe. 'Simon's a big softie.'

Rachel shook her head. 'No,' she said firmly. 'I've made my bed and all that. I can't go back now; I couldn't do that to Simon.'

Just then Alfie started to cry.

'Or Alfie,' Rachel added, heading out of the door. 'It's much better for him to be here.'

'It didn't do me any harm, growing up in London,' called Zoe up the stairs.

Yes it did, thought Rachel, to herself. Zoe was cynical and hard and streetwise. She'd had to be. But Rachel didn't want that for her baby. She lifted Alfie gently out of his cot and watched as his angry little face softened as he felt his mother's arms around him. She was determined to give her little boy every chance she could for a happy life, and if that meant putting up with village life, so be it.

'He's still a bit odd-looking, isn't he?' said Zoe, peering down at her godson. 'He won't be winning any bonny-baby contests.'

Rachel took a deep breath, counted to ten and waited for the anger to subside. For years she had put up with Zoe's insults, and that was fine, she could take it. But to insult Alfie, that was way out of line. Rachel counted to fifty, but still the anger wouldn't leave. She gazed adoringly at her beautiful, perfect little boy as Zoe's words swam around her head. Odd-looking? How dare she? No one was allowed to criticize her baby. For the first time in her life Rachel answered back.

'He's not odd-looking,' she said as calmly as she could.

'Eh?' Zoe's head was already elsewhere and she'd almost forgotten what she'd said about the baby.

'Alfie is gorgeous and there's no way I'm going to let you say that about him,' Rachel glared at Zoe.

'But he is,' insisted Zoe. 'He's got a cone head and six chins.'

'And you've got short legs and a slight squint in your left eye, but I don't go around shouting about it!' yelled Rachel.

Zoe's hand flitted automatically to her left eye. Her shoulders crumpled and her head bowed. At last she'd found Rachel's insult threshold. She'd crossed it without even realizing she was there, and now she knew where she stood: behind Alfie every time. She felt wretched, not because she'd upset Rachel, but because Rachel had upset her.

'That was cruel, Rach,' she said in a tiny, hurt voice. 'And anyway, I was only teasing.'

'Yup, well now you know how it feels,' replied Rachel.

Rachel watched Zoe's broken expression and found she was softening despite herself. Zoe had never really grown up, and it felt like telling off a naughty toddler.

'Look, I'm sorry, Zoe,' she said, more gently now. 'That was out of line, but, you really mustn't ever say anything nasty about Alfie. He's my baby and I'd do anything to protect him, even if it's just from your teasing. Friends?'

Zoe pouted for a moment and then nodded, somewhat petulantly.

'Friends,' she said.

But an invisible line had been crossed, their relationship had shifted in the changing sands of time and their friendship would never be the same again. When Zoe watched Rachel wave goodbye in her rear-view mirror, she felt as if it might be for good.

Chapter Three

Meet the neighbours

When the doorbell rang one Tuesday morning in April, Rachel nearly dropped the baby in surprise. For most people this wouldn't have been a momentous event, but for Rachel, who had been living in the village for over a month and had yet to have a single visitor other than Zoe, it was both an exciting and scary proposition. Who could it possibly be? The postman had already delivered a phone bill and a free prize draw that morning. She glanced in the mirror in the hall and was, as always, shocked by the haggard, puffy-faced vision before her. Where the hell had Rachel gone? And who was this frumpy, middle-aged hag who had invaded her once beautiful body? Oh well, there wasn't much she could do about it before answering the door. Rachel hurriedly brushed her hair with one hand while balancing Alfie over her shoulder with the other, then she took a deep breath and opened the door. There, on the doorstep, stood the Porsche girls. Their teeth glistened, their skin glowed and their hair gleamed.

'Hello,' said Rachel nervously.

'Hi, hon,' gushed Porsche girl No. 1, who was resplendent in baby-pink velour. She had teamed her Juicy Couture tracksuit with vertiginous Gina mules, a crocodile-skin Hermès bag – which had cost £8,000 and had a three-year waiting list. Rachel knew this for a fact, having written a press release about it in the course of her work – and a shiny black dog. 'I'm Bianca,' she explained in a friendly Scottish accent.

There had been no need for an introduction. Up close, Rachel recognized Bianca Mills instantly. She was, after all, Britain's most famous page-three model (now retired) and since marrying TJ Mills (aging Eighties pop icon) she had become a regular in the 'at home' slots in *OK!* and *Hello!* magazines. Rachel hadn't realized that her faux Tudor dream home was actually in the village of Combe. Bianca Mills was the kind of brunette who made blonde and blue-eyed look bland. She was short, like Rachel, but perfectly formed in a pneumatic Pamela Anderson kind of way, while Rachel was now short in a jolly Dawn French kind of way. Bianca's tracksuit top was unzipped just low enough to display her most famous assets. And Rachel had to admit that, in the flesh, they really were magnificent. Whether or not they were real was debatable, and had indeed been debated in the tabloids many, many times, but the fact that they were beautiful was not open to question.

'And I'm Harriet Lilywhite Smythe,' said the tall, skinny, haughty-looking young woman behind her.

Harriet's voice was as sharp and clipped as the

blunt blond fringe that fell heavily over her arched eyebrows. She had the kind of lean, taut, athletic body that looked equally at home in jodhpurs and an haute-couture evening gown, but mildly uncomfortable in anything else. Today, she wore tight jeans, tucked into knee-high brown leather boots, a cream cashmere poloneck and a coffee-coloured pashmina wrapped several times around her unnaturally long neck. It was the kind of understated but very expensive look that Rachel had seen often on Sloane Street. Stealth wealth they'd called it in fashion circles. Harriet's eyes were the palest grey-blue and utterly impenetrable. Everything about her screamed 'Ice Queen' and even her dog had a rather snooty air about him. Rachel recognized Harriet, too, and suddenly realized why the name Lilywhite Smythe had been so familiar when she'd first heard it. Harriet had been one of the handful of aristocratic young models who'd made it big in the Nineties – Jodie Kidd, Stella Tennant, Jasmine Guinness, Sophie Dahl and Hattie Lilywhite Smythe. She had never been a household name like some of the others, and her pale face rarely graced *Vogue* these days, but Harriet had been successful enough on the catwalk and in Burberry ad campaigns for Rachel, as a fashionista, to know her work well. In fact, Rachel had rubbed skinny shoulders with Harriet at several after-show parties, but they'd never been introduced.

'Rachel,' said Rachel, cringing in the presence of such groomed perfection. She cursed herself for pulling on her baggy maternity jeans that morning – there was no hope of squeezing back into her pre-pregnancy wardrobe – and teaming them with a voluminous T-shirt that shouted 'Big Mama' across her matronly bosom.

'We thought it would be neighbourly of us to pop over and say hi,' announced Bianca chirpily.

Harriet rolled her eyes.

'Bianca thought it would be a good idea,' she corrected her companion quickly. 'I said you were probably far too busy looking after your baby, or something like that.'

Harriet frowned as she realized she didn't actually know what ordinary people did with their time.

'Anyway, we can go if you're in the middle of something.'

Harriet eyed Alfie suspiciously, as if Rachel had a boa constrictor on her shoulder rather than a baby, and took a small step back down the garden path. She'd told Bianca that it was a stupid idea. This woman looked so dull, with her shapeless clothes and drooling baby, they should have gone to the gym at Babington as she'd suggested. But Bianca was fretting about this new arrival in the village.

'Her husband works in London and she doesn't know anybody,' Bianca had recounted after getting the gossip from Mrs Bell in the village shop. 'We really should take her under our wing, hon.'

Harriet thought it was bad enough having to hang out with Bianca, let alone make friends with a dowdy housewife. The sooner Daddy let her move back to the Chelsea apartment the better. She was twenty-nine and had been out of rehab for months now. She was perfectly capable of living in London without getting back into her old ways with the old crowd. But Daddy didn't trust her. He said he needed her close by so that he could keep an eye on her. He treated her like a naughty kid who'd been expelled from boarding school – which, incidentally, she had been on several occasions. He said he didn't want to find her dead one morning, having choked to death on her own vomit like that young Hurlingham Jones character. She knew he was determined not to lose Hattie, his youngest. In the absence of any meaningful career, it had become his project to keep her in one piece. It did Harriet's head in. Just because he'd driven her mother away – to the other side of Bath, at least – and had lost his older daughter to anorexia when she was just 23, it didn't mean he had to keep her on a lead. But Daddy was determined that Harriet would beat her addictions for good and that he would be her saviour. When he told her that he couldn't face burying another daughter before she was thirty, Harriet felt she would collapse under the pressure of being the only one left.

'Are you busy?' continued Bianca hopefully. 'Shall we come in?'

'Yes, yes, do,' Rachel flustered, worrying about the weekend's newspapers on the living-room floor and the numerous half-drunk mugs of coffee that littered the room.

'Rachel, I brought you some home-made jam,' announced Bianca, fishing out a jar from her Hermès bag. 'As a house-warming pressie.'

Harriet looked incredulous. 'Bianca, you brought her some jam?'

'Uh-huh,' Bianca nodded happily. 'Raspberry. I made a whole larder full of it last autumn.'

'Oh – my – God. What are you going to think of us, Rachel? I mean, in London people bring wine, or champagne, or cocaine even. Here, we bring home-made jam. I do apologize. We're not all complete fuckwits. It's just that Bianca has decided to become Wiltshire's answer to Nigella Lawson. I expect a cookery book to come out at any moment. It will be called *The Faux Tudor Kitchen*.'

'No, really, it's lovely,' said Rachel, genuinely touched. 'Thank you, Bianca.'

Bianca smiled smugly at Harriet, who shook her head in disdain.

Rachel ushered the Porsche girls into the living room.

'Sorry about the mess,' she apologized. 'Sit down.'

Harriet picked up a multicoloured plastic rattle from the couch and looked at it reproachfully before perching uncomfortably on the edge, as if she didn't intend to stay long. Moriarty sat obediently at her feet, and didn't move a whisker, like a stuffed hound in a taxidermy shop. Jock, meanwhile, made himself at home, snuffling around the furniture, tail wagging, and helping himself to stray bits of Hobnob which had fallen on the floor.

'And who are you little man?' Bianca cooed.

'Alfie,' explained Rachel proudly. She knew she looked a fright and her house was a bomb site, but at least her baby was awe-inspiring. He was the most beautiful creature that ever breathed, of that she was quite certain.

'Aren't you just the cutest little boy I've ever seen,' gushed Bianca.

Alfie smiled up at the lovely lady with the big boobies and thought, Lunch!

'Let me have a cuddle,' insisted Bianca, 'while you put the kettle on, Rachel. I know how hard it is to make a cuppa while holding a baby. I've got twins.' All that and twins too, thought Rachel enviously as her son snuggled dreamily into the most famous chest in the country.

Over tea and biscuits, Bianca filled Rachel in on the village gossip while Harriet stared disinterestedly out of the window. Combe, it transpired, was a hotbed of sex, scandal and debauchery. Well, almost. Problems included the lack of a bowler for the village cricket team, due to the poor vicar's triple heart bypass – this news would later make Simon's day. Several wealthy occupants had had their houses ransacked last Christmas by some hoodlums from Frome who had now thankfully been arrested and jailed. The local hunt, run by Harriet's father, was up in arms about the proposed government ban on fox hunting and were proudly displaying their Countryside Alliance stickers in their Range Rovers.

'Except for that silly woman opposite you,' said Harriet, nodding her head towards Rose Cottage. 'She's got animal-rights posters on her windows. Don't know where she came from, but she'll soon learn that that sort of namby-pamby Liberal non-sense doesn't cut much ice around these parts. She'll be trouble.'

Bianca laughed and shook her pretty head.

'What, Summer? Don't be silly Harriet. Summer is—'

'A freak,' concluded Harriet.

'No,' argued Bianca. 'A sweet young woman who is just a little unorthodox.'

'And completely unwelcome in this village,' announced Harriet. 'With her incense and her bare feet and her cats.'

Moriarty's nose twitched at the mention of the enemy – cats.

'Well I like her,' Bianca explained to Rachel. 'She hasn't been in Combe long either and she's about our age, so I'm sure you two will be friends.'

'Summer isn't friends with anybody.' Harriet snorted. 'She doesn't even speak to me.'

'That's because you accused her of being a hunt saboteur.'

'Yes, because one of the sabs had a long blond ponytail under her baseball cap that looked un-cannily like Summer's.'

'Whatever,' said Bianca half-heartedly. She was used to disagreeing with Harriet and knew there was no point in arguing. Harriet was as stubborn as the rich and over-indulged come.

'But the biggest news around here,' said Bianca, eyes flashing with excitement, 'is that there's a new house being built at the top of the lane.'

Well, hold the front page, thought Rachel. Village in new house shocker.

'Really?' she feigned interest.

'Oh yes, hon,' enthused Bianca. 'It's going to be *huge*! Bigger than The Beeches, bigger than my place, even. And nobody knows who it belongs to or who's going to move in. But Mrs Bell in the shop, well her son's a plumber and he's done some work there and he says that it'll be ready any day now. Oh, I'm so excited about who it's going to be. TJ heard a rumour that it might be Madonna and Guy.'

'Don't be ridiculous, Bianca. They already have a place in Wiltshire, why would they buy another one?'

'I don't know, hon,' said Bianca. 'But TJ heard it from a good source in the music industry.'

'Darling,' replied Harriet. 'TJ's contacts in the music industry died during the last ice age.'

'Harriet, I will not have you talk about my husband like that. TJ is a very gifted musician; he's just having a few problems finding his market at the moment.'

'That's because they all live in nursing homes these days.' Harriet gaffawed.

'Hobnob?' interjected Rachel diplomatically.

Harriet finished the round-up of Combe's comings and goings.

'Basically.' She yawned. 'The place is full of rich, boring old farts who play bridge and bitch about each other. I have absolutely no idea why you wanted to move here.'

Rachel didn't have an answer to that one. Right now she didn't know why either. Alfie was trying his best to latch on to Bianca's protruding nipples through her tracksuit top and he'd left an enormous dribble mark on the pink velour.

'I think someone's hungry,' said Bianca, gently handing Alfie over to Rachel for a feed.

Rachel hated breastfeeding in public. She'd read somewhere that a carefully placed scarf could conceal the manoeuvre but she'd tried it once in a café in London and had almost suffocated Alfie in the process. The poor baby had gagged on a mouthful of pale pink pashmina. She considered using a tea towel – the only thing close to hand – but decided it might make her look even less sophisticated. She wished the perfectly groomed women would leave now and let her get on with feeding in peace, but they didn't budge. There's something humiliating about having to get your boobs out in front of virtual strangers. She knew Harriet had no children, and even though Bianca had twins, Rachel wrongly assumed she was the sort of celebrity mother who'd had an elective caesarean at the Portland Clinic, followed by a tummy tuck and a boob lift. The babies, she decided, had probably been handed straight to a nursery nurse the minute they were lifted out of their mother's womb and bottle fed to a strict four-hour regime ever since.

Bianca beamed at Rachel while Harriet's eyes bulged in horror. She visibly winced when Rachel unleashed her veiny breast from its hideous nursing bra and attached a greedy Alfie to a huge purple nipple.

'I could never do that,' she announced with a shiver. 'In fact, I can't think of anything more horrific than giving birth. Except, perhaps, giving birth to twins.'

'Harriet,' scolded Bianca. 'You really do talk nonsense. Becoming a mother is the single most important thing I have ever done in my life. And breastfeeding is the most wonderful bonding experience you will ever have with your child.'

Rachel realized that despite her plastic appearance, Bianca Mills was actually an earth mother extraordinaire.

'Is that why you're going to keep feeding your two until they're eighteen?' Harriet sneered; she thought it was disgusting that Bianca continued to breastfeed her twins now that they were two.

'You still breastfeed?' asked Rachel in surprise.

'Oh yes, hon,' enthused Bianca. 'It's funny, isn't it? I made my fortune with these babies.' She cupped her perfect breasts in her hands and Rachel wondered how on earth they had defied gravity after feeding twins. 'They brought joy to many an old man and now they're out of retirement, bringing pleasure to my two little girls.'

'How ironic,' said Harriet flatly. 'It must have been quite a shock for you when you discovered they had uses other than decorating *Playboy*. Were your tits that size before you had the baby?' she asked Rachel bluntly.

Rachel blushed. 'No, none of me was this size before I had Alfie.'

'How horrid for you,' said Harriet with genuine pity. There were two things Harriet feared in life, losing money and gaining weight.

'Oh, I was huge after I had the twins,' said Bianca sympathetically.

'Really?' asked Rachel doubtfully.

'No you weren't,' interjected Harriet. 'I saw you the weekend you came out of hospital and you were back in your Earl Jeans.'

'I was nearly ten stone,' announced Bianca in disgust.

'Were you?' asked Harriet. 'That's disgusting. Thank God you've got your own gym.'

Bianca nodded earnestly. Rachel thought she would walk over hot coals to be as light as ten stone again.

'You can use my gym whenever you want, Rachel,' offered Bianca. 'Here's my card. It's got the home number and my mobile on it. Call me any time.'

Rachel didn't know whether to be grateful for the offer or insulted by the insinuation that she desperately needed a good workout. When the Porsche girls left, Alfie was asleep on the sofa. Rachel sat on her window seat and thought about Bianca and Harriet. It had been nice to have some unexpected adult company and she'd appreciated the visit, but now they'd gone, Rachel felt even worse about herself than before they'd arrived – their wealth, beauty, wardrobes and skinniness had made her feel wretchedly inadequate in comparison. Bianca seemed very nice, if a bit dizzy, but Harriet was a total bitch. Rachel wondered why on earth Bianca wasted her time on Harriet. Maybe rich, skinny girls just gravitated towards each other in some sort of mutual appreciation society. Why else would Bianca put up with all that sniping from Harriet? Then Rachel thought about her own relationship with Zoe and the abuse she had to put up with. Perhaps these rich women weren't so different, after all.

It was a brave thing to do, to call Bianca, who she barely knew, and ask her such a big favour. Rachel was relieved when it was Bianca's cheerful Scottish voice on the other end of the line. She'd been worried that she might just hang up with fright if TJ Mills picked up the phone. She'd had his poster on her walls as a teenager. Aged thirteen, she planned to marry Bianca's husband herself.

'Hi, Rachel.' Bianca sounded genuinely happy to hear from her.

'Bianca,' said Rachel nervously. 'I need to ask you a favour.'

'Of course,' sing-songed Bianca. 'Anything I can do to help.'

'I wondered if I could take you up on the offer of using your gym some time,' started Rachel tentatively. 'I know it's really cheeky to ask, but I really need to do some exercise and it's difficult to go very far with Alfie and, oh god, it's far too much to ask, isn't it? I'm really sorry. Forget I even mentioned it.'

'Rachel, it's fine.' Bianca giggled. 'No probs at all. In fact, I'd love you to come over and see our place anyway. Listen, why don't you come for lunch tomorrow. We'll have a nice light salad and then I'll take care of Alfie while you do your workout. You could have a swim and sauna as well, if you like. It'll be lovely. How about twelve thirty?'

'That would be great,' replied Rachel.

'It's a date,' announced Bianca.

After Bianca had hung up, Rachel held on to the phone for a moment and sighed a breath of relief. That had gone even better than she'd hoped. Not only did she feel sure that Bianca was a potential friend, but now she'd get a workout, a nose around the Mills's mansion, and maybe she'd even get to meet TJ. Life was looking up.

How the plans for Millsborough ever got past the planning stage in a beautiful village like Combe was a mystery to everyone but the Mills themselves. TJ and Bianca's four-storey faux tudor monstrosity made Beckingham Palace look modest. As Rachel pushed Alfie's buggy up to the electric gates she was completely taken aback by the complete, unadulterated tastelessness of the place. If Millsborough was Bianca's dream home, it was Rachel's idea of a nightmare. The house itself stood 200 metres up a tree-lined avenue from the main road, but it was so massive that it seemed to dominate the skyline even from that distance. The brickwork was too red, the paintwork too white, the grass too green, the towers too tall and the windows too plastic for any of it to look remotely authentic. It looked like a doll's house on steroids.

'Oh my goodness.' Rachel giggled to herself.

She was buzzed in through the video entry system and made her way slowly up the driveway towards the house. As she approached she was greeted by a scene straight out of an executive home advert in a Sunday newspaper supplement. Bianca, TJ and their two gorgeous daughters stood snugly together in the doorway, beaming their Colgate smiles, waving enthusiastically to their visitor and wearing white to show off their year-round tans. Bianca had on another velour tracksuit, TJ wore a shirt undone to his waist with white linen trousers and the little ones were dressed in white fairy costumes, complete with wings and wands. Rachel thought it the most surreal scene she'd ever encountered.

'Rachel,' gushed Bianca, embracing her warmly and planting a delicate, vanilla-scented kiss on each cheek. 'Meet TJ, my husband.'

'Hi,' said Rachel sheepishly.

TJ's star might have waned two decades earlier, but the man was still gorgeous – drop-dead, pant-wettingly gorgeous. Just like he had been twenty years ago when he was the king of the New Romantics. His jaw was square, with a slight dimple in the cleft of his chin, his cheekbones high and sharp enough to cut glass, his honey-coloured hair was on the long side of cropped and mussed-up sexily, and his bare chest was smooth, muscular and tanned. He had to be on the wrong side of 40, but Rachel didn't think she'd ever seen a better specimen of manhood.

'Pleased to meet you, Rachel,' said TJ with a warm smile and a hint of a Brummie accent.

Rachel held out her hand, but TJ moved closer and kissed her on both cheeks. She felt a flutter of butterflies in her tummy as his skin touched hers. It wasn't every day she got to meet – hell touch – her childhood hero.

'And this is Lotte and Poppy.' Bianca beamed with obvious pride.

The toddlers were adorable miniature versions of their mother. They grinned with tiny, shiny white teeth and jumped up and down so their dark-brown ringlets bounced around their heads. Rachel couldn't believe that Alfie would be that big in two years' time.

'Baby,' shouted Lotte, spotting Alfie in his buggy.

'Baby,' echoed Poppy, who was twenty-three minutes younger.

'They're really into babies at the moment,' explained TJ fondly. 'And they might get one of their own before too long if I get my way.'

He kissed Bianca on the lips and squeezed her firm, round bottom. 'Eh, missus?'

'Not yet, TJ.' Bianca blushed. 'I've told you, I want to wait a few more months. I am sorry, Rachel, my husband is obsessed with getting me pregnant again.'

Lucky you, thought Rachel, surprising herself.

As the Mills ushered Rachel into their vast, shiny entrance hall, TJ fondled his wife's bum again.

'You're a sex pest,' she teased him.

Rachel felt a pang of envy at this public display of mutual attraction. Why did Simon's sexual advances seem so sinister when TJ's appeared so sweet?

Rachel made a mental note to make love to her husband the following weekend. Maybe she was just out of practice. Perhaps the idea of sex was much worse than the reality. Before the pregnancy, their love life had been healthy enough. Nothing earth-shattering, granted, but perfectly normal in a once-a-week kind of way. The problem was, she'd recently discovered that the less she had, the less she wanted. Now she'd been out of the saddle for so long that she was seriously rusty. But once they got down to it, she'd begin to fancy her husband again. Maybe.

Millsborough reminded Rachel of a Las Vegas

hotel she'd once stayed in with Simon on one of their weekend breaks. It was golden and glitzy and incredibly naff. Proof, if proof were needed, that money cannot buy good taste. Every surface gleamed with well-scrubbed cleanliness – testament to the army of cleaners that scoured and polished each day. There were deep shagpile carpets in various shades of pink; gold fixtures and fittings; family portraits the size of billiard tables on the shiny, patterned walls, and even a gilded statue of Bianca as a mermaid, naked from the waist up, in the entrance hall. There was a twelve-seater cinema, a twenty-five-metre swimming pool with a retractable roof for the summer, a state-of-the-art gymnasium, a solarium, a sauna and steam room. Not to mention nine bedrooms, all of them ensuite, two kitchens, a wine cellar, a 'boy's room' with a pool table, Subbuteo, pinball, jukebox and full-sized bar, and an entire recording studio in the basement. Each room was more tasteless than the last, but what it lacked in style it made up for in atmosphere. However offensive the décor, no-one could deny that the house echoed with laughter and love.

'What do you think?' asked Bianca expectantly after giving her new friend the guided tour.

'It's incredible,' said Rachel truthfully. 'It feels like a very happy home.'

Bianca smiled broadly. 'Thank you, Rachel. That means a lot to me,' she said. 'Hattie says this house looks like a Barbie brothel, but then you should see The Beeches.' Bianca dropped her voice to a conspiratorial whisper. 'I mean, I know shabby chic is fashionable, but the Lilywhite Smythes take the look to extremes. The place is filthy and all the furniture is so old. Harriet says they're family heir-looms, antiques I suppose, but honestly it's all so dated. You know, they don't even have double glaz-ing. The place must be worth, oh' – Bianca thought for a moment – 'well, not as much as this place because ours is a new build and theirs is ancient, but a couple of million at least, and they haven't even bothered getting the windows replaced.'

Rachel pictured the beautiful, ancient leaded windows that she could see over the hedge from her attic room in Ivy Cottage and thanked god that Lord Lilywhite Smythe hadn't given in to the charms of a door-to-door double-glazing salesman.

After a delicious lunch of chicken and mango salad, prepared by the Mills's resident Malaysian chef, Rachel ventured into the gym, behind Bianca who insisted, 'Use everything. Take your time.' It had been a year since she'd done anything more strenuous than carrying her own weight – which was a workout in itself – and within two minutes of starting the running machine, her face had turned puce. Bianca had covered the walls and the ceiling of the gym with mirrors, presumably so that she could check out her perfect body from every angle as she kept it in shape. For Rachel, this was torture of the cruellest kind. She hadn't seen her back view in a long, long time, and it was not a pretty sight. The flab on her bum had experienced a landslide towards the back of her knees and there were rolls of fat above her bra strap that she'd never seen before. Even her ankles looked overweight.

The view was enough of an incentive to keep Rachel running for twenty minutes and to make her pledge never to buy chocolate Hobnobs again. Afterwards, she swam ten lengths and then had a long, luxurious sauna, where she hoped she might sweat off another pound or two. Rachel wondered if Bianca would allow this to become a regular event.

Alfie had been more than content to snuggle up to Bianca for an hour or two. The girls had dressed him as a baby fairy, so Rachel found her son gurgling happily between Bianca's boobs, wearing a silver leotard over his nappy and a tiara on his head. He looked drunk with happiness.

'Better?' asked Bianca as Rachel appeared, red-faced and damp-haired in the kitchen.

'Much better.' She smiled. 'That was bliss. I'm really grateful, Bianca. I haven't had any time to myself since Alfie was born.'

'It's tough, isn't it?' Bianca's beautiful face was full of empathy. 'I found it so hard when these two were tiny – I still do – but I had TJ here and we coped together. I don't know how you're managing on your own.'

Rachel had meant to put a brave face on things – she didn't want to scare her new friend away by being miserable and needy – but there was something soft and beguiling about Bianca, and under her doe-eyed gaze, Rachel felt her face begin to crumple and a lump form in her throat. Before she knew it, she'd completely lost control of her emotions and tears were streaming down her face.

'I'm not, Bianca.' She sobbed. 'I'm not coping at all.'

If tea and sympathy were an art form, Bianca Mills would be a grand master. She hugged Rachel like a life-long friend and stroked her wet hair. 'Shh, Rachel. It's OK. Everything will be OK.'

Rachel had been holding back so many emotions for such a long time that once the floodgates opened there was no stopping the pent-up frustrations from flowing out in a torrent of sobs and sniffs. She told Bianca how lonely she felt, how ugly and how fat. She explained how scared she was of losing Alfie because she loved him so damn much. She told Bianca how much she missed Simon when he wasn't there and how much she resented him when he was. How she didn't feel sexy and didn't want sex, which in turn scared her because Simon might look elsewhere. How could he want her now when she looked like this? She explained how much she missed her friends and that she was scared they'd just forgotten her. They never phoned her any more, and when they did it was like some sort of torture because all they talked about was the parties they'd been to, the clothes they'd worn and the good time they'd had. But most of all, she told Bianca, she was just tired. So, so tired. And if only she could get some sleep then maybe everything else would seem better.

When Rachel woke up, she was confused about where she was. The first thing she saw when she opened her eyes was the Sistine Chapel ceiling. Or at least a gaudy, small-scale reproduction of the Sistine Chapel ceiling, which was actually the ceiling of Bianca Mills's favourite guest room. Ah, Bianca's house. Lovely, kind, amazing Bianca. Bianca who'd mopped up her tears, kissed her head and then fished out her old expressing machine. Expressing breast milk – there hadn't seemed much point in trying it before because Simon wasn't around to feed Alfie a bottle anyway, but Bianca had insisted it was a brilliant idea.

'That way, Simon can do the night feeds at the weekends and you can catch up on some sleep.'

Rachel had sat there at Bianca's shiny breakfast bar, plugged into an electric milking machine while the twins pointed noisily and shouted, 'Whazat?' She hoped that TJ would stay in his studio as Bianca promised he would. Being caught in this uncompromising position by TJ Mills would be too humiliating to bear. Alfie's huge eyes looked like they were going to pop out of his head as he watched mummy being milked. It took nearly an hour to fill two bottles and then Bianca said, 'Go to bed.' So she did and now it was getting dark outside and Rachel felt as if she'd slept for a thousand years. Ouch. As she tried to stand up, she realized her muscles had already seized up from their earlier workout, but her mind felt clearer than it had done for weeks. In fact, there was a vaguely familiar warm feeling in her belly, which she realized might be happiness. She descended the sweeping staircase from the second floor, feeling like an extra from *Dynasty*, and headed towards the laughter rising up from the ground floor of Millsborough. She found Bianca, cuddling Alfie on a white leather sofa in the family room and laughing at TJ, who was rolling around on a huge sheepskin rug tickling his hysterical daughters.

'More!' shouted Poppy. 'Daddy more!'

The Mills family looked up and greeted their guest cheerfully, and Rachel was overcome with gratitude towards her new friends.

'Simon phoned you,' said Bianca, waving Rachel's mobile at her. 'Hope you don't mind me answering it, but he'd tried three times. I think he was getting a bit worried because you weren't at home. I introduced myself and told him you were getting some well-earned rest. And I invited him to the dinner party next Saturday. He said he'd be delighted to come.'

'Dinner party?' asked Rachel. It was the first she'd heard of it.

'Oh yes.' TJ smiled. 'We've decided to throw a party for our new neighbours. You're the guests of honour, so you'll probably need a new outfit. I know what you girls are like. Why don't I look after the kids tomorrow while you two go into Bath? I'm a dab hand with a bottle, so you don't have to worry about Alfie. It'll be nice to have some male company for a change.'

As she left Millsborough, Bianca handed her a carrier bag.

'What's that?' asked Rachel.

'The expressing machine. You'll need to do a few bottles' worth for our shopping trip tomorrow. TJ is a man of many talents, but even he can't lactate!'

The plan was that Rachel would walk up to Millsborough in the morning and settle Alfie in with TJ, before heading off to Bath in the Porsche. Rachel was a level-headed woman who was not normally impressed by the trappings of wealth, but she couldn't help but feel excited by the prospect of a ride in Bianca's car. And, much as she appreciated her new Honda 4x4, she didn't feel switched-on enough to drive it safely herself at the moment. As she wandered slowly back down Chillyhill Lane in the half light of dusk, Rachel listened to the evening bird song and smiled happily to herself. Alfie was fast asleep in his buggy and the lights of Combe twinkled prettily below her. It wasn't such a bad place she decided. Rachel's thoughts were interrupted by the headlights of an on-coming vehicle approaching at speed. She pulled the pushchair onto the grassy verge quickly, worried for a second that the driver might not see them in the dark. The jeep slowed down as it passed her and a man she'd never seen before waved his thanks. In the twilight, the man's eyes seemed to flash emerald green, and for a second Rachel felt dazzled by their brightness. That night, Alfie slept from midnight until 5 a.m.

Chapter Four

The Dinner Party

'You went to Bath with the housewife?' Harriet was not happy.

'Yes. With Rachel,' sing-songed Bianca. 'We had a lovely time. I persuaded her to buy a dress from Whistles, we had lunch at the Moon and Sixpence and then we popped into Baby Gap to buy some summer clothes for the children.'

'And you didn't think to invite me?' Harriet was worried that she had been replaced.

'Well no,' said Bianca honestly. 'There's only room in my car for two. And anyway, you said you thought Rachel was boring.'

'She is,' answered Harriet petulantly. 'But hanging around here on my own is more boring. It just would have been nice to be asked.'

'Are you jealous?' teased Bianca gently.

'No, don't be stupid. It's just, well, I've kind of got used to hanging around with you lately and I don't know what to do with myself when you're busy.' Harriet took a deep breath and blurted out what she really meant. 'Bianca, you're my only acquaintance – OK friend – in Combe and I don't want you to be friends with her instead of me. I know I can be difficult, and I'm not very nice sometimes, but that's just my manner. It doesn't mean I don't like you, OK?'

'OK,' said Bianca, smiling to herself. 'But why can't we all be friends? Rachel's very nice, you know. And she used to work in fashion, so you two have got loads in common.'

'Fashion?' Harriet was confused. 'I didn't think they let fat people work in fashion. That's why designers make clothes in such tiny sample sizes. It's to keep ordinary people reliant on M&S.'

'Hattie, don't be a bitch,' warned Bianca. 'That's why you don't have any friends.'

'I have got friends,' said Harriet defensively. 'It's just they're not here. They're in London and New York and LA . . .' She trailed off. 'Anyway, I'll see you tomorrow night at this stupid party of yours. That's if I'm still invited, now that you've got a new friend to play with.'

'You're still invited,' confirmed Bianca patiently.

'Are you wearing Versace?' asked Harriet automatically.

Bianca said yes.

'I'll go for Prada then.'

Bianca thought that was a good idea.

'I'm not going,' announced Rachel, slumping onto the bed in her new dress. 'I look like a milk maid from a Thomas Hardy novel. And a fat one at that.'

The dress Bianca had persuaded her to buy was a whimsical ensemble of frothy cream broderie anglaise, with a very revealing neckline. It was so tight around the torso that it scooped Rachel's enormous breasts up until they spilled over the top. It would have looked beautiful in a small, she concluded, but in a large it was verging on the pastoral.

'You look fine,' said Simon as he straightened his tie in the mirror. He didn't sound convinced. Actually, he didn't sound as if he gave a toss.

'Fine?' pouted Rachel. 'I don't want to look fine. Fine isn't good enough.'

Simon turned round and looked his wife up and down.

'You look nice,' he concluded.

'Nice? Just nice? Argh! I'm getting changed,' shrieked Rachel.

'What's wrong with nice?' asked Simon, perplexed. It seemed the longer he was married to Rachel, the less he understood her.

Half an hour later the bed had disappeared under a mound of clothes, all of which had been tried on and discarded by their owner, who couldn't do up their zips. Alfie was lying comfortably on a silk jersey Joseph frock. Rachel was back in the milk maid's outfit but, having swathed herself in a large cream wrap, her assets were no longer on show. To finish off the outfit, she'd forced her swollen toes into a dainty pair of beaded Jimmy Choo mules.

'My feet look like pig's trotters,' she concluded.

'If you say so, darling,' said Simon, who had decided it was easier to agree with his wife than to attempt to give her a compliment.

Actually, he thought she looked delicious – all

plump and inviting and oozing with naughty delights, a bit like a chocolate éclair. He prayed silently to himself that sex might be on the agenda later that night.

'So who's going to be at this dinner party?' he asked as the Travis family trooped up the lane towards Millsborough. Simon was pushing Alfie's buggy while Rachel struggled to keep up in her heels. She'd forgotten how to walk in girlie shoes. She'd worn nothing but slippers or wellies recently.

'I don't know,' replied Rachel nervously. 'Lots of rich, glamorous people I expect.'

Simon pushed the all-terrain buggy with one hand and held out the other to his wife. She grabbed it gratefully.

'Have you remembered I have to go back to London first thing tomorrow?' he asked.

'Yeah.' Rachel sighed. 'I wish you didn't have to.'

'I know, love,' he said gently. 'But I'm off to New York on Monday and I've got a mound of work to do in the office before I go.'

Rachel was gutted about missing a precious day with her husband, but she was trying desperately to be brave. She knew Simon didn't want to leave her and Alfie. It was work. He was the boss now. It had to be done.

The evening started badly for Rachel. TJ welcomed them in and led them to the formal drawing room, where the guests were assembled. Rachel walked in just in time to overhear Bianca and Harriet talking about her.

'I think Rachel's about the same age as us,' Bianca was saying. 'Late twenties.'

'Really?' Harriet mused. 'I can never tell how old fat people are. Most just look frumpy and middle-aged, but some of them look quite young, I suppose. All that fat does seem to ward off wrinkles. It must work like a filler for fine lines. Flab,' she said thoughtfully. 'Nature's botox. Maybe old Portly Paws is on to something . . . Ouch!'

Bianca stabbed Hattie in the ribs with her bony elbow.

'Rachel. Hi,' she gushed warmly, hoping that Harriet's hurtful comments had not been overheard by Rachel and Simon. 'You look lovely.'

Harriet and Bianca looked far from frumpy and middle-aged. Bianca was a glistening vision of loveliness in her one-shouldered Versace gold dress and Harriet looked haughty but elegant in a simple black Prada shift and pearls. Rachel shrank back towards the doorway, wishing she could turn tail and run. 'Portly Paws?' How nasty was that? Simon squeezed his wife's hand reassuringly. He was normally drawn to attractive young women, but in Harriet's case he made an exception. He hated her on sight.

By the time the main course was served Rachel had relaxed and was beginning to enjoy herself. This was partly due to Bianca's talents as a hostess – knowing how low Rachel's self-esteem was, she had deliberately placed her new friend between TJ and Harriet's dad, both of whom were ridiculous flirts and would make Rachel feel special. In fact, Lawrence Lilywhite Smythe – 'Darling, do call me

Larry' – hadn't been able to avert his gaze from Rachel's cleavage since she'd discarded her wrap. He was practically slobbering with delight at having been sat next to this buxom young wench. Simon had also been helping his wife to relax by constantly topping up her glass with champagne without her knowledge in the hope that a drunken wife might be more accommodating to his needs than a sober one.

Rachel was not the only one getting sozzled. Marjorie, a greying, bespectacled horse of a woman with a weak chin and protruding nose, had never been very good at socializing, preferring to spend time with thoroughbreds and Labradors and could only cope with the horror of having to make small talk by getting quietly smashed in the corner. Harriet, meanwhile, had consumed enough champagne to tranquillize an elephant and was beginning to get somewhat lary as a result. She had already sniped at her stepmother and was now glaring at her father, who was also becoming increasingly pissed and opinionated.

Larry was an amiable old bigot. He had already held court on the subjects of fox hunting: 'I'll bloody well keep on hunting even once it's illegal. They can send me to jail for all I care.' And Europe: 'We Brits must fight for our independence. If we give in to Brussels we'll become a German colony before we know it. Is that why we fought Hitler? Is it? Or worse, a French colony. We'll be forced to eat garlic and play that damned stupid game boules. You know they already have an annual boules championships in Bath? You see, it's started already.' And immigrants: 'Bleeding our economy dry.' And Londoners: 'They come here, buy up property, making it too expensive for my staff to own, and then leave it empty most of the time, which only encourages theft and vandalism. Then they come to visit for the weekend, take over a perfectly good village pub and loudly discuss their woolly, Liberal, city-dwelling ideas in front of the village youngsters, who are at a most impressionable age. We'll be left with a village full of Lefties at this rate,' he spluttered drunkenly.

'Oh Daddy, do shut up,' interjected Harriet suddenly. 'In case you hadn't noticed, no one is agreeing with you. We're all just sitting here, quietly letting you talk bollocks because we don't want to have an argument.'

'Harriet, that's no way to talk to your father,' snapped Lady Lilywhite Smythe.

The guests turned to stare at her in surprise. She had said nothing up until this point and most of them had almost forgotten she was there.

'You have no respect for your elders,' she continued, her voice breaking with wine-induced emotion. 'If you were my daughter . . .'

'If I were your daughter, what?' demanded Harriet. Her eyes flashed and her pale cheeks had become flushed with anger and alcohol.

Marjorie Lilywhite Smythe's face was long, thin and drawn at the best of times, but now, as she sucked in her sunken cheeks with disgust, she resembled the living dead. She dabbed at her narrow lips with her napkin.

'I'm not going to have an argument with you

here, Harriet,' she said coldly. 'Not when Bianca has gone to so much effort to give us all such a pleasant evening. You really are a rude young woman.'

The assembled group stared at their plates and shuffled their feet beneath the table in embarrassed silence.

But Harriet wouldn't, or couldn't, let it lie. 'The Temper' was as much a part of her genetic make-up as her blond hair or long legs. 'The Temper' had cursed generations of Lilywhite Smythes; it ate away at the family tree like hereditary cancer. Her father had it, and his father had had it before him. It was a huge, black monster of an emotion with a life of its own and Harriet's will power was no match for its ferocity. That evening, as usual, it was aimed at Marjorie.

'If I were your daughter I'd have topped myself by now,' said Harriet. Her voice cracked under the weight of her anger.

Bianca tried to catch Harriet's eye, to give her a friendly look and tell her it was OK, that people understood how difficult Marjorie could be and that it would be all right to back down. But Hattie's eyes were fixed firmly on her stepmother and she was oblivious to her friend's stare.

'Are you going to let her talk to me like that, Larry?' Marjorie demanded of her husband.

Larry took a long slug of his Scotch and said half-heartedly, 'Hattie, don't speak to your stepmother like that.'

He had given up trying to accommodate the two women in his life a long time ago. He knew full well that never the twain would meet. Harriet blamed Marjorie for her mother's absence at The Beeches. She'd decided long ago, as a hot-headed teenager, that if her father had never met Marjorie then Hermione would have come home eventually. Larry knew this was nonsense, of course. His first wife had left months before he'd met Marjorie and he'd tried to convince her to come home many, many times. But Hermione had got sick of his philandering and had fallen out of love. It was as simple as that. For once, Marjorie had not been to blame. Of course, his second wife was a frightful bore and he couldn't really blame Harriet for disliking her. Quite frankly, he'd forgotten what he'd ever seen in the woman. He vaguely recollected an inheritance of half a million pounds, which had been left to her by her recently deceased first husband. It had all gone now, of course. There wasn't a penny left. Marjorie was of little use to him these days and she certainly wasn't worth falling out with Harriet over.

'I'll speak to her however I like,' continued Harriet. 'She talks to me as if I'm a piece of dirt. Why should I show her any respect?'

'Harriet, please,' interjected Bianca. 'Forget it. Let's just have pudding.'

'Dessert would be delightful,' said Marjorie to her host. 'Somebody here could do with some sweetening up.' She glared at her stepdaughter.

And then 'The Temper' took over. The little switch in Harriet's head flipped to 'on' and all hell broke loose. She stood up suddenly, toppling her chair over as she did so and screamed, 'You are such a fucking cow, Marjorie! It's just snipe, snipe,

snipe, all day, every day. You do this act in public, like you're so hard-done-by, and I'm such a difficult person to deal with.'

Marjorie snorted and glanced around at her fellow diners with a knowing look-what-I-have-to-put-up-with expression.

'Harriet, darling,' she replied with venom dripping from her tongue. 'You're not difficult, you're impossible. No civilized individual would act like this at a dinner party. Once again, you've ruined a delightful evening for everyone else. In fact, I would go so far as to say that you're unhinged. I mean, everyone knows about your addictions, your criminal record, your temper—'

'Marjorie, leave it,' said Larry firmly. 'She's upset.'

'Oh, she's upset,' scoffed Marjorie. 'She's always upset. Poor little Harriet with all her problems. Perhaps if you and Hermione hadn't pandered to her problems quite so much she might have turned out to be a reasonable human being instead of this spoilt brat.' And then she turned to everyone else. 'I do apologize,' she said, 'for Harriet's disgusting display. Let's have dessert, Bianca.'

But Harriet was not going to let Marjorie have dessert. Harriet decided that Marjorie needed wine – a large glass of red to be precise, thrown right into her ugly old face. And so she did it, without thinking; she just grabbed her glass and threw its contents in the direction of her stepmother. Harriet watched in slow motion as the wine left the glass and splattered all over Marjorie's head. For a split second, as Marjorie gulped in disbelief, Harriet felt satisfied, and then the guilt set in, as it always did after the 'The Temper' subsided. She looked at Bianca's horrified face, Simon's look of disgust, the sadness in her father's eyes and TJ's glint of amusement. Only Rachel looked at Harriet with anything approaching sympathy, or was it pity, Harriet didn't know. And then the tears came, as they always did, and she ran from the table in shame.

Bianca stood up to follow Harriet as the waiting staff fussed around a horrified Marjorie, trying to mop up the mess.

'Leave her,' said Larry quietly to Bianca. 'Let her calm down. She'll feel wretched now. She needs to lick her wounds, then she'll come back and apologize. She always does.'

The table sat in uncomfortable silence while the staff changed the tablecloth and reset the table for dessert and coffee. Marjorie reappeared from the bathroom with damp hair and a red stain on her blouse.

'So,' said TJ in a blatant attempt to diffuse the situation. 'What do we all think about the new house on the hill? I hear it's finished now.'

'It has to be some new-money type,' said Larry with forced enthusiasm, keen to deflect attention from his troublesome offspring. 'I know of several stately homes on the market at present, and no one with any breeding would waste their money building some modern monstrosity when they could buy a house with character and history.'

Bianca's face fell. It mattered to her what Sir Lilywhite Smythe thought, and here he was in her house spouting off about new builds. TJ caught his wife's eye and gave her a reassuring wink. TJ didn't give a toss about what the old toff thought. He was likeable enough, old Larry, but he didn't half talk nonsense. TJ knew better, of course. Having been born into poverty, Terry John Mills was proud of what he'd achieved. He had millions in the bank, a huge house, a beautiful wife and two great little girls. Not bad for a kid from Wolverhampton. He was in awe of Bianca's father, Mario, who'd moved to Scotland from Italy aged fifteen, without a penny to his name and not a word of English. Now Mario owned a chain of ice-cream parlours, several fish and chip shops and an upmarket Italian restaurant in Glasgow's West End. To TJ, the man was a legend. Larry, on the other hand, was just a pissed-up old fart who'd been lucky enough to develop in a rich lady's womb. He didn't have any real power any more. He was a dinosaur, a relic, and soon his type would be extinct for good.

'Would you like another whiskey, Sir?' he asked Larry with a warm smile.

Bianca thought there was a lot to be said for new architecture, and as the daughter and wife of working-class boys done good, she had a lot to say about new money too. She also had strong opinions on fox hunting – cruel, disgusting, barbaric – and Europe – surely bringing down barriers is better than putting them up? – and immigration – her parents were immigrants, after all – but, as always, she said nothing. Bianca had been brought up to believe that pretty little girls should be seen and not heard. She'd been treated as an attractive accessory for so long that she feared her brain and her mouth

110

were no longer connected. She had all these thoughts racing round her head, but she never dared to utter them. It was OK for Harriet to voice an opinion. Christ, she could have a full-blown temper tantrum and her family hardly raised an eyebrow. People expected it of her. She had the confidence that comes with being born into money; she'd always been told she was part of the elite. She believed in her right to be part of society and to abuse it if she liked. Bianca believed only in her ability to decorate it.

'The problem is,' Larry continued drunkenly, 'that the only people who have money now are those who've made it through crime. I wouldn't be at all surprised if this new house isn't occupied by some drug baron or an International arms dealer. Isn't that so, Marjorie.'

'Quite so,' sniffed Lady Lilywhite Smythe in wholehearted agreement. 'Combe is not the place it once was.'

Rachel was now past the merely tipsy stage and had to stifle a giggle. She caught TJ's eye and the pair shared an amused grin at the thought of their presence having brought down the tone of the neighbourhood. Bianca wasn't finding the conversation quite so amusing. In fact, the dinner party wasn't going according to plan at all. She tried to change the subject again.

'More lemon torte anyone?' But it was to no avail. The Lilywhite Smythes were on a roll.

'I mean, we've always had slum housing in Combe,' continued Marjorie, sounding haughty, but looking bedraggled in her wine-splattered clothes.

'Oh yes, the cottages,' guffawed Larry. 'But we didn't mind those looking tatty when our staff lived in them.'

'That's our slum housing now,' said Simon coldly. He was beginning to see why Rachel was feeling so miserable about being marooned in Combe. The locals were bloody awful.

'I'm sure you're very comfortable there.' Marjorie smiled in a condescending manner. 'We're just used to something a bit grander, that's all.'

'So, my dear,' slurred Larry, returning his gaze to Rachel's chest. 'What's your story? Where are your people from?'

'Oh, I'm just the daughter of a couple of bleeding-heart Liberals from London.' Rachel smiled sweetly. 'We're pro Europe, anti hunting, New Labour-voting Lefties. And some of our best friends are immigrants.'

'Never mind, dear,' he replied cheerfully. 'You're very pretty and that's the main thing.' Lord Lilywhite Smythe was, after all, an amiable bigot.

Marjorie tutted. Simon smiled proudly and TJ realized he'd found an ally. Bianca felt a pang of jealousy towards her new friend. If only she had the courage to speak her mind like that.

It was a mild, clear spring evening, so after dessert Bianca ushered her guests out onto the verandah for some aperitifs alfresco. Harriet was still nowhere to be seen. As Simon chatted to TJ and Bianca fussed around filling her guests' glasses with port, Rachel excused herself.

'I'm going to check on Alfie,' she explained.

In truth she was sure Alfie was fine, it was

112

Harriet she was worried about. She wasn't quite sure why she was concerned about Hattie's well-being. The woman had been absolutely vile to her from the moment they'd met, but Rachel had always had a soft spot for the underdog and, right now, Harriet Lilywhite Smythe was definitely in the dog house. Rachel tripped, a little drunkenly, into the house.

'Harriet?' she called.

There was no answer.

'Harriet?'

Rachel listened carefully in the silence. From somewhere far away she could hear crying. It wasn't the high-pitched wail of a baby but the slow, sobbing gasps of an adult. She pushed open door after door until the sobbing got closer. Eventually Rachel realized that the sound was coming from the bedroom where she'd left Alfie sleeping. She pushed open the door as quietly as she could and was surprised to see the shadow of a figure sitting on the bed next to Alfie's pram. It took a while for her to focus through the half light and the fog of champagne, but eventually she realized it was Harriet holding Alfie in her arms. Hattie's shoulders shook gently and she was talking to Alfie through her tears.

'Don't grow up like me, little fellow,' she was whispering. 'Be a good boy for your mummy and daddy. Be happy. Make them proud.'

'Hello,' said Rachel, not quite sure what else to say.

Harriet jumped. 'Rachel. Hi,' she stammered. Her face was blotchy with tears. 'I'm sorry, I was in the loo and I heard him crying, so I just popped in to see if he was OK. Anyway, I gave him a bit of a cuddle and he's gone back to sleep now. I hope that's all right.'

'Of course it is,' said Rachel. 'Thanks.'

Harriet held out the sleeping baby to his mother. Rachel took her child and kissed him gently on the cheek – as always he smelled delicious – and placed him carefully back into his pram.

'He's OK, isn't he?' asked Harriet, wiping her eyes with the back of her hand. 'I did the right thing, didn't I?'

'He's absolutely fine,' said Rachel, 'but you don't look too good.'

Harriet sniffed loudly and shrugged. 'Oh, I'm OK,' she said with a flustered, embarrassed shrug. 'I always do that. I've got this terrible temper and I lose it at the most inappropriate times. I can't explain it. It's like having a little devil inside me that I have absolutely no control over. Some things and some people – especially Marjorie – just get to me. I get wound up and then I explode. I used to do it when I was a kid. You know, I was one of those children who would throw the Monopoly board across the room if I ended up in jail. Mummy used to say I'd grow out of it, but I never have. I try really hard to stay in control, but I always end up spoiling everything. Now they'll all think I'm this hideous monster. I really should just stay in my room and never go out. I can't be trusted.' She smiled weakly at Rachel. 'Are they all terribly cross?'

Rachel shook her head. 'No, they're fine. We're

114

having drinks on the terrace. Come back out with me.'

'No,' said Harriet firmly. 'I can't. I'm too ashamed to face them all. Especially Bianca. Poor Bianca. She really cares about throwing these silly dinners and playing the perfect hostess and I've gone and ruined it for her.'

'Bianca will understand,' said Rachel. 'She tried to go after you.'

'She did?'

'Yes, but your dad thought you should be left alone to calm down.'

'He's right. It takes a little while for my blood to stop boiling and then I just feel wretched and ashamed and about this size.' Harriet held her fingers a millimetre apart.

A stray tear meandered its way down her smooth cheek and paused for a moment before dripping off her chin. Rachel had found Hattie intimidating at first, but looking at her now, she seemed anything but – just vulnerable, messed-up and, despite her six-foot frame, very, very small.

'I've got a friend like you,' said Rachel, thinking about Zoe. 'On the surface she's totally cool and collected. Scary, even. And she does this whole act of being really hard and impenetrable but inside she's as soft as the rest of us.'

Harriet nodded.

'What you need,' said Rachel firmly. 'Is a hug. Come here.'

Harriet's bottom lip quivered as she threw her skinny body into Rachel's warm arms. The truth was, she hadn't had that much physical contact for a long time and it felt good. She stayed there, shaking quietly for several minutes until the tears dried up.

'I should apologize,' said Harriet sadly.

'You should,' agreed Rachel. 'Come on.'

As they walked slowly through the house together Harriet stopped suddenly and said, 'Thanks, Rachel. For listening. Most people just think I'm a waste of space.'

'Nobody is a waste of space, Harriet,' said Rachel. 'We all have our good and bad points.'

'I just keep my good points well hidden.' Harriet smiled sadly.

As they walked back out onto the verandah, they found Bianca waving her arms around excitedly and shouting, 'Look! Look!'

Above them, at the top of the hill, was a twinkling palace of golden light.

'It's the new house,' said Bianca in awe. 'Isn't it magical?'

Every light in every room of the huge house had been turned on, as if the new owner were announcing his arrival by lighting up the sky. The Mills were the closest neighbours, and from their verandah the fairy lights strung up on the trees in the garden of the new house could be seen dancing in the gentle evening breeze. At the end of the long garden was one particularly bright, white light. It had been strategically placed at the top of a huge cedar tree and now, in the darkness, it appeared like a lighthouse above the cliff which fell to the woods below. Rachel thought it was the most beautiful sight she'd ever seen.

'Wow!' she said. 'That's some house.'

'Who lives in a place like this?' joked TJ in *Through the Keyhole* style.

'Some obnoxious young oik, no doubt,' muttered Larry.

'I think it's quite wonderful,' whispered Bianca.

'It puts Millsborough to shame,' agreed TJ with a tinge of envy. 'Who on earth can it be?'

'It's the Great Gatsby,' grinned Simon.

Everyone laughed at his joke, except Bianca and TJ, who were not well read, but they smiled politely and pretended to understand.

Simon watched his wife undress with baited breath. As she slithered out of the tight dress her pale flesh tumbled free and he couldn't wait any longer. He grabbed her around her bare waist and squeezed her soft belly.

'Can we make love tonight, Rachel? Please?' asked Simon.

His eyes were pleading with her. Rachel thought Simon looked just like Alfie when he was desperate for a feed. Just the thought of her son put her straight off the idea of sex. All week she'd been planning on making love to her husband tonight. She'd been psyching herself up to the event – that's what the new dress had been all about, not to mention the new underwear she was now standing in – and she'd even drunk more at the party than is fitting for a breastfeeding mother just to help her loosen up. But now she'd gone and thought about Alfie again and the moment was ruined. Why did she find it so hard to be a mother and a lover simultaneously? She thought about all the sexy mothers out there – Kate Moss, Catherine Zeta-Jones, Victoria Beckham – and couldn't believe for a minute that they'd been celibate since giving birth. Rachel wondered if she should put an ad in the local paper 'Lost. One libido. If found please return to Rachel Travis. Hefty reward.'

Simon was kissing her neck in a way that used to make her squirm with delight, but now she just found it mildly irritating.

'Rachel, I love you so much.' He was slobbering into her ear. 'I can't wait to ravish you.'

Rachel took a deep breath and decided there was no way out. She closed her eyes and tried to get in the mood.

'I love you too,' she whispered.

And she did. She just didn't fancy him any more. It was no use. Simon's kisses felt all wrong – too wet, too desperate – and his touch made her cringe instead of turning her on. There was no going back, though, not unless she wanted to start the mother of all marital arguments. She was just going to have to lie back and think of England. So she did. Simon was not a selfish lover, he did everything he could to pleasure his wife. It wasn't his fault that her libido had gone AWOL, so Rachel oo-ed and ah-ed in all the right places and pretended to be having the time of her life. But when he tried to enter her it was too much to bear.

'Ouch!' she shouted.

'Are you all right?' asked Simon kindly. 'I'll be as gentle as I can.'

Rachel nodded and he tried again.

'Ow!' she screamed. It felt as though she was being ripped in two, just like giving birth again.

'I'm sorry, babe, it really hurts,' she explained.

Simon tried once more but there was no way his wife was letting him in.

Rachel watched as her husband slumped back into the pillows, his ego deflating quicker than his erection.

'I'm really sorry, Si,' she said softly.

Simon said nothing. He just turned his back on Rachel and pretended to go to sleep. Rachel turned off the light and wept silently in the dark. She felt so alone, as if she'd just had a meaningless one-night stand with a stranger. It was as if she didn't recognize Simon any more. She felt cold and ashamed, lying naked on the bed, unable to give her husband the one thing he needed. As her eyes became accustomed to the darkness she could make out the shape of Simon's bare back. His shoulders were shaking gently and she realized that he was crying too. Part of her wanted to take him in her arms and reassure him that everything would be all right, but she knew that would be a lie. Deep down she knew that nothing was all right; it wasn't all right at all.

Alfie had a disturbed night and Rachel spent the early hours sitting in the rocking chair nursing him and feeling numb. From the window in Alfie's attic room she could clearly see up the hill to the light at the end of the garden of the new house. She watched it twinkle in the moonlight and wondered why the owner had put it there. As it began to get light outside, she fell asleep in the chair still cradling Alfie, and when she woke up, Simon had gone. For a horrible moment she thought he'd walked out on her, but then she remembered about the work he had to do at the office and she was slightly relieved. On the kitchen table she found a note which read, 'Didn't want to wake you. Have had to go back to London. Will call this afternoon. Kiss Alfie for me. Simon.' There was no xxx at the end of the note.

That Sunday, Rachel went through the motions of being a mum. She changed nappies and fed Alfie. She washed clothes and sterilized bottles. She sang nursery rhymes in a sad little voice and smiled empty smiles at her baby. She waited for the phone to ring, longing to hear Simon's voice, needing to know that last night's aborted attempt at love-making hadn't meant anything to him. Something stopped Rachel from phoning him. He would be busy and short with her and that would just make things worse. She was sure that Simon would be miserable too, and she felt sorry for him being so far away from his family, working on a Sunday.

In the afternoon her mum called to find out how things were going.

'Everything's great, Mum,' she lied, and then kicked herself once her mum had hung up because she really needed to confide in someone.

She found it hard admitting to her parents that she was having problems. She was the opposite of Harriet Lilywhite Smythe. She had always been such an easy child – polite, well-mannered, studious. She'd sailed through school, passing exams and making friends easily. Her mum and dad had never had to worry about her. She didn't want to shock them by suddenly becoming a problem child at the age of twenty-nine.

By eight o'clock, Alfie was sound asleep and the house was spotless. Simon still hadn't called. There was no reply at his office and if he was home, he wasn't picking up the phone, and his mobile was switched off. Eventually, Rachel decided to call Zoe. They hadn't spoken since the Alfie incident, but Rachel needed to talk to someone and she realized, a little miserably, that there was no one else. Even though it was a Sunday night, Rachel wasn't at all surprised that her party animal of a best friend wasn't at home. When Zoe answered her mobile, Rachel could hear the boom, boom, boom of loud music and the cheerful chatterings of weekend bar life.

'Zoe, it's me,' she shouted, making sure she could be heard above the din. 'Where are you?'

'At a bar opening in Notting Hill,' she shouted back. 'It's excellent. Really cool place. You should be here. You'd love it.'

Rachel was about to explain to her friend what had happened with Simon when Zoe continued, 'Si's here. With some mates from work. Have you let him off his leash this weekend?'

'What do you mean?' asked Rachel nervously.

She felt a slight panic in her chest at the thought of Simon out partying in London after the events of the night before. Why wasn't he at home alone, licking his wounds and thinking about her and Alfie?

'I mean, have you let the poor guy have a

weekend off country living? I'm not sure it suits him. He looks so at home back here.'

'Right,' ventured Rachel tentatively. She felt as if she'd been smacked in the face. What the hell was Simon doing at a bar opening when she was here alone, worrying about their relationship?

'Does he seem OK?' asked Rachel, hoping that Zoe would say, 'No, he's really upset.'

Instead Zoe shouted, 'What? I can't hear you, babes. It's very loud in here. Oh my God, have you met Si's new secretary, by the way. She's called Grace and she's fucking hilarious.'

'Is she?' asked Rachel nervously. So Simon was out with the Rottweiler.

'Oh yeah, she's a hoot. Very young. Reminds me of us when we were that age.'

'What age?' asked Rachel desperately.

'Oh, I dunno. Twenty-two, I'd say. Fresh out of uni. Completely bloody mental. She's had a few tequilas and now she's doing a pole dance for the boys. Si and Anton are loving it, dirty old bastards.'

Zoe laughed while Rachel tried to swallow a lump in her throat.

'Zoe, Simon and I are having a few problems,' Rachel said, more loudly this time.

'You're breaking up, hon,' shouted Zoe.

'No, we're not breaking up. We're just having a few problems.'

'No, it's no good. I can't hear you. You're definitely breaking up. Listen, I'll give you a call tomorrow. And don't worry about Simon. I'll make sure he keeps out of trouble.'

In desperation, Rachel phoned Bianca, only to be

informed by the housekeeper that the Mills had decided to nip over to Marbella for a few days at the last minute. Rachel knew that Harriet's bony shoulders were not the sort to cry on, so she curled up into a little ball on the sofa and sobbed until her eyes throbbed.

'Mum,' said Tabitha. 'I think the lady across the road is crying.'

Summer turned away from her front door, which she was attempting to open with a rusty key, and peered across the street. Tabby was right. The girl who'd moved into Ivy Cottage could clearly be seen through her open curtains. She was lying on the couch, crying inconsolably.

'We should do something,' said Tabitha. 'When I cry, you always come and give me a hug. I'd hate to be crying on my own.'

Summer sighed. She was, by nature, the kind of woman who couldn't leave a hedgehog on the road without moving it to safety, so it went against all her instincts to ignore the sobs of a heartbroken neighbour, but there was nothing she could do. For a start, when Bianca Mills had invited her to her dinner party, she'd told her she was away for the weekend, and if anybody saw her here in the village, she'd be rumbled as the liar she'd become. Plus, if she went across the street and comforted the poor soul at Ivy Cottage, who knows what would happen. They might get on. Her new neighbour had a lovely warm look about her, which Summer suspected might lead to friendship. She couldn't risk making friends in Combe, Murphy had made that quite clear. The only reason she was here was for the isolation. 'It's a small village,' Murphy had explained. 'The kind of place where you and the kid can disappear.' And so Summer and Tabby stayed in their cottage, a self-contained unit of two, too busy hiding from their past to allow themselves a present.

'We can't go over there, Tabby,' said Summer.

Tabitha pouted. 'But Mum, that's mean. She's crying.'

'I know, my love,' agreed Summer. 'But we've talked about this, haven't we? It's just the two of us now. We don't need anyone else.'

'But we have to do something. She looks very sad.'

'There's nothing we can do, Tabby,' said Summer in as firm a voice as she could muster.

She opened the door with a thrust of her shoulder and ushered her daughter inside. Once the door of the cottage was closed to the world she felt safe again.

Tabitha spent the evening curled up on the window seat in the living room with three of the cats, gazing forlornly across the road while Summer sat at her sewing machine, mending Tabby's favourite skirt.

'She's closed the curtains now,' Tabby gave a running commentary. 'She's probably just in there on her own, crying her eyes out.'

'Her husband might be back now,' answered Summer.

'No, his car isn't there,' confirmed Tabitha.

'You're very nosy,' teased Summer.

'No.' Tabitha sighed mournfully. 'I'm just concerned.'

Summer smiled to herself. Her daughter was quite the little drama queen. But then, she'd witnessed more than her fair share of drama in her short life, so perhaps it was understandable.

'Mum,' said Tabitha suddenly. 'Why are there two moons tonight?'

'Don't be silly, my love. There can't be two moons.' Summer laughed.

'No, there are definitely two moons. Look.'

Summer picked up a cat and perched herself beside her daughter at the window. From their seat, Summer and Tabby had a clear view up Chillyhill Lane to the top of the hill. The moon was huge that night, and bright white. But to the left was another bright, white light, almost as big again. Summer stared at the light for a long time. It had to be in the garden of the new house, she decided. Somewhere deep inside a delicious, warm memory of a long-forgotten promise stirred.

'I'll find you,' he promised. 'When I've made my fortune. I will seek you out and I'll put a bright, white light at the end of my garden so that you'll know I've arrived.'

Of course it couldn't be him. It was just a silly dream, whispered by a teenager in the darkness. He wouldn't even remember her now. She'd walked out on him twelve years ago, not long after he'd made the promise. But she remembered him. She often wondered where he was, what he was doing, how lovely his life must be. If she closed her eyes, she could still see his

125

beautiful face as he kissed her goodbye.

'It's just a light,' said Summer softly. 'It must be from the new house.'

'Oh,' said Tabby, somewhat disappointed not to have discovered a second moon. 'It looks very pretty though.'

'It does,' agreed Summer with a sigh.

Simon called Rachel on Monday morning from the airport.

'Did you have a good time last night?' asked Rachel, her voice wobbling with barely contained anger.

'Oh, you've spoken to Zoe then,' said Simon sheepishly.

'Yes,' said Rachel more angrily. 'I can't believe you went out. I was worried about you. I felt sorry for you because you had to work on a Sunday and you were out on the razzle with your secretary.'

'Come on, Rach,' said Simon. 'It wasn't like that. Gavin had got tickets for this party; it was all very last minute, and Anton and Zoe were up for it and I felt bad about dragging Grace into the office at the weekend, so I invited her along too.'

'Do you fancy her?' demanded Rachel.

'What?' Simon was dumbfounded by the question. 'Do I fancy her? Of course I don't bloody fancy her. I'm married to you. Rachel, you've gone bonkers. Since when were you the jealous type?'

It was true that Rachel had never worried about Simon's fidelity before, but she felt vulnerable being so far away from him, and so fat and so frigid. The man hadn't had sex in months, he was bound to be gagging for it by now, and Rachel worried that he might start looking elsewhere – specifically in the direction of his pretty, young secretary.

'I just think it's really weird that we had that "thing" on Saturday night . . .'

'What? That "thing" about you not wanting to sleep with me?' Simon lowered his voice so that the other people waiting in the business-class lounge couldn't hear him.

'Yes,' said Rachel. 'No. It's not that simple. Anyway, you're changing the subject to get yourself off the hook. I was saying, I just think it's weird that we argued on Saturday night and then you went out with Grace, or whatever her name is, last night. It's like you want to punish me for not sleeping with you.'

'Rachel,' said Simon, exasperated. 'I'll admit I was upset. I'd been looking forward to us making love for ages and then it didn't work out and I felt like shit, but the only reason I went out last night was because the opportunity arose. Gavin thought I sounded as if I needed a few beers, one thing led to another and we all made a bit of a night of it. If you'd been in London, you would have been there too.'

'But I'm not in London.' Rachel sniffed. 'I'm here, on my own, and you're going out with my best mate and some sexy, young secretary, and it's not fair.'

Simon's head pounded. He had a hangover and he couldn't cope with this.

'Look, Rach,' he said softly, trying to calm her

down. 'You've got it all wrong. We'll talk about it properly when I get back, OK? But you have nothing to worry about.'

'Sure?' asked Rachel.

'Sure,' confirmed Simon. 'I'm going to have to go now, my flight's being called, but I'll call you from New York when I can. Is Alfie all right?'

'He's fine,' said Rachel. 'He misses you. We both do.'

'I miss you both too,' said Simon. 'Love you.'

'Love you too,' said Rachel, beginning to feel better.

After he'd hung up, Simon went to the bar for a hair of the dog. He'd told Rachel a little white lie. His flight wasn't for two hours yet.

In the weeks that followed, life conspired against Rachel and Simon. Simon's Friday morning meeting in New York was postponed until the following Monday, which meant that he stayed in America over the weekend and couldn't get back to Combe. Once he was back in London, business really picked up and he was constantly on conference calls or in meetings with clients, and whenever Rachel called him he was unavailable or too busy to speak. On the couple of occasions that Simon phoned Rachel, she had popped out to the corner shop or was in the garden hanging out the washing, and she missed the phone. Eventually, two weeks after the dinner party, Simon made it back to Wiltshire with a short fuse and a car full of paperwork. Rachel thought he was grumpy with her and ratty with Alfie. Simon, meanwhile, got irritated because Rachel wouldn't give him any peace to get on with his work. Again, he left early on Sunday to get back to the office, and to Grace, thought Rachel. And then there was another last-minute trip to New York over the weekend, and this time, to Rachel's horror, Grace was going too.

'I know you're having an affair with her!' she screamed down the telephone the night before Simon left.

'Rachel, you're being ridiculous,' Simon insisted. 'I am not interested in Grace.'

'I don't believe you!' Rachel shouted.

'But Grace is seeing—' Simon began to explain, but Rachel had hung up before he had a chance to finish his sentence. 'My brother,' said Simon to the dead telephone line as it buzzed in his ear.

Oh well, bugger you, Rachel, he thought as he headed to the fridge to grab another beer.

Rachel had changed almost beyond recognition in Simon's opinion. He didn't know whether it was having Alfie that had done it or the move to the country, or the fact that they hardly saw each other any more, but as far as Simon was concerned, his wife seemed determined to shove a great big wedge of resentment between them. He explained the situation to Grace during the long flight to New York, conveniently missing out the part where Rachel accused him of having an affair with his secretary.

'It sounds like post-natal depression,' said Grace. 'My sister Emily had it after her little girl was born. It was a nightmare, especially for her partner, but she's fine now. She just needed the right treatment and a lot of support from her family.'

Simon nodded thoughtfully. 'And I'm not really giving her enough support, am I?'

'Not really Simon,' she said. 'Not if she's got post-natal depression. She's going to need you around a lot more.'

'But she won't accept that she's got a problem,' said Simon. 'She thinks everything's my fault. She even thinks I'm having an affair.'

Grace laughed. 'That's ridiculous,' she said. 'The only women you see are me and Zoe. And it's not as if you're going to have an affair with either of us.'

'Exactly,' said Simon. 'Thank you, Grace.'

Chapter Five

The end of the beginning

'Hey, Padre,' Scarlett had called when TJ appeared. 'I've been expecting you.'

With TJ Mills came baggage. The baggage was called Scarlett, she was seventeen and she was the reason for their trip to Spain. Scarlett was the product of a champagne-fuelled one-night stand that TJ had had with an American actress in 1985 when Bianca was still in training bras.

TJ had received the phone call from Angelina half an hour after the guests had left the dinner party. He and Bianca had been enjoying a last drink on the verandah before bed when the peace had been shattered by his ex-lover's shrill American hysteria. Scarlett had run away. Angelina's husband, Victor, was a hotshot Hollywood movie producer. He'd allowed Scarlett, who, like most Beverly Hills teenagers, was an up-and-coming actress, to audition for his latest project, but he'd given the part to Kate Hudson instead. Scarlett was furious at this blatant disregard for nepotism and had taken off somewhere at breakneck speed in her convertible. This was not an unusual occurrence, and Angelina and Victor had assumed that she was staying with friends somewhere in the valley to cool off. Several days later there was still no sign. Angelina had spoken to all of her daughter's friends and the LAPD had had no luck finding her either, although her car had been discovered in a car park at LAX airport. A missing person's inquiry was underway when a postcard arrived from Spain which read, 'Go screw yourselves, fuckwits!' Since TJ owned a villa in Marbella, Angelina decided it was time to give her ex a call.

'I can't believe that Scarlett's been missing for a week and you haven't even had the decency to tell me!' TJ had shouted down the line. 'Christ, Angelina, I'm her father. Don't you think I've got a right to know these things?'

'She runs away all the time, baby,' Angelina had explained. 'You can't expect me to keep you in the loop every time.'

And so TJ, Bianca, Lotte and Poppy had boarded a 7a.m. flight from Bristol airport to Malaga and had found Scarlett three hours later, sunbathing by the pool of their Marbella villa. The maid, who'd known Scarlett since she was an angelic, blond-haired little angel of a girl, had happily let the prodigal daughter make herself at home. Which she had done with gusto. When the Mills family arrived, they found their luxury four-bed villa strewn with cigarette butts, empty bottles of San Miguel, exquisite haute-couture clothes and the sleeping body of a local waiter called Jose.

And so Bianca's few days in Marbella turned into

a month. Bianca tried very hard to love Scarlett, but Scarlett wasn't easy to love. She was like an exotic cactus: very beautiful to look at, but with spikes.

'Ouch!' cried Lotte. 'Scarla hit me.'

The toddler began to cry.

'I did not,' scoffed Scarlett in her transatlantic drawl.

'Did!' shouted Poppy, jumping to her sister's defence with a scowl so full of hatred that it made Bianca nervous for the future of her family. Both twins ran to their mother for a hug.

'It was a slight tap,' said Scarlett to Bianca, turning her smooth, nearly naked teenage body over onto its front. 'Because she was in my sun.'

'They're only babies, Scarlett,' explained Bianca patiently. 'And your father and I don't believe in smacking.'

Scarlett rolled her heavily made-up eyes heavenward. 'Gee, I'm so sorry I upset the precious little princesses,' she said sarcastically before replacing her headphones and lying back down on her sun lounger.

Bianca did not believe in smacking toddlers, smacking 17-year-old stepdaughters, however, might be satisfying. Scarlett was wearing a G-string. Her round, oily buttocks were completely bare and just asking to be spanked. Had TJ not walked out of the villa at exactly that moment, Bianca might actually have resorted to physical violence for the first time in her life. A month in Scarlett's company was enough to try the patience of a saint. She shot her husband a look that she hoped said, Control your daughter before I throttle her.

'Problem?' asked TJ, patting his tearful twins on their glossy, dark heads.

Bianca nodded in Scarlett's direction. 'There's the problem,' she said.

TJ sighed.

'I've just spoken to her mother,' he explained quietly so that Scarlett wouldn't hear. 'And Angelina says this whole attitude problem is my fault. If I'd been around more when she was growing up then she wouldn't be so difficult now.'

'You did your best,' whispered Bianca. 'But LA isn't exactly round the corner, is it? You see her when you can and she comes here every summer. And anyway, her stepdad has been around since she was a baby. It's not as if she hasn't had a steady family life.'

'Are you two done talking about me?' asked Scarlett. 'What did Mom say? I'm not going back. Did you tell her?'

'You've got to go back to school,' said Bianca. Then she saw the look on TJ's face and added, 'Or do you?'

'Actually, no,' said TJ, with an apologetic glance at his wife. 'Scarlett, your mother and I have decided that you're going to come and live with Bianca and me in Wiltshire for a while, OK?'

He turned to his wife. 'That is OK, isn't it?'

Bianca felt the colour drain from her face beneath her suntan. Scarlett terrified her, and the thought of having the teenage temptress from hell running riot in Millsborough made her blood run cold. And she couldn't believe that TJ would make such a monumental decision without consulting her. Whenever

Angelina said 'Jump', TJ replied 'How high?' Bianca shivered, even though it was thirty degrees in the shade.

'You should have asked me first,' said Bianca to TJ.

'Sorry,' he mouthed silently.

'Yeah, and you should've asked me, too,' interrupted Scarlett. 'Why can't I just stay here? It rains too much in England.'

'Because this is our holiday home,' explained TJ patiently. 'And you're too young to be on your own. You need to live with either me or your mother. The choice is Combe or Beverly Hills. You choose.'

Scarlett sat up and pulled off her headphones. She wore her usual expression of terminal boredom, a thong and absolutely nothing else. They had been at the villa for four weeks by now and Scarlett's skin was the colour of golden syrup.

'I guess I'll come to England with you guys then.' She sighed. 'I ain't going back to LA. The next time I see that fat mother-fucking – ha, mother-fucking! that's neat – lard ass, it'll be in his coffin.'

TJ rubbed his brow as if preparing for the months of headaches ahead and Bianca felt her heart drop into her stomach like a lead weight. If anything could ruin Millsborough's happy atmosphere it was the stepdaughter from hell.

'Don't talk about your stepfather like that,' said TJ lamely.

Scarlett had already put her headphones back on and could hear nothing but the Red Hot Chili Peppers' new track.

135

'Sorry, love,' said TJ, kissing Bianca's hair.

'It's not your fault,' she said gently. 'Maybe a few more weeks with us will do her good.'

'Maybe,' said TJ, but neither of them thought it would. The last four weeks had been tiresome to say the least.

'Why is my book in the pool?' asked Bianca, fishing out her new, and now very soggy, Judy Jones novel. 'Did either of you do this?' she asked the twins as sternly as she could.

'Scarla,' said Poppy with a frown. 'Naughty Scarla.'

TJ pulled the headphones off the fluffy blond head of his eldest daughter.

'Whadizit?' she shouted grumpily.

'Scarlett, why was Bianca's book in the swimming pool?' he demanded.

'Oh geez, that.' She sneered. 'I started reading it and it was bullshit, so I tossed it away. I didn't mean for it to end up in the pool. Christ, you guys need to take some chill pills.'

Rachel looked back into the mirk of her recent past and tried to understand how she'd come to be a virtual single mother, living in rural isolation with no family or friends around her. Rosie, the health visitor, was sitting expectantly on the couch, wanting to know. She had a kind, thoughtful face.

'My husband is having an affair,' explained Rachel calmly. 'With his twenty-two-year-old secretary.'

She said the twenty-two bit with added gravity, in order to convey the importance of this piece of information.

'Or at least I'm pretty sure he is. We're not really talking at the moment, so I don't know for sure.'

'Right,' said Rosie, bumping Alfie up and down on her knee. 'So is that why you two are arguing? Because of his affair?'

'No,' said Rachel. 'Mainly we're arguing because I wouldn't sleep with him.'

'O–K,' Rosie spoke very slowly and concentrated on every word, as if to make sure she never said anything that could be misconstrued. 'And how long have these problems in the bedroom been going on?'

'Since Alfie was born,' said Rachel with absolute certainty.

'When did you last see your husband?' asked Rosie gently.

'Last week,' answered Rachel. 'He came home to see Alfie and to talk things through with me, but I hit him over the head with my Manolo.' She nodded towards the designer stilettos by the fireplace. 'And he hasn't been back since.'

'Right,' said Rosie, speaking very carefully now. 'And was he hurt?'

Rachel shook her head. 'I didn't use the heel. I should have done, he needs some sense knocked into him, but I just kind of slapped him on the forehead with the sole. I did do it with some force, mind you. There was a big red splodge on his forehead when he left.'

'Have you always had a violent relationship?' asked Rosie.

Rachel smirked. 'No,' she scoffed. 'Don't be silly. We've never laid a finger on each other before. But he kept banging on about me having post-natal depression. He said I'd completely changed since I had Alfie. That my low self-esteem and lack of sex drive was all to do with a hormonal imbalance and that he'd been speaking to a friend at work about my problems. I asked him which friend and he said Grace. That's her, the twenty-two-year-old secretary – the one he's having an affair with. He said that her sister went through the same thing. That's when I lost it. I couldn't believe he'd been speaking to her about me. So I hit him.'

Rosie nodded sympathetically, but said nothing.

'Anyway, I told him I couldn't believe he'd been discussing me with his twenty-two-year-old mistress and he went absolutely ballistic, completely denied having an affair and even tried to tell me that she was going out with his brother. I mean, as if I'm going to believe that. Then he said I was deranged and paranoid and obviously needed medical attention.'

'Right.' Rosie stroked Alfie's hair softly. 'And then what happened?'

'He got up, rubbed his forehead, kissed Alfie goodbye and left. I haven't heard from him since. You see? What kind of father would walk out on his wife and baby like that?'

'Are you sure he's having an affair?'

Rachel nodded and then shrugged.

'I think so. I don't know for sure. But my best friend, Zoe, has seen him out with her a few times and it just kind of makes sense. She's young and pretty and I'm . . .' Rachel ran her fingers through her greasy hair.

'And you are?' asked the health visitor, confused. All Rosie could see was a young, attractive woman. A little tired and unkempt perhaps, but young and attractive all the same.

'And I'm not. I'm fat and ugly and I'm getting wrinkles.'

'Your husband's right about one thing,' said Rosie.

'What's that?'

'You do have a problem with low self-esteem.'

'But I don't have post-natal depression,' insisted Rachel as the tears began to flow again. 'I'm not depressed.'

Rosie looked at the sobbing wreck of a first-time mother in front of her. 'I think you need to see a doctor, love,' she said.

Simon looked at his Rolex – a wedding present from Rachel – and sighed. A quarter to six. He wondered what Rachel and Alfie were doing right now. He rubbed his forehead. There was still a bump where Rachel had slapped him with her shoe. For once, Simon didn't know what to do to make things right. How could he convince her that he wasn't having an affair? He thought about calling Rachel and telling her he still loved her, violent temper and all, but as always he held back. Rachel had changed so much since becoming a mother. He barely knew how to talk to her any more. There was hardly anything left that resembled the fun-loving, independent girl-about-town he'd fallen in love with. She was so miserable. No fun any more. He wanted the old Rachel back. He missed her. He was dragged from his thoughts by a knock on his office door.

'Come in,' called Simon.

Grace entered the room and filled it with Coco Chanel.

'Is it OK if I head off now, Simon?' she asked with a dazzling smile. She looked stunning in her tight black pencil skirt, fitted white shirt and high, high heels.

'Sure,' said Simon with a fond smile. 'Are you off on a hot date?'

Grace nodded enthusiastically. 'Gavin's taking me to some photography exhibition in Clerkenwell.' She grinned. 'So I'd better get home and change into something less corporate.'

'You do that,' said Simon. 'Can't keep that brother of mine waiting now, can we? He'll think I'm trying to monopolize his new girlfriend.'

'Are you doing anything tonight?' asked Grace.

Simon nodded. 'Just meeting Zoe for a quick drink,' he said.

'What, with Anton?' asked Grace.

'No, Zoe and Anton are having a few problems,' said Simon. 'Must be something in the air. I think Zoe and I are going to wallow in our mutual misery this evening.'

'Oh right ... but I thought Anton was your friend?' said Grace.

Simon shrugged. 'I miss Rachel,' he said. 'Going out for a drink with her best friend is the next best thing to having her around.'

Grace gave her boss a sympathetic smile.

* * *

140

It was as if a cloud of depression had descended upon the entire village. Millsborough's shiny façade had been temporarily tarnished by Scarlett's reign of terror. It was as if she'd cast a spell upon the once cheerful place. She had only been in the house for two days and already her sorcery had begun. There had been tears, tantrums, violence and mindless acts of vandalism. The twins had taken to hiding behind their mother's legs at all times for protection. Jock had decided that the most sensible thing for a dog to do would be to move into the basement permanently. He ventured upstairs for mealtimes only, casting furtive sideways glances at the teenage witch in his midst. TJ wore a mask of cheerful stupidity, pretending to be enjoying his newly extended family, while studiously ignoring the chaos all around. Bianca took on the role of protector: protecting the twins and the dog from random acts of violence, protecting her much-loved designer wardrobe from random acts of teenage customization, and protecting the house from random acts of redecoration, Scarlett style. It was kind of like *Changing Rooms* with a psychotic twist. TJ, being the guilt-ridden absent father that he was, had agreed that Scarlett could redecorate *her* room – otherwise known as Bianca's favourite guest room; the one with the Sistine Chapel ceiling – however she saw fit. Scarlett saw fit to paint the entire room black, ceiling and all.

Meanwhile, Rachel skulked gloomily around her cottage in a half-conscious state of zombification, while Alfie cried continuously with colic, or teething pain, or some other unidentifiable infant

141

malady. Zoe had been drip, drip, dripping information about Simon's London life to Rachel over the past few weeks and now she was sure that her husband was having an affair. It seemed that Zoe bumped into Simon out on the town with Grace at least every other day. At night, Rachel lay awake, tormented by visions of her husband writhing naked in the luscious, youthful limbs of his secretary. By day, she poured over old photographs of herself and Simon in happier times. She tortured herself with pictures of their wedding, of Rachel looking tiny and tanned in an itsy-bitsy bikini on a Maldives beach and of Simon clutching a miniature newborn Alfie, a look of sheer awe on his handsome face. Rachel soon learned that nostalgia can be as addictive as any drug – just as sweet and just as destructive. Her present was intolerable, she had no future to speak of and so she turned to the past.

On the other side of the hedge, the faded grandeur of The Beeches was the perfect environment in which to wallow in a mire of self-pity. The huge rooms were dark and crowded with crumbling antiques (and that was just Lord and Lady Lilywhite Smythe). Curtains and fabrics were worn and faded, wallpaper and paint peeled, scuffed wooden floors were no longer polished and everything was covered in mounds of dog hair. The Lilywhite Smythe menagerie included three hyperactive Jack Russells, two lazy, fat black Labradors, a nervous lurcher and Moriarty.

Harriet, like all imprisoned princesses, could be found in the highest room of the highest tower. Her circular bedroom had breathtaking, panoramic views of Combe and the surrounding Wiltshire countryside. Hattie had taken to opening all the curtains and lying on her bed all day, chain-smoking Marlboro Lights and drinking Jack Daniels while taking in the views. Moriarty lay faithfully across the foot of the bed, hoping in vain that his mistress might get out of bed and actually take him for a walk.

Harriet didn't bother with an ashtray or a glass, preferring to flick ash directly onto the Eighteenth-century hand-woven carpet and drink the liquor straight from the bottle. For some reason, Marjorie had sacked the cleaner and, as yet, there was no sign of a replacement. And so Harriet's room gradually turned into an oversized ashtray. There was nothing wrong with Hattie, as such, she was just bored to the point of terminal lethargy. She had friends, but they were all abroad. She had a car, but was banned from using it. She had Bianca, if she was desperate, but she'd been in the Costa del Crime for the past month and now she was back she had that irritating little bitch Scarlett in tow and was far too busy playing at being a stepmum. And she had her father, but he was far too busy arguing with her stepmother to notice her.

From one of her windows, Harriet could see directly into Rachel's back garden. Every now and again she would spot a pale and rather lifeless-looking Rachel shuffle outside with armfuls of babygrows to hang on her washing line. 'She looks how I feel,' said Harriet to Moriarty. Sometimes she thought about visiting Rachel, but she could never quite muster up the energy to make the journey next door.

But spring was turning into summer, and as the gardens in the village bloomed so too did the imagination of its newest resident. Jack Gatley had plans. Big plans. He was going to wake this sleepy little village up and sprinkle stardust on its streets. Sometimes he could barely breathe with excitement. His plan was almost complete. The dream was so close he could almost smell it.

Chapter Six

The Yummy Mummy

'Rachel, look at you, you've lost so much weight.'
Bianca whirled through the door of Ivy Cottage in
a haze of vanilla-scented enthusiasm, delighted to
see her friend again.

'Simon's left me and I'm too depressed to eat,'
announced Rachel flatly. 'It's doing wonders for my
waistline.'

'Simon's done what?' Bianca stopped in her
tracks as Rachel crumpled before her. 'Hon, I'm so
sorry. What on earth happened?'

Rachel explained the events of the past few
weeks tearfully to her friend.

'And then to top it all off, the doctor says I've got
post-natal depression,' said Rachel with a sigh.
'Which is what Simon's been saying for ages.'

'And are you sure about his secretary?' asked
Bianca, bewildered. Simon hadn't struck her as the
type of man who'd engage in sexual relations with
an employee. He was far too straight for that.

Rachel shrugged. 'Oh, Bianca, I don't know.
Sometimes I'm so sure he must be sleeping with her

and then other times I think I'm going mad. I feel as if my head's going to explode. I hope the anti-depressants kick in soon because I don't know how much longer I can cope with feeling like this. I mean, look at the place, Bianca. It's a complete tip, but I just don't have the energy to do anything about it. I've just kind of given in to the chaos.'

Rachel's living room was strewn with photographs of happier times. Dirty nappies had been discarded on the floor without being put in nappy sacks and disposed of. The curtains were drawn against the sunshine outside and the room was dark and musty. Baby clothes and toys were littered here and there, but the baby was nowhere to be seen.

'Where's Alfie?' asked Bianca nervously.

Rachel had a slightly manic look about her. She fidgeted nervously with the sleeves of her over-sized jumper and bit her cracked lips. The bags under her eyes were so dark that she looked as if she'd been punched.

'Upstairs,' replied Rachel. 'In his cot.'

'Is he asleep?' asked Bianca, hoping that this was his regular nap time.

Rachel shrugged absent-mindedly. 'Dunno,' she said. 'He keeps crying. I don't know what's wrong with him. I thought maybe he was tired so I put him in his cot.'

'I'll go and get him, shall I?' asked Bianca.

'Get who?' asked Rachel, slumping onto the couch.

'Alfie,' said Bianca.

'Oh. Right. Yeah. If you like.' Rachel drew her

knees up to her chin and stared blankly at the television. The *Teletubbies* were on, but the sound was off.

Bianca was scared. She ran upstairs as quickly as she could, desperate to check on the baby, but when she got to the door of the nursery she paused for a moment and took a deep breath. There was no sound coming from Alfie's room and somewhere in the darkest corner of her mind Bianca imagined a scene from a Romanian orphanage on the other side of the door. She pushed the door open with her fingertips and forced herself to look inside.

'Oh, thank goodness,' she declared as Alfie stared back at her with his huge brown eyes. 'You gave me a fright there, little man. You and your mummy. Come here, my little soldier. Come to Auntie Bianca.'

Alfie stretched his chubby arms up towards Bianca and smiled a gummy smile. Bianca was delighted to find Alfie not only still breathing, but fully clothed, well fed, pink-cheeked and smelling sweetly of baby products. Rachel had obviously been neglecting herself, but nobody could accuse her of not caring for her baby. The nursery was immaculate, the sheets on the cot pristine and a pile of Alfie's clothes sat washed and ironed on the rocking chair. The truth was that Rachel had gone on autopilot when it came to mothering. She had discovered that even in the darkest of times, there's something about a baby that just forces you to keep going. Nobody could say she was living life to the full, in fact, she was barely existing at all, but thanks to Alfie, at least she could just *be*.

'Hi, baby,' whispered Rachel as Bianca brought Alfie into the living room. She smiled at her son fondly, but her eyes were full of pain.

'When did you last have a nice hot bubble bath, hon?' asked Bianca, who could smell her friend from the opposite side of the room.

'About six months ago,' said Rachel. It was the truth. She hadn't had time for anything but a quick shower since Alfie was born, and in the last couple of weeks there hadn't seemed much point in bothering to wash herself. She hadn't left the house.

'Why don't I run you one?' suggested Bianca.

'Fine,' said Rachel without enthusiasm.

While Rachel was in the bath, Bianca started to tidy up, but the enormity of the task overwhelmed her. The truth was that she hadn't actually done any housework in years. That's what her army of cleaners was for.

'I need help,' she thought to herself, fishing in her Hermès bag for her mobile phone.

'Hattie? It's Bianca . . . Yup, yup, I'm back. But listen, hon, I need your help. I've got a bit of a crisis on my hands. It's Rachel, she's in a hell of a state and . . . What do you mean you're busy. Where are you? London? Oh that's a shame . . .'

Bianca had taken Alfie out to the back garden for some fresh air. She was standing below the beech hedge, directly underneath Harriet's bedroom, and when she glanced up she saw an interesting sight.

'Harriet,' said Bianca sternly. 'You're not in London. You're in your bedroom. I'm watching you. You're smoking a fag in your nightie. I'm in Rachel's garden. I can see you.'

148

Harriet peered out of her window and waved her hand lamely in Bianca's direction.

'So I am,' she said sarcastically. 'And it's not a nightie. It's a pure silk slip and it cost more than your entire outfit. What's the problem down there on planet housewife?'

'She's fallen out with Simon, she looks malnourished and she's almost certainly in the middle of a nervous breakdown. I can't cope with this on my own, Harriet. Please, get dressed, get down here and help me,' hissed Bianca as firmly as she could manage.

'OK, keep your hair extensions on.' Harriet was taken aback by the forcefulness of Bianca's demand. 'On my way.'

Two minutes later, a long, thin foot appeared through the beech hedge. It was well pedicured and wore a bejewelled flip-flop. A pale, smooth expanse of toned leg followed, then a protruding hip bone, a bony elbow and a head of sleek blond hair. And, with a slight rustle of leaves, all six feet of Harriet Lilywhite Smythe tumbled out of the hedge. She shook her head slightly and her hair fell back into place. She was still wearing her green silk negligée. Moriarty stepped neatly through the hedge behind her, wearing a red collar and an air of superiority.

'Harriet,' scolded Bianca. 'You can't just walk through Rachel's hedge.'

'It's our hedge,' said Harriet with a scowl. 'I'm a Lilywhite Smythe. I can do what I like. So?' Harriet looked expectantly at Bianca. 'What's the story?'

'Do you know anything about depression?' asked Bianca earnestly.

'Hmph,' said Harriet. 'I could write a book on it. No one could possibly be as depressed as I am. Do you know what? I'll be thirty in two weeks' time. That means I will officially be past my sell-by date, on the shelf, washed up, dried up and had it. I should be spending the last days of my youth partying with my friends in London and having drug-fuelled sex with young men whose names I can't recall. Instead, I live at home with my father and the Wicked Witch of the West Country, my friends have deserted me, I haven't had sex since I was twenty-eight, I've spent most of my twenty-ninth year in rehab, I have a criminal record for drunk driving and possession of a Class-A substance and I'm a virtual prisoner in this godforsaken shit hole of a village, stuck here with the likes of you – and her!'

Harriet pointed accusingly at Rachel's back door.

'So, if anyone has anything to be depressed about it's me.'

'It's always me, me, me, me, me,' teased Bianca. There was something about Hattie's blatant rudeness that always amused her. 'You're so self-obsessed. Rachel's world is falling apart and you're having a crisis because you're nearly thirty. Mind you, it's good to know you're older than me,' added Bianca, who wouldn't be thirty until August.

'Oh shut up,' said Harriet, pretending to be cross, but there was the beginning of a smirk appearing at the corner of her mouth. She'd never admit it, but she was delighted that Bianca was back from Spain.

'At least Rachel has a husband to fight with,' deadpanned Harriet as they walked down the garden path. 'I haven't even managed a marriage yet, let alone a divorce. I'm quite a disappointment to my family, you know: I come from an incredibly long line of divorcees. We're all so unspeakably horrid that no one can live with us, despite the family fortune.'

'Hattie,' asked Bianca sweetly as they entered the house. 'Have you really not had sex for two years?'

'Really, really,' nodded Harriet. 'It's a tragedy, B, my hymen is growing back.'

'So?' asked Bianca. 'What do you think we should do about this?'

Harriet surveyed Rachel's insanitary living conditions and shrugged. 'It doesn't look any worse than my place,' she said.

'Don't be silly. What about your cleaner?' scoffed Bianca.

'Marjorie sacked her,' explained Harriet. 'Nobody has washed so much as a teacup in the last three weeks. Daddy bought some plastic cups so he could drink his Scotch.'

'That's grim,' said Bianca in astonishment.

'Darling,' replied Harriet with a flick of her hair. 'It's called shabby genteel. It's what we old-money types are all about. Anyway, I am absolutely, bloody useless at tea and sympathy. Rachel will be suicidal in minutes if I try to give her any advice.'

'What about your mum?' suggested Bianca hopefully.

'What about my mother?' asked Harriet defensively.

'Well, this is right up her street, isn't it?' asked Bianca.

'And how do you know about Mummy?' demanded Harriet.

'Marjorie told me,' replied Bianca innocently.

'I bet she did,' spat Harriet. 'Look, I don't really want to get my mother involved. Anyway, she's in Chew Magna and it's miles away.'

'OK,' said Bianca, putting her hands up submissively. 'It was just a thought. Rachel could do with some help, that's all.'

Harriet chewed her lip thoughtfully for a few moments and said, 'All right, I'll get Mummy over, but you have to promise me that you won't laugh at her, OK?'

'Why would I laugh at her?' asked Bianca.

'People do,' said Harriet bitterly.

By the time the ancient Bentley pulled up outside Ivy Cottage, Rachel was curled up on the couch in her bathrobe. Bianca was wittering away chirpily in a vain attempt to lighten the mood while Harriet was awkwardly manhandling Alfie on her lap.

'That's mummy,' announced Harriet with glee as the gravel crunched outside.

She jumped up, with Alfie under her arm, and rushed to the door. Bianca was both shocked and touched by the obvious affection Harriet had for her mother. She looked like a little girl on Christmas morning, her face full of excitement and anticipation.

'Mummy!' Harriet exclaimed from the front door. 'Mwa, mwa.'

'Harriet, my dahling. That baby quite suits you.

You really must think about finding a husband quite soon.'

Nothing could have prepared either Bianca or Rachel for the vision that walked through the door. Hermione Lilywhite Smythe, for she had kept her married name, floated into the room as gracefully as a prima ballerina. She was as tall as her daughter, with the same blond hair and exquisite bone structure. At fifty-six, she remained a woman of breathtaking beauty and, in her prime, she would have made her daughter look quite plain by comparison. She wore a real chinchilla jacket – despite the fact that it was almost twenty degrees outside – a black pencil skirt and three-inch heels. Her black sheer stockings were seamed up the back, her eyes were rimmed in black kohl, her lips were painted scarlet and her long hair was pulled tightly into a bun. She looked like Diana Dors and sounded like the Queen.

'Dahlings,' she announced in the gravelly tones of a lifelong smoker. 'Such a pleasure to meet you both. I am so pleased that Harriet has made some friends.'

Harriet blushed and muttered, 'Mummy, I have had other friends.'

'Of course you have, dahling,' said Hermione breathily, 'but they have tended to be drug addicts and ne'er-do-wells, haven't they? These two look far more promising. Such pleasant girls.'

Rachel and Bianca shared a bemused look.

'I'm Hermione,' she added, holding out an elegant manicured hand. 'Such a great pleasure to meet you both.'

153

Bianca shook Lady Lilywhite Smythe's hand politely. It was soft and comforting and warm.

'Hello, I'm Bianca.' She beamed.

'Bianca, you're even more beautiful than Harriet described you.'

'Thank you,' said Bianca, shocked that Harriet would describe her as anything other than irritating.

'Hi,' said Rachel rather sheepishly, embarrassed that Harriet's mother had driven twenty miles to see her. 'I'm Rachel.'

'Now do tell me, Rachel?' said Hermione, perching neatly on the edge of the couch, knees tightly together, hands clasped on her lap. 'What is all this I hear about your ghastly husband leaving you in the lurch?'

She put a hand gently on Rachel's knee and, with eyes the colour of bluebells, implored her to tell all.

'Hattie,' she ordered. 'Do make some coffee, dahling. My mouth is as dry as a Saharan mistral. I cannot abide this hot weather. So many flies.'

Forty-five minutes, three cups of coffee and five French cigarettes later and Hermione had been fully informed of the events of the past month.

'How old is Simon?' asked Harriet's mother thoughtfully.

'He was thirty last January,' answered Rachel.

'Aha,' announced Hermione with certainty. 'A classic case of an early mid-life crisis. It really is much more common than you'd think. In some ways turning thirty is more painful than turning forty. By forty you are quite used to yourself. I think I actually quite liked myself by then. But thirty,

thirty is difficult. Just as you start to enjoy your youth, suddenly, poof!, it's gone. Men do tend to cope with this by sleeping with girls who are very, very young. Larry had his first affair at thirty, you know. Didn't he, Hattie?'

Harriet nodded solemnly. 'Anja, the German au pair girl,' she recalled bitterly.

'Then there was that frightful young woman from the pony club, do you remember, dahling?'

'Yes, she had a bigger arse than the horses,' said Harriet.

'And it only got worse,' continued Hermione, shaking her head sadly. 'By forty he was having an affair with his eldest daughter's schoolfriend. She was only seventeen. He'd known the girl since she was twelve. It was absolutely disgraceful and I'm quite sure that's when Ursula's problems started. Don't you think, Hattie?'

Harriet nodded silently.

'It did my girls no good at all, Larry's behaviour. It hit Ursula the hardest, of course. Harriet was always much stronger. Weren't you, dahling?'

Harriet nodded, but Bianca noticed that she didn't look very strong right now. She knew that Harriet's older sister had died, but wasn't sure of the circumstances.

'That's when I left him,' continued Hermione. 'The tight-fisted old blighter hardly gave me a penny, but I don't regret leaving him for a minute. It was best for me and it was best for the girls. If only Ursula could have seen that.'

'So there's no hope for Simon then?' asked Rachel with a wobbly bottom lip. 'If he's having an affair now, then he'll just keep having them over and over again?'

'Not necessarily, dahling,' said Hermione with a reassuring pat on her knee. 'Not many men are as caddish as Larry. He really does excel himself in that respect. Perhaps Simon just has to get this thing out of his system and then he'll be back with his tail between his legs and a dozen red roses.'

'I might not want him back,' said Rachel solemnly.

'Well, that's up to you, dahling,' answered Hermione gently. 'That is entirely up to you. Now, first things first. A clean house leads to a clean mind. Harriet, get my box from the car will you, dahling?'

Harriet nipped out to the Bentley and returned with a big, red, plastic box full of cleaning products. Hermione gracefully put on a pair of yellow Marigolds as if they were white satin evening gloves.

'What are you doing?' asked Rachel, bewildered. 'I can't have you cleaning my house.'

'But dahling.' Hermione laughed. 'That's what I do for a living. I'm a charlady. Didn't Hattie tell you? I'm the best cleaner in the West Country.'

'But the Bentley and the house in Chew Magna and . . .' Rachel was dumb-founded.

'The house is a two-bedroomed cottage – I bought it with what I got from the divorce settlement – and the Bentley is twenty-five years old. When I left Larry, that's what I used to escape. He didn't have the nerve to ask for it back. Dahling, I'm as poor as a church mouse. Didn't you know?'

156

Rachel shook her head in bemusement. Harriet Lilywhite Smythe's mother was a cleaner. Now that was a turn up for the books.

Hermione sprinkled her magic over Ivy Cottage like Mary Poppins on HRT. She preened and polished, swept and scrubbed, dusted and Dysoned the entire house with graceful ease while still wearing her stilettos. She had banished the younger women to the garden with the baby.

'I don't need any amateurs getting in my way, thank you,' she'd scolded, shooing them out the back door.

And when they were allowed back inside, Rachel was amazed at the results. The cottage gleamed with a new-found sparkle and Rachel realized that Hermione had been right. Now that her home had been spring-cleaned, her head would have to be next.

Before she left, Hermione kissed each girl lightly on the cheek.

'Harriet,' she said, 'I'll see you on your birthday.'

'When's your birthday?' asked Rachel.

'Two weeks today.' Hattie wrinkled her nose in disgust. 'I'll be thirty.'

'I'm thirty in September,' said Rachel with a depressed sigh.

'And my thirtieth is in August,' winced Bianca.

'My dahlings,' announced Hermione as she swept out of the door. 'You have absolutely no idea how young you are. Enjoy.'

And with that, she closed the front door behind her and was gone.

'Your mum is so cool,' enthused Bianca.

'She's incredible,' agreed Rachel, who was feeling much more human.

'I told you.' Harriet smiled proudly. 'Mummy always makes everything all right.'

Larry Lilywhite Smythe was walking the dogs up Chillyhill Lane when he spotted his first wife getting into his old Bentley outside Ivy Cottage. She looked as stunning as ever and his heart skipped a beat like a teenager's as he watched her ease her long legs into the car.

'Hermione! Hermione!' he called, running as fast as his aging legs would allow up the hill towards the Bentley, which was pulling out of the drive.

Hermione spotted the sad old man, huffing and puffing towards her, and smiled to herself. Her ex-husband had not aged well. His face was red and puffy and his body looked withered and old, but there was a look of sheer delight in his pale grey eyes as he hurried towards her. She knew he regretted losing her and, once or twice, a long time ago, she had almost gone back. But now she felt nothing. No hate. No love. No remorse. Just total apathy.

She wound her window down slowly and said, 'Hello, Larry,' as her ex-husband reached the car.

He leaned on the door as he tried to catch his breath and said, between gulps of air, 'Hermione . . . my dear . . . you . . . you look wonderful . . . How . . . how are you?'

'I'm very well, Larry,' replied Hermione coolly. 'How's Marjorie?'

Larry pulled a face. 'She's an old nag. She makes my life a misery.'

'Oh well,' said Hermione with a saintly smile. 'If one does make one's bed, one must lie in it.'

'Quite true,' agreed Larry remorsefully. 'Now look here, my dear. I was wondering whether you might like to join Harriet and myself for dinner on her birthday. Marjorie won't be there, she and Hattie can't abide one another as you well know, but I thought it might be nice for the girl to have both her parents there on such an auspicious occasion.'

'Nice try, dahling,' breathed Hermione. 'But no thank you. Harriet and I are going to have lunch together that day in Bath. It's all arranged. Now I must go. Goodbye.'

Larry stumbled out of the way as the Bentley pulled out onto the lane. He stood and watched it disappear down the hill and out of sight. 'What a silly old sod you are', he scolded himself, 'to let that fine filly get away.' He wondered if, perhaps, once Marjorie was dispensed with there might be a chance of winning back Hermione. Ever the optimist, he sauntered back towards The Beeches, humming to himself and remembering how it felt to have those magnificent legs wrapped around his thighs.

Chapter Seven

The Invitation

Rachel was much better. She was sure it was partly due to the Prozac, the unseasonably hot weather they were having that May and the company of Bianca and Harriet, but mainly it was to do with the flowers that had arrived from Simon with a card promising that he'd be home at the weekend. They'd had a long, emotional phone call the night before. Simon had promised that Grace was, very definitely, seeing his brother Gavin. He'd introduced them himself. And she was, therefore, not interested in Simon one little bit. And, he insisted, the feeling was mutual. They agreed that they needed to talk about their problems, but there was nothing between them that couldn't be resolved. By the time she hung up, Rachel was convinced that she'd been wrong about the affair. Well, about 95 per cent convinced anyway.

She wasn't exactly full of the joys of spring, but she was no longer staring at packets of paracetamol longingly, and wondering who'd look after Alfie once she was gone. And so, when the invitation had arrived, she'd felt remarkably upbeat about the prospect of a party. She'd even had a growing feeling of excitement and anticipation for the forthcoming event as it got closer. The one good thing that had come of her depression was the fact that she'd dropped two stone in weight without actually trying, and now that she was beginning to feel more human, a shopping trip to Bath beckoned. 'Posh frocks and black tie,' read the invite. She picked up the phone.

'Do you fancy going shopping to buy something new for tomorrow night?' she asked Bianca. 'You do? Can TJ babysit? Fantastic. I'll call Hattie.'

Half an hour later the girls were ready to hit the road.

'Rachel, why is the cellophane still on the seat?' asked Harriet as she climbed into the 4x4.

'Because I've only used the car once since Simon bought it for me,' replied Rachel.

'That is so sad,' scolded Hattie. 'I would give my Birken bag to be allowed to drive and you've got a brand-new car sitting in your drive getting rusty.'

Rachel shrugged. 'OK, I've been acting like a freak. So shoot me.'

Harriet laughed. She had discovered that, despite her initial reservations, Rachel was actually quite a cool chick. She was warm and friendly and really quite a lot of fun – when she wasn't on the brink of suicide, obviously. What's more, having had a sneaky look in Rachel's wardrobe, Harriet had discovered lots of exciting relics of her past life as a fashion PR. There was even a piece of vintage Chanel couture. How could she not want to be friends with such a useful person? One day, quite soon, Harriet hoped to borrow the gown in question. Of course, only a really good friend would allow her to do that.

'Handbags?' asked Rachel, squirming uncomfortably in the unfamiliar driver's seat.

'Check,' said Harriet and Bianca in unison.

'Lippie?'

'Check.'

'Sunglasses?'

'Check.'

'Credit cards?'

'Check.'

'OK then, we're ready. Bath, here we come,' announced Rachel as she kangaroo hopped down Chillyhill Lane, trying to get used to the car.

Summer watched them go from her window. They seemed to have become firm friends, the page-three girl, the rich bitch and the new neighbour from across the street. She saw them together almost every day now, sometimes with the kids, sometimes just the three of them, always smiling and joking around. Summer was glad that the young woman from Ivy Cottage was happier these days. Sometimes Summer felt a pang of envy for the friendship that had blossomed in the village and she wondered if there might be room for one more. But when she saw them out and about, designer handbags dangling daintily from their elbows and kitten heels clip-clip-clopping down Combe's cobbled streets, she would hide. She wasn't exactly in their league. And anyway, there was no room for friendship in Summer's world.

There was just her and Tabitha. And maybe, just maybe, there was him.

She read and re-read the invitation. There was no clue as to who had sent it.

You are cordially invited to a house-warming
party at High House on
Thursday 12th May.
Dress code: posh frocks and black tie.

Summer didn't own a posh frock.

'I'm Cinda-bloody-rella,' she said to her favourite cat, Mr Pickles.

She knew she shouldn't go. And it wasn't as if the host was going to be *him*, was it? How would he have found her? Nobody could find her. Murphy had made sure of that. And why would he *want* to find her when she'd finished with him so abruptly all those years ago? Just because she remembered a conversation about a fictional light in the garden of a make-believe house, didn't mean he would. It was all so long ago. They'd been kids. Kids who'd just read *The Great Gatsby* at school and been impressed by the plot. He was Jay Gatsby and she was his Daisy Buchanan. She smiled to herself at the memory, and thought for a moment how nice it would be to be that young and silly, naïve and romantic again.

No, Summer would not be going to the party. She didn't have any money to buy a new dress. Plus she'd spent the last few months going out of her way to avoid her neighbours. If she went to this party, she'd have to socialize with them and what would she say when they asked her who she was? Or where she came from? No, no, no, it was a really bad idea. Anyway, what would Murphy say? He certainly wouldn't approve. Summer fingered the invitation, flipped it over to see if there were any secret messages written on the back and then sniffed the stiff white card, just in case it smelled familiar. But there were no hidden clues. Nothing to suggest that the invitation had been sent by him.

Even if she did go to the party, she figured, the house was sure to belong to some middle-aged posh tosspot and the whole thing would be a complete waste of time, effort and money. But then again, she pondered, if there was even the smallest chance that maybe, just maybe, it was him, then she'd need a new dress, because he hadn't seen her for almost twelve years and she'd have to look her best. Perhaps it was a risk worth taking. Summer reached on top of the kitchen cupboard for her emergency money tin and emptied the contents onto the kitchen table.

'Twenty-three pounds and sixty-four pence,' she said to Mr Pickles, who pawed at the pennies playfully.

The money was supposed to be for Tabitha's new ballet shoes. Summer was constantly amazed at her daughter's never-ending list of talents. The poor girl had had the worst kind of upbringing imaginable, being dragged from hostels to bedsits and even, for six miserable, rat-infested months, a squat in St Paul's. She'd seen the worst kind of human misery in her eleven years, experiencing drug abuse, alcoholism and violence first hand. She'd been to the poorest schools in the most run-down areas of Bristol and yet, somehow, she continued to shine. She was polite, she never swore, she got consistently good grades and she was such a promising dancer that her ballet school gave her lessons for free.

While Summer had thrashed around in the gutter of life, Tabitha had somehow managed to rise out of the filth, clean and unscathed. Now Summer had managed to get her daughter into a first-rate Church of England school in Bradford-on-Avon, where the teachers raved about her and talked about GCSEs, A levels and even university. Summer's life had been a right-off up until now, and the only reason she'd managed to cling on was for Tabitha's sake. She hadn't lost her optimism completely though and she did allow herself to hope that the future would be brighter. But for now Summer lived vicariously through her daughter's successes, and was happy just knowing that she'd given life to such a special child. Summer had never once put her own needs before those of her daughter. Not until now.

'Does it make me a terrible mother if I spend this on myself?' Summer asked Mr Pickles.

The cat ignored her, as cats do.

'I can't,' said Summer to herself. 'I have to get the vegetables ready for the market on Saturday.'

Summer and Tabitha lived modestly. They scraped by on government benefits, handouts from Murphy and the few quid Summer made from selling her home-made jams, pickles and cakes and home-grown vegetables at the farmers' Market in

Bath. She'd had a job in the past, but it hadn't paid well and it wasn't a career she'd been proud of. Summer longed to get a proper job and make her own money – in a library maybe, or a music shop or, even better, in a florists – but Murphy said she'd have to wait until things settled down. This move would probably be temporary, he explained. There was no point in putting down roots. Summer returned the pound coins and twenty-pence pieces to the tin and placed it back on top of the cupboard. Then she made herself a camomile tea and sat at the kitchen table making towers out of two-pence pieces and wondering what she could get for £23. Tabitha was at school, and after school she had ballet lessons. The veg could wait until tomorrow. Summer had plenty of time to get a bus to Bath and be back again before her daughter was dropped home by her friend's mother. She eyed the tin greedily. If it was him, it would be worthwhile.

'Cinderella, you will go to the ball,' she announced to herself.

Summer grabbed the tin from the cupboard, threw it into her oversized cloth bag and ran out of the house before she had a chance to change her mind. Her cup of tea sat steaming on the kitchen table beside the mobile phone, which Murphy had warned her she should never leave home without.

Both Bianca and Harriet had bought designer one-offs from Square in Shires Yard while Rachel, who wasn't as flush as her friends, had plumped for a rather gorgeous strapless Fifties-inspired dress from Karen Millen.

166

'Why don't you wear one of your designer pieces that you've got back at the cottage?' asked Harriet, wondering if the Chanel couture might be going begging.

'They don't quite fit me yet,' admitted Rachel. 'I've still got another stone to lose before I'm back to my pre-pregnancy weight.'

'Oh,' said Harriet. 'Well, you look much better than you did when you were fat.'

'Thanks,' said Rachel. 'I think.'

Harriet was queen of the backhanded compliment. The girls were just enjoying a coffee outside a little café in The Corridor when Harriet spotted Summer.

'Look, it's the weirdo,' she announced. 'I wonder what she's doing out of her hovel. How did she get here? She doesn't have a car.'

'There is such a thing as public transport, hon,' replied Bianca. 'Perhaps she got the bus.'

'Or maybe she just jumped on her broomstick,' retorted Hattie.

'What's your problem with Summer?' asked Rachel. 'I mean, she keeps herself to herself, but she seems harmless enough.'

Harriet shrugged haughtily. She had a chocolate moustache above her top lip from her cappuccino, which neither Rachel nor Bianca felt compelled to warn her about.

'No come on, Harriet,' Bianca prompted. 'There has to be some reason why you don't like her.'

'She's just so, oh, I dunno, so sickeningly serene,' shrugged Harriet. 'I mean, she's poor, her clothes are disgusting, she doesn't have a bloke, she hasn't got any friends and yet she wafts around the village with this idiotic smile on her face. It annoys me.'

'You're jealous.' Bianca giggled.

'I am not,' scoffed Hattie. 'Why would I be jealous of that?'

The three women watched Summer as she looked in the window of a charity shop just down the lane. As always, she wore a tranquil but impenetrable smile. She hadn't spotted her neighbours.

'Because she's happy,' suggested Bianca.

'And beautiful,' added Rachel.

'I'm beautiful,' said Harriet petulantly.

'Yes, you are,' agreed Bianca. 'But you're not happy.'

'Yeah, right, whatever,' said Harriet in her usual dismissive tone. 'There's just something odd about her. I don't trust her. I think she pretends to be something she's not.'

'What are you talking about Hattie?' asked Rachel.

'I don't know.' Harriet frowned. 'It's the way she stays holed up in that cottage. She's been in Combe for ages now and nobody knows anything about her. She could be a serial killer for all we know. I wonder what she's doing in Bath?'

Bianca and Rachel shared a bemused look.

'Shopping?' suggested Rachel. 'That's what people do in cities, isn't it?'

'Or maybe she's going to do something really amazing like, oh, I don't know, visit the bank.' Bianca giggled.

'Nah, you need money to go to the bank,' said

Hattie. 'No, there's definitely something not right about her. I can't put my finger on it, but I'm sure there's more to Summer than . . . Look, she's off. I'm going to follow her.'

'No.' Rachel was appalled. 'That's ridiculous. You can't spy on people.'

'Whatever,' said Harriet, grabbing her bag from the table. 'I'm going after her. You two do what you like.'

And with that, Hattie swept off down The Corridor, dark sunglasses firmly in place, looking every inch the secret agent, chocolate moustache and all.

'Come on,' said Bianca to Rachel. 'We might as well go with her. She's safer when she's supervised.'

Summer walked quickly in her flip-flops, with her blond hair bouncing down her back. She zoomed down the main shopping street with Harriet, Bianca and Rachel teetering behind her, their kitten heels sliding on the cobbles.

'Oh no, she's going to the scuzzy part of town,' said Harriet in disgust as they passed Marks & Spencer and headed towards the shopping precinct where the cheaper shops were hidden away from the more monied shoppers.

Summer strode straight into Top Shop without a backwards glance.

'Top Shop,' said Bianca in amusement. 'I haven't been to Top Shop since I was fifteen.'

'No, it's OK,' Harriet reassured her. '*Vogue* says that Top Shop is actually quite cool these days. One is supposed to mix designer with vintage and high street apparently. Not that I have the patience. I usually find everything I need on Sloane Street.'

Rachel was amused by her friends' reaction to entering the alien environment of a high-street shop. The two women, who'd ordered the shop assistants around so masterfully in the designer mecca of Square, suddenly seemed to lose their confidence the minute they set foot inside the door.

'Fish out of water,' muttered Rachel to herself.

Harriet fingered a miniskirt warily, as if the high nylon content might cause a skin complaint. Bianca oohed and ah'd in patronizing tones, saying, 'This would be really quite nice if you didn't have much money,' and, 'Oh, this skirt is a rip-off of the Chloé version, but the finish isn't nearly as good.' Rachel who, like most fashion professionals, had regularly shopped at Top Shop pre-Alfie, decided to stock-up on some basic vests and buy herself a new pair of jeans.

'You're going to buy something?' asked Bianca incredulously. 'In here?'

'Yup.' Rachel smiled. 'I often do.'

Bianca and Harriet shared a mortified look. They had accidentally befriended a Top Shop wearer. How careless.

'Where's Summer gone?' asked Bianca when they got upstairs.

'She's in there, trying on some tarty dress,' said Harriet, nodding towards the changing rooms. 'Come on.'

Harriet grabbed an armful of T-shirts and headed for the changing rooms. Bianca and Rachel followed less enthusiastically.

'Psst, in here,' whispered Harriet from behind a curtain.

The three women squeezed into one tiny cubicle, designed for a skinny teenager. Rachel and Bianca had their backs hard against the mirror on the wall while Harriet peeked out from behind the curtain.

'Wow!' whispered Hattie.

'What is it?' asked Bianca.

'She looks quite nice,' said Harriet begrudgingly.

'Let me see,' hissed Bianca, elbowing Hattie out of the way.

Summer had been hiding a phenomenal body underneath her hippie garb. She stood in the Top Shop changing room, wearing a £30 nylon dress and making it look a million dollars. The dress was tight, red, knee-length and had one bare shoulder. Summer held her hair up on top of her head and twirled in front of the mirror. She looked like Marilyn Monroe, all obscene curves and platinum hair.

'She's got to buy it,' said Bianca quietly. 'She looks divine.'

Rachel, who had been pretending to be above this snooping, couldn't feign disinterest any more.

'Let me have a look too,' she whispered.

'No, I'm in charge of this mission,' hissed Harriet. 'I need to keep a look out.'

Hattie tried to push past Rachel, but got her foot caught up in the handle of Bianca's Hermès bag instead. Suddenly she crashed out of the changing room and landed in a heap at Summer's feet, with Bianca and Rachel tumbling out behind her.

'Harriet,' said Summer in surprise. 'Bianca. What are you doing here?'

171

Summer blushed to the same colour as the dress she was trying on. She wasn't sure the dress suited her – it was a bit young and trendy and made her look a little plump. The last people she wanted to see her trying it on were her rich, sophisticated neighbours.

Bianca was the first to get to her feet.

'The dress looks lovely,' she gushed.

'Do you really think so?' asked Summer in her soft Bristol burr. 'I think I'm a bit old and fat for it?'

Rachel nearly choked.

'Fat!' she shrieked. 'You're not fat. You've got an amazing body.' And then she blushed because she'd never spoken to Summer before and she realized that her comments were probably a bit personal. 'I'm Rachel, by the way,' she added, stretching out her hand. 'I live opposite you.'

'I know.' Summer smiled. 'Pleased to meet you.'

The women smiled sheepishly at each other.

'You really should buy that,' said Rachel eventually, breaking the uncomfortable silence. 'It looks fab.'

'Thank you,' said Summer with a smile, pleased with the compliment, despite the strange circumstances under which it had been given. 'Anyway, what are you lot doing in here? I thought you were a bit too upmarket for this place.'

Harriet coughed uncomfortably and muttered, 'Rachel's buying some jeans and vests. Bianca and I were just helping her choose.'

'But why were you all in one changing room?' continued Summer.

'Because we can't bear to be apart,' announced Bianca with an insane grin.

'Right,' said Summer uncertainly. 'You must be very close. Right, well, I'd better get out of this. Nice to, erm, bump into you. See you later. Bye.'

And with that she vanished back into her cubicle. As Bianca and Harriet bustled out of the changing rooms, bickering about who'd pushed who, Rachel glanced back over her shoulder. Through a crack in the curtain she could quite clearly see Summer counting out coins on the floor. Outside, Harriet lit a cigarette and sneered down her long nose at the ordinary people, rushing past, getting on with their ordinary lives. When Summer came out of the shop, Bianca pounced on her.

'Did you buy the dress?' she asked. 'Are you going to wear it to the party at High House?'

Summer shook her head. 'No,' she said defensively. 'It wasn't really me and I'm not going to the party.'

'Oh,' said Bianca. 'Why not?'

'I don't like parties,' replied Summer.

'Do you want a lift home?' asked Rachel.

Summer shook her head. 'No thanks. I've got things to do,' she said and walked off in the direction of the bus station.

'Where now?' asked Bianca chirpily.

Harriet shrugged. 'Home, I guess. That's the fun over. How dull, she was just shopping. And she didn't even buy anything.'

'Just a minute,' said Rachel. 'I've got to pop back in. I forgot something.'

* * *

173

When Summer got home much later, having had to wait an hour for a bus to Trowbridge and then another forty-five minutes for one to Combe, she found a Top Shop bag on her doorstep. Inside was the red dress with a note which read, 'Please come to the party and wear this. You looked beautiful in it. Best wishes, Rachel.' Summer didn't know whether to laugh or cry. She had so wanted to buy the dress, but she was not the sort of woman who accepted charity from virtual strangers. She still had her pride, if nothing else. She took the bag inside and hid it guiltily under the couch. She was always telling Tabitha that they couldn't afford luxuries and she didn't want her daughter to think she'd been spending money they didn't have. She fished the tin out of her bag and put it back above the cupboard in the kitchen. It was only slightly lighter than it had been earlier, having paid for Summer's bus fares. She would decide what to do with the dress later. As she picked up the mug of cold tea from the table, Summer noticed her phone. The colour drained from her face. 'Big mistake, Summer,' she scolded herself. 'Big, big, huge mistake.' With shaking hands she lifted up the mobile to check if she'd missed a call from Murphy. She would be in so much trouble if he realized she'd gone out without it. 'You have no new messages,' said the answer machine. 'Thank Christ for that,' said Summer as she placed the phone safely into her pocket.

Rachel watched Summer disappear into her cottage from her breastfeeding perch at the window and hoped she hadn't offended her with the gift.

Perhaps it had been a silly thing to do. But outside Top Shop, Rachel had been gripped by the urge to do something for Summer, to welcome her into the gang just as Bianca had welcomed Rachel herself. Seeing Summer alone, and seemingly friendless, had seemed so unfair when she and Bianca and Harriet had become so tight. She hoped Summer would accept the dress for what it was – an offer of friendship. Alfie guzzled away contentedly. The familiar comfort of nursing lulled them both into a state of deep relaxation. Rachel's mind wandered, as always, back to London, and she wondered what Simon was doing. She wanted to speak to him to plan the weekend, but the phone was lying on the couch, in sight but out of reach. She didn't have the heart to disturb Alfie, so she decided to call Simon the minute he'd finished feeding instead.

When the phone rang, Simon hoped it was Rachel. He felt much more positive after the conversation they'd had the night before and couldn't wait for the weekend when he'd see his wife and son.

'Si, it's me. Zoe,' said the female voice on the other end of the line.

'Oh hi, Zoe,' replied Simon, trying not to sound too disappointed.

'What are you up to this evening?' she asked.

'Not a lot,' he said honestly. 'You?'

'Nothing, I just wondered if you fancied grabbing a beer after work.'

'Yeah, why not,' agreed Simon. Zoe had grown on him recently. She was always up for a drink and a laugh, just like Rachel used to be.

The phone in Simon's office rang and rang. Damn, I've missed him, thought Rachel, cursing Alfie for taking so long to feed and then immediately feeling guilty for dissing her son. She tried Simon's phones, sporadically all evening, but there was never any reply.

That night, Rachel couldn't sleep. It had been a warm day and the temperature hadn't dropped much in the evening. Her bedroom was stuffy and airless, even though the window was open. Alfie slept peacefully on Simon's side of the bed. The marital bed seemed vast without Simon in it, and it was comforting for Rachel to sleep with the baby. Plus it made night feeding so much more bearable. She hardly had to wake up at all to breastfeed in the night these days. But tonight she couldn't sleep at all: she had a strange feeling that something, somewhere was going horribly wrong. Rachel tossed and turned and eventually went downstairs and got herself some water. It was 3 a.m. She sat on the window seat and watched the moon for the longest time.

Simon crept out from beneath the sheets as quietly as he could and fished around in the darkness for his boxer shorts.

'Shit, shit, shit!' he said to himself. 'What the fuck have I done?'

The whiskey had worn off and the hangover had begun to kick in, even though he'd only nodded off for an hour or so. As his eyes acclimatized to the gloom he could vaguely make out the shape of the sleeping woman in his bed. His heart thumped loudly and made his head throb.

'You are such a stupid man,' he said angrily to himself. 'You've just thrown your marriage away.'

Simon punched the bedroom door so the wood splintered and his knuckle bled. What he had just done, in the heat of a very drunken moment, was to push the final nail into the coffin of his marriage. Rachel could probably forgive just about anything, but she would never, never forgive this. Simon padded into the kitchen and turned on the light. He squinted in the brightness and tried to make sense of his surroundings. He was in his own flat, their flat. There was a collage of photographs on the wall above the table. Rachel's cute little face beamed proudly at him from a wedding snap. Alfie's huge brown eyes – his mother's eyes – stared unflinchingly, accusingly at him. Zoe and Rachel hugged each other fondly aged about fifteen. God, Zoe. Zoe. What was he thinking? He didn't want Zoe. All he wanted from her was to be reminded of how Rachel used to be: so full of life, ambition and opinions. Independent. Party loving. Good-time girl. Up for anything. Absolutely anything, it would appear.

'Here you are,' said a female voice from the kitchen door. 'Come back to bed and ravish me, you big stud,' it giggled provocatively.

Zoe stood naked in the light, proud of her tight, gym-honed body, licking her lips like the cat that had just got the extra-thick double cream. Simon shook his head. Why the hell did Anton have to say those things about Zoe being amazing in bed?

That's what had crept into his dirty mind the night before – stupid, irrational fantasies of a whiskey-fuelled, sex-starved, weak, shallow man. Oh Jesus, how was he ever going to face Anton again?

'We shouldn't have done that, Zoe,' he said darkly. 'What we just did was a terrible thing.'

'No it wasn't,' giggled Zoe. 'It was great fun. I didn't hear you complaining.'

She smiled broadly as Simon stared at her in horror. It occurred to him suddenly that Zoe's legs were a bit on the short side. Without her clothes on, she looked all out of proportion and wrong. But then everything about having Zoe naked in his flat was wrong.

'Don't you feel guilty?' asked Simon, whose mouth was so dry he could hardly spit the words out.

'Nope,' said Zoe nonchalantly. 'We're both consenting adults. What have we got to feel guilty about?'

'Rachel!' said Simon, with a look of complete disbelief on his face. 'Think what we've done to Rachel?'

Zoe shrugged. 'What Rachel doesn't know and all that,' she said.

'And Anton,' added Simon in horror. 'My best mate!'

Zoe shrugged. 'Anton doesn't need to know either.'

'I think I'm going to be sick,' said Simon suddenly, running in the direction of the bathroom.

Zoe followed and tried to stroke his bare back as he threw up, but he pushed her away quite roughly.

Zoe stood naked in the dark bathroom and shivered. Things were not going according to the plan. The plan involved seducing Simon, making him fall in love with her and the two of them running away together into the sunset.

'Get dressed,' ordered Simon, 'and go home. I can't face you now, Zoe. I can't face myself. We're shameless bastards. Just leave me alone, OK?'

Zoe dressed slowly and tearfully, alone in the bedroom while Simon sat hunched on the bathroom floor. She went to him before she left, and tried again to connect like they'd done the night before.

'I know you need time to think, Si,' she said. 'But give me a call later, yeah? Maybe we could meet up to talk about "us".'

Simon looked up at her and frowned, as if he couldn't comprehend her, as if she were talking Flemish.

'"Us"?' he asked incredulously. 'There isn't any "us", Zoe. We made a mistake. A horrific, nasty, dirty mistake.'

Zoe blushed and backtracked, realizing she'd shown too much. Simon's eyes bored into hers and she felt sure he could see the raw emotion hiding just beneath the surface of her nonchalant smile.

'Sorry, slip of the tongue. Didn't mean "us", just meant "this", you know? Just thought you might want to . . .'

Simon still looked uncomprehending.

'. . . Never mind. I'll be off. See you soon.'

She half bent towards him to kiss him goodbye, but he lurched away. Zoe pushed her fingers through her short blond hair, took a deep breath and left the flat. She wandered out into the darkness and down the street where Simon lived. It was 4 a.m. and even London was asleep. The sound of her heels clip-clopping down the road rang in her ears and merged with her hangover and wretched disappointment. Zoe's moment of triumph had been woefully brief. She had no idea where she was going or what she was going to do next, so she just kept walking. At the corner of Finchley Road she stopped in a bus shelter to light a cigarette. The normally bustling street was deserted except for a few lone bodies, stumbling home alone, lost in the misery of their lives. Zoe puffed hard on her cigarette, stepped out of the shadows and joined this army of lost souls.

Chapter Eight

Party Time!

Rachel gave her reflection a modest nod of approval. She'd scrubbed up pretty well, all things considered. The silvery blue dress sucked in her waist and pushed up her full, milk-laden boobs, while hiding her bum, which for some reason was both wider and flatter than before Alfie. At least her feet had lost their puffiness and suddenly her favourite shoes – satin, very pointy, silver with four-inch heels – fitted her again. She'd had her hair done at Bianca's favourite salon in Bath and sported a sleek, shiny, urchin cut, complete with the season's essential fringe. She'd opted for a long fringe which swept over one eye. It looked good, but she hoped it wouldn't make her mascara run. She applied one more generous coat of lip gloss to her pout, threw a delicately crocheted silver shawl over her bare shoulders, picked up the clutch she'd bought to match the dress and glanced once more in the mirror, before rushing back downstairs to check that the babysitter was coping with Alfie. Lynne, the babysitter, was Mrs Bell's granddaughter

– a plump, plain, pudding of a girl with a pleasant disposition. Bianca swore by Lynne and had reassured Rachel that if she could cope with the twins, she could cope with anything.

'Are you sure you'll be OK?' Rachel asked for the fifth time.

'Yes, of course, Mrs Travis,' said Lynne with a reassuring smile. 'I'm the oldest of seven. I could change a nappy before I could talk.'

'And you've got my mobile number? Just in case.'

'Yes, Mrs Travis. You've written it down here with your list of instructions.'

Lynne waved five sheets of A4 paper at Rachel.

'And you know I'm only up the road if you need me, don't you?'

'Oh yes,' beamed Lynne. 'You're going to the party of the year with the rest of the village. Even my nan's going to be there. Everyone's talking about this new house and its mysterious owner. I can't wait to hear all about it tomorrow.'

'I'm pretty excited myself,' admitted Rachel. 'From what I hear, it's the most exciting thing that's happened in Combe for years.'

'Centuries,' confirmed Lynne. 'It's the biggest event in the village's history since one Lilywhite Smythe brother murdered another during a dual in 1728.'

Rachel giggled, kissed Alfie goodbye, leaving a smear of pink lip gloss on his cheek and then, with a deep breath and a final check of her reflection in the hall mirror, she left the cottage and teetered up the lane towards the party of the year. Harriet was waiting for her at the gates to The Beeches. She leaned against the gate post, smoking a cigarette and looking divinely aloof in a slinky black dress.

'Tonight,' announced Hattie throatily, 'is going to be one hell of an event.'

They collected Bianca and TJ at the bottom of Millsborough's drive. The Mills wore white, as they often did. TJ was in a white tux and red bow tie while Bianca was poured into a tiny silk number encrusted with crystals.

'TJ is such an Eighties throwback,' Harriet whispered to Rachel as they carried on up the hill.

'I hope we're not too early,' TJ was worrying. 'It's only five past eight. Maybe we should wait here for a few minutes before we go in.'

Bianca screwed up her face. 'No, baby,' she squealed. 'I can't wait any longer to find out who it is. I know it's not Madonna and Guy, but I have a sneaking suspicion it might be Gwyneth Paltrow and Chris Martin. I heard a rumour they were looking for a property in the area, and who else would be rich enough to build a place like this?'

She swept her arm in the direction of the glorious new house.

Jack waited for the fun to begin. He gazed around his ballroom and smiled to himself. The house was perfect. The guests couldn't fail to be impressed. It had been designed by a Parisian architect friend, whose innovative designs had been hailed as works of genius by those in the know from New York to Tokyo. High House was loosely based on the ultra-modern mansions built in the Hollywood Hills during the 1920s. From the outside it looked low and sleek, its flat roof jutting from the side of the hill, level with the road, and the house itself perched below road level, clinging to the hillside. There was a winding drive down from the lane to the double garage that nestled under the house – just big enough for the Jeep and the Ferrari. The exterior was made of a state-of-the-art concrete compound which gave the appearance of solid marble. The enormous windows were the height of the building and offered panoramic views down to the village, over the river and across the valley below.

Jack checked his reflection in the vast Art Deco mirror and nodded to himself approvingly. Oswald Boatang had done a great job with the suit. He slid his hand subconsciously through his hair and gave the room a final once-over. The ballroom was airy and white, with a polished granite floor. Voices echoed in its near-empty vastness. The hired waiting staff hovered in the doorways, eager for the first guests to arrive, while the maitre'd fussed over whether or not he'd uncorked the champagne too soon. The pianist leaned casually on the grand piano, staring out of the vast windows and admiring the amazing dancing lights strung up on the trees outside. It was still half light outside and he looked forward to the sunset he hoped to watch from his perch at the piano. Meanwhile, the string quartet gossiped amongst themselves about last night's episode of *EastEnders*.

When the doorbell eventually rang, everybody jumped. The pianist quickly sat down on his stool and the other musicians stopped discussing last night's telly.

'Right,' said Jack, eyes shining in excited anticipation. 'Let's make this a night to remember. Give the guests anything they want and remember, enjoy yourselves. It's your party too. I couldn't do it without you. Let's go.'

While the butler – also hired for the evening – hurried off to answer the door, Jack sauntered off in the opposite direction.

'Ooo,' cooed Bianca, as she entered the ballroom. 'This is fantastic.'

'Jesus,' whispered TJ. 'It's like something out of a film set.'

'Who owns this place?' wondered Harriet a little too loudly. 'I must marry him and have his children – at once.'

Rachel entered tentatively behind them, feeling too ordinary to be in such a magnificent house. She gratefully accepted a glass of champagne from a hovering waiter and gazed around the room in wonder. They were the first ones to arrive and their voices bounced off the vast walls. There was no sign of the owner.

'So where's our mysterious host?' demanded Hattie.

'Hello,' boomed a deep, velvet voice in the distance.

Rachel peered into the fading evening light and eventually made out the silhouette of a man appearing through the doors from the terrace.

'So glad you could make it,' said the voice. 'I'm Jack Gatley, your new neighbour.'

As the man stepped out of the shadows and into the ballroom, Rachel had to catch her breath. He was breathtakingly handsome in his black suit, white shirt and black bow tie, but it was his smile that bewitched her. It was a rare smile of warmth and reassurance. The kind of smile that lights up a room. The sort of smile you come across only once or twice in your life. The others felt it too, and they basked in its warm glow.

Harriet was the first to pull herself together.

'Harriet Lilywhite Smythe,' she announced in her confident, clipped accent. 'Lord Lilywhite Smythe's daughter. He'll be here shortly.'

'Delighted to meet you, Harriet,' said the host.

'And we're TJ and Bianca Mills,' announced TJ enthusiastically. Jack was not only the kind of man women wanted to seduce, he was also the sort of man other men longed to befriend.

'Hallelujah,' whispered Harriet to Rachel. 'There is a God. And she *must* be a woman.'

Rachel was dumbstruck. Her feet were glued to the spot and she couldn't for the life of her make them move in Jack's direction in order to shake his hand. Although she'd never met him before, he looked strangely familiar. As far as Rachel was concerned, Jack Gatley was, without doubt, the most handsome man who'd ever lived. He had blond, floppy hair that danced provocatively into his green eyes and curled possessively over his shirt collar. It was messy and unbrushed and seemed deliciously at odds with his expensive, tailored clothes. His skin was tanned in a weathered kind of way, as if he spent most of his time outside. In fact,

186

Rachel decided, he looked like a surfer who'd accidentally stepped into a dinner suit instead of a wet suit. Jack was just a touch over six feet tall, broad-shouldered and slim-hipped. His even features fell together on his face in such a pleasing arrangement that, had it not been for his chipped front tooth and broken nose, the finished result might have been too pretty for a man. But Jack Gatley was perfectly flawed. Rachel let out an audible sigh of desire.

'And this is Rachel Travis,' TJ was saying.

Harriet gave Rachel a sharp prod in the ribs and hissed, 'Lift your chin off the floor, Rachel. Be cool.'

Rachel somehow managed to introduce herself to Jack. She lifted her eyes up to meet his and was once again dazzled by their emerald intensity. Suddenly she remembered when she'd seen him before. He'd passed her on Chillyhill Lane in his Jeep a few weeks earlier, when she'd been on her way home from Bianca's. She wouldn't forget those eyes in a hurry. Jack kissed her hand in a gesture of faux grandeur and Rachel hoped that he couldn't read her mind.

While the girls had been busy swooning, TJ had been quick to spot a fellow working-class boy done good. Jack's clothes were obviously expensive, but his accent belied a more modest past. It was pure West Country. He had, it seemed, been brought up in inner-city Bristol. TJ immediately monopolized the host, keen to become his friend, quizzing him about the house, gardens and cars parked in the drive. The girls sipped champagne, looked around their impressive surroundings and tried to catch their breath.

'Nice pad,' said Bianca.

'Nice pad?' scoffed Harriet. 'Is that all you can comment on? What about the owner?'

'Yeah, he's cute,' said Bianca breezily. 'Not as cute as my TJ, but not bad.'

Harriet and Rachel shared an is-she-mad? look.

'He looks like Robert Redford in his prime,' said Rachel wistfully. 'Only taller and better looking.'

'Don't you get any ideas, lady,' Harriet warned Rachel sternly. 'You're married. I'm the single one around here, so I get the first go, OK?'

Rachel shrugged. She didn't want Jack in that way. She had Simon. Rachel would be more than happy to worship her new neighbour from afar. Anyway, he was far too sexy to talk to without blushing.

Before long the ballroom was teaming with guests. It seemed the entire village, plus most of the rest of the county, had turned up for the party, despite the fact that they'd spent the last few months complaining about the building of High House. Larry Lilywhite Smythe, who'd actually started a petition to have the building work stopped, was schmoozing loudly with all and sundry and guzzling the free champagne, while Marjorie, ever the wallflower, waited awkwardly in his shadow. There were a handful of rent-a-celebs in attendance – the odd model, a couple of premiership footballers, a few soap stars and most of the England rugby team.

'I wonder what he does, this Jack Gatley?' said

Bianca thoughtfully. 'It's quite a good turn out for this part of the world. He must be pretty well connected, but I've never heard of him before, have you?'

Rachel shook her head, but then, being a nobody, she wouldn't have. Harriet looked pensive.

'I like Daddy's theory best. He's got to be a drug baron.'

'Or a human trafficker,' added Bianca with wide eyes.

'Or an International arms dealer, or a spy.'

'Or a legitimate but successful businessman,' suggested Rachel.

Bianca and Harriet shook their heads.

'No, we'd know about him if he was in business round here, wouldn't we, Hattie?' said Bianca.

Harriet nodded with certainty. 'Nope, it's got to be something dodgy but glamorous. He's too young to have made this much money legitimately.'

Hattie glanced around and suddenly made a grab for the arm of a passing villager, Lillian Chamberlain Banks. Lillian was married to the local MP – Tory, of course – and was infamous in Wiltshire for knowing everything about everyone.

'What's the story with Jack Gatley, Lillian?' she demanded.

Lillian shrugged. 'Do you know, I have absolutely no idea,' she replied in disbelief. 'I heard he was an Oxford man and that he's in "business", but other than that, I'm as clueless as the rest of you. Devilishly handsome, isn't he?'

The women nodded.

'I shall, of course, endeavour to discover more

this evening,' continued Lillian with gusto. 'I'll give you an update the minute I have any news. Now, must dash. People to see and all that.' She disappeared into the throng.

Rachel watched Jack Gatley from across the room. He flitted boldly from group to group, leaving each guest in fits of laughter, but every now and then he would glance at the door, as if waiting for the guest of honour. Rachel had never met anyone with such a mysterious aura before. People used the word charisma about Hollywood stars all the time, but Rachel had never fully understood its meaning until now.

'Oh no, what's she doing here?' asked Harriet with a frown. 'I can't get away from that bitch.'

Rachel and Bianca peered over their shoulders just in time to spot the supermodel Venetia gliding into the room on the arm of one of the footballers.

'I thought she was one of your friends,' said Bianca.

'She was,' said Harriet. 'Sort of. But if I learned anything in rehab it was to keep away from friends like that.'

'You were in rehab?' asked Rachel in surprise.

'Duh,' replied Harriet sarcastically. 'It was all over the tabloids. Everybody knows I was in rehab.'

'I didn't,' said Rachel. 'What were you in there for?'

Harriet shrugged her bare, bony shoulders. 'Oh, the usual – booze, coke, smack.'

'Right,' said Rachel rather nervously. She'd always been far too much of a good girl to dabble in even soft recreational drugs, and the fact that one of her friends was an ex heroin addict came as a bit of a surprise.

'Why do you think Daddy keeps me locked up in The Beeches?' asked Harriet with a sulk.

'He doesn't,' argued Bianca. 'You go out shopping and horse riding and to yoga and Pilates.'

'Uh, yeah right,' said Harriet. 'Like that's a worthwhile existence. I mean, he won't even let me drive.'

'Yes but you're banned,' Bianca reminded her firmly. 'So you know you mustn't drive.'

'Should you still be drinking if you're in recovery?' asked Rachel, eyeing Hattie's fourth glass of champagne.

'I don't have a problem with alcohol,' scoffed Harriet. 'It's the most innocent of vices.'

'I know, but if you have an addictive personality alcohol can be completely destructive,' said Rachel with genuine concern.

'God, you two are so square,' snapped Harriet. 'I'm going to talk to Venetia.'

'But I thought you hated her,' said Bianca, confused.

'No, I said she was a bitch, which she is. But at least she's a *fun* bitch. Unlike you two. God, it's like being out with a couple of maiden aunts.'

And with that she was gone.

'What did we do to deserve that?' asked Rachel, offended.

'Oh, don't worry about her,' said Bianca with a knowing smile. 'She finds it difficult being out at a party without drugs. It's early days for her, but she's definitely on the mend. Addicts are never fully cured though. Even TJ has off days and he's been clean for sixteen years.'

'TJ used to be an alcoholic?' asked Rachel.

'No, hon. TJ used to be a cocaine addict. They all were in the Eighties, you know.'

'Right,' said Rachel, wondering how she'd managed to live such a clean existence for twenty-nine years.

Summer had managed to get halfway up Chillyhill Lane, without turning back. She had seriously considered cancelling the babysitter – an expense she couldn't really afford and a risk Murphy had warned her not to take – and having a quiet night in instead. But curiosity and longing had propelled her forward, into the red dress, which she had planned to give back to Rachel, out of the cottage and halfway up the hill. She was so nervous she was shaking, despite the warm evening air. The sun was setting over the valley and now she could clearly see the bright white light at the end of his garden, willing her to keep going, up the hill to the house.

'It's not him,' she said to herself. 'Don't get too excited.'

But she hoped. How she hoped.

'Please let it be him,' she begged any God that would listen.

Jack was in his bedroom upstairs. From the window he watched his guests spill drunkenly out onto the terrace below and into the garden, where wrought-iron tables and chairs had been arranged for their convenience. The caterers had laid out a spread of delicacies on a vast table on the terrace and everyone was tucking in with relish. He could see his friend, Mack, a DJ, setting up his decks in the garden. Soon the real fun would begin.

Jack's head buzzed with the whispered questions of a hundred guests. He'd heard them all around, wondering to each other. 'Who is he?' 'Where does he come from?' Jack smiled to himself and shook his sore head. He kicked off his new shoes, which were killing his feet, and discarded his jacket on the bed. He undid his bow tie, loosened the collar of his shirt and replaced his brogues with a pair of battered black Birkenstocks. He pushed his hand through his hair so that it stood up in messy blond tufts. This was the real Jack Gatley.

He could hear the thumping of music downstairs and, despite a headache, forced himself to rejoin his guests. It wouldn't do for the host to go to bed early with a couple of Ibuprofen. And anyway, he had work to do. He'd spotted a few potential 'victims' at the party. The three glamorous young women who'd arrived first were almost certainly perfect candidates. He would have to find them and start working on them immediately.

In the garden, Bianca and Rachel were getting giddily drunk on the free-flowing champagne. The party seemed to be buzzing with rumour and speculation about Jack Gatley. It seemed nobody knew him. No one had a clue where he was from, what he did for a living or how he'd managed to afford to build a house as impressive as this.

Harriet had not been seen since she disappeared off to speak to Venetia and Bianca was getting worried about her.

'I think she might lapse,' she confided in Rachel. 'Let's go and find her.'

'Where?' asked Rachel. The garden was mobbed.

'Follow me,' said Bianca. 'I know where she'll be.'

They pushed their way through the crowds, and back into the house. Bianca asked a waitress where the nearest Ladies' was.

'She'll be in here,' announced Bianca as she pushed the door. It was locked.

'Harriet! Open up!' she shouted.

'Bugger off!' came the reply.

'Hattie, I mean it. Let me in,' insisted Bianca.

Eventually there was a clunk as the bathroom door was unlocked and Bianca barged her way in. Rachel followed uncertainly, feeling like a gate-crasher. Harriet sat on the bathroom floor with Venetia, who wore a haughty sneer and a tiny wisp of a dress.

'We're just talking,' said Harriet petulantly.

'Yeah right,' replied Bianca. 'Have you done any?'

'Any what?' snapped Harriet.

'I dunno, coke, smack. Whatever it is she's taking these days.' Bianca pointed accusingly at Venetia.

'Bianca Mills,' said Venetia slowly in her Transatlantic drawl. 'How are you, you cheap little tart?'

'I'm fine thank you, you skinny old bint,' said Bianca in a broader Glaswegian accent than Rachel had ever heard her use before. It was a fact that, although Bianca had worked hard at losing her Scottish accent, when she was angry it came back tenfold.

'Do you two know each other then?' asked Rachel.

'Let's just say, our paths have crossed,' said Bianca. 'Right, come on Hattie. Come with us.'

'Who are you, my mother?' asked Harriet, sounding like Kevin the Teenager.

'No, I'm your friend,' said Bianca patiently. 'And I really don't think you want to be doing what she's doing, do you?'

To Rachel's surprise, Harriet got slowly to her feet and patted Venetia on the head.

'I'm going to go with the nuns,' she said to Venetia. 'I think it's best I leave you and your narcotics alone. Much as I'd love to indulge, I know where it leads, and I really don't want to go there again.'

'Good for you, Hattie,' said Bianca with a broad smile.

'OK, Mother Superior,' said Harriet. 'Get me to a nunnery.'

'Oh, I think we can do better than that.' Bianca smiled, taking Harriet's hand and leading her back towards the garden. 'There's a rather lovely young DJ who's just started a set out here and I think he might be just your type.'

Half an hour later, the girls were dancing on the lawn as their heels sank into the dewy grass.

'I really can't decide,' Harriet was saying, 'whether Jack or the DJ is more handsome.'

'Oh look, there's Summer!' shouted Rachel above the din.

'And she's wearing that red dress,' said Bianca. 'I thought she didn't buy it.'

195

'She must have gone back for it later.' Rachel grinned.

'She looks gorgeous,' gushed Bianca. 'Let's go and talk to her.'

'Must we,' moaned Harriet.

'Yes!' shouted Bianca and Rachel in unison.

Summer hovered nervously at the top of the stairs that led down to the lawn from the terrace. She hadn't spotted him inside, and now she studied the sea of faces in the garden below her, searching desperately for him. He'd have changed in twelve years, but she was sure she'd still recognize him in an instant. Her heart began to sink. He wasn't here. It wasn't him. It had all been too good to be true.

'Summer! Summer!' shouted Bianca, waving maniacally from below. 'Come and join us.'

Summer took a deep breath and began to descend the stairs.

Jack watched the girl in the red dress from behind. There was an aura of magic about her. She had the curved body of a Roman sculpture and the long blond hair of a fairy-tale princess. Jack willed the girl to turn round, but she kept on going down the stairs towards her friends. His eyes followed her hungrily.

'Hi,' said Summer sheepishly to Rachel, Harriet and Bianca. 'Good party?'

'Oh yes,' enthused Rachel. 'It's fab, and you should see the host. Wow! He's a total babe.'

'Where is he?' asked Summer nervously, trying not to give herself away.

'There,' replied Rachel, 'at the top of the stairs.'

Summer was almost too scared to turn round. All

she could hear was the thump, thump, thumping of her heart. Her head swam and her stomach lurched, and for the life of her she couldn't catch her breath.

'Are you OK?' asked Rachel. 'You look a bit pale.'

Summer nodded and swallowed hard. She could feel his eyes on her now. They were boring into her back, willing her to look. Slowly, very slowly, she swivelled her head and raised her eyes. And there he was. Jack. Her Jack. There could be no mistake. Summer's world stopped turning. The party-goers around her seemed to freeze in mid motion; she could no longer hear the music pumping out of the sound system, everything became a blur, except for him. His smile lit up the night sky. Relief washed over Summer like a tidal wave. Suddenly, for the first time in years, she felt safe. There, at the top of the steps, was a man who truly cared about her. Jack held up his champagne glass and silently toasted his guest of honour.

Rachel and Harriet were oblivious to the love story unfolding before them, but Bianca had witnessed the scene. They knew each other, Summer and Jack, that was for sure. But somehow, Bianca sensed that this was a private moment and that she mustn't tell the others what she had just seen. Not yet anyway, not until she'd got the situation sussed. Summer dragged her eyes from Jack's and attempted to pull herself together. It had been so long, she had absolutely no idea what to say to him – everything or nothing? She sipped nervously on her champagne and tried to make polite chit chat with Bianca, Harriet and Rachel, but all the time she was wondering when Jack would come. It seemed to take an age before she finally felt his warm hand on her bare shoulder. She hoped he couldn't see the goose bumps.

'Hello,' he said. His eyes searched hers for years of unanswered questions.

'Hello,' she said. Her eyes flashed but gave nothing away.

'This is Summer,' interrupted Harriet, assuming the two were strangers.

'Summer?' Jack frowned.

'Yes, Summer,' repeated Summer firmly.

'Well, it's lovely to meet you . . . Summer,' said Jack with a quizzical look.

His hand squeezed her bare shoulder gently.

'I, I, I . . .' began Jack.

'Shh,' whispered Summer in his ear. 'Later.'

He nodded. Later would be better. He'd waited twelve years, he could wait another hour or so.

Rachel and Harriet were both incredibly drunk by now and, having managed to corner Jack, were desperately trying to outdo each other. Harriet had one obscenely long, bare leg jutting out in Jack's direction while Rachel was frantically pushing her cleavage towards him. They were like a couple of over-enthusiastic puppies. 'Play with me now,' they were saying with their body language at least. Bianca could see that while Jack was mildly amused by her friends' attention, he had eyes only for Summer. His eyes had glazed over and he kept snatching furtive glances at Summer, who was standing a few steps away with Bianca.

'You know him, don't you?' said Bianca to Summer.

Summer nodded. 'We've met before,' she said vaguely.

'Where?' Bianca continued digging, determined to get to the bottom of the mystery.

'At school,' replied Summer rather coolly, 'if you must know.'

'What's he like?' asked Bianca.

'You're very nosy, aren't you?' replied Summer. She was still smiling, but her icy blue eyes were hard.

'No,' said Bianca. 'It's a fair enough question. Jack's turned up in the village, built a huge house and invited us all to a party. Everybody's fascinated by him and no one knows the first thing about him. I just wondered what he was like at school, that's all.'

Summer realized she'd been overly defensive and tried to backtrack.

'Sorry, Bianca,' she apologized. 'I'm not very good at parties. The crowds make me nervous. I get a bit ratty.'

Bianca nodded but she wasn't convinced.

'Jack was a good boy,' added Summer with a nostalgic smile. 'He was really bright and all the teachers loved him.'

'Popular?' asked Bianca.

Summer nodded. 'What do you think? Everyone was gutted when he left.'

'Left?' Bianca fished.

'He got a scholarship to Clifton College when he was sixteen and then went on to Oxford,' explained

Summer. 'He was the first pupil from our school who ever made it to Oxford.'

'Were you close?' asked Bianca, although she was sure she already knew the answer.

Summer shrugged dismissively.

'We grew up on the same estate, that's all,' she said. 'That's why I know all this. Everyone round our way was really proud of him. I'm not surprised he's done so well.'

'Do you know what he does for a living?' Bianca probed.

'No idea,' she replied truthfully. 'Something very important, I'm sure.'

'Do you still see his mum when you go to visit yours?' Bianca wondered if she was pushing her luck.

'No,' said Summer quietly. 'I don't go back there. My mum's dead.'

'Oh,' Bianca blushed. 'I'm sorry. I didn't realize.'

'Why would you?' asked Summer directly. 'You don't know anything about me.'

'True,' said Bianca. 'Very true.'

They stood for some time in awkward silence. Bianca usually made friends easily – Christ, she'd even managed to strike up a relationship with Harriet Lilywhite Smythe – but Summer was an enigma. She was so closed off from the world that Bianca had absolutely no idea what was going on in that angelic-looking head of hers. She was beginning to wonder if Harriet had formed the right idea about Summer after all. She certainly seemed to be a cold fish.

'I'm going to find TJ,' Bianca announced after a while.

'OK,' said Summer dismissively.

Jack spotted her, standing alone, and managed to escape the clutches of Rachel and Harriet. He made his way back towards Summer, with his two drunken fans following close behind.

'Sharon,' he said.

'Her name's Summer.' Rachel giggled drunkenly. 'You called her Sharon.'

'No he didn't,' snapped Summer.

'Yes he did,' argued Rachel. 'Didn't he, Hattie?'

'What?' asked Harriet.

'Jack called Summer Sharon,' Rachel repeated.

'I dunno,' slurred Harriet. 'I dunno anything.'

'You did,' insisted Rachel, turning to Jack. 'You called her Sharon.'

'Did I?' Jack looked confused.

'Oh, I've had enough of this,' snapped Summer, walking off down the garden.

'Sha— I mean Summer, wait.' Jack shouted and then ran after her.

'What the hell's all that about?' asked Rachel, bewildered.

Harriet shrugged. 'No idea. I'm going to dance. Come and dance.'

Rachel shook her head. 'I can't,' she explained. 'Usually I love to dance, but tonight my legs are too drunk. Where's Bianca?'

But Harriet didn't answer. She'd already disappeared into the throng of dancers.

Rachel stumbled on shaky legs through the crowds, banging into tut-tutting party-goers on the way. She wished Simon was there to lean on. It felt a bit scary being this drunk at a party on her own. A wave of relief washed over her as she slowly focused on Bianca and TJ, chatting to a rugby player and his wife on the terrace.

'Bianca,' said Rachel, tripping over her high heels. 'I need help.'

'I can see that, hon.' Bianca giggled. 'Let's go and powder our noses, shall we?'

Bianca steered a giddy Rachel through the house and into the loo.

'I think I love Jack,' announced Rachel.

'No you don't,' said Bianca patiently. 'You've only just met him. And anyway, you love Simon – your husband, remember?'

'Vaguely,' said Rachel with a wave of her hand. 'But Simon's rubbish. I don't like him any more. Jack's much nicer.'

Bianca giggled at her friend's nonsense. 'You just think you love Jack because you've drunk about three gallons of champagne,' she said patiently.

Rachel flopped onto the toilet floor. Suddenly her world began to spin.

'Bianca,' she said in a small, pathetic voice. 'I think I'm going to be sick.'

Chapter Nine

The Morning After
The Night Before

The following morning, Rachel discovered that babies and hangovers don't mix. Alfie, who was probably drunk on his mother's milk, was being particularly cranky and demanding. Rachel, who'd had about three hours sleep, thought her poor head would explode every time he cried, and when she sat him on her lap to feed him, his weight (all of 18 lbs) made her stomach churn and she'd have to run to the bathroom again to throw up. She realized that her alcohol tolerance level had plummeted since becoming a mother and thought that nine months of enforced abstinence during pregnancy must have been to blame. 'Or maybe I just can't handle my drink any more, now that I'm getting old,' she wondered. By lunchtime she felt strong enough to phone Bianca. There were certain holes in her memory of the previous night and she thought that her friend might be able to fill them in.

'How did I get home?' she asked, bewildered.

'TJ carried you.' Bianca giggled. 'And dropped you a couple of times.'

'Is that what happened to my shoes?' asked Rachel, looking forlornly at her shredded satin stilettos on the living-room carpet.

'Yes, I think so,' Bianca confirmed. 'He tried his best, but he is forty-three and you were wriggling.'

'Oh no,' squirmed Rachel. 'Tell him I'm really sorry. Was I a total disgrace?'

'No, you were hilarious.' Bianca laughed.

'Did Harriet and Summer leave with us?' asked Rachel.

'Nope,' said Bianca. 'We lost them both. I've tried phoning Hattie, but her dad says she's still in bed, and as for Summer, well, the last I saw of her she was disappearing down the garden path with Jack.'

'Really?' asked Rachel. 'Lucky Summer.'

'I'm sure it was all very innocent,' said Bianca, although she was far from convinced. 'They were at school together. They probably just wanted to catch up.'

'Probably,' said Rachel. 'God, did I make a complete idiot of myself? With Jack, I mean.'

'No, hon,' lied Bianca kindly. 'You were just being, um, neighbourly. I'm sure he appreciated it.'

'But Hattie and I were having a flirt-off,' continued Rachel, getting flashbacks of the night before. 'The poor guy must have been terrified.'

'Yeah.' Bianca giggled. 'And then you christened his new bathroom with vomit.'

'Oh no!' shrieked Rachel, who'd forgotten about throwing up. 'I can't believe I did that. I'm not even thirty yet and I'm already growing old disgracefully.'

She and Bianca laughed for a long time.

Despite the hangover, Rachel felt great. She couldn't wait for Simon to get home and decided to clean up the house so that everything would be perfect for when he arrived. She laid Alfie under his baby gym on the play mat, turned the radio up and plumped up the sofa while singing and dancing to Justin Timberlake. Alfie grinned up at her.

'D'you like Mummy's moves, Alfie?' she asked him, wiggling her bum to the beat. 'Mummy used to be a great little mover, you know. I used to go to all the best clubs in Brighton and London. I'd wear funky clothes and I'd shake my booty, and men would fall at my feet.'

Alfie chuckled, showing his gums.

'You don't believe me, do you?' she teased him. 'You think Mummy just hoovers and washes and feeds you. But I used to be really something, baby. That's why Daddy still loves me.'

Alfie kicked his chubby legs to the music.

'I think you've inherited my rhythm, little one,' said Rachel. 'Which is just as well, because Daddy can't dance to save his life.'

The music was so loud that Rachel almost didn't hear the phone.

'Hello?' she said rather breathlessly.

'Rachel?' The male voice sounded familiar, but Rachel couldn't quite work out who it was. 'Rachel, it's Anton.'

'Anton, hi,' said Rachel, a little surprised. Anton was not in the habit of calling when Simon wasn't at home. 'How are you?' she asked.

'Actually, Rachel, I'm not so good. I'm not so good at all.' Anton's voice sounded strange, and for a horrible moment Rachel assumed something dreadful must have happened to Simon or Zoe.

'Anton, what's wrong?' she asked nervously. 'Has something happened to Simon? Or Zoe?'

There was silence on the other end of the line. Rachel couldn't bear it.

'Anton,' she pleaded. 'What's the matter? Tell me?'

'It's not what you're thinking,' said Anton eventually. 'Nothing bad has happened to Simon. Or Zoe. Not yet anyway.'

Rachel scratched her head and wondered if Anton was drunk. 'You're not making much sense, Anton,' she said. 'What do you need to tell me?'

'God, Rachel, I don't want to be the one doing this and I'm sorry, OK?'

'Anton, what are you talking about?'

'Simon and Zoe slept together,' Anton announced, just like that.

'Don't be stupid.' Rachel laughed. 'That's ridiculous. Anton, have you been drinking?'

'Rachel,' said Anton, very slowly and very seriously. 'Your husband – my best friend – and my girlfriend – your best friend – have slept together.'

Rachel couldn't take it in. It was a crazy idea. Simon would never do that to her. Not with Zoe. And Zoe. Zoe was her best mate. It was mental. It didn't make any sense.

'Anton, you must have got it wrong,' said Rachel. 'Who told you this?'

'Zoe,' said Anton coldly. 'Zoe told me that she'd slept with Simon.'

Rachel's mouth had gone completely dry. She

opened her mouth to speak, but no words would come out. The enormity of what Anton was saying was too much to take in. It couldn't be true. Eventually she managed to squeeze a few words out.

'Anton, is this some kind of sick joke?' she asked croakily. 'Because it's not very funny. Is this Zoe's idea? Put her on. Tell her I'm not laughing.'

'Rachel, Zoe's not here and this isn't a joke. I've never been so serious about anything in my life. They slept together. I know it seems mad, but it happened and I had to tell you. I'm sorry, Rachel.'

'No,' said Rachel in a very small voice. 'No.'

She felt her knees give way beneath her and she sank to the floor in a very small ball. 'No, Anton,' she pleaded. 'No. Tell me it isn't true.'

'I'm really, really sorry, Rachel.' Anton sniffed. 'I didn't want to do this to you, but I had to, didn't I? You had a right to know.'

Rachel leaned her head back against the cold wall and felt the full force of her world falling in around her.

'Thank you for telling me, Anton,' she said in a strange little voice that seemed to come from somewhere outside of her body. 'Goodbye.'

And then Rachel fell apart. She lay on the floor and writhed in an agony that felt almost physical it was so intense. She understood what it meant now, to be stabbed in the back. Her body shook with gasping sobs and she moaned like a wild animal caught in a trap. Alfie sensed his mother's pain and he felt it too. Soon the whole cottage was filled with pain.

Rachel didn't know whether she'd been crying for twenty minutes, two hours or two days, but slowly she became aware of Alfie's cries through her own. She opened her eyes and saw her son, lying rigid with anger. His tiny face was bright red and his little fists were clenched so tightly that his knuckles had gone white. She scrambled off the floor and ran to her baby, scooping him up in her arms and kissing his furrowed, clammy forehead until his screams died down to a whimper. Some deep primeval survival instinct kicked in and her pain congealed in her throat, turning into a steel ball of anger and settling uncomfortably in the pit of her stomach.

Harriet woke up at 2 p.m. feeling rested and calm. She remembered the night before and smiled contentedly to herself. There was a new man in the village, a much-needed injection of young blood, and it made her feel so much happier about her enforced exile in Nowheresville. What's more, she'd resisted Venetia's treats. Or at least Bianca had made her resist them. She wasn't sure she'd ever had a friend who'd cared that much before. The old gang used to give her drugs, not take them away from her, and that wasn't exactly a loving thing to do to an addict, was it? No, the truth was Bianca was pretty cool. It wasn't as if she hadn't been tempted by what was on offer. She still found it hard to go out socially without a chemically induced buzz. Venetia had hardly had to drag her into the bathroom kicking and screaming, and she'd known that her old friend would have a handbag full of narcotics, but she hadn't taken any, and for that she felt proud. She could see through her window that it was another glorious day, so she pulled on an old pair of denim shorts and a vest and padded down three flights of stairs to make herself a coffee.

'Oh, so Sleeping Beauty has awoken, then?' said Marjorie sarcastically.

'Yup,' replied Harriet.

She was in far too good a mood to have another argument with her stepmother. Harriet rummaged around the kitchen for a clean mug. The cupboards were empty and both butler's sinks were piled high with dirty crockery, cutlery, pots and pans.

'When are we getting a new cleaner, Marge?' asked Harriet, who knew perfectly well that Lady Lilywhite Smythe couldn't bear to be called Marge.

'When we win the lottery,' snapped Marjorie.

'Don't be silly.' Harriet laughed. 'Daddy has stacks of money.'

Marjorie raised an over-plucked eyebrow and said, 'Oh really? Does he now?'

'We've at least got enough for a cleaner, surely,' said Harriet.

'Why don't you ask your father about that,' snapped Marjorie.

'I will,' replied Harriet, trying to find the kettle among the mess.

She half-heartedly rinsed out a bone china teacup, which didn't appear to have any mould growing inside, and made herself a coffee. She noticed that there was no real coffee in the house, just a cheap jar of instant. Things had certainly gone downhill at The Beeches lately, but surely they couldn't have money worries. The Lilywhite Smythes had been loaded since before the Magna Carta was written. She wandered outside and spotted her father on the lawn, sitting at the rusty wrought-iron table in the shade of the cedar tree. It suddenly hit Harriet that now, in the bright light of May, everything around her seemed rather worn out and old. Her father was wearing a moth-eaten cream linen suit that had seen better days and a battered old panama. For the first time, Harriet realized that her dad was becoming an old man. He was drinking Scotch from a plastic cup with a shaky hand and surveying his land. The once manicured gardens had become overgrown that spring, and the plants, which had been tamed by generations of gardeners, were beginning to run wild. The lawn looked both patchy and a little too long. It would be no good for croquet that summer. Lord Lilywhite Smythe was staring intently at the gardens with a very strange look on his face. Harriet couldn't quite make out if it was a look of extreme pain or exquisite pleasure, or perhaps a little of both.

'Hello, Daddy,' she called as she joined him at the table.

Larry jumped.

'Oh, Hattie darling, good morning.'

'Afternoon,' she giggled.

'Is it?' asked her father absent-mindedly. 'I have absolutely no idea of the time.'

'What were you looking at, Daddy?' asked Harriet.

Larry shook his head, a little mournfully.

'I see ghosts, Hattie,' he said. 'On days like these, I can see them playing and I can hear their laughter. It's as clear to me now as it was back then.'

Harriet smiled sympathetically at her father.

'I know, Daddy,' she said softly, putting her hand over his. 'Sometimes I see them too.'

Father and daughter sat together silently and watched the ghosts of summers past as they played on the freshly mown lawn of yesteryear. The Beeches had not always been such a tired old place. When Harriet was a child the house had been full of laughter. Hermione and her two little girls had filled its rooms with their beauty and Larry had laughed a great deal. Friends would come and stay with their children and The Beeches would be full of kids running riot through its halls, hiding in the cellars and climbing into the tree house in the cedar in the garden. Croquet contests would be hotly contested by the children, while the adults grew lazily tipsy in the midday sun.

Every summer, Larry's dearest friend, James Hurlingham Jones, would come to stay with his wife, Beatrice, and their only son, Richard. Richard, or Ricky as he was known, was the same age as Larry's eldest daughter, Ursula. Larry had envied James for fathering a son. The Hurlingham Jones name would carry on down the generations, but Larry, with his two girls, would be the last of the Lilywhite Smythes. Hermione couldn't have any more children after she had Harriet. Indeed, Harriet had been a problem child before she was ever born and had nearly killed her mother with

211

her premature entrance into the world. It was the reason Larry had affairs. He had a half-hearted notion that if one of his mistresses bore him a son, his ancestors might approve. After Hermione left and he'd married Marjorie, Larry had hoped there might be more children. There had been a pregnancy early in the marriage, a brief one, but even back then Marjorie had been no spring chicken and she'd miscarried in the third month. They kept trying for a while after that but eventually Marjorie lost all hope. A light went out in her eyes, the corners of her mouth became permanently downturned and she insisted upon separate beds. Even now she refused to discuss the lost baby.

Back in the good old days, Larry and James had both hoped that one day Ursula and Ricky's childhood friendship would develop into something more long term. It wasn't exactly an arranged marriage, just a mutual dream of two silly romantic old sods. But, of course, it wasn't to be. Ursula died at 23, Ricky at 27. Ricky had been such a charming child before he became a rock star, a heroin addict and a beautiful young corpse. Now, there would be no more Hurlingham Jones's either. No one could blame James and Beatrice for packing up their country pile in Buckinghamshire and retiring to St Barts. There was nothing left for them here, not now that Ricky was gone.

Larry could see his angel now, with her long golden hair floating behind her in the wind as she ran into his arms. Ursula had always been the golden one – prettier than Harriet, better at school, a more talented ballerina, a more dedicated equestrian;

sweeter, kinder, more charming, easier to love. Why on earth had a child so special wanted to take up so little room in the world? She could have filled it with her talents, instead she shrunk away from it and eventually disappeared.

'I miss her so bloody much,' whispered Larry. A tear ran in a zigzag down his weathered face, following the contours of his wrinkles.

'I know, Daddy,' said Harriet quietly. 'Me too.'

Harriet wished she could be more like Ursula but no matter how hard she tried, she could never fill the gaping hole her big sister had left in their world. She just kept screwing up, disappointing them, pissing them off. If only she could make them proud.

'Daddy,' she said, in the voice of a little girl seeking parental approval. 'I bumped into an old friend last night.'

'Oh,' said Larry. 'Which old friend?'

'Nobody you know. She's not a nice girl,' continued Harriet. 'But she's a user and she had drugs with her.'

Larry's face fell. 'Oh no, not again, Harriet,' he began to scold.

'No, Daddy, I didn't,' explained Harriet desperately. 'That's what I'm trying to tell you. I was offered drugs, but I said no. I think it's a good sign, don't you?'

Larry's old face broke into a smile, but his eyes were still sad. He ruffled his daughter's blond hair fondly and said, 'I think things are looking up, Hattie. I'm very proud of you.'

Father and daughter sat in comfortable silence,

young hand clutching old, each lost in their own thoughts.

'Daddy,' said Harriet eventually. 'Have we run out of money?'

Larry snatched his hand away from Harriet's and shouted, 'What? That's preposterous. Who told you that?'

His face had turned puce and there was a vein throbbing in his temple. Harriet recognized 'The Temper' as it reared its ugly head. She knew instinctively that he was lying – and equally instinctively not to pry.

'Oh no one, Daddy,' she backtracked quickly. 'It was just something Marjorie mentioned about the cleaner.'

'Stupid woman,' muttered Larry under his breath. 'She'll be the death of me.'

'Don't be silly, Daddy.' Harriet laughed, trying to lighten the mood. 'You'll outlive the battleaxe.'

'Oh, I doubt it,' said Larry with a wry smile. 'I suspect she's not even mortal.'

'Why don't you just divorce her?' pleaded Harriet, not for the first time.

'I certainly can't afford to do that,' said Larry. 'As you know perfectly well, her brother is one of the best divorce lawyers in the country. When I go, this place becomes yours. If I divorce Marjorie, she'll fight me for every last brick and there will be nothing left for you. I won't have that.'

Harriet shrugged. 'So kill her then.' She giggled. 'Or I will.'

Larry sighed and then started sniffing the air.

'Someone's having a bonfire,' he announced, looking around him.

Harriet followed his gaze and was horrified to see huge, billowing clouds of black smoke coming over the beech hedge.

'Has that pretty little friend of yours at Ivy Cottage set the place on fire, do you think?' asked Larry, looking a little alarmed.

'I don't know,' said Harriet, jumping out of her seat. 'But if that's a bonfire, it's a hell of a big one.'

Harriet ran towards the hedge and squeezed through where the branches were thin. There on the other side was a dreadful sight. A fire took up most of the lawn in the cottage garden. It was piled high with books, clothes and photographs. Expensive-looking suits were turning crisp and then bursting into flames, shiny hard-backed books were melting in the heat, their words gone for ever. Wedding pictures were curling at the edges, images of smiling faces were contorting in the flames. Behind the bonfire stood Rachel. Harriet thought she looked like a witch. She was so close to the flames that her clothes had turned black, her tear-stained face was covered in soot and there was an insane look of rage on her face. In her arms, she was holding a huge, ivory meringue of a dress. As she tossed it onto the bonfire she let out a loud grunt, a bit like a tennis player.

'Rachel,' said Harriet from the other side of the flames. 'What are you doing?'

'Spring-cleaning,' announced Rachel matter-of-factly, wiping her face with the back of her hand and smearing soot into her hair.

'Was that your wedding dress?' asked Harriet.

'It certainly was,' announced Rachel in a voice that could only be described as triumphant.

'And was that a wise thing to do?' Harriet continued tentatively from the other side of the flames.

'Definitely,' said Rachel. 'Right, that's everything. Do you fancy a cuppa?'

'Is everything all right through there?' came Larry's voice from the other side of the hedge.

'Yes, Daddy,' said Harriet. 'I think so. I'm just going to talk to Rachel. I may be some time.'

'What's going on, Rach?' asked Harriet gently as she negotiated the bonfire.

'I've just found out that Simon is sleeping with my best friend,' announced Rachel. She looked almost defiant. 'But I'm OK. Honestly, I am. I'm furious and I hate them both, but I'm better off without them and anything that reminds me of either of them. So I've burned the lot. It's done now. It's finished.'

Rachel stood over the flames as they died down and watched the smouldering remains of her past. Harriet could see a photograph of a couple of young girls, aged maybe twelve or thirteen, with their grinning faces cheek to cheek, as it melted into the ashes. Rachel's look of triumph dissolved and turned into one of despair.

'How could she do that to me, Harriet?' asked Rachel desperately. 'She was my best friend.'

The expression on Rachel's pitiful face made Harriet want to cry in sympathy. She wasn't normally one for spontaneous acts of kindness, but she grabbed Rachel to her and hugged her sobbing body until it stopped shaking.

'Now listen to me,' said Harriet sternly as they let go of one another. 'That girl was no friend, OK? I mean, I wrote the book on how to be a total bitch and even I would never do that.'

'I know you wouldn't, Hattie.' Rachel smiled up at her weakly. 'You just pretend to be a bitch. Zoe is the real deal.'

Jack strode down his garden purposefully, although there was no specific purpose for the journey, and nodded his thanks to the staff, who were collecting discarded wineglasses and cigarette butts from the lawn. He was so excited that he couldn't keep still and had spent the day pacing the rooms of his lovely house, trying to decide what he should do next. Now he'd exhausted the inside of High House and was trying out the exterior for size. He walked to the very bottom of the garden and stopped at the edge of the cliff. He looked down the valley to the village and stared at the thatched roof of Rose Cottage. Just knowing she was there made him happier than she would ever know.

His mobile vibrated in the pocket of his surf shorts and startled him. It was Gerry.

'So?' asked Gerry. 'Did everything go according to plan?'

'Oh yes,' replied Jack. 'She came and she was amazing.'

'She came?' Gerry laughed. 'I should hope so too. A stud like you shouldn't have any problems pleasuring a lady.'

'No, you idiot. Not like that. We didn't *do*

217

anything. We just talked for hours and then she went home.'

'Oh, how sweet,' scoffed Gerry sarcastically. 'And what about Plan B? Any suitable candidates?'

'Oh yes,' enthused Jack. 'I've never met so many bored young women in my life. There's one group in particular. They live in the village. Three of them. Perfect fodder for the next project.'

'Oh good,' said Gerry. 'Well, I hope you worked your charm.'

'Oh, I did indeed,' said Jack. 'They were putty in my hands.'

'So, what now?' asked Gerry.

'I thought I might invite them to my book club,' replied Jack.

'Oh, that's good,' cackled Gerry. 'That's really good.'

Summer sang to herself as she hung out her washing. She felt just like she had done after their first kiss when she was fifteen. Not that they had kissed, not properly. There had just been a goodbye embrace that had lingered a little too long. But the chemistry was still there, buzzing away, sparkling between them after all those years. It had all been such a long time ago that Jack was a virtual stranger really. He still had those same naughty green eyes, and God was he good-looking. She'd never been able to resist him. But things had changed a great deal. They were both adults now, with responsibilities and baggage, no doubt, and she certainly had a few skeletons in her closet.

Summer watched Tabitha play with the cats on

the daisy-covered lawn. She hadn't told Jack about Tabby and she wasn't quite sure why. She had never been ashamed of her daughter. She wasn't one of Summer's dirty little secrets – and she certainly had plenty of those that she wouldn't be telling Jack in a hurry. But for some reason she hadn't mentioned her daughter the night before. She suspected it had been more for Tabby's benefit than for Jack's. Summer had never had a proper boyfriend since Tabitha was born, and Tabby wasn't used to sharing her mum with anybody else. Summer thought it might be best to suss out the man her childhood sweetheart had become before introducing Tabitha to the equation. Maybe they would never meet. That would keep things much simpler, certainly. But was it fair on Tabitha? Or Jack? Summer didn't know.

He'd invited her up to High House for dinner that evening, but Summer had declined. Firstly because she couldn't afford another babysitter, and secondly because she wanted to take things slowly. Maybe she would never take it further than a polite flirtation. It would be so much safer that way. Nothing could ever go wrong if they never got serious. There was something so beautifully romantic about being his one that got away. Surely, the reality of her could never live up to his expectations. She was bound to disappoint him, and then she'd have to give him up again. That would be too painful to bear. Maybe she'd just enjoy those delicious early, heady days of the relationship and then run away, like she'd done before.

But he'd found her this time, despite all the odds,

and Summer suspected that if she left again he would follow. Was it fate? Her mum used to say, 'You can't escape your destiny,' but she had been destroyed by hers. Could Summer's destiny really be that perfect? Surely it was a thought too beautiful to be true.

When her mobile rang, Summer jumped, but there was no need to wonder who it would be.

'Everything all right?' demanded Murphy in his gruff Irish accent.

It was always Murphy. No one else had the number.

'Yeah fine,' said Summer a little too enthusiastically.

But Murphy always knew when something was up.

'Something's happened, hasn't it?' he demanded. 'You sound weird.'

'Weird?' asked Summer. 'In what way?'

'Skittish, excitable, edgy,' said Murphy.

'Oh, it's no big deal,' answered Summer quietly, aware that Tabitha was trying to eavesdrop. 'I just bumped into an old friend from school, that's all.'

'How can you bump into anyone in the back of beyond?' asked Murphy darkly.

'Murphy, there's no need to be paranoid,' soothed Summer. 'It's just this guy I know from years ago; he's moved into the village. There's nothing to worry about.'

'Well, we'll have to move you,' responded Murphy without emotion. 'I'll set the wheels in motion right away.'

'No, Murphy,' pleaded Summer. 'I don't want to

move again. We're happy here. Listen, I can handle this.'

'No you can't,' replied Murphy. 'This guy, he knows your name, right?'

'Yeah, but—'

'But nothing,' Murphy interrupted. 'What else does he know about you?'

'Nothing,' lied Summer. 'We haven't seen each other since we were teenagers.'

'And he's just a friend, right?'

'Yes, well, no, sort of ... OK, he's an old boyfriend. But what does that matter?'

'Mary, mother of Jesus!' Murphy was getting het up. 'An ex-boyfriend just turns up out of the blue and happens to move into your village and you think it's just a coincidence.'

'It wasn't exactly a coincidence,' admitted Summer sheepishly.

'No?'

'No, he came looking for me. It was unfinished business, you know. A first-love thing. He always said, when he was older and he had some money behind him, that he'd track me down. And he has.'

'Shitting hell, Sharon,' spat Murphy. 'Doesn't that freak you out?'

'No, I think it's really romantic.'

'Sharon, you're a pretty girl but you're not *that* pretty. You honestly believe that this guy has tracked you down because he's still in love with you?'

'Yes,' said Summer, but she was starting to doubt herself. Murphy was such a pessimist that it tended to rub off.

221

'Don't be silly. You are so well hidden that I couldn't find you without a map. How the fuck has this ex boyfriend managed to get your address? Now, think, Sharon, do you know who he works for?' Summer could tell that Murphy was beginning to panic. 'Christ, we're going to have to move you tonight. He might be working for Mr Big.'

'He doesn't work for Mr Big, Murphy,' whispered Summer, turning her back towards an inquisitive-looking Tabby.

'No? So what does he do for a living then?' demanded Murphy.

'I don't know,' replied Summer. 'But he's legit, OK. I promise you. I trust him.'

'Sharon, listen to me,' said Murphy. 'Even if this guy is above board – and as far as I'm concerned that's a big "if" – we still have a major problem here.'

'Why?' asked Summer.

'Think about it,' said Murphy darkly. 'If some old boyfriend can find you, *anyone* can.'

Summer shivered despite the sunshine. How could she be so naïve? The thought hadn't even crossed her mind. She'd been so excited about seeing Jack again that she hadn't considered her own safety. She wondered if she should tell Murphy about Jack's friend Clinton MacDonald. He'd been at the party too. He'd smiled over at her and waved. They hadn't seen each other since school, but he had definitely recognized her. What if he blabbed?

'Now, what's this guy's name?' demanded Murphy.

'Jack Gatley,' replied Summer obediently.

'From?'

'Bristol, St Paul's, originally, then Oxford University, then London, I think.'

'Age?'

'Thirty-one,' said Summer. 'His birthday is on Christmas Day. It's not the sort of thing you forget.'

'I'll do some research,' said Murphy gruffly. 'But in the meantime, you lie low, OK? Keep the doors locked and don't take your eyes off Tabby for a second. And whatever you do, stay away from this Jack Gatley.'

'OK,' whispered Summer.

The old feeling of raw fear crawled over her skin, giving her goose bumps. Fear smelled familiar and vile. Summer felt the bile rise in her throat.

'I'll call you back the minute I have any news, but Sharon . . .'

'Yes?'

'You are going to have to move on. Soon. So start getting your head round the idea.'

'I don't want to move,' said Summer sadly.

'And I don't want you and Tabby to turn up dead,' replied Murphy flatly. This comment was the nearest he ever got to showing affection.

Summer put her phone back in her pocket and took several deep breaths before turning round to face Tabitha.

'What did Mr Murphy want?' asked Tabby with a frown, taking in her mother's pallid complexion. She was sick of Murphy. Murphy meant trouble.

'He was checking we're OK,' said Summer with a forced smile.

'And are we?' asked Tabitha.

'Of course we are, my love,' replied Summer, praying that it was the truth.

Bianca was walking Jock up the lane when she heard the Jeep approaching. She smiled her winning smile at the driver as she recognized Jack's handsome face. He slowed down and drew up beside her.

'Hi Bianca.' He grinned. 'Did you enjoy yourself last night?'

'Oh yes,' enthused Bianca. 'It was fab. Thanks so much. Actually, hon, TJ and I were wondering if you'd like to come to dinner at our place some time soon?'

'That would be lovely, Bianca.' Jack smiled. 'I'll check my diary. Actually, I've got a proposition for you too.'

'Oh yes?' flirted Bianca automatically.

'A book club,' announced Jack. 'I'm very interested in literature and I wondered if, maybe, you and some of your friends might like to join me, maybe once a week, for a few glasses of wine and an informal chat about books we've all read.'

Bianca thought she would burst with pride. Nobody had ever wanted to discuss literature with her before. Not since her English teacher at school, at least, and even he'd written her off as an imbecile. In fact, nobody ever wanted to discuss anything with her. The problem with being a glamour model is that everyone assumes you're brain dead.

'Jack, I would love to join your book club.' Bianca

beamed. 'I'm crazy about reading. I do it all the time. I'm really into all those chick-lit ones, you know?'

'I hoped you'd say that.' Jack grinned. 'Do you think your friends might be interested too?'

'Oh yes,' enthused Bianca. 'I'll ask Rachel and Harriet, and maybe even Summer too.'

'Now that would be an interesting group.' Jack smiled. 'How about you round up the troops and we say Wednesday, my place, for lunch.'

'Cool,' enthused Bianca.

'Any suggestions for our first novel? What was the last book you read?' asked Jack.

'Oh, it was the latest Judy Jones bestseller,' Bianca replied. 'I read it in Spain. It was fantastic.'

'Well, that will be perfect,' agreed Jack. 'I'm quite familiar with her work, actually. I like a bit of chick lit myself.' Then he lowered his voice conspiratorially and whispered, 'Just don't tell TJ, I've got a reputation as a real man that I'd like to preserve.'

Bianca giggled. 'Your secret's safe with me, hon.'

Jack tooted goodbye and continued down the lane and out of Combe towards the M4. He had decided to go back to London for a couple of days to clear up some unfinished business from his last project. Sharon had said no to dinner that night but had promised to see him later in the week. She said she wanted to take her time. Jack thought twelve years of waiting should have been long enough, but his arrival must have been a shock for her. He understood that she might need a bit of time to get her beautiful head around the idea that he'd done all this for her. Well, most of it for her.

There were other reasons why Combe was the perfect place to build a house. Approaching Bianca had been a good idea. She had been flattered by his invitation and her choice of book was perfect. Rachel and Harriet had both flirted with him outrageously the night before so he felt sure they'd be easy targets too. So now the next project was up and running and Jack felt good. This one might be fun. They were all good-looking women and hardly a drag for a young guy to have around. Hell, maybe he'd end up actually liking them. Not that that mattered, as long as they served their purpose, Jack would be a happy, and even richer, young man.

She knew it was him the moment she heard the gravel crunch on the front drive. She'd been expecting him and she was fully prepared. Alfie was safely tucked up in her bed. There was no way Rachel wanted him to witness the final showdown between Mummy and Daddy. She'd done her make-up and washed her hair. Put on the jeans that he said made her look sexy and a tight scarlet V-neck top. If she was going to go down with the ship, she'd bloody well look good in the process. Simon needed to see what he'd lost. She opened the door and tried to fill as much of its frame as she could.

The minute he saw her face, Simon knew that she knew. He'd already decided that he'd have to tell her. It would have got back to her anyway. He'd spent the last three hours, stuck in traffic on the M4, planning what to say. But someone else had got there first. Anton probably.

Simon took a deep breath and got out of the car with his arms open in an apologetic shrug. 'What can I say, sweetheart?' he began tentatively. 'I fucked up.'

'You're right,' said Rachel coldly. 'You fucked up. You ruined everything. It's all gone. So, what are you doing here?'

'Come on, Rach,' said Simon. 'Let me in. We need to talk about this. I mean, it's nowhere near as bad as it sounds. I was drunk, she took advantage of me—'

'Oh please, Simon,' spat Rachel in disgust. 'Credit me with some intelligence. I'm not going to fall for that one. Look, there is nothing to discuss. Our marriage is over. You've killed it. You've killed any feelings I ever had for you. Now please leave and let me get on with getting over you, OK?'

Rachel could feel her lip begin to wobble again and her eyes begin to sting. She was not going to let him see her cry. She started to close the door but Simon was so much bigger and stronger than she was. He managed to get his shoulder between the door jam and the door itself and shoved it back open, sending Rachel flying onto the hall floor.

'Oh shit, Rach. I'm so sorry,' said Simon, holding out his hand to help her up.

Rachel ignored his offer of help and struggled to her feet herself.

'Get out of my house,' she shouted, pushing his broad chest as hard as she could. Simon didn't budge.

'Look, sweetheart, I know you're angry, but we need to talk about this,' said Simon desperately.

The look of sheer hatred in Rachel's eyes broke his heart.

'Babe, I know you must hate me right now, but believe me, you can't hate me any more than I hate myself,' he said. And he meant it.

'Oh for fuck's sake, cut out the clichés,' snapped Rachel. 'And get out.'

'No,' said Simon.

'Yes!' screamed Rachel, feeling the angry ball rise up into her throat. 'Simon, leave now before I do something I regret,' she warned.

'No,' repeated Simon. 'You've got to hear me out. You've got to hear what happened from my point of view.'

'Why?' asked Rachel, amazed at his utter conceit. 'Why on earth would I want to hear any of the sordid details about the night you shagged my best friend? It might make you feel less guilty, but it won't make me feel any better and it won't change anything. Our marriage will still be ruined, I'll still hate you and I will still want you to leave this house.'

Simon took a step towards his wife. 'Please, Rachel.' His eyes were full of tears and she could see that he was genuinely sorry, but it made no difference. The damage had been done.

All Rachel wanted was to get the bastard out of her house. She pushed and shoved him backwards towards the front door, grunting and screaming as she did so. By the time she'd moved him to the threshold her pushes had turned into punches. She hammered her fists against his chest until she had no strength left and she collapsed against the warmth of his jumper. Simon wrapped his arms around his wife and for a moment she breathed in the familiar scent of his aftershave and her washing powder. Briefly, she was filled with longing for the days when those smells meant safety, comfort and love, and then she remembered what he'd done and, with one final push, Simon stumbled back out of the door and onto the driveway.

'Go!' she demanded. 'Fuck off! Don't come back.'

'Rachel, please?' cried Simon with tears pouring down his handsome face.

Rachel could feel her face crumple. 'No, Simon,' she said as firmly as she could. 'It's too late.'

She sat silently on the floor in the hall with her back against the door and listened to Simon's pleas.

'You don't have to let me in, sweetheart,' he said, sobbing. 'I'll stay out here. Just listen to me, OK?'

He took her silence as a sign that she would listen and collapsed onto the doorstep. The couple sat back-to-back with a solid wooden door between them.

'I've been lonely.' He snivelled. 'I know that's no excuse, but I miss you.'

'I missed you too,' screamed Rachel from behind the door. 'Do you think I wasn't lonely? But I didn't go off and shag a local farmer, did I? Christ, if that's your excuse, Simon, you might as well piss off back to Zoe and live miserably ever after.'

'No, no, no,' continued Simon desperately. 'I wasn't just lonely because you weren't there during the week. I was lonely because I missed the old you. The you before all this happened . . .'

'You mean before our son was born.' Rachel

snorted. 'You really are a pathetic, selfish pig. Babies change things Simon. For ever.'

'I know that,' said Simon. 'But it's as if you and Alfie are this tight little unit and neither of you need me any more.'

'And that gives you the right to sleep with my best friend, does it? The fact that you were feeling a little bit shut out.'

'No, Zoe was a mistake. A drunken, stupid, horrible mistake,' insisted Simon. 'I don't want Zoe. I don't even find her attractive.'

'Oh, and that makes it OK, does it?' demanded Rachel. 'You sleep with someone you don't even find attractive. Heaven help me if you actually fancied someone.'

'Rachel, listen to me, OK. This is how it is. We used to go out a lot, yeah?'

'Yeah.'

'And we had fun, right?'

'I suppose so.'

'And we drank too much and we laughed and danced and stayed up way too late and it was great.'

'Yes,' said Rachel coldly. 'And then I got pregnant and we had a baby and our priorities changed. Jesus, Simon, didn't you realize that you'd have to make sacrifices once you became a father?'

'I didn't think you'd change as much as you have. You're no fun any more. And you've been so depressed.'

'Right.' Rachel's blood was boiling. 'So you shagged Zoe because I'm no fun any more and I'm depressed. It's all my fault, is it?'

'No,' Simon cried in frustration. 'Zoe just reminded me of how you used to be, and in the fog of inebriation I had this nostalgic urge to have sex with a willing partner.'

'Oh, I get it. This is all about my lack of libido, isn't it?' Shouted Rachel. 'I've heard teenage boys say that they'll explode if they don't get laid but, Simon, you're a married, thirty-year-old father and the head of an advertising agency. You're supposed to be a grown-up.'

'I know, I know,' sobbed Simon. 'There are no excuses. I just wanted to explain. Listen, Rach, we've been together for five years and this is the first time I've ever fucked up, isn't it?'

'Yeah, but what a fuck-up,' retorted Rachel. 'This is the mother of all fuck-ups. You never did do things by half.'

'I know you'll need some time to calm down and get over this, sweetheart,' pleaded Simon. 'But we can get through this. I promise. I will never, ever hurt you again. Just say you'll give me another chance. Please, darling. I'm nothing without you. And what about Alfie? You can't shut me out of his life, can you? I'm his daddy.'

'Simon,' said Rachel in a calm voice that belied her agony. 'I'm not an unreasonable person. You know that. You can see Alfie whenever you like. It's not his fault that his father is a philandering toss pot. But you can't have me any more. I meant it. It's over. I can never forgive this.'

'Rachel, please.' Simon's voice was desperate. 'I love you. You can't throw away what we've got.'

'You threw it away, Simon,' said Rachel sadly.

'Not me. Look, just go, Simon. You're not welcome here. Just leave me alone. I've got nothing else to say to you.'

Rachel ignored the pleas coming through the letterbox and walked on shaky legs to the living room. She lay on the sofa in the dark and cried silently into a pillow while Simon banged on the door, shouted through the letterbox and knocked on the windows. Part of her wanted to let him in and tell him that everything would be OK. But this was too big. There was no way her pride would ever let her forget what he'd done.

Much, much later, she heard his footsteps slowly walk away, the car door opened and shut, and then Simon left the village.

'I don't think he's going to come back this time,' said Tabitha forlornly.

'Pardon, love?' asked Summer. Tabby was back at the window seat, spying on the neighbours.

'The man across the road,' she explained. 'I think he's gone for good.'

Chapter Ten

The Book Club

Everything had turned sour for Rachel – all her dreams of marriage and motherhood and living in the country had turned into a nightmare. The sun shone over Combe, the pale Cotswold stone of its buildings twinkled in the dappled Spring light and the blossom on the trees danced prettily in the breeze. But Rachel couldn't see any of this beauty. She just saw broken promises, shattered dreams and a lonely, solitary existence. She felt as if her future had been snatched away from her and there was nothing left for her in this village. As she squeezed the travel cot into the boot of the car, she wasn't sure if she'd ever come back to Ivy Cottage. It would be hard to leave the house she'd fallen in love with, but nothing would ever be as difficult as leaving Simon. If she could turn her back on the man she adored, she could walk away from bricks and mortar. Harriet had become a surprise ally, helping her pack up, fielding phone calls from Simon (or 'The Bastard' as Hattie now called him) and promising to water the garden while she was gone.

'I don't know if I'm coming back,' said Rachel quietly as she hugged Hattie goodbye.

'You'll be back,' replied Harriet confidently. 'We need you.'

Rachel smiled weakly at her friend. 'Thanks, Hattie,' she said. 'You've been a real friend.'

As she pulled out of the village, Rachel didn't look back. She drove in silence through the country lanes towards the M4. She couldn't bear to turn on the radio in case a song came on that reminded her of Simon. Everything reminded her of Simon. Not least Alfie, who she could see in her rear-view mirror, sleeping soundly in his car seat, the image of his father. She sped quickly, much too quickly, past Swindon, Reading and Slough. London was the last place on earth she wanted to be. It was where he was, and where she was – her ex husband and her ex best friend. But it was also where her parents were, and if ever a girl needed her mum and dad, this was it. Rachel hadn't told them what had happened. She knew that the minute she began to explain she would dissolve into tears and she wanted them to be there when that happened. More than anything she needed to feel their arms around her, because they loved her un-conditionally. Not like Simon, he only loved her when she was young and pretty and fun and thin.

'Rachel?' said Sally Rodgers in excitement and surprise as she saw the silver 4x4 pull up outside the house. 'Bill. Bill. Rachel's here.'

Rachel caught sight of her mum's beaming face at the living-room window. She could feel tears welling up behind her eyes, just waiting to roll down her cheeks the minute her mum was nice to her. She unfastened Alfie's car seat and struggled on shaky legs up the garden path, where her parents were bursting out of the front door with faces full of love.

'Rachel,' gushed her mum cheerfully. 'What are you doing here? What a wonderful surprise.'

And then Sally saw the drawn face, the bags beneath her daughter's eyes and the tears streaming silently down her cheeks.

'What's wrong, poppet?' she asked. 'What on earth has been going on?'

Rachel handed the baby seat to her confused dad and said, 'Please, can we just go inside. Quickly.'

Rachel didn't want Zoe's mum, who lived next door, to see this miserable homecoming. The house smelled strongly of Rachel's childhood. A certain brand of furniture polish, toast and marmalade, strong tea and a faint whiff of damp dog. Molly, the third generation of cocker spaniel to live with the Rodgers, sniffed excitedly around Rachel's knees, her tail wagging so enthusiastically that her entire body shook.

'She's a bit wet,' explained Bill Rodgers, not knowing what else to say. 'I hadn't quite finished drying her after her bath.'

'That's OK, Dad,' said Rachel weakly. 'I'm just glad to be home.'

'Has something happened?' asked Sally as she unbuckled her grandson and clasped his sleeping little body to her with expert ease.

'Yes,' said Rachel. 'Simon has had an affair.'

Sally and Bill had been together so long that their

mannerisms were indistinguishable from one another. They both shared exactly the same, open-mouthed look of sheer disbelief.

'No!' said Sally.

'No!' said Bill.

'Oh yes,' confirmed Rachel tearfully. 'With Zoe.'

The Rodgers' jaws fell open further. For a second or two there was silence and then both Rachel's parents said at once, 'Not Zoe.' They seemed to be even more shocked by the news than Rachel had been.

'Come here, poppet,' said Bill softly, ushering his daughter towards his chest with his right arm. 'Come here.'

Bill held his daughter close with one arm and his wife and grandson with the other. He was not a man of great stature, but he did have a huge heart. For a long time the family stood in a group embrace, drinking in each other's familiar, re-assuring smells.

That afternoon they sat at the enormous family table in the kitchen and dissected the events of the previous week.

'I can't believe Simon would do that to you,' said Bill sadly.

'I can't believe Zoe would do that to you,' said Sally angrily. 'You've been like a sister to that girl.'

'I can't believe they'd do that with each other,' said Rachel in disgust.

Sally and Bill had no easy solutions for their daughter but they had an abundance of empathy and Earl Grey tea. Later, Rachel had a broken nightmare-filled sleep and woke up confused and damp with sweat in her childhood single bed. She found her mother in the kitchen, bouncing a giggling Alfie on her lap.

'Do you feel any better, love?' asked her mum hopefully.

'A bit,' lied Rachel, taking her son and kissing his button nose.

'You know,' said Sally in a strange little voice. 'An affair doesn't have to mean the end of a marriage, especially not when there are children involved.'

Rachel looked quizzically at her mother. Sally was a petite brunette with a tidy bob and a neat little figure for her age. She had the same enormous brown eyes that Rachel and Alfie shared, which gave her an air of childlike innocence, unusual in a woman of fifty-seven.

'Mum, I know you're trying to help, and I realize that you love Simon to bits, but how can you possibly understand what it feels like to go through this?' asked Rachel, slumping down onto a chair.

'I know more than you might think,' said her mum in a quiet uncertain voice.

'OK, so you deal with this sort of thing for a living, but that doesn't mean you understand how it feels first hand.'

'Don't I?' asked Sally.

Sally glanced furtively at her husband. Rachel followed her mother's gaze. Bill sat in the conservatory in his favourite battered leather arm-chair, sipping from an oversized mug and reading the *Guardian* with his glasses on the tip of his nose. Molly was curled up comfortably at his slippered feet. He looked, as always, the picture of kindly contentment. Rachel tried to read her mother's face. What was she trying to say?

'What Dad?' Rachel gasped. 'Dad had an affair?'

Sally shook her head and looked sheepishly at her daughter. 'No, poppet. Not your dad. Me. I had an affair.'

'What?' Rachel was surprised to realize that there was still a bottom to fall out of her world, and it fell with a thud on the kitchen floor.

'I had an affair,' repeated Sally. 'When you were a girl. Your father forgave me.'

'Mum, how could *you* have an affair?' demanded Rachel angrily.

This went against everything she knew. Her mother was a sweet, well-meaning, kind, considerate, compassionate and loyal woman. Not a philandering harlot who had extra-marital affairs. She was a marriage-guidance counsellor for Christ's sake! She mended relationships for a living, she didn't destroy them. Rachel looked back on her childhood and watched her memories of domestic bliss disintegrate.

'I'm sorry, love,' said Sally. 'But it's time I told you so that you can perhaps understand what Simon is going through.'

'I don't give a toss about what Simon's going through,' scoffed Rachel. 'God mum, I came home because I thought you and Dad would make me feel better. But you're making me feel worse. How could you do that to Dad?'

'I know this is difficult for you, poppet,' said Sally. 'But just let me finish. As I was saying, an affair doesn't have to mean the end of a relation-ship. In fact, given time and patience, it can make you stronger as a couple.'

'Don't spout your marriage-guidance crap at me Mum,' snapped Rachel. 'What right have you got to comment on anyone else's marriage? Shit! Your entire career is a sham. My childhood is a sham. Your marriage is a sham.'

'Rachel,' scolded Sally gently. 'Don't be melo-dramatic. Your father and I have always, and still do, love each other very much. But once, a very long time ago, I made a mistake. That mistake eventually strengthened our relationship and it led me into my career. Getting through that difficult period made me want to help others in the same situation.'

'How very worthy of you,' replied Rachel curtly.

'All I'm saying is, don't write Simon off so easily. I know you're hurting, darling. And I'm not making excuses for his behaviour, but people, couples, do get through difficult times. I see it all the time. You need space to lick your wounds, but it's very important that once you feel stronger, you and Simon talk all this through because—'

'Who was it?' demanded Rachel, interrupting her mother in full flow.

'Pardon?' asked Sally.

'You heard me, Mum. Who was it that you had an affair with?'

'It was nobody you know,' replied Sally. 'And it doesn't matter anyway. It was a lifetime ago.'

'No, Mum,' said Rachel firmly. 'I want to know.'

'OK, OK,' Sally held her hands up. 'I'll tell you,

but there's no point in being angry with me because you can never make me feel any more guilty about what happened than I already do. It was the darkest time of my life, OK? And if your father can forgive me, then so can you.'

'Go on,' urged Rachel.

'OK, you were eleven or twelve maybe. We were living just outside Dorking. I don't know if you remember, but your Dad was completely embroiled in his career at the time. He used to leave for work on the six-thirty train and we were lucky if he got back before you went to bed.'

Rachel cast her mind back and vaguely recalled a time when her dad had been a fairly absentee father. His work as a policy adviser for the Labour Party had been time-consuming and stressful while Thatcher ruled the country. Rachel remembered having to leaflet the true-blue streets of Surrey with socialist literature in the run-up to elections. She'd believed in her dad's policies, but it had still made her cheeks burn with embarrassment when her Tory-loving friends had sniggered at her from behind their curtains.

Sally continued, 'We'd been trying for another baby for years and I'd just found out for sure that I could never have another child. I was devastated, but your Dad seemed more concerned about mines closing in Scotland and shipbuilders losing their jobs in the Tyne.'

'Yeah, those things were important,' said Rachel.

'I know they were, darling, but I was heartbroken and he wasn't there for me. I needed him too.'

'Sorry, Mum.' Rachel thawed slightly. She had always wondered why she was an only child.

'Anyway,' Sally sighed. 'There was this man at work.'

'At the animal refuge?' Rachel's mum had worked part time at a dogs' home before retraining as a marriage-guidance counsellor.

'Yes. His name was Geoff and he was so gentle with the dogs,' remembered Sally somewhat wistfully. 'He pursued me for years and I kept saying, "No. no. I'm married. I'm not interested," but one night, just after I'd found out about my infertility, we all went out – you were at your gran's in Kent for the weekend – and I drank far too much. I cried on Geoff's shoulder, told him all about your dad never being around and about how I couldn't have any more children and he was very kind and attentive.'

'I bet he was,' said Rachel.

'And one thing led to another and anyway, I'm sure I don't need to elaborate.'

'Please don't,' snapped Rachel. 'That's quite enough detail. So when did you tell Dad?'

'The next morning,' said Sally tearfully. 'Poor Bill. He was devastated. He blamed himself, of course, because, you know, that's what he's like.'

'I don't blame myself for Simon's behaviour,' said Rachel darkly.

'No, no, and you're right not to.' Sally stared into nothing, reliving painful memories.

'Then what happened?' asked Rachel.

Sally shrugged. 'We went to Italy, do you remember? To that lovely farmhouse in Umbria. We drank Chianti and talked all night, and by the time we

241

came back to the UK we were OK. Your father is a very reasonable, forgiving man.'

'I wouldn't have forgiven you,' said Rachel, still angry.

'No,' agreed Sally. 'I wouldn't have forgiven me either.'

'Is that why we moved here?' asked Rachel.

Sally nodded. 'A fresh start seemed like a good idea. It meant your dad was closer to work and we could spend more time together as a family because there was less commuting.'

'So all this is your fault,' said Rachel.

'Pardon?' Sally looked confused.

'Well, you had an affair, we all came to Wandsworth, moved in next door to a little girl called Zoe and two decades later she sleeps with my husband. Cheers mum.'

'Rachel, I don't think that's fair . . .' Sally started, and then she noticed there was a faint glimmer of a smile on her daughter's lips. 'You're teasing me, aren't you?'

'Yup,' said Rachel. 'Christ, Mum! This is going to take some digesting. You hussy.'

Sally blushed and then placed her hand gently on Rachel's arm.

'Rachel,' she said. 'Please don't mention this conversation to your father. We don't talk about those days very often and I'd hate to drag up painful memories.'

Rachel nodded.

Bianca took her new role as unofficial chairperson of the Combe Village Book Club very seriously

242

indeed. Immediately after her conversation with Jack, she scurried home and, with a quick shout to a bemused TJ that she was going into Bath on 'important book-club business' – TJ had scratched his head and thought, What book club? – she jumped in the Porsche and headed to town. At Waterstones she bought five brand-new copies of Judy Jones's No. 1 bestseller, *Bright Lights, Big City* – a sexy tale of four young women and their madcap adventures in London – then she headed to Paperchase for her stationery. As self-appointed chairperson of the book club she would need some groovy notepads and pens with which to take notes. Then she nipped into Square to invest in a suitably literary new dress. Prada had done some 1940s-inspired tea dresses that season and they were just *so* Sylvia Plath. Not that Bianca had ever read any Sylvia Plath – it was all a bit too dark for her tastes – but she had recently read in *Elle* that Gwyneth Paltrow was playing her in a film and that the woman had had exquisite taste in floral frocks. As she walked she talked on her mobile, not so much inviting, but conscripting members for the book club. Rachel wasn't answering her phone and Harriet was predictably downbeat about the idea.

'Oh God, how boring.' She yawned. 'I can't bear all the lit-lite nonsense. I was very expensively educated, you know. I do have quite high-brow tastes.'

'But you'll be there, right, hon?' Bianca railroaded her.

'If I'm not too busy,' Harriet had agreed without

enthusiasm, but secretly relishing the idea of an afternoon in Jack's company.

On her way home, Bianca screeched to a halt outside Rose Cottage and knocked on the door, leaving Jock in the car for the sake of Summer's cats.

'Who is it?' asked Summer somewhat nervously from behind the closed front door.

'It's me, hon. Bianca!' shouted Bianca. 'Why don't you open the door?'

The door opened a fraction and Summer peered out.

'Oh, it's you,' she said, looking relieved.

'Yes, that's what I said, it's me,' replied Bianca, confused. 'Can I come in? I have a proposition for you.'

'Oh goodie,' said Summer without enthusiasm.

Summer undid the chain and let Bianca in, somewhat reluctantly. Bianca had never been to Summer's house before and was appalled at the dated, tired furnishings and hippie paraphernalia strewn all over the place. It looked – and smelled – like a cross between an old people's home and a student hovel. The furniture had seen better days – the covers were faded, worn and shredded by the Ashton family moggies. There were candles, mirrored throws, Indian tie-dyed cushion covers and carved wooden animals all over the place. Plus the entire cottage reeked of incense.

'There's no television!' exclaimed Bianca, who had a TV in every one of the twenty-three rooms at Millsborough.

'No,' said Summer defensively. 'I don't want Tabitha's mind warped by the media.' And anyway,

I can't afford to replace the one that broke last year, she added silently to herself.

Bianca accepted the offer of a camomile tea, although she preferred Colombian coffee, and perched on the edge of a battered armchair, nervously fearing that she might get some horrible stain on her white miniskirt if she made herself too comfortable. A huge ginger tom-cat called Mr Pickles decided her lap looked rather comfortable and made himself at home there immediately. Bianca loved animals with the same passion that she loved children and, as Mr Pickles purred loudly, she began to relax.

'He likes you,' said Summer in surprise. 'He's not normally very friendly.'

'Oh, he's gorgeous, hon,' gushed Bianca. 'I'm bonkers about animals and I'm sure they can sense it. I'd have an entire menagerie if TJ would let me.'

Bianca made a big deal about formally inviting Summer to join the book club. Summer hadn't heard back from Murphy yet, and wasn't sure whether she'd still be in Combe for the first meeting. His phone call had unnerved her and filled her with paranoia.

'I guess I could come,' mused Summer. 'But why does Jack want to start a book club?'

Bianca shrugged. She wasn't a cynical woman and assumed it was for the simplest of reasons: Jack loved books. Summer was more sceptical.

It wasn't until Murphy called later that evening that things began to make sense. The good news was that he had grudgingly agreed to let her stay at the cottage. The bad news was that it was only 'for

245

now'. But she would be able to make it to the first meeting of Jack's book club and, having heard what Murphy had had to say on the subject of Jack Gatley, Summer had a feeling it would be a rather entertaining event.

'You came back,' said Harriet, stating the obvious.

'So I did.' Rachel smiled.

'Better?' asked Harriet.

'A bit,' said Rachel.

'Good-oh.' Harriet grinned. 'I've brought you a home-coming present. She'll be more reliable than Simon.'

There, wrapped in Harriet's pashmina, was a tiny, wriggling ball of fur.

'The dogs have been at it again,' shrugged Harriet. 'We've got more Jack Russells running around the stable block than we know what to do with. You'd be doing us a favour if you took this one off our hands. Daddy doesn't think she'll be any good at ratting or digging out on the hunt and her mum's taken an instant dislike to her, so either you have her or we'll have to take her to the dogs' home in Bath.'

This was a lie. The puppy in question came from great working stock that went back over a hundred years and could be traced to the Revd Jack Russell himself. She could easily have been sold to any number of farmers in the area and the proceeds put towards the reinstatement of a cleaner at The Beeches. But, much to Marjorie's disgust, both Harriet and Larry had agreed over Sunday dinner that there was nothing like a terrier to cheer you up. Rachel was to have Delilah, and that was that.

'She's called Delilah,' said Harriet sheepishly. 'Daddy's a big Tom Jones fan.'

She kissed the little bundle of fluff on its wet nose and handed it to Rachel.

'Hello, Delilah,' said Rachel, holding the velvety-soft puppy to her cheeks. 'You are so cute.'

Rachel sniffed back tears of joy. She was over-whelmed by Harriet's generosity. She'd wanted a dog of her own ever since she'd left home and she'd never got over the death of her beloved spaniels, Milly and Mandy. Then Simon had said they could have one once they moved to the country, but then Alfie had come along and they'd never quite got round to it. They'd been far too busy arguing.

'God, I love her, Hattie. Thank you so much,' she gushed.

'Oh stop it,' Harriet scoffed. 'Or you'll get me started and I don't do tears, OK?'

Rachel grinned and nodded her head.

'You know, there's nothing on this planet that compares to the smell of a puppy's ears,' said Harriet. 'Go on, try it.'

Delilah's ears smelled as sweet as Bianca's signature scent. That night Rachel didn't cry herself to sleep. She curled up in a ball with Alfie beside her and Delilah in the crook of her arm and, as she fell into a deep, comfortable slumber, she was vaguely aware of the faint aroma of vanilla filling the warm evening air.

When Wednesday arrived, Bianca could barely contain her excitement. It had been a long time since she'd felt she had a purpose other than mother and lover, and the book club promised hours of intellectual stimulation. More than anything in life, Bianca Mills wanted to educate herself. Only TJ knew that underneath the air-head exterior lurked a capable brain, trying to escape. And he wasn't exactly an intellectual mastermind himself, so he wasn't much help when it came to bettering herself. But at least he listened to her. Nobody else had ever given her poor brain a chance to develop. So many other body parts had developed so beautifully that her brain had been overlooked.

Her mum and dad, who she worshipped, were old-fashioned Italian and very Catholic in their views. While her brother, Anthony, had been privately educated, encouraged to go to university and then trained to take over the family business, she had just been expected to decorate the family with her exquisite prettiness. Good money had been spent on dance lessons, elocution classes, expensive clothes and even modelling lessons and photo shoots. Her father had been a little disappointed when her modelling career took off without the need for a bra, but he'd soon come round and been a very proud Papa indeed, especially when Bianca became the *Daily Record*'s Flower of Scotland when she was sixteen. She'd gone on to become a National sweetheart, GQ cover girl and had even been invited to a party at No. 10. Then she'd dabbled in a bit of TV presenting for Scottish Television. Not that her TV career had ever really taken off. Bianca had struggled with the autocue and was prone to talking too loudly and being a little overfamiliar with the guests, insisting on calling them all 'hon'. Then she'd met and married TJ who, to Papa's delight, was also a Catholic, and both parents felt their job with Bianca had been successfully completed. Nobody had ever considered for a moment that the poor girl might have liked to get an education somewhere along the line.

When the book club arrived at High House for their first meeting, they were all surprised by Jack's attire. Having only seen him in a dinner jacket, his usual laid-back dress sense came as a bit of a shock. His hair was even more sexily unkempt than before, he wore surf shorts that clung provocatively to his pert round bum cheeks as he walked and a navy T-shirt that said 'Oxford University Yacht Club 1991' on the front. It was just tight enough to show off his pecs. He'd bounded enthusiastically to the front door in bare feet and warmly welcomed his guests inside, ushering them into his office, where he'd had a Thai banquet delivered for lunch from Bath. It was exquisitely laid out on white bone china platters with silver chopsticks on the side.

Rachel, Bianca and Harriet searched the office for clues as to what Jack did for a living, but even Inspector Poirot would have struggled to come up with any definite conclusions with the evidence on display. Summer just stared out of the window and took in the breathtaking view. The office itself felt a little like a garage. It was very basic, very square and had a polished concrete floor. The walls were white and bare but for three surf boards, which were well worn and obviously hung there for storage rather than for decoration. There was a huge glass desk top on steel trestles, and on top of the desk was a state-of-the-art flat-screen computer, two digital phones, a bubblegum-pink Roberts radio, a half-eaten banana and a mug of half-drunk coffee. A massive glass bookshelf housed a vast array of novels, autobiographies, textbooks and magazines, plus a dozen files housing sheets and sheets of A4 paper. One wall was made up entirely of sliding glass doors that led directly onto the terrace. In the middle of the room was a solid oak table, and this is where the book club assembled for its first meeting. Bianca handed out glossy editions of *Bright Lights*, *Big City* and glittery silver notebooks and pens to the others. She felt rather overdressed in her Prada dress – the other women were all wearing jeans.

'Who are you? The milk monitor?' asked Harriet, bewildered.

Bianca shrugged shyly.

'I just thought I'd take charge.' She blushed.

'You've been shopping for stationery.' Harriet snorted in amusement. 'Oh my God, Bianca, you're taking this seriously, aren't you?'

Bianca stared at Harriet with a look of complete incomprehension.

'You're actually here to learn, aren't you?' demanded Hattie.

'Of course I am,' replied Bianca, po-faced. 'Why else would we be here?'

Harriet could barely squeeze the words out because she was laughing so hard. 'That is the funniest thing I have ever heard. Bianca, you don't come to a book club to learn about books, it's just something bored people do to fill in their time.'

Summer and Rachel stared at their silver note-books in an attempt to avoid Bianca's hurt expression. The truth was, neither of them were there for the books either.

'Perhaps that's why you're here, Harriet, but I'm here to discuss literature,' retorted Bianca, holding her head high, despite feeling very small. 'That's why I bought the stationery, so we can all make notes.'

'And what's with the Miss Marple frock?' giggled Harriet, on a roll.

Bianca tugged at her floral dress self-consciously.

'You look like Jordan trying to prove she's got A levels,' continued Harriet.

Rachel picked up her pen and made her first notes in her book, then held it up so that Hattie could see what she'd written.

'Stop being mean,' it warned.

'What?' asked Hattie incredulously. 'Has no one got a sense of humour around here except me?'

'I was just trying to create the right atmosphere for learning,' muttered Bianca in a hurt little voice.

'Thank you, Bianca,' said Jack warmly. 'I knew I could rely on you to organize things. And I think you look lovely, by the way. OK, everyone, let's tuck in to lunch while I explain my plans for this group.'

Jack explained, between mouthfuls of noodles and prawns, which he neatly popped into his mouth with the chopsticks, that he had a bit of spare time on his hands and, as a new resident of Combe, felt he wanted to give something back to the village that had welcomed him so warmly.

Bianca, too, was an expert at eating oriental cuisine, having holidayed in that part of the world so often, but Harriet, Rachel and Summer were struggling, rather messily, with their chopsticks. Bianca tried to hide her agitation as she watched the others splatter satay and oyster sauces onto their pristine novels and notebooks.

'Today we'll just talk about reading and writing in general, then we'll all go away and read Judy Jones.'

'I've read her already,' interjected Bianca proudly.

'And next week,' continued Jack, 'we'll discuss the novel. We'll try to do a novel a week but, if everyone fancies it, we could spend some time writing stories ourselves, and I thought, maybe, we could throw in a few outings if the weather stays nice.'

'Fab,' enthused Bianca.

'Why?' asked Summer bluntly.

'Pardon, Sh— I mean Summer?' asked Jack.

'Why are you doing this?' she persevered.

Rachel and Harriet, who were also wondering about Jack's motives, eyed him suspiciously.

'I've just explained,' said Jack. 'I like books, I thought you guys might like them too.'

He stared at Summer, wondering why she was being so difficult. She stared back with unflinching, questioning blue eyes.

'It just seems a bit odd,' she continued. 'A young bloke like you, spending his time talking about girlie books with a bunch of women.'

'I like women,' said Jack.

Summer raised her eyebrows. 'I bet you do,' she said.

Jack had butterflies in his stomach. Not because he thought he was about to be found out, but because that's what Sharon's voice had always done to him. Her voice was pure vocal velvet. She sounded exactly like the Cadbury's Caramel rabbit.

'So what exactly is it you do for a living, Jack?' asked Harriet suddenly. It was the question Bianca and Rachel hadn't had the nerve to ask.

Jack shrugged. 'It's all very boring,' he said casually. 'I'm in sales.'

'What do you sell?' Harriet persevered.

'Oh, this and that,' Jack mumbled. 'Paper, amongst other things. Nothing very interesting.'

Summer snorted.

'What's funny?' asked Jack.

'Nothing,' replied Summer. 'I just choked on my Bok Choi.'

'Right,' interrupted Bianca. 'Let's get on. Shall I clean up the lunch things first?'

Bianca couldn't abide mess, and she feared for her stationery. Rachel hid a yawn behind her hand and wondered how TJ was coping with Alfie, the twins, Scarlett, Jock and Delilah. Harriet, meanwhile, was reading the blurb on the back of the book with a look of sheer indignation.

'This sounds rubbish,' she announced.

'Oh?' said Jack. 'I thought it was quite good. It's a bestseller.'

'Yes, but the type of people who buy this crap aren't exactly discerning, are they?'

'I bought it,' said Bianca cheerfully.

'I rest my case,' Harriet said.

Jack studiously ignored the bitching and searched

for an ashtray for Harriet, who was flicking her cigarette ash onto his brand-new polished concrete floor.

'Do any of you ever write?' he asked hopefully.

'I used to write press releases in my job,' said Rachel. 'I was a fashion PR. But it was all pretty brainless stuff about which celebrities were wearing what labels. I'd liked to have written more creatively. I loved English at school.'

'That's good.' Jack smiled, glad to have an ally of sorts.

Summer twirled a tendril of golden hair around her finger and said, 'I make up stories for Tabitha.'

'Who's Tabitha?' asked Jack.

Summer realized, too late, that she'd said too much too soon.

'Her daughter,' announced Bianca.

'You've got a daughter?' Jack was surprised that Summer hadn't mentioned the fact sooner.

Summer nodded but refused to catch Jack's eye.

'And what sort of stories do you make up for her?'

'Fairy stories,' said Summer. 'Magical tales of poor little princesses getting rescued by handsome rich princes, but with a modern twist.'

'Lucky princesses,' said Jack.

'And lucky princes,' added Summer with a smirk.

'I write poetry,' added Bianca rather nervously. She had never admitted this to anyone before.

'Pardon?' Jack dragged his gaze away from Summer and tried to refocus on the rest of the group.

'I said I write poetry,' repeated Bianca.

'No you don't,' scoffed Harriet.

'Yes I do,' insisted Bianca. 'I mean, I'm sure it's rubbish, but I do it. I've always done it. Since I was a little girl.'

Harriet laughed cruelly.

'And what about you, Harriet?' asked Jack. 'Do you write?'

'The odd email,' replied Harriet. 'And a couple of cards at Christmas.'

Bianca shook her head. She wished she'd never invited Harriet. She was ruining everything.

'OK,' continued Jack cheerfully. 'And what do you all like to read. Harriet?'

'Oh, you know, *Vogue, Tatler, Harpers & Queen*,' said Harriet, trying to maintain her air of bored superiority.

'Any favourite authors?' continued Jack hopefully.

'Not really,' shrugged Hattie. 'Except Jane Austen. I must admit I do have a soft spot for her.'

'Brilliant,' said Jack. 'And what exactly is it that you love about Austen's work?'

'Well, she just knew how to write a bloody good story,' replied Harriet. 'She's witty, observant, romantic. And I suppose I can relate to the characters.'

'In what way?' asked Jack.

'Oh, all those beautiful young heiresses going to balls and shopping in London and Bath. They're just like me really.' Harriet grinned to show she was joking. 'And they all have trouble finding decent men, which I've certainly found to be a problem.'

'I'm sure your Mr Darcy is out there somewhere, Harriet.' Jack smiled. Then he turned to Bianca. 'And, Bianca, you like modern chick lit, don't you?'

'Love it,' confirmed Bianca. 'Can't get enough. Especially Judy Jones. The woman's a genius.'

Summer snorted and Harriet rolled her eyes.

'What?' demanded Bianca. 'What's wrong with liking girlie books? Just because it's light-hearted and fun doesn't mean it's no good.'

'I agree,' said Jack. 'And, in a way, Jane Austen was the Judy Jones of her day. She appealed to the masses too.'

'Yeah right,' said Harriet sarcastically. 'Just because lots of people like something, doesn't mean it's any good. I mean, that would make TJ the Eighties equivalent of Beethoven.'

'Leave TJ alone,' warned Bianca. 'Anyway, you haven't even read the poor woman's stuff yet. Read the book and then criticize, OK.'

'OK,' agreed Harriet grudgingly. 'But I bet it's bollocks.'

'Rachel?' Jack turned to Rachel, who was miles away, thinking about Simon, wondering what he was doing.

'What?' asked Rachel, dragging herself back to the here and now.

'What do you like reading?' asked Jack.

'Um, a variety of things,' replied Rachel vaguely. 'I used to read a lot, mainly books that got good reviews in the papers or that won prizes – Captain Corelli, Memoirs of a Geisha, White Teeth, Twelve Bar Blues, that sort of thing. But since Alfie was born I don't seem to have time to read much, other than my baby manuals, of course.'

She smiled apologetically. 'I haven't read Judy Jones before but I'm sure I'll enjoy this. I could probably do with something light and frothy at the moment.'

'It's not *that* light and frothy,' said Jack. Then he turned to Summer, who was twirling a blond curl around her finger and smiling to herself knowingly. 'And you, Summer? What do you like to read?'

'Thrillers,' replied Summer flatly. 'I like a good mystery. I'm very good at unravelling the plot.'

'Are you now?' asked Jack.

He kept getting the feeling that Summer was talking in code. He looked into her eyes for answers but got none.

'I always know who "done it" very early on,' continued Summer with a knowing smile.

'Right, let's break for coffee?' suggested Jack suddenly, jumping up out of his chair.

Over coffee, conversation drifted away from literature and towards Combe and Bath. Jack wanted to be filled in on the comings and goings of the village and wanted to know which bars and clubs were worth visiting in town. Harriet and Bianca happily took him on a verbal tour of the area, while Rachel daydreamed about Delilah and Summer wondered how much she should tell Jack about Tabitha. Suddenly it was four o'clock and Rachel realized she'd have to go to give Alfie his afternoon feed. Bianca and Harriet reluctantly agreed to leave with her, but Summer showed no signs of leaving High House.

'I wonder what kind of "sales" he's into?' said Harriet as the girls wandered back down the lane. 'He said something about paper. Maybe he launders money. That's some pad he's got there.'

'No,' scoffed Rachel. 'I'm sure he's all above board.'

'Or maybe he's a drug trafficker and he's recruiting Summer as one of his mules,' mused Harriet. 'I mean, she could do with the money.'

'No,' said Bianca firmly. 'Those two know each other.'

'Yeah, they were at school together,' said Rachel.

'No, it's something more than that,' insisted Bianca, remembering the look she'd seen them share at the party. 'There's some story there. I'm sure of it.'

'So,' said Jack the minute he was alone with Summer.

'So?' Summer looked up at him and smiled ruefully.

'What happens now?' he asked.

'Now I ask you how you found me,' she replied.

'What do you mean?' Jack broke away from her gaze; he couldn't lie to her face.

'You know exactly what I mean.' Summer put her hands on Jack's cheek and turned his head towards her so that his eyes could no longer escape hers. 'You must know I wasn't supposed to be found.'

Jack shrugged. 'I have friends in high places.'

'I bet you do,' she said. 'How high?'

'Right up to the top,' he replied. 'That's what happens when you go to Oxford. Your friends grow up to be very influential people.'

258

'I need to know that I can trust you,' continued Summer, her eyes boring into his soul.

Jack stared right back and said with complete sincerity, 'You can trust me with your life.'

'I might have to,' said Summer.

'I know,' he replied.

Summer kissed him softly on the cheek and said, 'Now I have to go home because Tabitha will be getting in from school.'

Jack's face fell.

'When will I see you again?' he asked.

'Soon,' she said. 'Very soon.'

Summer turned and started towards the door and then she stopped.

'By the way,' she called over her shoulder. 'I know your secret too.'

'What secret?' asked Jack with faux innocence.

'Let's just say that neither of us is exactly who we seem and leave it at that.'

It had taken Rachel a while to feel ready to confront Zoe, but now she needed some answers. She knew that Zoe wouldn't take her call if she recognized the number on her mobile, so she called her at work instead.

'Hello, Zoe Parks speaking,' said the chirpy voice on the other end of the line.

'Hello, Zoe,' said Rachel without a trace of emotion.

'Oh shit!' said Zoe, any hint of chirpiness now gone. 'It's you, Rachel.'

'Look, Zoe, I don't want an argument, or a long, drawn-out conversation about the intimate details

259

of your affair with my husband, but I do need some answers, OK.'

'OK,' said Zoe. Rachel thought that Zoe sounded nervous, scared even, and it gave her the courage to continue.

'I just want to know why,' she continued. 'Why would you sleep with my husband? With all the men in London, why would you choose to shag the one who's married to your best friend.'

There was silence for a while and then Zoe sighed.

'I don't know, Rachel,' she said quietly.

'Yes you do,' spat Rachel. 'You're a control freak. You always know what you're doing and why. So why did you sleep with Simon?'

'I wanted to see if I could,' Zoe blurted out. 'That's all. I felt like your life was better than mine. As if you'd overtaken me and I was being left behind. You got married first, had a baby first, and you and Simon have more money than I do, a bigger house, better cars, all that sort of stuff. It began to bug me, that's all.'

'You were jealous, so you thought you'd shag my husband?' Rachel said incredulously. She was appalled at just how shallow her so-called best friend had become.

'I suppose so,' muttered Zoe. 'I needed to prove to myself that I was as good as you. I'm sorry, OK. It was a shitty thing to do.'

'Zoe,' said Rachel. 'I don't need your sympathy. The only thing you've proved is that you're a complete slut who's not worth the shit on my shoes. How can sleeping with your best mate's man make you feel anything other than cheap?'

'I feel terrible,' whined Zoe.

'Good,' said Rachel. 'That makes five of us.'

'Five?' Zoe sounded confused. 'You, me, Simon, Anton . . .'

'And Alfie,' Rachel said with venom. 'He hasn't even crossed your mind, has he? And you're supposed to be his godmother. What you and Simon did was to steal a huge chunk of his child-hood. He doesn't have a dad at home now, Zoe. Does that make you feel good? Now he's in exactly the same position that you were at his age. But I can promise you one thing, Zoe, my son's not going to end up fucked up, like you.'

'I didn't think of it like that,' said Zoe in a very small voice.

'No, you didn't think about anyone except your-self. Well I hope you have a very miserable little life and that I never set eyes on you again. Bye.'

When Rachel put down the phone she let out a huge sigh of relief. She'd done what she had to do. Now she could get on with the rest of her life.

Zoe bit her lip so hard that it began to bleed. She dug what was left of her bitten nails into the palms of her hands and tried desperately not to break down at her desk in the middle of the office. In her line of work appearance was everything and she didn't want to appear weak. She blinked back the tears and swallowed the pain just as she had swallowed the truth. There was no way she was ever going to admit to Rachel that she was actually in love with Simon. She still had her pride if nothing else. And so now there would be no Rachel, no Simon and no Anton. Zoe took a deep breath and stared down at her chewed fingernails. She'd let herself go lately. 'Get a life woman,' she muttered to herself. She was losing her grip. It was time to start again. Zoe made an appointment for a manicure straight after work and then sent a circular email around the office inviting everyone out for a piss-up that night. She would find a new circle of friends, a new best mate, a new boyfriend, a new life. One day she might even find happiness.

Chapter Eleven

The Full Monty

Harriet stared in the mirror and decided that thirty didn't appear to look any different to twenty-nine. Despite years of smoking, drinking and drug-taking, her English-rose complexion remained pale, smooth and blemish free. She had often been criticized for being moody and not smiling enough, but having a rather dark disposition had its benefits, and she'd escaped laughter lines as a result. Of course, good breeding came into it, too. She'd always felt hard done by that she'd inherited both her father's weak chin and 'The Temper', but that was a fair pay-off for the perfect skin and long limbs her mother had bequeathed her. Thirty years old and a day. According to her mother, it was time to start acting like a grown-up. Harriet had taken the advice on board and promised to try to behave responsibly from now on.

But for today, at least, she was going to indulge in her childhood passion, riding. Monty was back at The Beeches, having had his wicked way with four mares that spring. That was four more rolls in the hay than Harriet had had. She rummaged through the growing mound of clothes on her bedroom floor and eventually found her jodhpurs, creased and stained at the bottom. She pulled them on and stood naked from the waist up, surveying the floor for a clean(ish) bra. There wasn't one, so she threw on a white T-shirt over her bare breasts. One riding boot was hiding under the bed, the other eventually turned up on top of the wardrobe. Harriet liked to live dangerously and had never worn a riding helmet; instead she pulled on a battered old baseball cap. She ran downstairs, out of the house and towards the stables, desperate to be reunited with her favourite horse.

'I know you've missed the old boy, darling,' said her father as he leaned against the fence of the paddock, observing his daughter through the open stable door. 'But there's no need to French kiss the beast.'

Harriet was kissing Monty hello and whispering about how much she'd missed him. Larry watched his daughter tack up her favourite horse and wondered if there was any way they could afford to keep him. Marjorie was adamant that he had to go. Monty was worth a small fortune and his sale would keep the bailiffs from the door for quite a while, but it would break Harriet's heart to lose him. Larry hoped he had bought some time for Monty with the stud fees he'd made that spring, but he was sure that eventually Marjorie would get her way. She always did. Just at that moment Marjorie appeared from nowhere with her young stable girl in tow. Why, wondered Larry, didn't his wife get rid of the staff and do the mucking-out herself? Perhaps that way they could keep Monty. Marjorie had a dreadful habit of turning up unannounced just as her husband was cursing her. Larry felt sure sometimes that she could read his mind at fifty paces.

'It's such a shame you two love birds will have to be parted,' quipped Marjorie to Harriet. Larry shot her a warning look, but she ignored him, as always.

'What do you mean?' asked Harriet, mounting Monty for a morning run.

'Well, he'll have to go. I've told your father. There's no way we can afford to keep him.' Marjorie was enjoying herself, torturing her stepdaughter.

Harriet looked confused for a moment and then upset and then, of course, angry.

'You can't sell Monty,' she shouted down at Marjorie. 'He's not yours to sell. He's mine. Tell her, Daddy.'

Harriet flashed Larry a pleading look. Larry dropped his head and studied his wellies. He was too ashamed to face his daughter's wrath. The stable girl busied herself at the back of the stable and tried to ignore the brewing argument.

'You can't afford a thoroughbred,' scoffed Marjorie with a look of defiance. 'You haven't worked – if you can call modelling work – for a couple of years. And you're too old for that game now. You're pathetic, Harriet. Thirty years old and your poor father still has to keep you. Why don't you get a job?'

'Why don't you?' asked Harriet, desperately

trying to remember her mother's advice about rising above Marjorie's jibes, but failing to beat the anger welling up inside. 'You live off Daddy's money, too.'

'I'm his wife,' said Marjorie with grave pomposity. 'I run the estate.'

'Yeah, you run it into the ground.' Harriet was getting agitated. She could feel her cheeks burning and tears of indignation welling up in her eyes. 'Anyway, Daddy says there are no money worries, so we don't need to sell Monty, all right.'

Larry had selective deafness and chose not to hear the rest of the argument, concentrating instead on a balloon flying over.

'No money worries? Is that right?' sneered Marjorie. 'Well, we'll see about that once we've sold Monty. Perhaps then we'll have fewer money worries.'

'Fuck off, Marge!' screamed Harriet. 'It has nothing to do with money. Monty's mine. You can't sell him.'

Monty's ears were back and his nostrils flared. He stamped his hooves aggressively in Marjorie's direction, as if he could understand the conversation. Marjorie took a step back. She loved horses and had two mares of her own, but the black stallion always made her nervous. He'd spent too much time with Harriet and seemed to have inherited her flighty, wild temperament. He wasn't to be trusted, and the sooner they sold him the better.

'Harriet, my dear.' Marjorie smiled. 'It has everything to do with money. Your father and I paid for that beast and now we need to sell him. If you want to buy him from us at the full market value, then fine. Otherwise, enjoy him for now, because he won't be with us for much longer.' Marjorie's voice dripped with saccharine malice.

Marjorie knew Harriet didn't have a penny of her own and it wasn't as if she'd be able to borrow it from her mother, Hermione, the charlady of the Chew Valley. Oh how that made her laugh.

Harriet walked Monty forward and pinned Marjorie to the door of the stable. She looked down at her stepmother with a hatred so intense that it frightened the older woman.

'I promise you, you gold-digging old bitch' spat Harriet. 'That if you ever, *ever* sell my horse, then I will kill you. Do you hear me? I will find you and I will rip you limb from limb.'

And with that, Harriet pulled sharply on Monty's reins and galloped him out of the stable, missing Marjorie by a whisker.

'Did you hear that, Larry?' demanded Marjorie. 'She threatened me.'

Larry shook his head gloomily. How had things got to this? He would have to do something drastic. And he would have to do it soon.

'Did you hear that?' Marjorie turned to the young stable girl, who was studiously trying to ignore the incident by shovelling horse shit. The girl shrugged, not quite sure what to say.

'Gloria,' repeated Marjorie sternly. 'I asked you if you saw what just happened.'

Gloria was terrified of Lady Lilywhite Smythe. She nodded sheepishly. She wasn't particularly keen on Harriet, but she much preferred her to her stepmother and felt somewhat disloyal for having to act as Marjorie's witness.

'She threatened me, didn't she, Gloria?' Marjorie persevered.

'I s'pose so,' said Gloria shyly. 'But I'm sure she never meant it. It were just said in the heat of the moment, weren't it?'

'Oh do shut up, you silly girl,' snapped Marjorie. 'I didn't ask for your opinion.'

Harriet rode Monty straight up the path, onto the driveway and out onto Chillyhill Lane. Moriarty ran obediently behind. He would have followed his mistress into the fires of hell if that was what she desired. Tears of rage stung Harriet's cheeks as she gripped the stallion with her thighs and pushed him faster and faster up the hill. Monty's hooves pounded the lane, throwing dust up into Harriet's face, while Moriarty's paws struggled to keep up behind. The sun burned down on them, and through the red mist in front of her eyes, Harriet could see that the road ahead had disappeared into a haze of steaming tarmac. She turned off into a field to the right of High House and kept going through the farmer's prized oilseed-rape crop into the woods beyond, over tree stumps and bogs, and then down, down into the valley, until both woman and beasts were dripping with sweat. She pulled Monty up when they came to the river bank. Moriarty dived straight into the water and lapped up as much of the Avon as he could swallow. Harriet slumped over Monty, hugged his powerful neck and cried into his mane.

'I won't lose you, boy,' she whispered. 'I promise.

They won't take you from me. We'll run away if we have to.'

Monty snorted his agreement and sniffed Moriarty's nose affectionately. It had always been this way for Harriet. She couldn't get on with people. They caused her nothing but grief, but animals, they were loyal, they had always been her best friends.

Jack Gatley and his best friend Clinton MacDonald – Mack as Jack called him – were lounging on the lawn, smoking a joint at the end of the garden and enjoying the early summer sun.

'Geez, you've done well, J,' said Mack, stretching his strong black legs out in front of him. 'Look at this place, man. It's like fucking Southfork.'

Jack smiled proudly at his friend. 'I know, it's mad, isn't it, Mack?' He grinned.

'You don't even do a proper job, man,' Clinton continued. 'You're one lucky bastard, I'm telling you.'

'I know,' said Jack, lazily drawing on the spliff. 'All this and I've found Sharon again, too.'

Clinton had spotted Sharon Ashton – or Summer as she was known now – at the party a couple of weeks before. It was the first time he'd seen her in years, but he'd heard rumours. Everybody had. Bristol wasn't such a big city. And even though he'd long since left the estate where they'd all grown up and moved to leafy, genteel Clifton, stories had filtered back to him on the grapevine. Nasty stories from the wrong side of town. Stories about Sharon having a kid at eighteen, about her mum dying, about how their old haunts were being run by crack dealers and pimps, about how Sharon was living in a squat and then there was the big story. Everyone knew about that. And then nothing. No one seemed to know where she was. Clinton, like everyone else, had sadly assumed she was dead.

Mr Big didn't forgive his enemies. And that was what Sharon Ashton had become by all accounts. Christ, Clinton had heard bad things about Mr Big: a headless corpse found washed up on the beach at Weston-super-Mare, a fifteen-year-old boy who'd been thrown from a bridge onto the M32 at rush hour, an ex wife who'd vanished into thin air, knee-capping, face-slashing, stabbings, beatings and murders. He hadn't told Jack that Sharon had got mixed up with Mr Big, of course. He hadn't known how. It was a huge relief to find her here, full of life, in genteel middle England. Clinton found it romantic that the childhood sweethearts had found each other again, but it troubled him too. So much had gone on in the meantime. They were both such different people to the kids they were back then. Could it ever work out now they were adults?

'Sharon Ashton,' mused Clinton. 'Now there's a turn up for the books. How did you find her, Jack?'

Jack shrugged. 'Friends in high places,' he replied, as he had done to Summer.

'Scotland Yard?' asked Clinton.

Jack shook his head. 'The Home Office,' he replied.

'Right,' said Clinton as if this piece of information was no big deal. He'd long since stopped being amazed by Jack's glamorous existence.

'You know you can't tell anyone you've seen her, don't you?' asked Jack, suddenly realizing how complicated things were becoming.

'Yeah, man,' nodded Clinton. 'I'd figured that much out for myself.'

Jack handed Clinton the joint and the two men lay back and enjoyed the view over the valley.

'Are you back together, then?' asked Clinton. 'You and Sharon.'

Jack shrugged. 'I don't know,' he replied, staring into the distance. 'Not really. I kissed her at the party. Sort of. And we've talked a bit, but I think she's rather freaked out by me turning up like this.'

'No wonder.' Clinton laughed. 'You're a nutter. What was the idea with the light and all that?'

Jack shook his head and laughed at the ridiculous flashiness of his own gesture. 'Oh, I don't know. It was something I promised I'd do for her when we were younger. I said I'd run away and make my fortune and then I'd come back and find her and put this huge white light at the end of my garden. Like *The Great Gatsby*, you know?'

'The Great Gatley,' giggled Clinton.

'Exactly.' Jack grinned. 'That was the joke.'

'But mate,' continued Clinton. 'She might have been married, or a lesbian, or just not interested in you any more. She did dump you when you were eighteen.'

Jack shrugged. 'I know. It was a gamble, but I think it might just pay off. I've been with loads of women over the years, you know that, but I've never felt anywhere near as close to any of them as I did with Sharon. I needed to know if it was as special as I remembered it and if that feeling was still there.'

'And is it?' Clinton turned round to look at his friend.

'It is for me,' replied Jack. 'I'm not sure how she feels yet, but if I'd never found her, I'd always have wondered. You can't spend your whole life wondering, "what if?" Can you?'

Clinton shook his head.

There were now three balloons floating over their heads. Clinton watched them until he became aware of a movement in the woods below. He could hear the clip-clopping of hooves and eventually a vision of a sexy blonde and a huge fuck-off great black horse appeared out of the undergrowth and onto the track at the bottom of the cliff. A dog, like a hunting hound, followed behind. The girl was soaking wet and her transparent white T-shirt clung to her torso. She was quite clearly wearing no bra and Clinton could easily make out the shape of her small, pert breasts as they rose and fell with the horse.

'That's not a sight you see often in Bristol.' Clinton sighed, nodding towards the vision below.

'No,' agreed Jack. 'That's Harriet Lilywhite Smythe and you certainly wouldn't catch her in St Paul's.'

'D'you know her?' asked Clinton hopefully.

Jack nodded.

'She's beautiful.' Clinton sighed.

'Oh yeah, she's beautiful all right,' said Jack. 'But she's fierce. You're not used to girls like that, Mack. She's got spikes.'

It was true that Clinton MacDonald was not used to girls like Harriet Lilywhite Smythe. He was used to pretty little students handing him their phone numbers on empty cigarette packets in Bristol clubs once he'd finished his DJing set. Sometimes, if they were exceptionally pretty, he'd give them a call a week or two later, take them for a drink, give them a kiss, maybe even a shag, but it never went any further and he liked it like that. He was also used to his friends' sisters having crushes on him, flashing him those looks with their big brown eyes while they sang in the gospel choir at church on Sundays. But he knew their fathers and their brothers. Hell, he'd known most of those girls since they were in nappies, and he was too smart to mess around with any of them. He thought that probably, one day, he'd marry a girl like that. A good, clean, God-fearing, family-loving girl. A black girl. A girl his folks would approve of. In the meantime, Clinton was keen to sample as many exotic delights as he could. And he'd never seen anyone like Harriet before. Not in the flesh. She was the kind of haughty young woman you saw in the pictures at the back of *Hello!* magazine, photographed at a society wedding or polo match, or some other posh people's do. The kind of rich bitch that the likes of Clinton had been brought up to despise and yet there was something weirdly appealing about her.

'Get her up here,' Clinton said to Jack.

'What?' asked Jack.

'Shout to her, man,' insisted Clinton. 'Get her up here. I want a closer look.'

Harriet could hear someone calling her name, but it took her a while to work out that she was directly below Jack's garden. She'd ridden these paths since she was a child but High House was relatively new and she'd forgotten it was there. She looked up. Jack was standing at the edge of his garden, wearing a pair of shorts and nothing else. He was waving his arms around frantically.

'Come and visit,' he shouted.

'I'm on a horse,' Harriet called back.

Jack shrugged. 'Bring the horse too,' he hollered. 'And the dog.'

'OK.'

Harriet could think of nothing better to do than visit a half-naked young man in his garden. It beat going home to face the stepmother-fucker, that was for sure. She wiped her tear-stained face with her arm and hoped that Jack wouldn't notice she'd been crying. She rode Monty up to the top of the path where it met Chillyhill Lane and then snaked down Jack's steep curved drive. The stallion stepped neatly over the planted borders into the garden and trotted casually down the manicured lawn.

'Won't he mess up your garden?' asked Harriet, somewhat concerned, as she approached Jack.

Jack shrugged. 'No big deal,' he said lazily. 'I'll just get someone in to fix it.'

Harriet was surprised to see that Jack was not alone. She immediately recognized his handsome companion as the DJ from the party. Close up and in daylight he was even better looking than she'd remembered. He was also naked but for a pair of

274

baggy combat shorts. He was taller than Jack which, for Harriet, was a good thing. At just over six feet tall, it was quite difficult for her to find a man of suitable stature. The DJ was lounging on the lawn, but even lying down Harriet could tell he was at least six foot three. His muscles were well defined without being pumped up and his smooth dark skin glistened in the sun. He looked as if he were sculpted from mahogany.

'This is Clinton MacDonald,' said Jack with a grin. 'Or Mack. He's my oldest friend.'

'Jack and Mack,' said Harriet with a hint of a sneer. 'How cute.'

Harriet dismounted Monty gracefully, pulled off her baseball cap to reveal her shiny blond mane and stretched out a pale, soft hand. 'Harriet Lilywhite Smythe,' she said in her clipped accent.

'It's a pleasure,' said Clinton, flashing his winning smile.

'The pleasure's all mine,' insisted Harriet, with a firm handshake.

She looked down at him, he looked up at her, holding each other's gaze for just a little longer than was necessary.

'Is that a joint I can smell?' asked Harriet, pulling herself together.

Jack nodded as he sat back down.

'Oh do pass it here,' she said, flopping onto the grass between the two men. 'I've had a fuck of a day.'

Of course, smoking a joint was supposed to be completely off limits to Harriet, since her stint in rehab, but Hattie had never been one to stick to the rules. She puffed hard and felt the marijuana begin to dull the pain. That's what she loved about drugs, they stopped her feeling anything at all, and that was the best way to be – numb.

As he watched her full lips suck hard on the joint, Clinton wondered if he might have met his match in Harriet.

'Harriet,' asked Jack, staring at her intently. 'Have you been crying?'

Clinton forced himself to look more closely at Harriet's face. He found her so beautiful that it was hard for him to stare without blushing and giving himself away. It was true, her pale blue-grey eyes were tinged with red and the grime on her cheeks was smeared with tears.

'Not really,' said Harriet as dismissively as she could. 'As I said, I've just had a fuck of a day.'

'So tell us about it,' Jack implored her with his green eyes. But Harriet's love for Jack had been fleeting and she no longer felt compelled to tell all.

'Nah,' said Harriet. 'It's not important.'

'Go on,' said Clinton softly.

He forced himself to meet her eyes, and as he did so they both felt a buzz of electricity pass between them. Suddenly, despite being stoned, Harriet felt very emotional again, and before she could stop herself, she heard the words tumbling out of her mouth. She told them about Marjorie and how horrid she was, wanting to sell Monty. About how scared she was that her father had somehow frittered away the family fortune and that yesterday, on her thirtieth birthday, all Daddy had given her was a measly cheque for fifty pounds.

'I'll buy the horse,' said Jack cheerfully.

'But I don't want you to have Monty,' whined Harriet. 'He's mine.'

'Anyway, Jack,' added Clinton. 'You can't ride.'

'No,' continued Jack. 'I won't keep him. I'll buy him from Marjorie and then I'll give him to you as a birthday present.'

Harriet smiled as she realized that Jack was joking.

Harriet had managed to studiously avoid Marjorie for several days, but on Tuesday morning, at the crack of dawn, it became impossible to avoid her any longer. Harriet woke with a start to find her ugly stepmother's sneering face about three inches above her bed. For a moment she assumed she was having a nightmare, but then Moriarty growled and she became aware of the stench of stale breath in the air and, to her disgust, Harriet realized that Marjorie was actually there, inches from her face.

'What are you doing, you mad woman?' asked Harriet, startled. 'Were you trying to suffocate me?'

'Don't be ridiculous, Harriet.' Marjorie smiled.

There was nothing that repulsed Harriet more than her stepmother's smile. For a start the woman had teeth like iron railings, and then there was the halitosis. Yuk! Harriet's delicate stomach churned.

'What do you want, Marge?' asked Harriet, pulling the duvet up over her nose.

'I just wanted to tell you the good news,' said Marjorie.

'Oh yeah, what's that?' Harriet yawned. 'Have you got terminal cancer?'

'No, my dear. I've found a buyer for Monty,' she said. 'I thought you should know. He's going tomorrow, so you'd better get up now if you want to have one last day with your beloved horse.'

'No!'

'The Temper' took over. Harriet threw back the duvet and launched herself at Marjorie as she turned to leave the room. She grabbed her step-mother's short, grey hair and pulled it back hard until she had her in a headlock. Marjorie's eyes nearly popped out of her head with fright. She was not a big woman, and her stepdaughter was almost a foot taller than her. She realized, too late, that she might have pushed Harriet too far this time. Harriet stared at Marjorie for a long time and fought back the urge to punch her in the face. They stayed there, locked together, for what seemed like an eternity, staring at each other with such hatred that it filled the room. Moriarty scrambled under the bed to hide. And then, after counting to ten, like her mother had always told her to do, Harriet let go.

'That, my dear,' spat Marjorie. 'Was assault. And now I'm going to go downstairs and call the police.'

Harriet said nothing. There was nothing left to say. Marjorie had done her worst. She couldn't hurt Harriet any more.

'I'm not coming to the stupid book club,' snapped Harriet when Rachel arrived to collect her for their weekly meeting.

'Why not?' asked Rachel gently. She could see that Harriet was upset about something.

'Because I don't feel like it, OK?' She started to close the door, but Rachel put her foot in the way.

'You've got to come today,' she insisted. 'Jack's got a surprise for us.'

'Well bully for Jack,' said Harriet. 'I hope you enjoy it.'

'Harriet, please,' begged Rachel, who was under strict instructions from Bianca to get Harriet to High House by one o'clock, come hell or high water.

'Look, Rach.' Harriet sighed, thawing slightly under Rachel's warm gaze. 'I won't be much fun to be around today. You see, Marjorie has sold Monty. The people who bought him took him away this morning. I didn't even say goodbye. I couldn't bear it, so I hid in my room and just listened to them trying to force him into the horsebox instead. It was hellish. I could tell he didn't want to go any more than I wanted him to. He was making an awful fuss and he kicked Marjorie in the thigh and now Daddy's taken her to A&E in Bath and Monty's gone who knows where with Christ knows who. So, you see, I can't come to the book club because I'll just depress everyone. It's best if I'm on my own.'

'Oh, poor, poor you,' said Rachel, rubbing Harriet's bare arm. 'What a cow that woman is. I hope Monty did her leg some serious damage. But listen, Hattie, you mustn't be on your own. Come to Jack's. You know how good he is at cheering us up.'

Harriet shrugged. 'Maybe,' she said.

'Definitely,' insisted Rachel. 'It'll do you good to be with your friends.'

'I suppose so,' agreed Harriet grudgingly. 'But I'm not going to stay long, OK.'

'Fine,' said Rachel.

Harriet's birthday had somehow got lost in the chaos of her friends' lives. Rachel had been submerged in the hell of her marriage break-up and Bianca had had her own problems to deal with, namely an incident involving Scarlett, Bianca's Porsche and a postman on a bicycle. Nobody had been badly hurt, but the car needed a new front wing and the bicycle was a right-off. Bianca had been far too busy dealing with insurance companies, the police and the Royal Mail to manage to organize anything for Harriet.

'I feel bad,' she'd confided in Jack when she and TJ had bumped into him and his friend Clinton in the Fox and Hounds one night.

'Don't,' Jack had said, eyes shining with a bright idea. 'I'll throw her a surprise party at my house on Wednesday. We'll make her think she's just coming up for the book club. It'll be brilliant. I've even thought of the perfect present for her.'

'I know exactly what you're thinking,' Clinton had said. 'And you've got more money than sense, man.'

'What? What?' Bianca had jumped up and down, desperate to be let in on the secret.

'You'll just have to wait and see,' Jack had said with a winning smile. 'Drink anyone?'

Harriet followed Rachel up the hill reluctantly. She wasn't stupid and she knew that Jack and the girls had some silly little birthday bash planned for her. But she was in no mood to celebrate and she just wanted to get the whole charade over and done with so that she could retreat back to her room and mourn Monty's departure in peace.

'Come on,' coaxed Rachel. 'They'll be waiting for us.'

Harriet dragged her feet, kicking the dusty road in her open-toed sandals and studying the layer of grime on her pedicured toes.

'It's hot for May, isn't it?' she said, feeling the sun on her bare shoulders. 'They say we're going to have a long, hot summer.'

'Let's hope so,' said Rachel. 'You and I could both do with some cheering up.'

The women smiled affectionately at one another, each understanding the other's pain.

Rachel rang the bell several times but there was no answer at High House. She peered through the windows but could see no sign of life.

'I guess they're in the garden.' She shrugged at Harriet.

'Or maybe they've forgotten,' suggested Hattie hopefully.

'Let's look round the back.'

Harriet mooched moodily behind Rachel as they made their way round the house, still staring at her feet. She heard the words before she took in the scene.

'Surprise!' sing-songed Rachel, Bianca, Summer and Jack.

Harriet looked up at her friends' grinning faces and was just about to say an ungrateful thank you when she spotted her present. There, in the middle of the garden, grazing happily on Jack's lawn, was Monty. The stallion had a red satin bow around his neck.

'Happy birthday, Harriet,' said Jack, kissing her affectionately on the cheek.

'I–I–I thought you were joking about buying Monty for me,' she stuttered, in shock.

'I never joke about true love.' Jack grinned. 'Now, go get him. He's been missing you and you've only been apart for a few hours.'

'Thank you,' gushed Harriet tearfully. 'No one has ever done anything like this for me before.'

She ran to Monty and threw her arms around his powerful neck. The horse nuzzled into his mistress happily as the others looked on with goofy smiles and a warm glow in their bellies.

'Why did you do that for her?' whispered Summer in Jack's ear.

'Because I like her,' replied Jack truthfully.

'Well, if that's how you treat people you like, I hope you like me,' she teased.

'No,' he said so quietly that she could hardly hear. 'I love you.'

They were the words she'd been waiting to hear.

Chapter Twelve

Naked Ambition

A warm May had given way to a scorching June. Bianca found Scarlett lounging by the pool, smoking a cigarette and looking divinely nubile in one of her stepmother's favourite bikinis.

'Scarlett, you're flicking ash into the water,' scolded Bianca. She could hear the whine in her voice and it upset her. She didn't want to be a nag, but Scarlett's behaviour was pushing her to the edge.

'So-ree!' snapped Scarlett with a bored toss of her peroxide head.

'I thought you were supposed to be looking for a summer job,' said Bianca, sitting down on the lounger beside Scarlett's and trying to sound interested rather than irritated.

'What's there to do around here?' said Scarlett, rolling her eyes in acute boredom.

'There are lots of shops and restaurants in Bath,' suggested Bianca, enthusiastically. 'I know some people, perhaps I could pull a few strings, get you some work waiting tables or as an assistant in a clothes shop.'

'Oh, purlease,' scoffed Scarlett rudely. 'Do I look like a skivvy to you?'

'Well, what do *you* want to do?' asked Bianca patiently.

Scarlett sat up and looked Bianca straight in the eye.

'I want to try some modelling,' she said. 'You could help me. You've got contacts, haven't you?'

Bianca nodded. 'Yes, but I was a glamour model, Scarlett. You know what that means, don't you? It's topless stuff. Not *Cosmopolitan* cover-girl shots.'

'Yeah, I know,' said Scarlett. 'That's what I want. I want to look sexy, not emaciated like that horrible friend of yours.'

'Harriet,' said Bianca. 'Her name's Harriet.'

'Harriet, Schmarriet.' Scarlett waved her hand dismissively. 'She looks like she hasn't eaten in years.'

Bianca shrugged. 'That's what works for fashion modelling. Glamour modelling is different.'

'Yeah, you can be short,' retorted Scarlett, looking Bianca up and down critically. 'All you need is a pretty face and some big titties.'

Bianca studied Scarlett's body with an expert eye. She had the face of a cherub – huge blue eyes, full swollen lips, a cute button nose and a crown of fluffy white-blond hair. Her legs were good – curvy and well-defined, like an athlete's – and her bum was high and round and perfect. Her stomach was toned and flat, with just enough muscle definition, and her breasts, well, Bianca had never looked very closely at her stepdaughter's breasts, despite the fact that they were often on display.

'Take your top off,' she said.

'What?' demanded Scarlett.

'I said, take your top off. I need to see your boobs, so I can tell whether they're any good.'

Scarlett blushed and slipped Bianca's bikini top off shyly, covering her chest with her arms.

'Come on,' urged Bianca. 'Let me see them.'

Scarlett dropped her arms awkwardly and sat naked in front of Bianca. She looked uncomfortable, but her breasts were round and full and perky. A C cup, Bianca estimated, and perfect for glamour work.

'I'm sure you'd get work,' said Bianca truthfully. 'If that's what you want.'

Scarlett beamed. 'Do you think so, Bianca?'

For once the teenager's face was full of life, and Bianca felt good that she'd at last got through to the girl. She handed her back the bikini top and helped to do it up again.

'You'd be fantastic,' gushed Bianca. 'If you're sure it's what you want to do then I could set up some test shots for you. My favourite photographer is a great friend *and* she's a woman.'

'Then what?' asked Scarlett excitedly.

'Well, if Gillian – that's the photographer – thinks the test shots are good, she'll approach the tabloids and lads' mags. Oh, and you'll need an agent, but you can have mine, he's fab, and—'

'What are you two gossiping about?' asked TJ as he wandered out of the house with a twin on each side. He was delighted to see Bianca and Scarlett deep in conversation, chatting happily to each other. Was this a thaw in the cold war at last?

'Daddy, Bianca's going to turn me into a model!' exclaimed Scarlett with genuine delight.

'Is she now,' said TJ carefully. 'What kind of model?'

'A glamour model, of course,' retorted Scarlett. 'I'll be the second Ms Mills to grace the cover of *Loaded*.'

'Over my dead body,' replied TJ.

Scarlett's face fell, as did Bianca's.

'Why? What's the problem, hon?' asked Bianca, confused. She was aware that some fathers might not approve of such a career for their daughters, but TJ was different. He was married to the most famous topless model in the country. He understood the business.

'She's too young,' he said sharply.

'No she's not,' Bianca argued. 'She's seventeen. It's the perfect age to start. I was younger than that when I began modelling.'

'She's not doing it and that's that,' snapped TJ.

'I hate you Daddy!' screamed Scarlett, bursting into tears and storming off into the house. 'You never let me have any fun.'

'What the hell are you doing putting ideas like that into her head,' TJ demanded of Bianca.

Bianca was dumbfounded. TJ never spoke to her like that. He was always kind and gentle with her. That's why she loved him so much. The twins were equally taken aback by their father's aggressive tone. They crept quietly behind their mother's legs and hid.

'TJ, I don't understand,' said Bianca. 'What's wrong with Scarlett doing some modelling.'

286

'Listen to me, Bianca, because I'm only going to say this once.' TJ's eyes narrowed angrily. 'No daughter of mine is going to make a living by taking her clothes off, understand?'

Bianca's mouth dropped open. 'Excuse me?' she said. 'It's OK for your wife to do it, but not your daughter? Is that what you're saying?'

'Aha, the penny finally drops,' said TJ, shaking his head, as if Bianca was the one being thick.

'But why?' continued Bianca. 'Why is it not OK for Scarlett to do it?'

'Because it's demeaning and degrading and she's worth more than that,' said TJ.

'And I'm not?' demanded Bianca. Her eyes were wide and watery.

'I didn't say that,' said TJ.

'Yes you did,' said Bianca in a sad little voice. 'Yes you did.'

She walked off slowly with her head bowed, looking utterly defeated. The twins followed her, casting accusing looks back over their shoulders at their dad.

'I didn't mean it like that, Bianca!' TJ shouted after her. 'Listen, babes, don't get upset.'

But it was too late. Bianca was clearly devastated.

'Oh shit!' said TJ to himself. 'Shit, shit, shit, shit, shit!'

He ran into the house after her and caught up with her at the front door.

'Where are you going, babes?' he asked.

'To Rachel's, or Harriet's or Jack's,' replied Bianca quietly.

'Why?' asked TJ.

'Because they're my friends,' she said quietly.

'You're always with them these days. You're never at home. And what about the girls?' demanded TJ. 'Are you just going to dump them on me again, because I have work to do. I'm a musician not a house husband.'

Bianca sighed. 'No, TJ. The twins are coming with me,' she explained patiently. 'And if spending time with them is too much for you, then just tell me, because I can do it on my own. I was just under the impression that we shared the childcare in this house. I thought it was what we both wanted.'

'It is,' insisted TJ. 'Look, babes, I'm sorry OK. I hate arguing with you. I didn't mean what I said before. I just don't want Scarlett to get involved in the whole tabloid machine, you know? You're level-headed and sensible and you could always look after yourself and keep out of trouble, but she's different. If there's trouble within a five-mile radius she'll find it. And if there's no trouble, she'll cause it herself. Do you know what I mean?'

Bianca shrugged sadly. 'That's not what you said though, TJ. You said it was OK for me to make a living from taking my clothes off, but it's not OK for your daughter, because she's better than that. That hurts, baby. Don't you understand?'

TJ nodded. 'I'm sorry,' he said, and he meant it. But the words were out there now, doing their damage, and he couldn't take them back.

'Don't go out, Bianca,' he said gently.

'I want to,' said Bianca firmly. 'I want to see my friends.'

TJ watched the door close behind Bianca, Poppy and Lotte and felt Millsborough fall silent. He made his way down to the recording studio in the basement, poured himself a Jack Daniels and waited for inspiration to strike. So far, he'd been waiting fifteen years.

In the days that followed, the sun continued to shine, but a chilly gloom descended on Millsborough. Scarlett had refused to talk to her father since he'd poured cold water on her plans to become the next Jordan. Neither would she speak to Bianca, who she blamed for not changing her dad's mind. Bianca, in turn, had sent her husband back to the Midlands – to Coventry to be exact – convinced that he loved her less than he loved Scarlett. The twins, whose language had been coming along beautifully, had suddenly turned mute, traumatized by the bad atmosphere in their home. TJ had taken to living in the basement with Jock, Scarlett stayed in her black room listening to suicidal rock bands and Bianca frantically scribbled poems for Jack to read at the book club. She sat, hour after hour, bent over a notepad, pouring out her heart.

She was desperate for Jack's approval. She had decided to write a poem about TJ and the problems they were having. Bianca thought it was the best thing she had ever written.

'Great art is often created during an artist's bleakest time,' Jack had told them at the book club that week while discussing *Jude the Obscure*.

Bianca was sure that her poem's depth was

heightened by the pain she was feeling inside. When it was finished, she neatly typed out the final version, folded it in two and placed it carefully in her handbag. She hid the rough draft under her pillow. The last thing she needed was for TJ or Scarlett to find her poem. She was sure they'd only laugh at her. Then she scurried up to High House to show Jack what she'd done.

'Read it out loud,' urged Jack.

He was lounging on a stripy deckchair on his terrace, iced margarita in hand, suntan oil on his smooth, muscular chest. The sun had bleached his hair a bright white blond and turned his skin nut brown. He seemed even more cheerful than usual and kept flashing her his megawatt smiles. Bianca sighed involuntarily. She was scared she was falling in love with Jack a little bit, despite her earlier protestations that he wasn't a patch on TJ. It wasn't just his appearance that made her weak at the knees, it was the way he listened to what she had to say. The way he introduced her to books that swept her off into far-away worlds she'd never imagined before. It was the way he told her how clever she was. It was these secret little meetings they had about her poetry. It was everything about him. He was magical.

Summer watched the scene from behind the bedroom curtains upstairs. She'd just made love to Jack Gatley for the first time in years and she felt as if her head and heart would explode with happiness. Summer had tried so hard to resist him, to take it slowly, to be sure she was doing the right thing. But even as kids there had been an invisible bond

between them. Oh, the adults had scoffed and said
they were too young, that it wasn't real love. But it
had been, it was and it would be for ever, Summer
hoped. She watched Jack as he chatted easily with
Bianca in the garden below. Every now and then he
glanced up at the bedroom window and smiled.
What would his guest think if she knew that
Summer was hiding upstairs?

'Come on.' Jack grinned at Bianca. 'I can't
wait.'

'OK,' said Bianca nervously, standing before Jack
like a child before a teacher at a school recital. 'It's
called "My Love" and it's about TJ.'

Jack nodded enthusiastically.

'My Love,' began Bianca tentatively.

My love gave me flowers and said I was fine,
He wooed me with words and expensive wine.
He got into my head and my heart and my bed,
And in the morning he said, 'Now you're mine.'

He taught me to fly, showed me how to be free,
My love was so much smarter than me.
He said it was love and that that was enough
For a good Catholic girl like me.
A good Catholic girl like me.

He took me to parties and told me to shine,
So I danced and I flirted and drank too much wine.
My love showed me how to live my life,
And our worlds became one when he said
  'Be my wife.'

My love made me grow and he gave me my girls;
He showered me with diamonds, wonder and pearls.
And when I felt giddy and silly and small,
My love said, 'Babe, you're ten feet tall.'

But my love loves another girl, younger than me,
She's witty and pretty and wild and free.
He says there's room in his heart for three,
But it feels too crowded for a girl like me.
A good Catholic girl like me.

He swears we're OK, says there's room for us all,
But he's slipping away and I'm beginning to fall.
Without him I'm nothing, I'm nothing at all;
I want my love to be ten feet tall.

So I push him away, try to break free;
If he's got her why does he need me?
But if I lose him, what will I be?
It'll break the heart of a girl like me.
A good Catholic girl like me.

Jack placed his drink on the ground beside his deckchair, stood up and, with a grave face gave Bianca a long, loud round of applause.

'That, Bianca, was beautiful,' he said.

Bianca grinned so widely she thought her mouth would split.

'So, what was Bianca's poem like?' asked Summer later, once she'd gone.

Jack looked pensive. 'Naïve, clichéd, repetitive,' he said. 'And the syntax was all wrong, of course.'

292

Summer shrugged. 'Bianca doesn't strike me as a poet.'

'But, you know,' continued Jack. 'It was honest and from the heart. And the sentiment was very sweet. And, actually, when you think about it, that girl left school at sixteen with no qualifications at all. Yet she's sat down and she's written a seven verse love poem that actually makes sense. That's quite something. I think, in her way, she actually has a talent.'

'You like her, don't you?' asked Summer hopefully.

She hated the thought of Jack using her friends purely for his work.

'Yeah,' Jack nodded. 'I really do. I like them all, you know. They're my girls.'

'I thought I was your girl,' teased Summer, kissing his bare brown chest.

'You're my number one.' He smiled. 'The others are all equal second.'

'Where have you been?' asked TJ forlornly when Bianca returned.

'With Jack, discussing literature,' replied Bianca curtly, pushing past her husband and heading for the stairs.

'Why don't you talk to me any more, Bianca?' he asked.

Bianca shrugged and started climbing the stairs. TJ followed, tugging at her T-shirt from behind, like one of the twins.

'Babes, I need you. I can't handle it when you're not there for me.'

'Tough,' said Bianca.

'What have I done that's so wrong?' pleaded TJ.

They were on the landing now. Bianca turned round and faced her husband. Her eyes flashed angrily.

'You made me feel small and cheap,' hissed Bianca. 'Lots of people have made me feel that way over the years, but never you, TJ. I truly believed that you saw past the boobs and the make-up and the short skirts. I thought you saw in here.'

She pointed to her heart.

'But you don't,' she continued. 'You're just like all the rest. I should have known it from the start.'

'What do you mean?' TJ looked confused.

'TJ, you got your agent to call my agent and ask me for a date after you saw my picture in the Pirelli calendar. It's not exactly a romantic start, is it?'

'No, but what does it matter how we met? It's what we've got now that counts.'

'It does matter,' cried Bianca. 'It matters because it makes me see that you were never interested in my brain. You just thought I looked nice without my clothes on.'

'Sweetheart,' said TJ, placing his hand on the small of her back. 'There were hundreds of pretty girls before you. You know that. They all looked great without their clothes on. But you were the only one I wanted to marry. Doesn't that tell you anything?'

'Yeah. It tells me that you were getting a bit long in the tooth and you thought it might be time to settle down. I was just the sucker you were shagging when you realized it.'

TJ shook his head in disbelief. 'Do you really believe that, Bianca?' he asked. 'Because you couldn't be further from the truth. You are my other half. You're my sun and my sea and my moon.'

'TJ, you're reciting one of your songs,' said Bianca sadly. 'If you're going to pay me a compliment, at least try to come up with something original.'

'I can't come up with anything original,' he said desperately. 'That's the problem. I'm an old has-been with no new ideas. I can't get a record deal, my wife's lost interest in me. No wonder you've fallen in love with the young guy up the road.'

'Don't be ridiculous, TJ,' said Bianca impatiently. 'I'm not in love with Jack.'

'Well why are you there all the time, instead of here with me and your kids?' demanded TJ.

'Because he makes me feel clever,' admitted Bianca. 'For once in my life I've found someone who talks to me like a grown-up. I'm nearly thirty, TJ. But everyone treats me as if I'm fifteen.'

'I don't,' said TJ with a look of sheer despair on his handsome face. 'You're my rock, Bianca. I know I might not show it all the time, but honestly, babes, without you I'm nothing.'

He collapsed onto his knees, threw his arms around Bianca's tiny waist, buried his head in her stomach and began to sob. Bianca's heart melted. She stroked his hair fondly and whispered, 'I do love you, TJ. I just need some more space to be me.'

There was a creak of a door and, in a haze of cigarette smoke, Scarlett appeared from her bedroom. She sneered at her father and stepmother, tenderly holding each other on the landing.

'You guys make me want to barf,' she announced.

It was the first time she'd spoken in a week.

Chapter Thirteen

Truth or Dare

'Right,' said Jack with a mischievous glint in his emerald eyes. 'Truth or dare.'

'What?' shrieked Harriet. 'I'm not playing that. Truth or dare is for teenage girls having sleepovers.'

Jack grinned in the candlelight. His teeth and the whites of his eyes glistened eerily. He looked dangerously handsome.

'I'm up for it,' said Rachel. 'I haven't got anything to hide.'

'Yeah, whatever,' shrugged Summer nonchalantly.

'Fab,' enthused Bianca. 'I love games.'

'You would,' said Harriet, and then added, 'Oh, all right then. If we must.'

'How shall we decide who goes first?' asked Bianca excitedly.

Jack emptied the remnants of a bottle of champagne into his mouth and then lay the empty bottle on the grass.

'We'll spin the bottle, of course,' he said.

The book club had long since forgotten about literature that day. Their afternoon meeting had disintegrated in the heat of the sun into a champagne-fuelled picnic in the garden of High House. A sense of freedom had overcome them all – Tabitha was staying at a friend's house that night, Alfie was having his first visit to his dad's and the twins were asleep in Jack's huge bed, having run themselves ragged in his garden earlier that afternoon.

Now it was dark, after ten o'clock, and the group remained slumped on the lawn under the lights that danced in the tree tops. It was a hot, sticky night and the air was thick with the sound of crickets. Jack took the bottle in his right hand and made a grand gesture of spinning it hard and fast. The group watched, giggling as it turned and turned, ever more slowly, and finally came to a rest before Harriet.

'Oh fuck a duck,' she protested. 'I didn't even want to play.'

'Tough.' Rachel giggled. 'Truth or dare.'

'OK.' Harriet took a deep breath. 'I'll tell the truth. What do you want to know?'

'Each of us has to tell the others something that nobody knows about them,' stage-whispered Jack dramatically. The women giggled.

'All right,' said Harriet. 'I used to be a heroin addict. There, that's a secret.'

'No it's not,' scoffed Bianca. 'Everyone knows that. That doesn't count. It's been in the newspapers and everything.'

'Oh pants,' huffed Harriet. 'I haven't got any other secrets.'

'I bet you have,' teased Jack. 'There must be

something intriguing going on beneath that mysterious exterior.'

Harriet blushed, flattered.

Jack leaned closer and whispered into her ear, 'Tell them what you told me the other day. About having to sell Monty . . .'

His warm breath tickled her cheek. She met his eyes with a questioning stare, wondering whether it would be a good idea. Jack nodded his encouragement.

'Go on,' he urged.

'Oh all right, I'll tell you a real secret,' she conceded . . .

They all nodded. Bianca could barely contain herself. There was nothing she loved more than other people's secrets.

'We're broke,' she announced.

'What?' Bianca asked, confused.

'We're broke,' repeated Harriet. 'Skint, penniless, bankrupt. However you want to put it. The Lilywhite Smythes are piss poor.'

'But you can't be,' said Bianca, reeling. 'Your family have always been loaded.'

'I know,' said Harriet. 'I haven't a clue what we're going to do but, hey-ho.' She took a large glug from a bottle of champagne. 'I'm sure I'll survive.'

The group stared open-mouthed at Harriet. Rachel squeezed her friend's knee reassuringly.

'Thank you for being so honest,' said Jack.

'Yeah, follow that,' said Summer, handing Jack the bottle so that he could spin again.

This time it stopped facing Rachel.

'Gosh, I don't think I've got any secrets,' she said.

'Come on,' urged Harriet. 'There must be something. Something that will shock us to our very cores.'

'OK,' said Rachel, taking a deep breath. 'I'll tell you my deepest, darkest secret.'

'Go on then,' said Bianca, jumping up and down.

'I've never had an orgasm,' announced Rachel.

There was a deafening silence. Rachel looked around at her friends' shocked expressions and said, 'What? It's not that bad, is it?'

Harriet's hand had covered her mouth, Bianca's eyes were popping out of her head and Summer was shaking her head sadly.

'That,' said Jack gravely, 'is the most tragic thing I have ever heard.'

'Oh don't be daft,' said Rachel, blushing now. 'It's not a big deal. I just don't think I'm made that way.'

'Darling,' said Harriet, 'everyone is made that way.'

'Don't get me wrong,' Rachel continued. 'I like sex. I enjoy it. Or at least I used to, before Alfie. But I just don't come. Never have done.'

'Have you never tried DIY?' asked Bianca in a sweet, concerned voice.

'No, Bianca,' replied Rachel. 'I've never had the urge.'

Bianca and Harriet shared a concerned look. Rachel was obviously not normal.

'What about Simon?' asked Jack. 'Didn't it worry him?'

Rachel shook her head. 'Oh, he didn't know,' she

300

said. 'I used to fake it every time. I've seen *When Harry Met Sally*. It's quite easy to do.'

'Fucking hell, Rachel,' cried Harriet. 'We're going to have to get you some action with a serious love god.'

'It wouldn't make any difference,' replied Rachel. 'I'm telling you, I haven't got the right anatomy. It just doesn't work.'

'It'll work,' said Summer suddenly. She hadn't spoken for some time, and the group watched her closely. 'It's hard for some women, but once you learn how to relax properly, with the right partner, it'll happen for you.'

'Really?' asked Rachel. 'Are you sure?'

'Oh yes,' insisted Summer. 'You just need to find a man who knows exactly which buttons to press, then you need to let go.'

'And what makes you such an expert?' asked Harriet.

Summer shrugged. 'I just know about these things.' She smiled sweetly. 'OK, Jack, who's next.'

Jack spun the bottle one more time and it landed facing Bianca.

'Right,' said Bianca. 'This is a huge secret, because TJ doesn't even know yet, but I'm pregnant.'

'Oh that's wonderful, Bianca,' gushed Rachel. 'I'm so pleased for you.'

'Christ, you're a sucker for punishment,' said Harriet. 'Three children under three and no nanny.'

'Why haven't you told TJ yet?' asked Jack softly.

'I'm punishing him,' said Bianca with an embarrassed little smile. 'We had a bit of an argument the other day and I felt as if he didn't deserve to know until he said sorry. Then he said sorry, but I still didn't tell him. It's as if I want to be selfish. To keep the baby to myself for a little while before it becomes his property too.'

'What did you argue about?' asked Rachel. She was surprised to hear that Bianca and TJ ever fell out. They seemed so sickeningly together.

'Scarlett, of course,' replied Bianca. 'She wants to get into glamour modelling and TJ's dead against it. He thinks it would be demeaning for her to do topless work, but he's never had a problem with me doing it. That just showed me that he cares more about her than he does about me. It was very hurtful.'

Jack shook his head. 'I'm sure it's not that,' he said. 'It must be a father/daughter thing. He sees you as a fully grown woman who makes her own choices in life, but Scarlett's still his baby. He doesn't want men looking at his little girl like a sex object.'

'But it's OK for men to look at his wife as a sex object?' asked Bianca, confused.

'Yes, but only because he knows you're all his in here,' Jack pointed to his heart. 'He's scared that he could lose Scarlett to some lowlife bastard. That's what every father fears for his daughter, I'm sure.'

'I'd never thought about it like that,' said Bianca quietly.

'Bianca,' said Rachel. 'I have never seen a man so in love with his wife as TJ is with you. You should tell him about the baby. He'll be so happy. It's not fair to keep it from him.'

'I will,' nodded Bianca. 'Very soon.'

Jack picked up the bottle and began to spin it again. This time he did it slowly and softly, expertly controlling it so that it stopped facing Summer.

'Truth or dare?' he asked with a questioning smile.

'Dare,' said Summer with certainty.

'Dare?' asked Bianca. 'You can't say dare. Everyone else has done truth.'

'Well I don't want to tell everyone my secrets, so I'll do a dare. Those are the rules, aren't they, Jack?'

'Those are the rules,' he agreed. 'But you won't like the dare.'

'What is it?' she demanded, holding her chin high. 'I can take it.'

'I don't know yet. Any suggestions, ladies?' asked Jack, looking from Harriet to Rachel to Bianca with a demonic grin. 'Something really nasty.'

He watched Summer closely, but there was no reaction.

'I've got an idea,' said Harriet.

'You would,' retorted Bianca. 'And I bet it's awful.'

Harriet fished around in her handbag and presented Summer with her house keys. 'Here,' she said, chucking them to Summer.

Summer caught the keys. 'What are these for?'

'Your dare,' announced Harriet, grinning. 'I dare you to go to The Beeches, help yourself to Marjorie's undies and string them up from trees and bushes all over the village.'

Summer rolled her eyes in exasperation. 'That's stupid, Harriet. I'm not doing that.'

She looked at the others for support, but even the usually sensible Rachel looked amused by the idea. 'Oh come on, guys, think of something else.'

'You could always tell us a secret,' Jack reminded her.

'OK, I'll do it,' said Summer, standing up with a shrug of resignation. 'Will she be in?' she asked Harriet.

Harriet shook her head. 'No, they're at some charity ball at Highgrove,' she said. 'They won't be back until after midnight.'

'So where will I find Marjorie's underwear?' Summer sounded rather bored, as she found the whole idea more tedious than nerve-racking.

'In her dressing room,' explained Hattie excitedly. 'First floor, third door on your left. Her knickers are in a kind of big antique chest of drawers thingy. Oh, and get some bras too. And bring us back a girdle as proof.'

'I will,' called Summer over her shoulder as she sauntered off casually in the direction of The Beeches.

'She's not worried about doing it at all,' commented Rachel. 'That girl's got no fear.'

'That's not true,' replied Jack, watching Summer disappear into the darkness in bare feet. 'She just keeps her fears well hidden.'

'So, Mr Gatley,' said Harriet, turning her attention to Jack. 'I believe it's your turn for truth or dare. What are your secrets? I suspect you have a few.'

Jack leaned into the group so that the women could feel his warm breath on their faces. 'I'll tell

304

you a secret,' he whispered in the darkness. 'Something no one else knows.'

'What? What?' demanded Bianca giddily.

'I think I've got a daughter,' he said solemnly.

'What do you mean, you "think" you've got a daughter?' demanded Harriet. 'Either you've got one or you haven't.'

'Well,' whispered Jack, glancing around, as if checking for spies in the garden. 'I've got this ex girlfriend and she has a daughter. I've done my sums and, well, I could theoretically be the father, if you know what I mean.'

'So why don't you just ask her if the girl is yours?' asked Bianca, wide-eyed.

'It's complicated,' explained Jack. 'Surely the mother would tell me if she wanted me to know.'

'Does the girl look like you?' asked Rachel.

Jack shook his head sadly. 'I have absolutely no idea. I've never met her.'

'She can't be yours,' said Harriet.

'Why not?' Jack looked a bit put out by the assumption.

'Because you're loaded,' she explained. 'The mother would have had lawyers onto you within minutes of the birth. She'd be owed a fortune in alimony or palimony or whatever it's called when absent fathers have to pay zillions of pounds for not using a condom.'

'True,' conceded Bianca. 'TJ's paid a fortune for Scarlett over the years and her mum was a multi-millionairess even before she married into Hollywood royalty.'

'No,' said Jack. 'This woman isn't like that. She's

not interested in material things. I don't think she wants money for her daughter.'

'Was it just some one-night stand?' asked Rachel gently.

Jack shook his head. 'No, I loved her very much, but she left me.'

'So what are you going to do?' asked Bianca. 'You need to know.'

Jack shrugged. 'I'm working on it.'

He sat silently, staring out to space for a while, and then he said, 'Don't mention this to anyone, will you?'

The women shook their heads. Bianca wondered if Summer was to be excluded from the secret too. But no, Jack and Summer were so close, she was bound to already know about his dilemma.

Summer felt the deep summer grass beneath her feet. It was warm from the day's sunshine and slightly damp with dew. She approached The Beeches from the paddock behind and crept around its ancient stone walls until she reached the imposing wooden front door. Her heart thump, thump, thumped in her chest and her hand shook as she began to open the door. The key Harriet had given her was large, old-fashioned and rusty. It took a few tries before the door unlocked with a satisfying clunk. Summer thought it was strange that the Lilywhite Smythes had no security. There was no alarm, no mortice lock, not even a security chain like she had at the cottage. She guessed that the family were used to more innocent times, when the Lord of the Manor could trust his villagers not to break into his property and steal his wife's underwear. Summer shut the door behind her and sighed with relief to find that there were no lights on. Harriet was right, Larry and Marjorie were definitely not in. Summer was just acclimatizing to the darkness when she felt a hard blow to her stomach. It knocked her backwards so that she fell onto her back on the cold tiled floor and winded her so that she couldn't catch her breath. She felt an immense weight on her chest as a huge black shadow lurched towards her. She tried to scream, but before any sound could escape, a hot, slobbery tongue was thrust into her open mouth. Her nostrils were filled with the unmistakable stench of dog breath.

'Get off. Get off, you silly mutt.' Summer laughed, pushing the Labrador off her chest and sitting up. 'Christ, you scared me.'

She rubbed the dog's ears affectionately and the dog wagged his tail enthusiastically and gave Summer a paw. She could hear more paws skidding on the bare floor and suddenly another dog appeared, and then another and another. They all licked her face and her bare feet and snuffled excitedly at her skirt, which must have reeked of cats.

'No wonder they don't have a burglar alarm,' said Summer to the dogs. 'You lot would kiss an intruder to death before he could steal anything. Now let me up.'

The dogs followed Summer excitedly up the creaky staircase. Summer felt along the wall at the top and counted the doors on her left – one, two, three. She opened the door and sneaked into

Marjorie's dressing room. Just as Harriet had described, there on the back wall was a large chest of drawers full of Lady Lilywhite Smythe's smalls. Summer gathered handfuls of underwear and then shut the drawers neatly behind her.

'Come on, you lot,' she said to the dogs. 'Let's go.'

She shut the door behind her and crept back down the stairs.

'I'm going now,' she said to her new friends as they panted expectantly at her feet. 'Don't tell your mistress it was me, OK?'

She kissed the Labrador on his head and let herself out of the front door with a deep sigh of satisfaction. Summer was surprised to find that she'd almost enjoyed the experience. It had given her a naughty, frivolous little thrill. It had been such a long time since she'd had fun just for the sake of it. She felt bad that she couldn't share any secrets with her new friends and she was well aware that such behaviour made her appear cold and withdrawn, but she had no choice. Murphy had made that perfectly clear. Maybe doing this silly little dare would be like some sort of initiation ceremony. The other girls would see that she could be fun to have around and they would accept the bit of her that she was able to give them.

Summer jogged towards the village green, giggling to herself and being careful not to drop any knickers on Chillyhill Lane. She checked to make sure no one was looking. It was after closing time at the pub, and the beer garden was empty. The coast appeared to be clear. Summer began to hang sensible big knickers onto the branches of the oak trees on the village green. She placed a huge boulder-holder of a bra on the cricket club's score board and hung another on the sign outside the pub. She stood back and admired her work. The village looked strangely pretty, decorated as it was with her Ladyship's smalls. Summer wiped the sweat from her forehead and laughed out loud. She couldn't wait for the others to see her handywork. She shoved a greying corset into her pocket and began to make her way slowly back up the hill towards High House. The gravel hurt her bare feet.

Just as she was beginning to catch her breath, Summer heard a car approaching in the distance. Worried that it might be the Lilywhite Smythes returning from their ball, she crouched down behind a bush and waited for the headlights to appear. The sound of the engine got closer and closer, but Summer couldn't see any lights. She peered down the hill and tried to see what was going on. She could just about make out the shape of a car creeping slowly up the hill towards the village. Whoever it was had forgotten to put on their lights. Perhaps it was Larry. Maybe he was drunk. Summer waited behind the bush for the car to pass. She waited and waited. The sound of the engine was quite clear in the silent night air, but it wasn't getting any closer. Summer peered out from her hiding place again. The car sat still, fifty metres down the lane. It waited in the darkness right out-side Rose Cottage. Summer could feel the panic rising in her chest. Adrenalin pumped through her veins and she chose flight not fight. Summer's bare feet pounded the rough road as she ran with her heart in her mouth towards High House. She checked behind her to see whether the car was following, but it remained in its position outside her house. Summer ran at full speed up the hill, round the corner, and was just passing the gates to Millsborough when a figure appeared in the shadows.

'Don't touch me, you bastard,' shouted Summer, backing into the verge. 'Look, I've got my phone here. I'm calling the police.' She held her mobile phone up in the air and waved it at the figure.

'Summer?' said the shadow. 'Is that you? Are you OK?'

'Who's that?' demanded Summer, squinting in the darkness and wishing there was a moon that night.

'It's me,' said the voice. 'TJ.'

'TJ,' gushed Summer gratefully. 'Thank God. I thought you were somebody else.'

She threw herself into TJ's arms.

'Summer, what on earth's going on? You're shaking,' said TJ, confused. He was used to women throwing themselves at him, but not normally under these circumstances.

Summer breathed deeply, trying to catch her breath. 'I was doing a dare,' she explained, panting. 'I think I just freaked myself out in the dark.'

'You girls,' teased TJ as he placed a protective arm around Summer's shoulders. 'I thought you'd have grown out of games by now.'

'It wasn't our idea,' explained Summer breathlessly as they continued up the hill towards High House. 'It was Jack's.'

'Oh, he's a real joker that Jack Gatley,' said TJ.

Summer thought she could detect a hint of something strained in TJ's voice. Not quite anger, but perhaps mistrust. Or was it envy?

'Look who I found,' announced Summer as she appeared back on the lawn at High House. 'He jumped out of the bushes and scared me half to death.'

'TJ!' shouted Bianca cheerfully. 'Have you come to take me home? Is it past my bedtime?'

'Hi guys,' said TJ sheepishly to the others. 'I hope I'm not intruding. Just thought I'd come and find my wife, make sure she remembered where she lived.'

'Don't be silly, hon.' Bianca giggled. 'I was going to call you in a minute anyway. The girls are asleep in Jack's bed and I need you to carry one of them home.'

Bianca turned to Summer. 'Did you do it?' she asked, brown eyes shining.

Summer nodded solemnly and made a big deal out of slowly pulling the corset out of her pocket.

'Brilliant,' said Harriet smugly. 'Marjorie's going to feel like a right tit.'

'She's going to feel like a droopy tit,' said Summer. 'All her bras are hanging in the village green.'

'What have you lot been up to?' asked TJ. 'I thought this was a book club.'

'We got a bit side-tracked.' Jack grinned. 'I'm afraid I've been leading your wife and her friends astray.'

TJ forced a smile. That's what I'm worried about,

he thought to himself as he held out a hand to Bianca and pulled her to her wobbly feet.

'I'm going to get going too,' said Rachel. 'I'm tired. You coming, Harriet?'

Harriet nodded. 'Can I stay at yours tonight, Rach?' she asked. 'I don't think I want to be at home when Marjorie tries to get dressed in the morning.'

'Course you can,' said Rachel. 'If you're good, I might even make you breakfast. Are you coming, Summer?'

Summer shook her head and slumped down onto the grass beside Jack. 'I need to get my breath back,' she said. 'I just ran all the way up here from the village green.'

TJ and Bianca trod softly down the hill with a sleeping twin draped over each of their shoulders. Harriet and Rachel tip-toed as quietly as they could behind. Combe was deathly silent, except for the sound of the odd cricket in the stale night air.

'There's a car outside your house,' said Harriet as she and Rachel approached Ivy Cottage.

'So, there is,' said Rachel. 'That's weird.'

The car revved its engine, did a hasty three-point turn and disappeared into the night.

'Must have been lost,' decided Rachel.

'No wonder,' retorted Hattie. 'Stupid man forgot to put his lights on.'

Back at High House, Summer rested her head on Jack's chest and bit her lip. Jack could feel her heart pounding.

'Are you OK?' he asked. 'You seem edgy.'

'I'm scared,' whispered Summer. 'I think there was a car waiting outside my house.'

'When?' asked Jack with a frown.

'Earlier, when I did my dare. It didn't have any lights on, but it was definitely just sitting there, outside the cottage.'

Jack sighed deeply. He wasn't sure how to cope with the situation, but he knew he had to do everything in his power to protect Summer.

'Stay here tonight,' he urged. 'Tabitha's at a friend's house, isn't she?'

Summer nodded.

'Then stay here with me, and in the morning you can call Murphy.'

'OK,' said Summer in a small voice.

He stroked her golden hair gently until her breath softened a little and she began to relax. Summer and Jack lay together in the grass, whispering in the darkness, sharing their secrets now that the game was over.

'Do you think the others know about us?' wondered Summer suddenly.

'No,' said Jack. 'They haven't got a clue.'

'Do you think we should tell them?' Summer said thoughtfully. 'I'm sure we can trust them.'

'No. Let's just leave things the way they are.'

'Why?' asked Summer, turning her head to look Jack in the eye. 'Are you ashamed of me?'

'Don't be silly,' Jack rebuffed.

'You should be,' said Summer forlornly, laying her head back on his chest. 'I'm a bloody disaster area. I'm an unemployed, poverty-stricken single mother, with a colourful past and half of Bristol's gangland villains baying for my blood. Hardly a good catch.'

'Summer, I'm not ashamed of you. You're the only woman I've ever loved, but as I explained before, it's better if the others think I'm single. I need to get as close to them as possible or my plan won't work. If they think I'm only interested in you, they might lose interest and stop coming round here so often. I need to study their every move, get inside their heads. Anyway, I thought you wanted to keep me secret too.'

'I don't *want* to.' Summer pouted her bee-stung lips. 'I can't tell Murphy because he'd do his nut, and because I haven't told Tabby about you yet, it isn't really fair to tell anyone else. What I want to do is shout it from the church roof.'

'Why haven't you told Tabitha yet?' asked Jack.

Summer shrugged and stared into the black night. 'I suppose I'm waiting to see whether you're going to stick around.'

Jack kissed her golden hair and whispered, 'It took me twelve years to find you, I'm not going anywhere.'

Rachel had fallen into a deep, velvety sleep and was now enjoying a luxurious, semi-conscious lie-in – a rare treat since becoming the mother of a milk-thirsty son. She languished in the half-awake, half-asleep dreams of the morning with Delilah curled up in the crook of her neck. It was total bliss. Suddenly her fuzzy brain was bombarded by the sound of a persistent banging on the front door. She turned over and tried to ignore it, but it wouldn't go away. Soon the banging was accompanied by a screeching voice, shouting, 'Harriet! Harriet! I

314

know you're in there. Come down here this minute!' Rachel opened her eyes reluctantly and winced at the brightness of the day. Memories of the night before crept into her consciousness and she realized that the screeching must be coming from Marjorie. With a sigh of resignation, she dragged her weary body out of bed, slipped her feet into her slippers and padded in her pyjamas downstairs to the front door.

'Good morning, Marjorie,' she said, rubbing her eyes. 'Can I help you?'

'Yes you ruddy well can,' snapped Marjorie.

Her normal pallid face was crimson with rage. Rachel noticed that she had her arms full of underwear and had to disguise a smirk as a yawn.

'I presume my stepdaughter had something to do with this.' Marjorie held out a greying bra for Rachel to examine.

'Marjorie, I have absolutely no idea what you're talking about,' lied Rachel. 'Harriet and I were at High House together last night and then she came home with me. Alfie's with his father so she kept me company.'

'A likely story,' sneered Marjorie. 'And where is she now? Still in bed, no doubt. Lazy blighter.'

'I'm here, Marge,' said Harriet, appearing at Rachel's shoulder, wrapped in a very small towel. 'I was in the shower. Now bugger off, will you. You've got no right to come thumping on her door this early on a Sunday morning.'

'I have every right to find out who is responsible for this, this, this . . .' Marjorie held out handfuls of knickers and bras. '. . . this barbaric behaviour. I

315

have a reputation in this village, and I do not need the residents to see the contents of my underwear drawer. How could you do this to me, your own stepmother?'

Harriet shrugged nonchalantly and said in a rather bored tone, 'Marjorie, it wasn't me.'

'I don't believe you,' snapped Marjorie. 'You're a lying little toad.'

Harriet rolled her eyes heavenward and sighed. 'Listen, Marge, I don't really give a flying fuck whether or not you believe me. It wasn't me and that's my final word on the subject. Now piss off, leave us alone.'

'But, but, but,' Marjorie spluttered. 'I hate you, Harriet. Do you hear me? I hate you.'

'The feeling's mutual, Mummy dearest,' hissed Harriet. 'Just go. Bugger off. Leave me alone.'

'You've not heard the last of this,' shouted Marjorie as she walked reluctantly down the garden path. 'You can't hide here for ever. Wait until your father gets hold of you.'

'Ooh, I'm shaking,' laughed Harriet, and then for good measure she shouted, 'Don't get your knickers in a twist,' and shut the door firmly.

'Sorry about that, Rachel,' said Harriet. 'I might have known she'd come looking for me. Bloody madwoman.'

'She really is quite vile, isn't she?' said Rachel thoughtfully. 'Whatever does your dad see in her?'

Harriet shrugged. 'I have absolutely no idea. He certainly didn't marry her for her looks, or her personality, or her body.'

'Well, I'm awake now,' said Rachel with a stretch. 'Breakfast?'

Harriet nodded enthusiastically.

They were just tucking into croissants filled with scrambled egg and crispy bacon when there was more frantic knocking on the door. Harriet stopped short, a croissant suspended in front of her open mouth.

'What the hell does she want now?' she demanded. 'Christ, can't I get any peace?'

'Don't worry,' said Rachel, getting to her feet. 'I'll get rid of her.'

The knocking became more and more desperate as Rachel walked down the hall.

'All right, all right, I'm coming,' she said rather impatiently as she opened the door.

There on the doorstep, with tears streaming down her face, was Tabitha. She looked up at Rachel with imploring green eyes and sobbed, 'Rachel, I can't find my mummy and I've forgotten my house keys and I'm scared.'

Rachel ushered the tearful child into the house and sat her at the kitchen table next to Harriet. The pair eyed each other suspiciously.

'Hello,' said Harriet.

'Hello,' sniffed Tabby.

'Where's your mum?' asked Harriet.

'Don't know,' frowned Tabby. 'I stayed at my friend's house last night and her mum dropped me off just now and then I realized I don't have my keys, so I knocked on the door and mum isn't there. She promised she'd be home and now I don't know where she is and she's probably dead.'

317

Tabitha threw her head onto the table and dissolved into tears.

'Drama queen,' mouthed Hattie silently to Rachel.

Rachel crouched down next to Tabitha and rubbed her heaving back. 'She won't be far away,' she said soothingly. 'She's probably just popped out to the shop or something.'

'But you don't understand,' whined Tabby. 'Mum and me, we always know where the other one is. It's safest like that.'

'That's very sensible,' replied Rachel, 'but I'm sure your mum is OK. We were with her last night and she was fine then.'

'Was she?' Tabitha looked up at Rachel with watery emerald eyes. Her stare felt somehow familiar.

'Yes, we had great fun.' Rachel smiled. 'Honestly, she won't be far away. Why don't we call her mobile. She has a mobile, doesn't she?'

'Yes,' answered Harriet with certainty. 'I've seen her with it.'

'I don't have the number,' said Tabby.

'Oh,' said Rachel, thinking that was strange. 'Have you got Summer's number, Hattie? I don't think she's ever given it to me.'

Harriet shook her head.

'Well, you wouldn't have it because it's a secret number for Mr Murphy . . .' Tabby's voice drifted off as she realized she'd blurted out too much information.

'Who's Mr Murphy?' asked Harriet, smelling a good story.

Tabitha shrugged. 'Just a man my mum works for. He looks after us.'

Harriet and Rachel shared a look that said, 'Interesting.'

'I know Tabitha. Why don't you have a croissant with egg and bacon and by the time you've eaten that I'm sure your mum will be home, OK?'

'Thanks,' said Tabby. 'But I don't eat pigs. I'm a vegetarian.'

'Of course you are,' remembered Rachel. This was Summer's daughter she was dealing with, after all. 'Scrambled eggs then?'

Tabitha nodded sadly. Just then, Delilah scurried excitedly into the kitchen and jumped up at Tabitha.

'You've got a puppy!' exclaimed Tabby in delight. 'She's gorgeous.'

Within thirty seconds, all traces of misery had been wiped from the girl's face.

Summer sauntered cheerfully down Chillyhill Lane, singing 'Dream A Little Dream of Me' to herself and smiling at the cows in the field. She'd spent the night with Jack, lazily making love under the cedar tree, indulging in memories of their childhood romance and planning their future together. Jack might have wealth and success and all the trappings that came with it, but underneath it all Summer had discovered that he was still the kind, vulnerable boy she'd fallen in love with. He knew why she'd left him all those years ago and he seemed to understand. She'd told him about what had happened in Bristol, about Murphy and Mr Big, and he'd promised that he'd protect her from harm. There was only one more secret that she'd kept from him, and soon, very soon, it would be time to tell all.

Summer didn't wear a watch, so she checked the time on her phone. It was half past ten.

'Jesus! Tabitha!' shouted Summer out loud and broke into a sprint.

Tabby would have been home alone for thirty minutes by now. The poor girl would be starting to worry.

'Stupid, selfish, irresponsible idiot,' Summer scolded herself for languishing in Jack's arms and forgetting her daughter in the process.

She arrived, huffing and puffing, at Rose Cottage and hurriedly unlocked the door.

'Tabby. Tabby, my love. I'm home. I'm so sorry I wasn't here. I had to nip out to the shop.'

The cottage was eerily silent. Summer ran upstairs to Tabby's bedroom. It was empty. She looked out into the garden. No one was there. Summer's stomach turned uneasily as she spotted Tabitha's keys on the kitchen table. She must have been home. Her keys were there. But if she'd come home, where was she now? Or perhaps she forgot her keys. Maybe Sarah's mum was running late. Call Sarah's mum. What was her name again? Debbie. It was Debbie.

'Debbie, hi,' said Summer, trying not to sound too fraught. 'It's Summer here, Tabitha's mum. Is she still with you?'

'No, I dropped her off about half an hour ago. Why?'

'Oh, I just popped out to the shop and I got chatting to a neighbour and now she's not at home. She must be around here somewhere. Nothing to worry about. Thanks for having her to stay. Goodbye.'

Summer flapped frantically around the cottage, checking in cupboards and under tables like a mother hen who'd lost her chicks. The cats eyed her warily. She felt sick with fear. She had a vision of the car she'd seen parked outside her house the night before and she could imagine some big, burly man shoving Tabitha in the back and driving away. With trembling hands, Summer called Murphy.

'Murphy, she's gone!' screamed Summer. 'Tabitha's gone.'

'Calm down, calm down,' said Murphy patiently. 'Don't panic. Tell me what happened.'

'I popped out to the shop for bread, OK,' she continued the lie. Murphy would be furious with her if he knew she'd spent the night at Jack's. 'When I got back, Tabby wasn't here.'

'Was she there when you left?'

'No, no. She stayed the night with a friend. I know it's against the rules, but she's eleven, that's what eleven-year-olds want to do. I thought it would be OK. And it was. Her friend's mother dropped her off here half an hour ago. I must have just missed her. Anyway, her keys are here but she's not. And last night I saw a car.'

'A car? What do you mean you saw a car? Where?'

'Outside my house,' explained Summer desperately. 'Just sitting there watching, with the engine running and the lights turned off.'

'Mary Mother of Jesus, why didn't you call me straight away?' demanded Murphy.

'I thought I was being paranoid,' said Summer

apologetically. 'I don't know. I thought if I ignored them they'd go away. But Murphy, what are we going to do about Tabby? Where's my daughter?'

Summer was screaming now. She paced the living room, pulling at her hair, biting her nails, feeling her skin crawl. And then she saw her, as clear as day, sitting on the window seat at Ivy Cottage with a puppy on her knee.

'Murphy,' said Summer suddenly. 'It's OK. I can see her. She's across the road with my neighbour. I've got to get her. I'll call you later.'

'Sharon? Sharon, we need to talk.'

But Summer had already gone.

'It's like Piccadilly bloody Circus in here today,' commented Harriet as Rachel answered the door for the third time that morning.

'Morning,' said Rachel cheerfully as Summer pushed past her.

'Tabby? Tabby?' called Summer, barging into the living room. 'Oh thank goodness, I thought I'd lost you,' gushed Summer, grabbing her daughter and squeezing her tightly to her chest.

'I forgot my keys, Mum, and you weren't there. I was scared, Mummy,' explained Tabitha. 'So I came over here and Rachel and Harriet made me breakfast and I played with Delilah.'

'That's good, my love,' whispered Summer into Tabby's silky hair. 'That's so good.'

Mother and daughter stood motionless together, clinging to one another for dear life.

'Drama queens,' mouthed Harriet to Rachel.

Rachel smiled.

Chapter Fourteen

Perfect Skin

Since separating from Simon, Rachel had found new levels of maturity and self-restraint. It was less than two months since she'd told him to go, and already the two could manage a near civilized conversation, as long as they stuck to safe subjects, such as Alfie or the unseasonably mild weather they were having.

'It's so hot, isn't it?' noted Simon politely as he stood patiently on the doorstep. Rachel would still not allow him into the cottage.

'It's boiling,' agreed Rachel, pulling uncomfortably at her flimsy summer dress, which clung to her damp skin.

'You look well,' said Simon, taking in his wife's tan, her newly gym-toned body and the tiny dress she was wearing. Her bare thighs looked soft, brown and enticing and he had to fight the urge to stroke them.

'Thank you,' said Rachel. 'You don't. You look pale and tired.'

Rachel wondered why it was that so few

Englishmen could dress properly in hot weather. Simon looked ridiculously foppish and Hugh Grantesque in baggy khaki shorts, a floral shirt and navy deck shoes. His skin was blue-white and his face was thin and drawn.

Simon shrugged. 'I've been stuck in the office. We lost a big contract a couple of weeks ago and I've been trying to minimize the damage.'

'I'm sorry to hear that,' said Rachel, wondering whether her husband's mind had been off the job because of her. She hoped so. 'Is the company in trouble?'

'Oh, it's nothing to worry about,' insisted Simon. 'We're fine.'

'Because I could live on less quite easily,' she suggested. Rachel thought that Simon was trying to compensate for breaking her heart by putting ridiculously large sums of money into her bank account every week. Guilt money.

'No, no, no,' insisted Simon. 'I'm not going to shirk my responsibilities.'

Rachel snorted. 'I think it might be a bit too late for that, Si.'

'Financially, I mean,' he said apologetically. 'I'm happy to support you. You're my wife.'

'Estranged wife,' Rachel reminded him coldly.

Simon shrugged with open palms. 'I guess so.'

'I'll get Alfie,' said Rachel suddenly. 'His bags are ready. Why don't you put them in the car.'

Simon watched his wife retreat back into the family home. Rachel looked amazing. Healthy, beautiful, sexy, strong. She seemed to be coping with the break-up so much better than he was.

324

There were a million things he wanted to say to her, but he didn't know where to start. They'd spoken at length once, over the phone, after she'd been to see her parents. She'd explained that she was too angry to talk about what had happened for the time being, that she needed time to get her head around everything, and that when she was ready, she would let him know and then, only then, they would talk. The balance of power in their relationship had shifted so that Rachel called the shots. All Simon could do was wait. For now he was living in limbo.

Rachel reappeared carrying Alfie in his car seat.

'Ooh, I'm going to miss you, little man,' she cooed tearfully to the baby. 'You be a good boy for Daddy and Mummy will see you on Monday, OK.'

She handed the car seat rather reluctantly to Simon. This was Alfie's third visit to his father, but Rachel was still not convinced about Simon's child-rearing skills. Last time, Alfie had returned wearing a back-to-front nappy. This time, the baby was going to London for a long weekend. Simon would have plenty of time to mess up.

'There are more than enough bottles of expressed milk to last all weekend in that cool bag,' Rachel fussed. 'Make sure you put them in the freezer the minute you get home. And remember to sterilize everything. Oh, and he's started solids now, you know that, don't you?'

Simon nodded obediently.

'You sent me a detailed email earlier in the week,' he reminded her.

'There are frozen home-made purées in ice-cube

boxes in the freezer bag and I've packed spoons, bowls and bibs. Make sure you wind him properly after every feed and give him a bath every night because he gets sweet potato in his hair, OK? And if you have any problems, any problems at all, phone my mum. I mean, phone me too, of course, but mum's closer, she can be with you in twenty minutes. And Simon,' she added nervously.

'Yes?'

'Take care of him. He's so little and he's not used to being away from me for this long.'

'It's only three and a half days,' Simon reminded her gently.

'I know,' she said. 'But we're so used to it being just the two of us, aren't we, Alfie?'

Rachel bent down and kissed her baby one last time. He smiled up at her.

'So what are you doing with your weekend of freedom?' asked Simon as he fastened Alfie's seat into the car with Rachel hovering nervously behind.

'I'm going to Cornwall with some friends,' said Rachel absent-mindedly, frowning at the car seat. 'You're doing it wrong, Simon. The padded bits have to go over his shoulders.'

'I know,' said Simon patiently. 'I haven't finished yet. So, who are you going away with?'

'Bianca, Harriet, Summer and Jack,' replied Rachel.

Rachel watched the colour drain from Simon's face and she wondered, for a moment, if it scared him: the thought of her having a new life without him.

'Are the straps tight enough?' she demanded.

'Yes,' said Simon. 'We're all done.'

Rachel stroked Alfie's soft cheeks one more time before dragging herself away.

'Such perfect skin,' she muttered to herself.

'Well, have a nice time,' said Simon a little too politely, a little too formally. He leaned forward to kiss Rachel on the cheek, but she pulled away and he found himself kissing her hair instead. It smelled of lemons.

'I will,' she said in as cheerful a voice as she could muster. 'I'm going to have a ball.'

Simon had noticed that Rachel refused to catch his eye. There was nothing more to be said. It was time to go. He watched her in the rear-view mirror as he pulled out of the drive. She was wiping her eyes, crying for Alfie, not for him, of that he was sure. Her dark citrus-smelling hair gleamed in the sunshine and her thin dress flapped in the slight breeze. The fabric was almost transparent in the brightness and he could easily make out the form of her body underneath. Simon thought that she had never looked more enticing in her life. The image stayed with him as he drove back to London and he was haunted by the thought of other men seeing her in the same way. She was going away for the weekend with a man he didn't know. What if she fell in love with someone else? What if she slept with another man? The thought horrified him. Rachel belonged to him.

'Ready?' asked Bianca excitedly from behind *Thelma and Louise*-style sunglasses.

'Ready,' confirmed Rachel, jumping into the passenger seat of the Porsche with Delilah under her arm. Jock snuffled at the puppy lovingly from his perch in the back.

'How was Simon?' asked Bianca.

Rachel shrugged. 'It was weird,' she admitted. 'It's like we're strangers in a way – all polite and formal with each other. But then, he's still Simon, my Simon, do you know what I mean?'

Bianca nodded. 'You're being very brave, hon,' she said.

'No, I'm not,' scoffed Rachel, staring at the countryside as it whizzed by. 'I still cry over him nearly every night, and when he left today I felt as much longing for him as I did for Alfie. Not that I let him know that, of course.'

'Good for you. Anyway, this weekend will do wonders for you,' announced Bianca enthusiastically. 'It's time you had some fun. Oh look, the others are right behind us.'

Rachel turned round and waved at Jack, Summer and Harriet in the Jeep behind. Jack had the top down and two surf boards were sticking out the back behind Hattie.

'They look like something out of a film.' Rachel laughed. 'All tanned and gorgeous, wearing their shades and their bright summer clothes.'

Bianca checked out her friends in the rear-view mirror. The three blonds did indeed look very glamorous. With a hoot and a wave, the Jeep sped past the Porsche. Summer's long golden hair trailed behind her like a flame.

'Poor Hattie.' Bianca giggled. 'Having to play gooseberry all the way to Newquay.'

'Do you think?' asked Rachel. 'I'm not sure you're right about Summer and Jack. Why wouldn't they just tell us if they were together? They're both single. It's not as if they'd be doing anything wrong if they were seeing each other.'

Bianca raised her eyebrows knowingly. 'I'm telling you, hon. Those two are at it big time. I have absolutely no idea why they're trying to keep it a secret, but they are completely loved up, believe me.'

'They do whisper a lot,' conceded Rachel.

'And Summer always finds some excuse to stay behind after the book club,' added Bianca.

'True.' Rachel nodded. 'And he's always touching her. Just a little pat on the arm here, or a squeeze of her hand there.'

Bianca grinned conspiratorially. 'We should spy on them this weekend. Find some concrete evidence.'

'Bianca,' scolded Rachel. 'I'd expect that sort of behaviour from Harriet, not you.'

'Oh come on.' Bianca laughed. 'Aren't you dying to know what they're up to?'

Rachel shrugged. 'It's their business, not ours.'

'But they're our friends,' said Bianca. 'And friends shouldn't have secrets.'

'You're a fine one to talk. Wives shouldn't have secrets from their husbands, either, but you still haven't told TJ that you're pregnant.'

Bianca shrugged. 'I will when I'm ready.'

'How do you think TJ will cope with all the kids?' asked Rachel, changing the subject.

'With difficulty. Poor TJ – a couple of screaming toddlers, a psychotic teenager and a pre-pubescent girl who's not used to leaving her mum's shadow.'

'I was surprised that Summer agreed to leave Tabitha at your house,' said Rachel.

'Me too,' agreed Bianca. 'That's another reason why I'm sure she's having an affair with Jack. She wanted some time alone with her lover.'

'Maybe,' said Rachel pensively. 'Or perhaps she's just decided to loosen the apron strings a bit. That poor child hardly goes anywhere without Summer. She's very overprotective, don't you think?'

'Sometimes it's as if she's scared to let Tabby out of the house,' agreed Bianca. 'But what harm could come to her in Combe?'

'I don't know,' said Rachel. 'I suppose she might get bitten by a rabid badger or get bored to death by Mrs Bell in the shop.'

'Summer asked all sorts of questions about our security system,' Bianca continued. 'In fact, it wasn't until she'd checked out the CCTV cameras that she actually took us up on our offer of baby-sitting. I mean, Tabby's a lovely girl and everything, but she's hardly going to be up there on a kidnapper's list of suitable victims, is she? My girls are far more at risk. Especially after that fiasco over Posh and Brooklyn Beckham. If a gang of criminals wanted to snatch the twins, TJ and I would pay out every last million to get them back.'

Rachel smiled to herself. Sometimes she forgot that Bianca inhabited a completely different planet from her own. It was only at moments like this that the gulf between them became apparent.

'I think I'd be less worried about Alfie if he was with a gang of villains right now.' Rachel giggled. 'At least they might know how to put a nappy on the right way round.'

'Oh, come on,' said Bianca. 'Simon can't be that bad, surely.'

'Oh he is,' said Rachel with certainty. 'You've got to remember, he doesn't get much practice. Not like TJ the Wonderdad.'

Bianca smiled warmly. 'He is good, isn't he?'

'He's the best. I just don't understand why you haven't told him about the baby yet.'

Bianca shrugged. 'I'm not sure either. It just hasn't felt like the right moment. We never get any time together, just the two of us any more. I'm planning a special dinner for two one night next week. I was thinking Babington, maybe, as we hardly ever make use of our membership. I'll tell him then.'

TJ had let Bianca go with a smile and a tender kiss, but inside he was in turmoil. He sensed that his wife had a soft spot for Jack and, for the first time in their marriage, he felt scared that he might be losing her. How could any man resist Bianca? She was so beautiful and sweet, kind and funny. If Bianca wanted Jack, TJ was sure that she'd get him. He watched the kids playing in the garden. Tabitha had made an obstacle course for the twins out of tents and tunnels and was now bossily giving them directions on how to play the game. Scarlett was sunbathing with her headphones on as usual, lost, no doubt, in some teenage world of angst, where parents are the enemy, there to be abused.

TJ noticed one of Bianca's handbags lying on the kitchen floor. Guiltily, he emptied the contents onto the granite worktop, looking for, well, he didn't know what – just something that would give him a clue as to why she'd suddenly become so distant. There was nothing out of the ordinary – a Chanel lipstick, a packet of chewing gum, the spare keys to the Porsche, a copy of *The Great Gatsby* and an appointment card for a private clinic in Bath. Why did Bianca have to see the doctor? He hoped she wasn't considering plastic surgery. She was worried about turning thirty, but she didn't need botox or a face lift or liposuction. He'd have to ask her when she got back. Nature had given Bianca the body of a goddess and it would be sacrilege to tamper with such perfection. TJ wandered aimlessly upstairs to the bedroom and began to check the pockets of Bianca's clothes for anything unusual, but her skirts and trousers were all hung up neatly, with their creases pressed and their pockets bare. If his wife was up to something, she'd left no trail.

TJ felt exhausted. The air was so hot and thick with humidity that he felt as if he were swimming through soup. He lay down on the enormous marital four-poster bed and placed his head on Bianca's cool cotton pillow, breathing in her vanilla perfume and missing her madly, although she'd only been gone for an hour or two. He slipped his hand under the pillow to stroke the silk nightdress that she always kept there and was surprised to find a piece of paper instead. What was it? A love letter to Jack, perhaps? He felt the panic rise in his chest. Or a note to tell him she was leaving? TJ unfolded the paper with trembling hands and read what it said. It was a poem. A love poem. And it was written for him. TJ thought they were the most beautiful words he'd ever read. Suddenly everything made sense. With a surge of energy and a flash of inspiration, he jumped to his feet and made his way hurriedly downstairs to the recording studio, clutching the poem in his hand. He could feel the blood pumping through his veins and the creative juices flowing to his brain. It had been a long time coming, but at last TJ Mills had a new song to work on.

Bianca followed Jack's Jeep round the sweeping coast road north of Newquay as far as Watergate Bay.

'I wonder where we're staying?' she said excitedly to Rachel. 'It's beautiful, isn't it?'

Rachel took in the cloudless blue sky, the wide yellow beach that stretched as far as the eye could see, the waves rolling into the bay and the black dots of the surfers riding them to shore.

'It looks like Hawaii,' she gushed. 'I can't believe this is Britain.'

'That's because it's thirty degrees outside,' said Bianca. 'It's a bloody miracle, hon. Now where is Jack taking us?'

They turned left up a steep hill and followed the Jeep as it climbed away from the beach.

'Watergate Bay Camp Site,' read Bianca

thoughtfully. 'The hotel must be along this lane, past the campsite.'

'Or maybe we're camping,' suggested Rachel.

'No,' scoffed Bianca. 'Don't be ridiculous, hon. Jack wouldn't make us slum it with surfers.'

They drove along the bumpy dirt track, past row upon row of artistically hand-painted VW camper vans, until they reached an empty plot. Jack pulled the Jeep into the space and indicated to Bianca to pull up beside him.

'Oh Jesus, we really are camping,' said Bianca, growing pale beneath her tan. 'I've never been camping. I've never stayed anywhere without air con and an en suite.'

Summer and Jack climbed out of the Jeep beaming. Harriet lingered behind with a perplexed look on her face.

'Isn't it wonderful?' asked Jack. 'I love this place. I come down every summer to hang out and catch a few waves.'

'It's perfect,' said Summer with a wistful look on her face. 'Sheer heaven.'

'It's very nice,' agreed Rachel, stretching her arms above her head in an attempt to get rid of the cramp in her shoulder from travelling such a long way in such a small car.

Bianca and Harriet shared a nervous look.

'We're not seriously staying here, are we?' asked Hattie.

'We sure are,' replied Jack. 'I've got a couple of tents in the back here – a three-man and a two-man, so one of you will have to share with me.'

'I will,' said Summer, a little too quickly.

'Told you,' whispered Bianca to Rachel.

'This is ridiculous,' said Harriet. 'I'm not staying here. I'll book into a hotel. Where will I find civilization?'

Jack said, 'Newquay's that way and Padstow is back the way we came. Or Rock isn't far away.'

'That's where Prince William goes, isn't it?' asked Harriet hopefully.

'I believe so,' replied Jack.

'Come on Bianca, let's go. Rachel, do you want to stay here at the student hovel or would you rather come back to the real world with Bianca and me?'

'Um, I'm quite happy here,' said Rachel truthfully. 'I like camping. I backpacked all over Asia, so I think I can manage a couple of nights in Cornwall.'

'Three,' retorted Harriet. 'Three nights sleeping on an inflatable mattress. Three nights of using communal loos. Three nights of sharing one metre square of a poxy field with you two. And we've got three dogs. Do you seriously think we'll squeeze six bodies into one tent?'

'I think it might be fun,' said Bianca suddenly, spotting the disappointment on Jack's face. He obviously hadn't been expecting a mutiny.

'What?' Hattie was furious. 'Bianca, you told me you can't sleep anywhere if it doesn't have a water bed.'

'We could always fill the air bed with sea water,' suggested Summer cheekily.

'I'll be fine,' said Bianca defensively. 'You're the one who wants to run away to a five-star hotel, Hattie.'

'Well I'm warning you, Moriarty farts like a trooper,' she huffed. 'It'll be like sleeping in a gas chamber.'

Harriet sat down on the ground with a thud and pushed her fine blond hair out of her eyes. She lit a cigarette and drew on it deeply, surveying the campsite with critical eyes. Then she spotted the neighbours.

'Well, would you look at that,' she said lustfully. 'I think I might be staying after all.'

Rachel, Bianca, Summer and Jack followed Harriet's gaze. There, just across the makeshift lane, was a butt-naked man in his prime. He was struggling to peel a wet suit off his foot and was hopping on one leg while pulling at the other. He was clearly displaying his dangling manhood as he did so. His jaw-length wet black hair was obscuring his face, but his body was to die for.

'It's Keanu in *Point Break*.' Rachel sighed.

'I saw him first,' snapped Harriet. 'Finders keepers.'

'Ladies, ladies.' Jack laughed. 'This is Watergate Bay in the height of summer. That kind of totty is ten a penny round here. There's no need to fight over the first guy you see.'

'I love it here,' announced Harriet. 'I think I might move in permanently.'

'OK, let's erect our tents,' suggested Jack.

'I'd rather erect the neighbours,' muttered Hattie.

Rachel stole one last look at the surf boy opposite. He had managed to get out of his wet suit and was just tying a tiny towel around his waist. He looked up and caught Rachel's eye. She blushed and turned away. For the first time in her life, Rachel had come face to face with her fantasy man.

Harriet, Bianca and Rachel wrestled with their tent poles for fifteen minutes before giving up and collapsing in a heap on the spot where their new home should have been. The three dogs lay sparked out on the grass, tongues hanging out, panting loudly.

'It's too hot for hard work,' announced Harriet, lighting another fag. 'Look, Jack's right, the surf dudes are multiplying.'

It was true, Rachel's dream boy had now been joined by three more sinfully attractive, near-naked young men. They were helping themselves to cold beers from the mini fridges they had in the back of their two camper vans.

'I'm going to ask for a beer,' announced Hattie.

'You can't,' protested Bianca. 'That's rude.'

But it was too late, Harriet was already approaching the boys with her best catwalk wiggle, and with a toss of her hair and a flick of her cigarette, she was introducing herself, accepting a can and sitting down beside them. Moriarty followed. Rachel watched enviously. Keanu Reeves looked up and caught her staring again.

Jack and Summer, meanwhile, had expertly erected their two-man tent, pumped up their air beds and were now finishing off their canopy.

'Do you need a hand?' asked Jack.

The girls nodded gratefully.

'Where's Harriet?'

'Chatting up the surfers,' replied Bianca.

Jack looked over to where Harriet was holding

court. Three handsome young men were hanging on her every word, eyes on stalks, taking in those endless supermodel legs and gently patting the pointer, wishing, no doubt, that it was her mistress they were fondling. The fourth, Jack noticed, was too busy eyeing up Rachel to pay much attention to Harriet.

Only once her tent was up did Harriet see fit to join her friends.

'We're all going to a beach party tonight,' she announced gleefully. 'Luke, Dan, Joshua and Ben have cordially invited us to join them. They're from London, by the way,' she added. 'Law students.'

'Which one is Keanu?' asked Rachel shyly.

'I can't remember which one's which,' scoffed Harriet with a dismissive wave of her hand. 'They're all cute and as keen as puppies.'

Later that afternoon, the group drove down to the beach.

'Who's going to join me in the water?' asked Jack.

Harriet, Bianca and Rachel shook their heads.

'We're just going to sunbathe, hon,' said Bianca. 'But we'll watch you. We'll all swoon at your expertise.'

'She's better than I am,' he said, nodding his head towards Summer, who was slithering her curves into a wetsuit.

'How do you know?' asked Bianca, still in detective mode.

'Because she's told me,' replied Jack.

'There is *so* something going on between those two.' Bianca sighed as she watched Jack and Summer run down the beach and into the waves, carrying their surf boards. 'Did you notice how quickly Summer volunteered to share his tent?'

'You're just jealous because you've got a little crush on Gatley yourself,' retorted Hattie.

'No I haven't,' argued Bianca. 'I'm very fond of him, yes. He's opened my mind up to all sorts of things I'd never thought of before, but I don't like him in that way. He's like a wonderful big brother.'

'Yeah, right.' Harriet yawned, looking around the beach. 'This place is teeming with fit young men. I think I've died and gone to toyboy heaven.'

The three friends lay back on their towels and melted into the sand. Rachel let the sea air flood her nostrils as she stared up into the blue, blue sky. She watched the gulls circle above her until her head began to spin. The blissful warmth of the sun soaked into her bare skin, and as she closed her eyes and started to drift off, she realized that she felt happy. Really, truly, positively happy for the first time in months.

'Oh–my–God. They are both seriously good,' announced Harriet loudly.

Rachel dragged herself back to full consciousness and sat up. Her head was spinning.

'Summer's amazing,' Bianca was saying, with a look of sheer awe on her face.

Rachel blinked into the brightness and tried to focus on the surfers. She placed her hand on her forehead to shield her eyes and gradually began to see what Bianca and Harriet were talking about. Summer and Jack glided side by side on the crest of a wave and then cruised to shore before diving into the water and paddling their boards back out to where the water was dark and deep. She could just about make out their faces as they waited, like basking seals, for the next good wave to come. They bobbed up and down together. Now you see them, now you don't. As their heads reappeared, Rachel could have sworn they were kissing, but they were so far away, so far out in the ocean, and with all the white horses dancing around them it was impossible to tell where Jack began and Summer ended.

'Baz, I've got something for you,' said TJ with barely concealed glee. 'And it is seriously good.'

'TJ, man, it's six o'clock, it's Friday and it's like the Costa Del fucking Sol outside. I was about to leave the office to meet a delightful lady friend for some liquid refreshment in a nearby beer garden when the phone rang. Who can that be? I asked myself. Well, I'll tell you who it's not. It's not my good friend TJ Mills, that's for sure, because he hasn't called for, oh, six months. No, everything's gone very fucking quiet in Wiltshire, so it won't be him on this fine summer's evening . . .'

'Baz, Baz, Baz,' interrupted TJ. Baz never used two words when twenty-two would do. 'I know I've been struggling, but I've got a cracker here. I've discovered this new songwriter and she is so bloody talented. I've been down here in the studio all day with her lyrics, jamming away, trying to find the right melody to do the words justice, you know?'

'If you say so, my good man,' shouted Baz. Baz always shouted. He only had one volume and that was full blast. 'But I've waited this long, I'm sure I can wait until Monday to hear this masterpiece.'

'No, no, no,' argued TJ. 'You have to listen to it now. It'll blow you away. I'm telling you, Bazza, with this song, I'm back. I can smell the vinyl.'

'TJ, we've moved onto CDs now,' shouted Baz. 'It was an invention that revolutionized the music biz a decade or so ago and—'

'I know, Baz. It was a turn of phrase. Now imagine this song with a slightly Celtic vibe. It's a ballad, a love song, and it really rocks.'

Baz sat silently – for once – at his desk in Soho as his oldest client crooned down the phone from the sticks. He gazed out of his window at the sunshine and let the words penetrate his brain. TJ had a great voice, that had never been in doubt. It was as velvety smooth as the cold pint of Guinness waiting for him at the pub. After a few seconds, Baz realized he was tapping his fingers involuntarily on his desk. It was a good sign. By the time TJ had got to the last verse he was wiping a tear from his eye.

'TJ, my man, you're a legend,' shouted Baz. 'A living fucking legend. Get yourself up here on Monday. I think you've got yourself a single.'

'I knew it!' exclaimed TJ, punching the air. 'God she's good.'

'Who is she?' demanded Baz loudly. 'Is she cheap? And does she have an album's worth.'

'Baz,' said TJ. 'It was Bianca. Bianca wrote it.'

For once, Baz was lost for words.

Rachel took an age deciding what to wear for the beach party. The tent was littered with outfits belonging to all three women – both Harriet and Bianca had offered to lend her their clothes.

'What about this?' she asked, scrambling out of the tent in a tight white minidress of Bianca's.

'Too tarty,' announced Hattie. 'And you'll never manage the sand in those heels.'

Rachel sighed and disappeared back into the tent.

'This?' she asked five minutes later, reappearing in a long, floaty red Gypsy Rose Lee number belonging to Harriet.

'Nah, you're too short and dark for that. You look positively Romany, as if you're going to read people's fortunes at some fairground in Skegness,' snapped Harriet impatiently.

The others leaned against the Jeep, waiting to go.

'Just wear something you feel comfortable in,' suggested Jack.

'I don't want to look comfortable. I want to look sexy. Christ, no one tells you that you squeeze your sex appeal out with the baby.'

'Don't be silly, Rachel,' said Jack honestly. 'You're very sexy. You'd look just as good in a cloth sack as you would in that frock.'

'I would not.' Rachel pouted. 'I look crap in everything.'

'You haven't lost your sex appeal,' commented Jack. 'You've just lost your confidence. You've got great legs, wear something short but not tarty.'

'OK,' replied Rachel. 'Thank you, Jack.'

Rachel crawled back into the tent and eventually poked her head out again.

'What about this?' she asked tentatively, standing

342

up and revealing her outfit – a denim miniskirt, a white cotton vest top and a pair of pink Birkenstocks.

'Perfect,' said the others in unison.

'You're just saying that because you're bored of waiting,' moaned Rachel.

'Shut up and get in the car,' demanded Harriet.

Rachel did as she was told.

The beach was teeming with very young people. The air was thick with the smell of marijuana, bonfires and barbecues. A sound system had been set up and thrash rock was fighting with the sound of the waves crashing to shore.

'I feel old,' complained Bianca. 'Everyone looks about sixteen.'

'That's because they are,' replied Jack patiently.

'Let's get drunk,' suggested Harriet. 'I always feel younger when I'm trashed.'

It didn't take long for Hattie to achieve her goal. An hour and several bottles of champagne later – Harriet had not left home without a good supply of chilled Veuve Clicquot in a cool bag – she and Rachel were dancing giddily to The Strokes, while Bianca watched them and smiled. Summer and Jack had long since disappeared into the crowds and the dogs were excitedly going from group to group, making friends and begging for burgers.

Rachel flopped down into the sand beside Bianca and said, 'Phew, I'm puffed. It's hard work dancing on the beach.'

Harriet joined them. 'I feel fifteen,' she declared loudly. 'Oh look, there's Dan and Luke and whatever their names are. Coo-ee! Boys! Over here.'

She waved frantically at the boys from the campsite. Rachel felt her cheeks burn as Keanu approached with his friends.

'Evening, ladies,' said a tall blond boy. 'Mind if we join you?'

'Be our guests,' said Harriet. 'Champers, darlings?'

Keanu sat down beside Rachel. He was so close that she could feel the hairs on his arm brush hers.

'You're Bianca Mills,' said the shorter blond boy in amazement. 'Oh–my–God. You're Bianca Mills. Look, guys, it's Bianca Mills.'

Bianca smiled sweetly.

'Will you sign my T-shirt?' asked the smaller of the blonds.

Harriet's face fell.

'Hello,' said Keanu to Rachel. 'I'm Ben.'

'Rachel,' said Rachel with an embarrassed smile.

'Are you a model too?' he asked.

Rachel laughed. 'Don't be silly,' she said. 'Do I look like a page-three model to you?'

Dan glanced briefly at Rachel's chest and said, 'Yes.'

'Harriet says you're a law student,' said Rachel, trying to keep the conversation going.

Ben nodded. 'What about you. What do you do?'

'I'm a mum,' she replied. 'I used to work in PR, but now I'm just a mum.'

'Oh.' Ben's sweet young face fell. 'So you're married.'

'Yes, well, no, well, sort of. We're separated,' explained Rachel. It still felt strange saying the words out loud.

Ben looked pleased.

'OK, everyone,' announced Harriet, keen to draw attention back to her good self. 'Let's play a drinking game.'

So they did. They drank themselves into oblivion and beyond. They drank themselves silly until they were writhing in fits of hysteria in the sand. And when Ben handed Rachel a joint she took it without a second thought and, for the first time in her life, got stupidly, dizzily stoned. After that, the night was a blur. Rachel vaguely remembered seeing Harriet snogging Dan, or Luke or Josh, which one she wasn't sure. She could barely recollect that Summer and Jack joined them at some point and ended up on their backs too. She knew that they all walked back up the hill to the campsite together, just as it started to get light, and when they got back they drank and smoked some more. She could just about remember a conversation that went something along the lines of:

Dan: 'How old are you girls, then?'

Harriet: 'How old do you think we are?'

Josh: 'About 25.'

Luke: 'No, I'd say 23.'

Cue fits of giggles from the girls.

Ben to Rachel: 'So how old are you?'

Rachel to Ben: 'Nearly thirty.'

Ben: 'God, you don't look that old.'

Rachel: 'Tonight I don't feel that old.'

Bianca: 'So how old are you guys?'

One of the boys: 'We're almost twenty.'

Cue fits of giggles from the girls.

At some point Ben whispered, 'I like you,' to Rachel.

'No you don't,' Rachel had scoffed. 'I've got stretch marks and saggy boobs.'

'I like stretch marks and saggy boobs,' Ben had declared drunkenly, desperately, so that everyone could hear.

Rachel remembered the look in Ben's eyes. He'd meant every word. He really did like her. And then it all went blank. The next thing she knew, Rachel woke up with a paw in her mouth and a dead leg. The tent smelled of regurgitated dog food and was so hot that Rachel felt as if she were being microwaved. It took a while to realize that Jock was the one with his foot in her face and that Moriarty was asleep on her leg. Bianca lay facing her with her eyes wide open.

'Morning,' she said in her usual chirpy fashion. Despite sleeping with her make-up on, Rachel noticed that Bianca still looked radiant.

'Is it?' asked Rachel croakily. 'I need a drink. Have you got any water? Dogs, get off me.'

Bianca handed Rachel a bottle of Evian. Sitting up was painful. Rachel's forehead felt as if it had an axe embedded in it and, thanks to the dogs, she no longer had any feeling in her limbs.

'Where's Hattie?' she asked, bewildered.

Bianca nodded her head towards the outside world.

'She slept with one of the surfer boys.' Bianca grinned.

'Did she?' asked Rachel with glee. 'Which one?'

Bianca shrugged. 'I don't remember. I doubt she will either until she wakes up next to him.'

Rachel giggled and then frowned. 'It wasn't Ben, was it?'

'No,' said Bianca kindly. 'He only had eyes for you.'

Bianca and Rachel made their way to the communal showers, blinking in the sunshine. There was no sign of life from Summer and Jack's tent, or from the boys' camper vans opposite. In fact, the entire campsite was eerily quiet.

'We must be the only ones here with children,' commented Bianca. 'No one else has lost the art of sleeping in.'

'Summer has a child,' Rachel reminded her. 'And she's still asleep.'

'Maybe the knack returns when your children get older,' suggested Bianca.

But Summer wasn't asleep and neither was Jack.

'I can't believe you brought me back here,' Summer whispered, keeping her voice low in case the others could hear through the canvas. 'It's so romantic.'

'This was where I made my promise to you,' said Jack quietly.

Summer's mind wandered back through the years to a hot summer's evening in Watergate Bay. She was seventeen, Jack was a year older. Sharon Ashton was out of care and had been back living with her mother in the squalor of their flat in St Paul's. Her mum was pretty sick by then. Years of poverty, prostitution, beatings and bad times had taken their toll and she'd had no resistance to the cancer that ate away at her withered body. She wasn't even forty, but there was no life left in her.

Sharon could barely remember a time when there had been any life in her mum.

She and Jack had been together for two years, but his family didn't approve, nice clean-living, hard-working people that they were. The Ashtons were notorious on the estate. A family of whores and petty criminals. The sort that gave the area a bad name. Nobody could blame the Gatleys for wanting to protect their prodigy of a son from people like that. And so, Sharon and Jack kept their love a secret, meeting whenever they could in other areas of Bristol, where nobody would recognize them.

Jack was about to go to Oxford and had arranged a final holiday for himself and Sharon before they were parted. He'd always been a keen surfer, having learned as a kid on holiday at his grand-parents' place in Devon. So he saved all his money from his summer job stacking shelves in a super-market, bought a cheap two-man tent, a couple of train tickets and three nights' accommodation at a camp sight just outside Newquay. On the last night, they realized they'd run out of condoms.

'It doesn't matter,' Sharon had said, desperate to have Jack completely before losing him for good. And so they'd had wonderful, wild and completely unprotected sex.

'This is where Tabitha was conceived,' whispered Summer nervously.

When Bianca and Rachel returned, cleansed if not entirely refreshed, Summer and Jack were fry-ing eggs on a camper stove. There was a strange, strained atmosphere between them and Bianca wondered if they'd had a fight.

'Everything OK?' she asked.

'Fine,' snapped Jack, angrily banging the frying pan onto the tiny stove. Summer's violet eyes were tinged with red.

Breakfast was almost over by the time Harriet eventually surfaced, looking beautifully dishevelled and devilishly satisfied.

'The drought is over,' she announced. 'I'm famished.'

'Which one was it?' asked Rachel, handing Hattie an egg.

Harriet shrugged. 'The tall blond one. Can't remember his name, but he was young and he had tremendous stamina.'

They all spent a lazy day on the beach. The sea was calm and the waves were no good for surfing, so they sunbathed and chatted and enjoyed a late lunch on the terrace of the café above the beach. Jack's earlier bad mood had thawed in the heat, but Summer remained subdued. It stayed hot into the evening and the five languished on their towels. Rachel snoozed, Summer sang sad little songs to herself, Jack scribbled in a notebook – 'Work,' he apologized – Harriet daydreamed about her new teenage lover and Bianca re-read Judy Jones.

'Why are you reading that crap again?' demanded Harriet suddenly. 'I could barely claw my way through it the first time.'

'It's brilliant,' said Bianca defensively. 'It's even better the second time round. There are jokes and clever observations that I missed the first time I read it.'

'Did you really hate it that much?' asked Jack, looking concerned.

Harriet shrugged. 'Like I told you at the book club. It was OK, I suppose. Nothing special. I certainly don't know why everyone makes such a fuss about her.'

'She's a multimillionaire,' announced Summer. 'She'd sold more books than anyone else this year. I think she's very gifted.'

'Well,' retorted Harriet. 'She should ask me about my life if she wants some decent plot lines. I'd tell her a few stories that would add spice to her sex scenes.'

'I bet you would.' Jack laughed. 'Come on then, spill the beans. About last night . . .'

Rachel woke up just in time to hear Harriet telling tales of cunnilingus in a cramped camper van.

As the sun set, the gang climbed into the Jeep and headed to Padstow for some fresh crab, except for Summer, of course, who chose the vegetarian option. On the way home, Jack pulled into the beach car park.

'What are we doing back here?' asked Bianca.

'Skinny-dipping,' announced Jack gleefully.

It was after midnight and the beach was almost deserted, except for a few couples making out in the sand. The moon was full and bright and a myriad of stars twinkled in the sky.

'All right, folks,' said Jack. 'Get your kit off.'

Harriet tugged at Rachel's arm, holding her back from the others.

'Now we'll see,' she whispered.

'See what?' asked Rachel, bewildered.

'Whether Bianca's boobs are real.'

Bianca dropped her skirt, kicked off her knickers and pulled her T-shirt over her head. Rachel and Harriet watched closely. The most famous breasts in the country stood perkily to attention, gleaming in the moonlight. There were no scars or hard, plastic bits, just perfect round globes of flesh.

'I don't believe it, they're bloody well real,' said Harriet a little too loudly.

'Of course they're real, hon,' replied Bianca breezily. 'I'm far too much of a coward to ever go under the knife. Come on, take your clothes off. We're waiting for you.'

Jack, Summer and Bianca stood together in their birthday suits.

'Christ, Jack,' exclaimed Harriet, staring at Jack's nether regions. 'You must be popular with the ladies.' Then she pulled off her sun dress to reveal that she was wearing nothing underneath.

Rachel took off her clothes slowly and shyly, aware that the others were watching. The excess weight of childbirth had gone, but her body had changed shape for ever – small bulges remained around her stomach and hips. She kept one hand shyly in front of her stomach as they ran towards the sea, and cupped her heavy breasts in the other. The friends whooped and skipped into the icy ocean, following the light of Jack's white bum ahead. When they got back to camp, sleepy and damp, Rachel was disappointed to see no signs of life in the camper vans opposite. She had hoped to see Ben.

Rachel and Bianca were almost asleep when the still night was disturbed by the shrill ringing of a mobile phone.

'Hello?' It was Summer's voice coming quite clearly from Jack's tent.

'No, everything's fine, Murphy. I'm in Cornwall with some friends . . . Tabitha? Tabitha's safe. She's staying with the husband of a very good friend of mine. It's the safest house in England, believe me . . . All right, I'll call you when I get home . . . Goodnight, Murphy.'

'What was that about?' whispered Bianca in the darkness.

'Beats me,' replied Rachel.

For the rest of the night, Rachel was vaguely aware of animated whispering coming from the tent next door.

'You should have told me,' huffed Jack. 'I had a right to know I was a father.'

'I did it for your own good,' explained Summer desperately. 'I didn't want to trap you. I had no hopes or aspirations. No one expected anything from me. It didn't matter if I was saddled with a kid at eighteen, but you, you were on the brink of this huge adventure. You were escaping, sweetheart. You were the only one with a chance of doing something good with your life. I didn't want to be the one who took that chance away from you.'

'But I wouldn't have gone to Oxford if I'd known you were pregnant,' whispered Jack.

'Exactly. That's why I didn't tell you. I couldn't have that on my conscience. That's why I finished with you, you idiot. Not because I didn't love you. Shit, Jack, I've never stopped loving you. But I wasn't going to drag you down to my level.'

'It did my head in when you didn't write back,' remembered Jack sadly.

'I didn't get your letters because I wasn't there. My mum died a couple of weeks after you left. I got kicked out of the flat by the council and ended up in a hostel in Eastgate for a while. Then I had the baby and I had to fight Social Services tooth and nail to keep her. I've been fighting to keep our heads above water ever since.'

'What did you do to survive?' asked Jack solemnly.

'Anything. Everything. I worked the massage parlours mainly,' she replied sadly.

'As a prostitute?' Jack could barely spit the words out.

'No! No!' Summer hit his bare back in frustration. 'Is that what you think of me? That I'm just like my mother? I'd never have done that. I did the books, looked after the girls, ran the office. That's how I ended up on Mr Big's payroll. I wasn't one of his girls, I was his secretary.'

'And that's why you knew so much when it all kicked off.' Jack sighed with relief as the pieces of Summer's jigsaw finally began to slot together.

'Exactly. That's why Murphy needed me. That's why I ended up in Combe.'

'I need to meet Tabitha,' said Jack quietly.

'I know,' replied Summer. 'It's time.'

* * *

It was their last night in Cornwall and the surf boys had asked Bianca, Harriet, Rachel, Summer and Jack to join them for a drink in a pub in Newquay. Rachel felt fourteen again, as if she was going on a first date. She was old enough to know where the evening would end. There was polite chit chat about music and bars they'd both been to in London. Ben asked questions about Rachel's old job and about what it was like in Vietnam, but he didn't listen to the answers. He just gazed at her longingly with enormous puppy-dog eyes that made him look even younger than his nineteen years. Rachel had been downing vodkas all night for Dutch courage, and with one final slug of her sea breeze, she looked Ben straight in the eye and said, 'So, your tent or mine?'

Bianca spent the night alone with the dogs. Harriet, she presumed, was with her blond surf dude, and Rachel, she knew, was with the sweet one called Ben. She'd seen them sneak into his tiny one-man tent between the camper vans earlier. The campsite was noisy that night. Bianca could quite clearly hear Summer squealing in the tent next door.

'Stop, Jack! Stop! You're tickling me!'

Why they didn't just come clean about their relationship was beyond Bianca.

Groups of surfers and holidaymakers were making a night of it, drinking, smoking joints and talking too loudly all around. Moriarty snored and farted sporadically. And then, from somewhere not very far away, Bianca could quite clearly hear Rachel's voice.

'Oh–my–God, Ben! Ben! Ben!' She was gasping. 'That's it. Just there. Keep going. Don't stop. Oh my God. That is so good. It's so good.' Her squeals got louder and louder: 'Oh my God. Keep going. I'm going to come. Oh my God. I'm going to come. I'm going to come.' And then finally she reached a crashing crescendo as she screamed, loud enough for the entire county to hear: 'I'm coming! I'm coming! I'm co–ming. I've come. I've come. I've come.' Rachel's voice turned into a loud sigh and then finally trailed off into silence.

Bianca stroked Delilah's soft, fluffy nose and said, 'Darling, either your mummy's just had her first orgasm or she'll be up for a best actress award at the BAFTAs.'

Rachel regained consciousness gradually and tried to make sense of where she was. A heavy tanned arm was draped across her stomach and she could feel hot breath on the back of her neck. It dawned on her that she wasn't wearing any clothes, not even her knickers. And she could feel the bulge of her companion's morning glory between her bare butt cheeks. The events of the night before started playing in her mind like a cheesy teen movie – she was snogging a gorgeous teenager in a pub, he was telling her how lovely she was and then they were in the back of a taxi, hands all over the place, and then crawling into his tent, ripping off each other's clothes, at it like sex-starved adolescents, rampantly grabbing each other's bodies, limbs everywhere, stretching the canvas, no room to manoeuvre but he was going down and then she remembered the feeling that she'd never had before. She'd held onto Summer's words – 'just relax, let go' – and she'd gone with it and got lost in the pure, heady wonderfulness of the feeling, and then she'd done it, she'd actually finally achieved an orgasm. Rachel blushed at the memory.

'Are you awake?' she whispered to her companion.

There was no reply. She moved his arm gently off her tummy and turned around uncomfortably in the tiny tent. Ben slept peacefully, with his tousled black hair falling on his face. He looked flawlessly beautiful and heartbreakingly young. She stroked his cheek softly.

'Perfect skin,' she muttered self-consciously to herself. 'Like Alfie.'

And then it hit her. Ben was a baby. Life hadn't knocked him around yet. There were no wrinkles or scars, no worry or laughter lines. He was as pure and untouched as her own son. Rachel had no right to be there. She fished around in the chaos for her knickers and began to get dressed. Then, fully clothed, she bent down to kiss him goodbye.

Rachel was about to leave when Ben began to stir. His lashes were so long and thick that it took an age for his eyes to open. He smiled an honest smile.

'Morning, sexy,' he said.

Rachel smiled back.

'I have to go now,' she said. 'But thank you for last night. It was wonderful. I won't forget it.'

A frown appeared on his perfect skin.

'Will I see you again?' he asked hopefully.

Rachel shook her head. 'No.'

'Why not?' asked Ben, sitting up. There was a whine in his voice.

'Because you're a teenage student and I'm a thirty-year-old single mum. Let's just call it a holiday romance and leave it at that.'

'Don't you like me?' He pouted.

'What's not to like?' she replied honestly. 'Of course I like you.'

'Well what's wrong with me?' he pleaded.

'Nothing, darling,' she said softly, kissing his forehead. 'You have perfect skin.'

'Can I text you?' he asked desperately as she backed out of the tent.

'Ben.' She laughed. 'I don't do text messages. I'm far too busy changing nappies.' If that didn't convey the enormity of their age gap, nothing would.

But Rachel didn't feel dirty or ashamed. In fact, she felt somehow liberated by the whole seductive experience. Her only regret was that she couldn't call Zoe and regale her with tales of sex with Keanu.

Chapter Fifteen

A Dish Best Served Cold

Bianca arrived back from Cornwall to find TJ waiting at the front door, wearing an excited expression and juggling two wriggling daughters in his arms.

'Mummy!' shouted Lotte, throwing herself into Bianca's arms.

'Mummy!' exclaimed Poppy, doing the same.

Bianca caught the twins with well-practised precision. TJ leaned over the girls and kissed his wife passionately on the lips.

'Babes, I missed you so much,' he announced.

Bianca thought he looked a bit odd. He was jiggling around with a slightly manic look on his face and he was wearing his best Versace suit.

'I have to go,' he said, picking up a Louis Vuitton holdall that was waiting at the bottom of the stairs.

'Where?' Bianca was confused. TJ never went anywhere further than the Fox and Hounds.

'London, my angel,' he explained. 'To see Baz. I've got a new single.'

'What do you mean?' Bianca placed the twins gently onto the floor. 'When did this happen?'

'Friday. I was hit by a bolt of sublime inspiration. And now I'm back, babes. With bells on. *Ciao Bella!*'

He kissed her again and then whizzed out of the front door.

'Oh hi, Summer,' he said breezily as he passed. He'd been so excited he hadn't even noticed his wife's friend in the doorway.

Bianca and Summer shared a bemused look.

'I don't know what's got into him,' said Bianca apologetically. 'I haven't seen him that excited about his music . . .' She paused to think and then added, '. . . ever.'

Summer smiled. 'It's good, isn't it?'

'It's fab,' agreed Bianca, 'if a little unexpected.'

'Hello, little ones.' Summer bent down and stroked the twins' heads. 'Do you know where Tabby is?'

'With Scarla,' explained Lotte. 'Tabby's a rock star.'

'Oh,' said Summer.

'Oh dear,' added Bianca.

They found Tabitha in Scarlett's blackened room, sitting on the black bedspread in a black outfit, wearing black eye make-up and a black beret.

'Hi, Mum. I've had a make-over,' she said with an angelic smile that was somewhat at odds with her demonic appearance.

'She looks cool now,' explained Scarlett proudly. 'She's my Mini Me.'

Summer's mouth fell open.

'Oh, Jesus, Summer, I'm so sorry,' apologized Bianca, casting Scarlett a look that said, 'You're dead meat, young lady.'

Summer took a few seconds to regain her composure and said, 'No, it's OK. They're kids and they're bound to want to experiment. Anyway, the make-up will wash off.'

'Yeah, but her hair won't grow back for years,' announced Scarlett, pulling the beret off Tabby's head and revealing a short, punky crop where once there had been a waist-length mane of golden curls.

Summer's legs buckled beneath her and she had to hold onto a dressing table for support. 'What have you done to my baby?' she gasped.

Bianca could feel her face turning puce. She dug her long nails into the palms of her hands and fought the urge to strangle her stepdaughter.

'You evil, spiteful cow,' she spat at Scarlett. 'How could you do this to poor Tabitha?'

'Keep your frigging hair on. She likes it.' Scarlett shrugged nonchalantly. 'Don't you, Tab?'

Tabitha nodded enthusiastically. 'It's way cool,' said the girl in Scarlett-speak. 'I look totally the business now.'

Rachel paced the living room impatiently, wondering how much longer Simon would be. She was desperate to get her hands on Alfie, to smell his delicious baby scent, to kiss those rosy cheeks and to squeeze his chubby thighs. God she'd missed him. And she wanted to see Simon, too. She had silently practised what she was going to say all the way back in the car and she now had the whole speech word-perfect in her head. Revenge, she knew, was a dish best served cold. And Simon was about to get what was coming to him. It would be so damn sweet to see the look on his face. Rachel couldn't wait.

'Come in,' she said to Simon when he knocked on the door.

'What? Into the house?' Simon was both surprised and flattered by the invitation. Perhaps this meant a thaw in relations with his wife.

'Give me my baby,' said Rachel impatiently. 'I need a hug.'

Alfie was sitting comfortably on his daddy's hip, nestled into the crook of his arm. They looked comfortable with each other, as if they fitted together suddenly.

Simon handed Alfie over to his mummy and smiled fondly as Rachel hugged him hard to her chest.

'We've had a wonderful few days, haven't we, son?' announced Simon, making cutesy faces at Alfie. 'We've been to the park and to Hamley's, and we saw Granny and Grandpa.'

'What? My mum and dad?' asked Rachel a little crossly.

'Yeah. They were dying to see him, so we spent the day there yesterday. It was lovely. I had a good chat with your mum too. She's a smart lady. She talks a lot of sense.'

Rachel raised an eyebrow. 'I'm not sure I like the idea of you hanging out with my parents. We're separated.'

'I'm well aware of that,' said Simon. 'But they wanted to see their grandson. That's OK, isn't it?'

'I suppose so,' said Rachel in a slightly huffy manner. 'But don't you try to get my mum on your side. She's a soft touch, but she's my mother and she's always going to put me first.'

'Don't be silly, Rachel,' said Simon, throwing himself comfortably into his favourite armchair. 'I wasn't aware that this was a war. We don't need to draw battle lines and recruit soldiers on each side.'

'You'd be fighting on your own if we were,' sniffed Rachel as she sat down to give Alfie a breastfeed on the couch.

'I'm sure you're right,' said Simon rather sadly.

He watched Alfie latch gratefully onto his mother's breast. The baby's hand felt around for Rachel's flesh and then stroked it gently as he fed. Simon's heart lurched. He wanted comfort and closeness from Rachel. He needed her too.

'I have something to tell you,' began Rachel. 'I think it's only right that you know.'

'Yes?' Simon hoped it was something good.

'I had sex with another man,' she announced formally. 'And I enjoyed it.'

Simon felt as if he'd been punched in the stomach by Lennox Lewis. He fell back into the chair and had to take a few moments for the room to stop spinning. His worst fears had come true, and quicker than he'd anticipated.

'Right,' said Simon, who eventually composed himself enough to form words. 'I suppose I asked for that.'

'Don't flatter yourself. It had nothing to do with you. I just met this guy. He was gorgeous, he fancied me and we had great sex. Fully protected, mutually consensual, fabulous, filthy sex. Simple as that.'

Simon shook his head sadly and stared out of the window. Rachel could see tears gathering in his eyes and she was surprised at how uneasy it made her feel. This is what she had planned. She'd wanted to tell him for precisely this reason. Her words had the power to hurt him and that was what he deserved. Wasn't it? She fought back this tiny pang of pity and concentrated on her anger instead.

'How did it come to this, Rach?' he asked sadly. 'With you boasting about your sexual conquests with other men as a way of getting me back?'

'I'm not trying to get my own back for what you did to me,' said Rachel defensively, although this was only half true. 'I'm a single woman. I have every right to have relationships with other men.'

'If you're so single, why are you telling me this?' asked Simon, wiping his eyes with the back of his hand.

'Because we're still married by law, if nothing else. And, as I said, I think you have a right to know.'

'Bollocks!' shouted Simon, jumping to his feet. 'You want me to suffer like you did. You must have done it for revenge.'

'No, I did it because I wanted to,' she replied, slowly and calmly. 'I enjoyed it. Ben was very nice. He restored some of the confidence that *you* knocked out of me.'

'Oh Ben. Ben is it?' demanded Simon, pacing the room like a demented tiger in a too-small cage. 'And what was Ben like?'

'Young, fit, sexy, virile.' Rachel continued as planned. 'Everything you used to be.'

'God, Rachel, you can be a total bitch when you set your mind to it.'

'You made me like this,' she reminded him. 'You and Zoe.'

'Fuck! I can't handle this!' roared Simon, punching the wall and leaving a smear of blood on the pale blue paintwork.

'Don't make a mess,' Rachel snapped. 'In fact, if you're going to be childish, you can leave now.'

'Oh I'm going,' spat Simon. 'I'm going all right. I'm not going to stay here and be punished. Rachel, do you think I don't beat myself up about what I've done every day? I hate myself for messing up this marriage. I can't bear being away from Alfie and, believe it or not, I can't bear being away from you. But you go on, you make everything worse if it makes you feel better. Sleep with as many men as you like, but it won't make you happy, because the truth is, you miss me as much as I miss you.'

Rachel snorted as if she found this thought ludicrous.

'Yeah, go on. Pretend you don't care. But this marriage isn't over, Rachel. We haven't resolved a thing. You won't even talk about it. You can run away as fast as you can, but all this bullshit between me and you will just keep catching up with you. The only thing keeping us apart is your pride. You think you'll look weak if you take me back. But running away's the easy option. The brave thing to do would be to forgive me and give it another try, for Alfie's sake as well as your own.'

'Are you finished?' asked Rachel calmly. 'Because you're disturbing Alfie's dinner. All this shouting will give him colic.'

'I'm finished,' said Simon angrily. 'Completely fucking finished.'

'Stop swearing in front of the baby and wash your knuckles,' scolded Rachel. 'You're dripping blood on the rug.'

Simon washed his hands and watched the blood circle the sink and disappear down the drain. The cold water stung his torn flesh and added to his pain. He looked at his reflection in the mirror and saw a broken man.

Rachel watched Simon's car leave from the window. Things hadn't gone exactly to plan. She'd said precisely what she'd planned to say and her words had had the desired effect and yet she felt horribly dissatisfied. She'd thought that seeing Simon crushed would somehow make her feel stronger but the entire experience had just left her feeling even more confused. A bit of her even felt sorry for him. The car disappeared out of the drive and Rachel felt a wrench. All the things he'd said about their marriage not being over were whirling around her head. Why did part of her desperately want them to be true?

'You have three messages,' Jack's answer machine announced.

'Message one: "Hi. Jack. Gerry here. Just wondered how it's going. I wanted to give you a gentle reminder that your deadline is looming."'

'Message two: "Jack, Gerry again. Why's your

mobile switched off? I need an update on your work. You've only got a month, remember." '

'Message three: "Gatley, it's Gerry. Where the hell are you? We need to talk." '

Jack smirked to himself as he dialled Gerry's office number in London.

'Gerry,' he said cheerfully. 'Jack.'

'Jack, where have you been?' demanded Gerry. 'I've been fielding phone calls left, right and centre. Give me the lowdown. When will you be finished.'

'Gerry, calm down,' soothed Jack patiently. 'Everything is going exactly according to plan. I've just spent a very enjoyable weekend away with my ladies, and now I have almost all the ammunition I need. I completed the first half last week and you'll have the rest by the end of the month, OK?'

'OK,' said Gerry. 'But you'd better not be bull-shitting, Jack, because there's a lot of money riding on this deal.'

'Would I let you down?' asked Jack cheekily.

'I suppose not,' replied Gerry. 'I realize you're a genius.'

Jack ambled upstairs, opened his wardrobe and wondered what a man should wear to meet his daughter.

Harriet heard the screeching before she reached the front door. Her father and Marjorie were at it again, shouting and throwing things at each other. It was, Hattie decided, like returning from paradise and stepping into The War of the Roses.

'Hi, honeys, I'm home,' she called sarcastically from the hall.

There was no reply, but she could tell from the direction of the bangs where her beloved family were fighting. Harriet walked into the kitchen to find Marjorie beating her father around the back with a riding crop.

'Good weekend?' she asked, sitting down at the kitchen table and making room for her elbows by shoving a pile of dirty plates out of the way.

Marjorie ignored her and carried on whipping Larry. Larry was crouched down with his arms protecting his head from the blows.

'Hello, Harriet,' he panted. 'Marjorie's a bit upset.'

'I can see that,' replied Hattie. 'Marge, leave him alone. He's an OAP.'

Marjorie threw the crop on the floor with a final scream of frustration and turned her venom on Harriet.

'Would you like to know what your beloved father has done now?' she demanded.

'Not really.' Harriet sighed.

'He's taken out a loan.'

'And?'

'From a loan shark. And he's missed three repayments. We've just had a visit from a couple of thugs who threatened us and then drove off in my Land Rover.'

'How tragic for you,' said Harriet.

'What are we going to do?' shouted Marjorie in desperation, looking from her husband to her stepdaughter. 'This family is going to the dogs and nobody seems to care except me.'

The dogs cowered under the table.

'Sell something,' suggested Hattie.

'Sell what?' asked Marjorie angrily. 'We could sell you to the white slave trade, but I don't think we'd get a very good price.'

'I'm going out,' said Harriet quietly. 'Come on Moriarty.'

'Keep still, Tabitha,' said Summer crossly. 'I can't get this muck off unless you let me scrub hard.'

'It hurts mum,' whined Tabby. 'You're rubbing too hard. My skin's coming off.'

'You're lucky I'm not spanking your backside, young lady,' said Summer as she took her frustration out on her daughter's flawless skin.

'But you don't believe in smacking children,' said Tabby, pushing her luck.

'I am just about ready to change my philosophy on that issue,' replied Summer angrily.

'I'm sorry about my hair, Mummy,' said Tabby gently. 'But it looks quite nice, doesn't it?'

'No, it's a complete abomination,' argued Summer. 'I can't believe you let that horrible girl near you with a pair of kitchen scissors. What were you thinking?'

Tabitha shrugged. 'I just fancied a change.'

'But you had such pretty hair.' Summer put her hand on Tabby's tufted head and looked dolefully at her daughter's reflection in the mirror. She still looked cute, in an impish kind of way, but she no longer looked like Summer's daughter. With her hair off her face, Tabitha's delicate bone structure was more apparent and her big eyes shone like emeralds from her tanned face.

'You're just upset because I don't look like your Mini Me any more.'

'Nonsense,' scoffed Summer. 'What's all this Mini Me business?'

'Oh it's just something Scarlett says,' replied Tabitha. 'It means being a miniature version of someone else.'

'Christ, she's a Mini Me of her father now,' thought Summer silently to herself.

'Where are we going, Mum?' asked Tabby, as she put some hair gel – borrowed from her new best friend, Scarlett – in her crop.

'Into Bath,' replied Summer.

'Why?'

'We're going to meet someone. Someone important.'

'Who?' Tabitha looked at her mother expectantly.

'Sit down, my love,' said Summer gently. 'I need to tell you something.'

Tabitha sat down on the window seat obediently.

'God, this is difficult,' muttered Summer, unable to meet her daughter's quizzical gaze. 'Right, it's like this, sweetheart. It's about your father.'

'He's dead,' replied Tabitha.

'Yes well, that's the thing,' stammered Summer nervously. 'He's not.'

'What do you mean? Of course he's dead. He died before I was born.'

'I told you a lie, Tabitha. I thought it was for the best. I didn't think we'd ever see your father again but, the thing is, he's here, in the village and he wants to meet you.'

Tabby shook her head desperately. 'No. No,

369

mummy. You're lying. He's dead. You said he was dead.'

Summer sighed and ran her fingers through her hair. This was really difficult, even more difficult than she'd imagined. She'd been telling lies and reinventing herself for so long that the truth had become terrifying.

'He's a lovely man, Tabitha,' Summer continued gently. 'You'll be so pleased when you meet him.'

'If he's so lovely why hasn't he wanted to meet me before? If he's so nice, why did you pretend he was dead?'

Tabitha's slender shoulders shook and her tears ran in dirty rivers down her cheeks.

'Sweetheart, he didn't even know you existed until now,' explained Summer, wishing she could make this easier for the child to understand. But she'd still been a child herself when she'd started the lie. It had grown up with her and mutated into a monster of a secret with a life of its own.

'Why not?' demanded Tabby, getting angry now. 'Why didn't you tell him about me?'

'I didn't know where he was,' explained Summer, knowing her answer was weak and insufficient and, in honesty, not even true.

'How could you do this to me, Mum?' demanded Tabby. 'You can't keep something like that from someone. It's not fair. I had a right to know that my dad was out there somewhere. And he had a right to know about me.'

'He was angry with me too,' said Summer, 'when I told him. He said exactly the same thing. But Tabby, my love, the thing you've got to understand is that I was seventeen when I got pregnant with you. I was only a kid. I didn't know what to do for the best so I just coped the best way I knew how.'

'Well you didn't do a very good job,' said Tabitha, staring out of the window, refusing to look her mother in the eye.

'I know, sweetheart. And I'm sorry, but nobody tells you how to be a good mum.'

Summer cried for Tabitha and her lost childhood. She cried for herself and the mistakes she'd made that had led them here. And she cried for Jack and the years of joy he'd missed out on as Tabitha's dad.

'Is he handsome?' asked Tabitha after a while.

Summer nodded, sniffing back the tears.

'Do I look like him?'

Summer nodded again and this time managed a smile. 'You're a Mini Me of him.'

Tabitha looked pleased.

Jack paced impatiently outside the Pump Rooms and searched the crowds for Summer's beautiful face. It was hot; hotter than it had been since records began. 'Bath hits 100 degrees,' shouted the Bath Chronicle from its stand. Jack was sweltering in his smart linen shirt and trousers. He wished he'd left his shorts on. He was meeting an eleven-year-old, not the queen. His palms sweated with heat and nerves and anticipation. What do you say to the child you never knew you had?

'Hello?' said a voice behind him.

Jack jumped and spun round to see Summer smiling nervously with an exquisitely beautiful young girl at her side.

'Jack, this is Tabitha, your daughter,' announced Summer. 'Tabitha,' she continued. 'This is your dad.'

Green eyes met green eyes. They stared at each other for the longest time, taking in the sight of their own flesh and blood, feeling the intangible bond that was somehow there, despite the years apart.

'I've seen you,' said Tabby, breaking the spell first. 'In the village. You're rich. You live in that big house at the top of the lane.'

'That's right,' said Jack, looking nervously at Summer for approval. Summer nodded, encouraging him to speak. 'You must come up,' he invited Tabby. 'Have a look around.'

'Cool,' she said. 'Can I live with you?'

Jack looked at Summer for help.

'One step at a time, my love,' said Summer to Tabitha. 'Perhaps you should get to know each other first before you talk about moving in.'

'But Jack's house is wicked,' enthused Tabitha. 'This is great. My dad's rich.'

Summer rolled her eyes at Jack and mouthed, 'Sorry,' but there was no need to apologize, Jack was already intoxicated by Tabitha.

'I like your hair,' said Jack. 'It's really cool.'

Tabby smiled proudly. 'Mum hates it,' she said. 'But she's not very trendy any more. She's too old.'

'Is that right.' Jack laughed. 'Well, that must make me old too.'

Tabitha nodded. 'But you look OK for an old man. Quite buff.'

'Buff?' Jack scratched his head.

'You'll need an interpreter for a while,' explained Summer grinning. 'But you'll pick up Tabitha-speak eventually.'

'I thought we could have afternoon tea,' suggested Jack. 'In the Pump Rooms. Do you like cakes, Tabitha? They do very good cakes.'

Tabby shrugged. 'Cakes are nice, but I don't like tea.'

'Well I'm sure you can have a Coke or something,' said Jack.

'Wicked!' exclaimed Tabby.

Summer shot him a cross look. 'She's not allowed Coke,' she explained.

'Not even today?' asked Jack. 'It's a special occasion.'

'OK,' Summer conceded. 'But just this once.'

'I think I'm going to like having you as a dad,' called Tabitha as she disappeared into the revolving doors of the Pump Rooms. 'You can be my bad influence.'

Jack followed her into the cool building. 'I was thinking more along the lines of being a responsible father figure,' he teased. 'You know, rules, discipline, punishment, that sort of thing.'

Tabitha shook her head and wrinkled her little nose. 'Nah. I get all that from Mum already. It's definitely a bad influence I need.'

'OK.' Jack grinned. 'I'll see what I can do.' Jack and Summer shared a knowing and pleased look behind their daughter's back.

Bianca was still lecturing Scarlett about the importance of other people's children's hair when the video-entry system buzzed, announcing the arrival of a visitor.

'Saved by the bell.' Scarlett grinned. 'Go on then, stepmommy dearest. You'd better see who it is.'

'I haven't finished with you yet,' promised Bianca, giving Scarlett her best scary stare.

'Ooh, I'm shaking,' replied Scarlett with a wink. 'Laters.'

Bianca sighed deeply and went to answer the bell. On the CCTV screen she could see Harriet and Moriarty waiting impatiently at the gates. Hattie looked as miserable to be back as Bianca felt.

'Hi, Bianca, it's me.' Harriet's voice crackled through the security system. 'I need to see a friendly face. Are you free?'

Bianca had never been so grateful to see Harriet in her life. They spent what remained of the afternoon arguing about what was worse, being the daughter of a ranting stepmother, or being the stepmother of a deranged teenager. The Mills's chef prepared a delicious dinner of seared tuna and tomato salsa, which the friends enjoyed on the verandah once the twins were safely tucked up in bed.

'I feel a bit sick,' said Bianca suddenly, halfway through her meal. 'And I've got a pain here.'

She pointed to the side of her stomach.

Harriet looked up and noticed that Bianca had grown scarily pale. Her normally perma-tanned face was as white as the summer dress she was wearing.

'Are you OK?' she asked. 'You look like shit.'

'I'll be fine,' said Bianca in a strange little voice. 'But I think I need to lie down.'

She stood up to leave the table, but was halted in her tracks.

'Ouch!' she cried, grabbing her stomach and doubling up in pain.

Harriet was on her feet and by her friend's side in an instant.

'What is it, Bianca? Is it the baby?' she asked with desperate concern.

'I don't know,' whispered Bianca breathlessly. 'But something's not right.'

Harriet could see beads of sweat forming on Bianca's pale brow.

'Let's get you to bed, darling, and I'll call your doctor.'

Harriet began to guide Bianca towards the nearest bedroom when Scarlett appeared in the hallway.

'What's wrong with Bianca?' she asked Harriet, looking almost concerned. 'And what's that on her dress? Oh my God, Harriet, she's bleeding. Do something, Harriet. Quick!'

Scarlett was screaming now, looking horrified.

'What's going on, Hattie?' whispered Bianca weakly. 'What's wrong with me?'

Harriet looked down and saw that Bianca's white dress had turned bright red with blood, which was pouring down her legs and dripping onto the floor.

'I've got to get her to hospital,' said Harriet, going on autopilot. 'Scarlett, where's your dad?'

'In London,' squealed Scarlett in a panic.

'Call him right now,' ordered Harriet in a calm voice that belied the sick feeling in her stomach. 'And tell him to get to the RUH in Bath, ASAP.'

'The what?' asked Scarlett, shaking.

'Just tell him to get to the hospital in Bath. He'll know where you mean.'

'What's wrong with her?' demanded Scarlett. 'Don't die, Bianca. I'm sorry I was mean to you. Please don't die.'

'I'm OK,' said Bianca in a tiny voice. She was lying on the hall floor, clutching her stomach in agony. 'Hattie, you can't take me to hospital, you're not allowed to drive.'

'Bollocks,' said Harriet. 'We haven't got time to wait for an ambulance. Where are the keys to your car?'

Bianca pointed towards her handbag on the floor and then lost consciousness.

'Scarlett,' ordered Harriet. 'Help me get Bianca into the car.'

It was pitch-black outside and they struggled to get Bianca into the tiny car.

'How do you drive this thing?' Harriet asked herself, struggling to get the key in the ignition, stalling it twice and then screeching down the drive with the engine screaming.

'Harriet, you've forgotten to put the lights on!' shouted Scarlett after them, but Hattie couldn't hear.

Bianca was half-conscious, muttering to herself, sweating profusely and thrashing her head against the car window. Harriet watched her friend as she drove down Chillyhill Lane. 'Please be OK, Bianca,' she was saying to herself. Bianca didn't look good. Harriet was so busy fretting about Bianca that she wasn't looking at the road ahead. Suddenly there was a loud bang from beneath the car and the vehicle stalled.

'Shit, I think I've hit something,' muttered Harriet, trying to restart the engine.

'What was it?' whispered Bianca. 'I hope it wasn't an animal. Go and see, Hattie. Check it's OK.'

'We've got to go,' explained Harriet.

'Please,' pleaded Bianca with her eyes closed in pain.

Harriet stepped out of the car into the darkness. The first thing she realized was that the car had no lights on. If she had hit something it was her own fault. Great, she thought. No licence, no headlights. I'd better not get caught. She wandered round the back of the car and peered into the black night. There was definitely something on the road and it wasn't moving. Harriet stepped closer nervously. She hoped it wasn't a dog. The car had stalled directly outside the gates of The Beeches. She hoped it wasn't one of her father's dogs. Christ, she'd never forgive herself. She stood over her victim and tried to make out what it was. It was too big for a dog; maybe it was a bin bag. She kicked it gently with her toe and it turned over onto its back. An arm appeared quite clearly on the road, splayed out away from its body. Harriet felt the blood drain from her face. Her eyes had acclimatized to the black night and she could now see quite clearly who it was. Marjorie's face stared up at her. Her eyes were fixed, cold and full of hate, and there was a tyre mark across her chest and a puddle of blood around her.

'Oh fucking hell,' said Harriet. 'I've killed Marjorie.'

Harriet stood silently for a moment, trying to

make sense of what was happening. Bianca was in the car, possibly bleeding to death, and her stepmother was on the tarmac, already dead. She took a deep breath and then did what she had to do.

'Are you OK, darling?' she asked Bianca gently as she leaned into the car for her phone. Bianca didn't answer. She was unconscious again.

Harriet calmly called 999 and said, 'Hello, police please. Yes, my name is Harriet Lilywhite Smythe and I've just run over my stepmother. She's dead. Her name is Marjorie and she's lying on Chillyhill Lane outside the gates to a house called The Beeches – that's our house, by the way. I can't wait here because I'm on my way to the hospital. My friend is seriously ill, that's why I wasn't looking where I was going. I'll be at the RUH in Bath if you need me. And please, somebody tell my father.'

Then she staggered to the verge and threw up. Harriet got back into the car, found the switch for the headlights and drove the rest of the way to Bath in a catatonic state.

TJ rushed into accident and emergency in a blind panic.

'Where's my wife?' he asked the woman behind the glass panel at reception. 'Bianca Mills, where is she?'

The woman looked on her computer screen and said, 'The doctor's with her now, Mr Mills. Please take a seat.'

'What's wrong with her?' demanded TJ. 'She was fine this afternoon.'

The waiting area was full. People recognized TJ

and watched with interest as he pulled at his hair and ranted at the receptionist.

'I need to know if she's OK!' he shouted.

'The doctor will be with you as soon as possible, Mr Mills,' said the receptionist patiently. 'Take a seat for now.'

TJ paced the waiting room until he spotted Harriet. She appeared through a set of double doors, flanked on either side by a couple of policemen.

'Harriet? What's going on?' demanded TJ desperately.

'Bianca's going to be fine.' She smiled sadly.

'Where are you going?' asked TJ. 'What's going on? Why are you with the police?'

'I ran over Marjorie,' replied Harriet quietly. 'On my way here. I was in such a rush to get Bianca to hospital that I didn't see her. I killed her, TJ.'

'Come on now, Miss Lilywhite Smythe,' said one of the policemen. 'We need to get you to the station.'

TJ watched as Harriet was led away from the building. Her head was hung low, her shoulders stooped and she looked painfully, pitifully sorry.

'Mr Mills?' asked a young female doctor with red hair and pretty pale blue eyes. 'You can see your wife now. Come with me.'

'Is she OK?' asked TJ.

'She's fine now,' replied the doctor gently. 'But I'm afraid she's lost the baby.'

TJ looked confused. 'What baby?' he asked.

'Oh, I'm sorry,' said the doctor. 'But your wife was fourteen weeks pregnant. She suffered a miscarriage this evening, but she's comfortable now. She's in here.'

The doctor showed TJ to a cubicle with the curtains closed. Bianca lay, pale and drawn, in the stiffly made hospital bed.

'Babes,' cried TJ with a wobbly chin. 'Are you all right?'

Bianca nodded bravely and said, 'I'm sorry, TJ. I lost our baby.'

TJ sat on the bed and pulled his wife's body towards his own. 'It's OK, my darling,' he whispered. 'Everything will be OK.'

The Wiltshire police were playing bad cop, bad cop with Harriet Lilywhite Smythe. She'd been sitting behind a desk in a small, badly lit room, chain-smoking cigarettes and biting her nails for almost six hours now. It had been dark when she'd arrived, but it had been light for a while now. The clock on the wall said it was almost 9 a.m., but it made no sense to Hattie.

'Look, Harriet,' said DS Price. 'You've admitted running over your stepmother, why don't you just tell us the whole story and this will be over?'

'That is the whole story,' repeated Harriet for the umpteenth time. 'I was in a flap because Bianca was so ill. I wanted to get her to hospital. I wasn't concentrating and I didn't see her.'

Harriet had run out of tears. She'd run out of every emotion other than sheer exhaustion.

DI Bennet drummed his fingers impatiently on the desk and continued. 'It doesn't look good for you, Miss Smythe,' he said darkly. 'Driving while

380

banned, taking a motor vehicle without the owner's permission and without insurance. And you've admitted that you didn't have your lights on, so let's add dangerous driving to the list.'

'She wasn't looking where she was going, either,' added Price.

'No, so let's add driving without due care and attention.'

'I had to get Bianca to hospital,' pleaded Harriet. 'What else could I do?'

DS Price and DI Bennet looked at each other and shook their heads.

'I put it to you,' said Price, 'that you saw your stepmother in the road and you took the opportunity to kill her. After all, there were no witnesses because Mrs Mills was out cold.'

'No she wasn't,' insisted Harriet. 'Not at that point. Ask her. We thought I'd hit an animal. She told me to check what it was.'

'You say that,' said Price, 'but Mrs Mills can't remember a thing.'

'You've questioned Bianca? In hospital? Have you people got no shame?' Harriet felt like she was watching herself in a particularly bad nightmare.

'It's no secret that you hate your stepmother, is it, Miss Smythe?' continued Bennet.

Harriet shrugged and lit another cigarette with shaking hands. 'I'm not, I mean I *wasn't* her biggest fan,' she admitted. 'But I didn't kill her. Well, not deliberately anyway.'

Harriet stared out of the window. 'Who told you that anyway?' she demanded suddenly. 'Who told you I didn't like Marjorie?'

'You did,' replied Bennet. 'We found your diary in your handbag.' He placed a clear plastic evidence bag on the desk. Inside was her Gucci diary.

'Oh fuck,' muttered Harriet.

What she'd written about Marjorie in her diary was certainly incriminating. She remembered one particularly malicious passage in which she'd fantasized about 'ripping the old hag's scrawny legs off and feeding them to the dogs'.

'Look, just because I hated her didn't mean I wanted to kill her,' explained Harriet desperately.

'That's not the impression I got from reading this,' continued Bennet, tapping the bag. 'You certainly had violent feelings towards the woman.'

'Look,' hissed Harriet. 'If you'd met her you would have had violent feelings towards her too. But I did not mean to kill her, OK? I didn't see her. It was a horrible accident.'

'Did you see her face as you hit her?' asked Price. 'Was she scared?'

'No, as I've just explained, I didn't see a thing. I just felt a bump. In fact, it was weird, as if she'd been lying in the road, because it all came kind of underneath, if you know what I mean?'

Price and Bennet looked at her blankly, as if she were talking Albanian.

'Check the car,' she demanded. 'I bet you won't find a bump on the bonnet and nothing touched the windscreen. Surely, if I'd run into her when she was standing up, she would have come through the windscreen.'

'The car in question is with our forensic team

now,' said Price. 'They'll be able to tell us exactly where your stepmother was when you hit her.'

'Good,' said Harriet. 'Maybe then you'll start listening to me. Where's my dad? Is he here yet?'

Bennet shook his head. 'We're trying to locate your father at the moment. Have you any idea where he might be.'

Harriet shook her head and looked blankly at the detectives. The whole world had gone mad.

Rachel stared out of the window and watched the village as it teemed with police officers. They'd already been round to see her. She'd had to admit that Harriet didn't like her stepmother but she'd been adamant that she wouldn't kill her. Poor Hattie; she wondered whether she should go to the police station and wait for her to be released. Perhaps not. Larry would be there for her, wouldn't he?

Rachel strapped Alfie into his pushchair and joined the other villagers, who'd congregated on the village green. Summer was there, and Jack too.

'Exciting, isn't it?' said Jack with eyes shining.

'Not for Harriet,' Summer scolded him.

'Or for Marjorie,' added Rachel.

'I had to be escorted past the murder scene,' continued Jack, unfazed. 'It's like being in an episode of *Midsomer Murders*. Chillyhill Lane has been sealed off around The Beeches and there are people in white suits poking around everywhere. It looks like aliens have landed. Look.'

The congregation all peered up the lane, and suddenly there was a collective, 'Ooh' from the crowd.

'What's happening now?' asked Rachel, who was too short to see above the others' heads.

'They're putting something in a black van,' said Summer. 'It's in a black bag. It looks like a body.'

'It must be Marjorie,' said Rachel sadly.

'No,' said Jack. 'They took her away hours ago. I watched them.'

'Well who the hell is that?' asked Rachel.

Harriet sat in her tiny cell and read the writing on the wall. 'All pigs stink,' said one message. 'Don't eat the food,' warned another. She'd already taken that advice. Her tray of breakfast sat untouched on the floor. Not that it looked unappetizing, it was just that Harriet had no appetite. Suddenly the lock on the door banged open and DI Bennet appeared in the cell.

'You're free to go, Miss Lilywhite Smythe,' he said.

'What?' Harriet looked at him, confused. 'You believe me?'

Bennet nodded. 'We know you didn't kill your stepmother,' he said gravely. The frown he had been wearing earlier had turned to a look of concern.

Harriet smiled. 'Oh, that's such a relief,' she said, wondering whether it would be against criminal etiquette to hug a detective. 'Is my dad here? Is he OK?'

Bennet took Harriet's elbow and led her down the corridor. 'Perhaps you'd like to come into my office for a few minutes, my dear,' he suggested.

Harriet shrugged. 'OK.'

Bennet ushered her into his office and pulled out a chair for her to sit on.

'The thing is,' he said, 'this case is a bit more complicated than it initially appeared.'

'Oh?' Harriet was emotionally drained and sleep-deprived. Nothing was making any sense any more.

'Harriet,' Bennet continued. 'The thing is, your father killed your stepmother.'

'What?' Harriet began to shake again. 'No, you've made a mistake.'

'There's no mistake, I'm afraid. He shot her, left her body on the road, which you then ran over, and then he shot himself.'

'What do you mean, he shot himself? Is he all right?'

'Harriet, I'm afraid your father is dead. He killed himself. He left a note explaining what had happened. But we didn't find the body for hours because it was dark. The note was in his pocket.'

Harriet could see her knees trembling in front of her, but she couldn't feel a thing.

'I know this must all be a terrible shock to you. Would you like a cup of tea?'

Harriet shook her head and gasped. 'Can I have a cigarette please?'

Bennet took a B&H from his pocket and lit it with a gold lighter, then passed it to Harriet.

'Are you OK, love?' he asked.

Harriet shook her head again.

'I want my Daddy,' she cried, rocking back and forth involuntarily in her chair. 'I just want my Daddy!'

Chapter Sixteen

–
The Truth Is Out There

Simon was trying to concentrate on the pitch he was working on for a Japanese car manufacturer, but his mind just wasn't on the job. It hadn't been for weeks, months even, not since Rachel kicked him out. Suddenly work seemed hugely insignificant in the grand scheme of things. The sad thing was that now he didn't want it, it was all he had left. Ever since Rachel had told him about that Ben bloke in Cornwall, Simon had been haunted by images of his wife writhing naked with other men. She'd told him that this Ben lived in London, so of course now he was eyeing every tube-traveller and pub-drinker in the Capital suspiciously, wondering if he was 'the one'. It was madness. Complete madness.

'You're a wreck,' Grace had said many times. 'Sort yourself out, Simon.'

She'd been trying to warn him, but he hadn't heard what she had to say. Now she was back in his office with that worried expression.

'You're needed upstairs,' she said solemnly.

'Am I?' asked Simon, confused. 'Is there a meeting? Did I forget again?'

'No, Simon,' replied Grace with a concerned little crease in her forehead. 'I think it's more serious than that. Wallis is here. From New York.'

'Oh,' said Simon, and then, as the penny dropped, 'Oh. Oh dear.'

'Gosh, Simon, I hope this isn't bad news,' gushed Grace suddenly. She looked more desperate than Simon felt. 'Explain to him about Rachel. He must have a heart somewhere under all that flab. Tell him it's just a blip in your performance record.'

'Grace, I've lost six clients in as many weeks,' Simon reminded her.

'A big blip,' she said with a pout.

Simon nodded and stood up. He squeezed Grace's arm gently, to let her know he appreciated her support, and then made his way to the lift. As he whizzed up to the top floor, Simon began to hum the funeral march to himself. Wallis was the boss, the head of the mothership – the US company that owned the smaller UK firm. Wallis only came to London for one of two reasons – hiring and firing. Simon knew which one this was going to be. The weird thing was, he didn't care.

Rachel was making a cup of tea in the kitchen, still sleepy from the night before, when something struck her as different. It took a while for her fuzzy head to work it out, but gradually it dawned on her that a chink of daylight was flooding onto one half of the room. This was very odd. No light ever managed to penetrate Ivy Cottage. She padded out to the garden wearing her knickers, the T-shirt she'd slept in and a pair of Simon's enormous slippers. Rachel looked up at the hedge and came face to face with an exotic-looking man with long black hair. He was swinging from one of the huge Beech trees in a harness and lobbing metres off the top hedge with a power saw.

'Good morning,' he shouted cheerfully above the din of the machinery.

'Good morning,' said Rachel, scratching her head and retreating back into her house to get dressed.

Rachel found the door of The Beeches ajar and let herself in.

'Harriet?' she called. 'Are you there?'

The dogs came running to greet her and were delighted to find Delilah in their hall. The puppy scurried after her mother and friends and disappeared off towards the East Wing. The house was eerily quiet and Rachel's voice echoed in its vast emptiness. Not a scrap of furniture remained. Harriet had to sell the lot.

'Harriet?' Rachel called again.

'In here,' said a voice, from the study.

Harriet sat cross-legged on the floor, surrounded by bills and invoices. She had a pair of spectacles perched on the end of her nose and her hair was pulled back in a bun. She looked alarmingly studious and straight-laced.

'I didn't know you wore glasses,' commented Rachel as she sat down beside her friend. 'They rather suit you.'

Hattie shrugged. 'I only wear them for reading

and, as you well know, I'm not a big reader, so I don't have much call for their services.'

'I came round to say thank you for having the hedge cut. It's amazing, my garden's basking in glorious sunshine and I have a great view of your house.'

'I thought it was about time your cottage got some sunlight. It's always so depressingly dark in there. Daddy refused to have the hedge cut, but I rather like the idea of being able to gossip with you over the garden fence. Did you get a great view of the tree surgeon too?' asked Harriet with a filthy twinkle in her eye. 'He's called Pete and he's half Burmese. He really improved the view for a while there. Married, unfortunately, with two kids. I was wondering about keeping him on as a permanent feature, but I'm not sure I can afford him, looking at these . . .'

'How are you getting on?' asked Rachel, eyeing the paperwork that covered the floor.

Harriet shook her head. 'Badly. Daddy had been ignoring bills for months. I've found whole drawers full of unopened envelopes from the bank. He sacked his accountant over a year ago and, as far as I can see, he just closed his eyes and hoped it would go away.'

'No wonder he felt so desperate,' said Rachel sadly. 'Your poor old dad. He must have been in a right state by the end.'

Harriet nodded. 'Silly old sod,' she said affectionately. 'He always did say that when an animal reached its use-by date, the kindest thing to do was shoot it, put it out of its misery, you know?'

Rachel nodded. She could imagine Larry saying that.

'But I thought he was talking about dogs and horses, not himself and Marjorie.'

Harriet made a brave attempt at a smile, but Rachel could tell that she was far from over her father's death.

'Mummy did a good job of cleaning the place,' said Harriet. 'She couldn't believe the squalor we'd been living in. She said it was the most disgusting thing she'd ever seen. She was furious at Daddy for letting the place fall into such disrepair. But, of course, she can't have a go at him about it because he's not here.'

She wiped a stray tear from her eye, as if it was irritating her, and continued. 'Had to sell all the furniture, of course. I've kept my bed, the fridge, the microwave and the kettle. I think that's it. I don't have a television, but that's OK because there's no chairs left to sit on and watch it. Sold my clothes. I'll be shopping in Top Shop with you and Summer next season. My shoes, bags, jewellery, Marjorie's jewellery – greedy old bag, she was going on about how poor we were and all the time she had twenty grand's worth of pearls and diamonds tucked away in a shoebox under her bed – and a couple of fox furs and a mink coat. Not to mention the Tiffany clock in a safety deposit box in London and the endowment policies she had hidden away. She doesn't have any family except me, so I'm allowed to use her funds, but they don't cover the debt. I don't get anything from Daddy's life insurance. It's because he killed himself. They won't give me a penny. Small print apparently. Bet Daddy didn't read it. He probably thought he was doing me a favour. I bet he thought his debts would die with him. He never was any good with money. And now I've got all this to deal with and I don't know where to start. There are death duties to pay and I haven't paid the undertakers for the funeral yet and that was nearly two weeks ago. Oh, Rachel, what am I going to do? I can't deal with this on my own and I can't afford to pay anyone to help. I'm scared I'm going to lose the house and Monty and everything.'

Rachel looked at her friend's desperate face and struggled to find a solution. Slowly, it dawned on her. There was one person she knew who might be able to help.

'I could ask Simon,' she suggested. 'You know he's been sacked, so he's at a loose end and he's brilliant with money. He'll know what to do.'

'Do you think he would help?' asked Harriet hopefully.

'If I ask him to,' said Rachel with certainty. 'And he'd jump at the chance of spending some time in Combe, because he could see more of Alfie.'

'Oh, Rachel, that would be ideal. I couldn't pay him, though.'

Rachel shrugged. 'As I said, he'll do anything I ask. He still feels as guilty as hell.'

'Are you thinking of giving him another chance,' asked Harriet.

Rachel shook her head and then shrugged. She wasn't sure. 'I don't know,' she said. 'I'm still so angry with him, but I haven't stopped loving him, and Alfie misses his daddy a lot. I feel as if he hasn't done enough to show me how sorry he is, though.'

'Rachel, the guy's apologized until he's blue in the face. He's lost his job because he was too busy being heartbroken to care about anything else and he's had to deal with you sleeping with a teenage surfer. Hasn't he been punished enough?'

Rachel thought for a moment and then said, 'Yes. He has been punished enough, but I still want something else from him. I feel like I deserve some grand gesture of love and commitment.'

'Like what?' asked Hattie.

'Oh, I don't know. I suppose I want a knight on a white charger to sweep me off my feet.'

'Can Simon ride?' teased Harriet.

Rachel shook her head. 'The man's never been on a horse in his life.'

She watched as Harriet flicked through a bundle of bills with a worried look on her face. 'Let me help,' she offered.

'Are you sure?' asked Hattie. 'It's brain-numbing stuff.'

'You should try changing nappies and watching the *Teletubbies*,' giggled Rachel. 'Now *that's* brain numbing.'

'Where is Alfie?' asked Harriet, suddenly realizing that Rachel had arrived without him.

'With Bianca,' said Rachel. 'She's got some theory about getting pregnant again if she spends lots of time around babies. She practically kidnapped him and ordered me to look after you.'

'The girl's a nutcase,' said Harriet. 'A lovely, bubbly, fruity nutcase. And what about Jack and Summer. How are they? I haven't seen them since the funeral.'

'Oh, they're fine,' said Rachel breezily. 'Still

pretending they're not an item, even though Summer and Tabitha have practically moved into High House full time. Jack's been working a lot, doing whatever it is he does. He still won't talk about it. And Summer, well Summer's been a bit edgy.'

'Summer's always a bit edgy,' Harriet reminded her.

'I know. She's a funny one. Every time I think I'm getting somewhere with her, you know, seeing the real Summer, she suddenly retreats again. She's like a little tortoise. She pops her head out for a while and then disappears back into her shell.'

Harriet laughed at the analogy.

'Oh, and that's another thing I wanted to ask you. Tomorrow, Jack's organized a book club outing to Babington – a swim, a sauna and then dinner. Are you up for it?'

'I'm not sure I can afford it,' said Harriet honestly. 'The food's pretty expensive there and Bianca will automatically order champagne instead of house white.'

'My treat,' offered Rachel. 'As a thank-you for returning the sunshine to my garden.'

Harriet bit her lip. She wasn't used to accepting charity. It was a weird feeling, not being able to pay her own way. She'd been born with a silver spoon in her mouth, but now there was nothing but plastic plates in the kitchen drawers.

'OK,' she accepted eventually. 'But I'll pay you back the minute I can. I'm so indebted to you already. You've all been such good friends to me over the past few weeks when everything's been so horrid. I don't know how I'm ever going to pay you all back. Even Summer's been sweet. She brought me some flowers from her garden and some vegetables she'd grown. Did you know she sells them at the Farmer's Market in Bath?'

Rachel shook her head.

'And you were all there for me at the funeral,' Hattie continued. 'Did you notice that none of my so-called friends from London turned up?'

Rachel shook her head again.

'Daddy's friends were there, even the Hurlingham Jones's, and they live overseas, but not one of my old gang. It's times like these when you find out who your real friends are, isn't it.'

'I guess so,' said Rachel. 'It's the same for me in a way. Since I left London, hardly any of my old friends stayed in touch. Well, apart from Zoe, but she only touched my husband.'

Rachel laughed sadly. 'I get the odd email from my old friends,' she continued thoughtfully. 'Telling me about who's sleeping with who and which bars they're all going to these days and who's been promoted or sacked. And they're always saying they'll come down and visit soon, but they never do. I doubt any of them ever will. No, I think we're just going to have to stick together, because nobody else seems to want us.' Rachel smiled at Hattie. 'Now, which pile does this go on, urgent or very urgent?'

'Are you nearly finished?' asked Summer, leaning over Jack's shoulders and peering at his computer.

'Almost there,' said Jack with a grin. 'Just another week and we'll be done here, then it's off to New York to start again.'

'I can't wait,' said Summer with a wistful smile. 'But we'll have to do something big before we go as a thank-you to the others – you know, for their help.'

'Sweetheart, they don't even know they've been helping,' Jack reminded her gently. 'And they don't know we're leaving either.'

'I know, but they're a good bunch and I think we should throw a party or something. On our last night. It would be a fitting end to everything.'

'It would indeed,' agreed Jack. 'A party to end all parties. I know, let's make it a thirtieth bash for you all. Harriet's birthday was a bit of a non-event and Bianca was in hospital for hers. Rachel's birthday is in a couple of weeks and yours, may I remind you, is only a month away.'

'Great idea,' enthused Summer. 'We'll get Mack to do a set and you could ask TJ to sing, Bianca would love that.'

Jack spun round in his swivel chair and held Summer around the waist. 'Have you told Murphy about our plans, yet?' he asked.

Summer shook her head. 'I'm a bit scared. I don't know how he'll take it. He's terrifying when he's angry.'

Jack shrugged. 'Once you're out of the country, you're no longer his concern,' he reminded her.

Summer was thoughtful for a moment, and then a look of sheer panic gripped her face. 'Oh my God, I've just remembered, Murphy's got my passport!'

The open-air swimming pool at Babington House was the perfect antidote to the scorching September sun. There was still no sign of summer ending and autumn felt light years away, despite the fact that the leaves had begun to turn orange on the trees.

'What a perfect girlie evening,' said Bianca as she floated motionless on her back in a white Bond girl bikini, her perfect breasts rising above the water like miniature islands.

'Except we're not all girls,' Harriet reminded her, nodding towards Jack who was doing manly lengths of the pool.

'Oh yes, and Jack, of course.' Bianca giggled. 'If he wasn't so utterly macho, I'd think he was gay. I mean, the way he hangs out with us girls and reads chick lit and gossips about sex, he's practically a woman.'

'Not quite.' Rachel giggled as she sat on the side with her legs dangling into the cool water. 'Remember, we saw the full monty in Cornwall. He's *all* man!'

Summer blushed and excused herself.

'I'm going to the steam room,' she explained as she pulled herself out of the pool.

Rachel noticed that Jack watched her go. Two minutes later, he got out of the water and disappeared.

'Fancy a sauna anyone?' asked Harriet.

The three friends sat in the sauna and sweltered.

'Why are we doing this?' asked Bianca. 'It's roasting outside. We've spent the last three months complaining about the heat and here we are sweating for pleasure.'

'It's good for you,' said Harriet. 'It gets rid of all those horrid toxins. We can detox in here and then retox in the bar afterwards.'

'Quite true,' agreed Rachel.

'Well, you two can stay here and detox if you

like, I'm going to try out the steam room.'

Bianca hummed cheerfully to herself as she left the sauna and headed for the steam room. She threw the door open and peered into the steamy heat. Nothing could have prepared her for the sight that met her. There before her stood Jack, butt naked with his back to the wall. Summer knelt in front of him, her swimsuit at her feet, beside Jack's shorts. Jack wore an expression of sheer ecstasy and Bianca was woman enough to know that he was in the throws of an orgasm.

'Summer,' he gasped.

Bianca felt her jaw crash to the floor. She wasn't surprised to discover that Jack and Summer were together, but to see them this together was a bit of a shock. Summer turned her head around and stared at their uninvited guest with obvious embarrassment.

'Bianca, it's not what it looks like,' she said, desperately searching for an excuse.

Bianca smiled angelically at her friends and waved her arm dismissively. 'Sorry to disturb you,' she said, backing out of the steam room and legging it back into the sauna.

Bianca fell into the sauna in a fit of hysterics.

'What's wrong with you?' demanded Harriet, keen to be let in on the joke.

Bianca could hardly catch her breath. 'I just,' she started, shaking her head in disbelief.

'Yes?' coaxed Rachel, intrigued.

'I just caught Summer giving Jack a blow job in the steam room!' she exclaimed. 'They are, very definitely, at it.'

'I bloody knew it,' said Harriet, shaking her head.

'Oh God, how are we going to face them at dinner?' Rachel cringed.

'Well, I won't be ordering sausage and mash.' Bianca giggled. 'That's for sure.'

Summer hid in the steam room, too mortified to go to the ladies' changing room, where she would have to face the others. She was dying of heat exposure, but she waited patiently long after Jack had left for his shower, until she heard the giggling voices of Bianca, Rachel and Harriet go past on their way to dinner. Jack waited outside the Ladies' for Summer, aware that there was safety in numbers. He and Summer had some explaining to do, and he didn't want to face the girls alone. Eventually, she appeared with damp hair and flushed cheeks.

'Ready?' he asked.

Summer nodded, but she didn't look too sure.

'Hello you two,' smiled Harriet a little too warmly when the lovers eventually joined them at their table. 'We were about to order starters. Are you ravenous? Or have you already eaten?'

Rachel kicked her under the table. It was too mean to tease them like that. They were obviously already mortified.

'Bread?' offered Bianca politely. 'Butter?'

Summer shook her head and stared into her lap.

'What's the matter?' said Harriet. 'Are you full?'

She and Bianca collapsed into fits of giggles again while Summer and Jack fidgeted nervously with their napkins.

'OK, let's stop this nonsense now,' said Rachel, banging her knife on the table to call for order. 'Right. Jack, Summer, we all know you two are seeing each other, so let's be grown up about it. It's no big deal. In fact, we're very pleased for you. Why wouldn't we be? You're two of our best friends and you like each other. In fact, it's great. The only reason these two are being so childish about it' – she glared at Bianca and Harriet – 'is that you chose to keep it a secret. I'm sure you had your reasons, but it's out in the open now, so let's all just forget about the incident in the steam room and enjoy a nice meal together, OK?'

'OK, Mum,' said Harriet, still giggling.

'OK,' muttered the others, still staring at their laps.

'I think we could all do with a drink,' suggested Rachel.

'Summer's already had one,' retorted Bianca with a cheeky grin.

Harriet laughed so hard that she fell off her chair and had to be helped back up by the waiter.

'Sorry,' said Jack suddenly. 'For not telling you. We've been together for a while, but we had to wait until Tabitha knew. We couldn't have her hearing about us from anyone else, and Combe is such a small village.'

He shrugged shyly, and looked so cute and endearing that the women melted and instantly forgave him.

'We told her a few days ago,' added Summer, still unable to meet the others' eyes. 'So now there are no secrets.'

'No secrets,' confirmed Jack as he squeezed Summer's hand under the table.

'Oh good,' said Rachel with a sigh of relief. 'Can we eat, drink and be merry now, please?'

Everyone nodded enthusiastically.

Jack dropped Rachel and Harriet off first. Hattie was staying at Ivy Cottage again. The Beeches was a big, and now empty, house to live in alone, and at night Harriet swore its floorboards creaked with the footsteps of ghosts. She was much happier tucked up in the cosy spare room at Rachel's in a house full of puppies, babies and good vibes.

'Oh, there's a car parked outside,' commented Jack as he pulled up between Ivy and Rose cottage. 'That's odd.'

He felt Summer's hand grip his arm in panic and suddenly realized what it might mean.

'Make sure you lock the door!' he shouted after Harriet and Rachel as they made their way to the front door.

Jack took Bianca all the way up the drive to the front of Millsborough, where Jock and TJ were waiting.

'Night, night, Bianca,' he said affectionately.

'Sleep well, you two.' She giggled. 'Don't do anything I wouldn't do.'

But Summer wasn't laughing. Summer was terrified.

'I have to call Murphy,' she said to Jack as soon as they were alone.

'I know,' he said gravely. 'Do it now.'

Chapter Seventeen

An Inspector Calls

'Detective Chief Inspector Murphy?' asked Jack when he opened the door to the short chubby man on his doorstep.

The man thrust out a clammy hand and shook Jack's outstretched hand warmly. He was ridiculously overdressed for the weather, wearing suit trousers and a golf jumper.

'Pleased to meet you at last, Jack. I feel as if I know you. Summer rarely talks about anyone else these days,' said the man in a gruff Irish accent.

'Likewise.' Jack smiled. 'You've been a great support to her through all this. I'd like to thank you for looking after her for me.'

'All in a day's work,' said the chief inspector, following Jack inside High House.

'Murphy!' cried Summer when she saw him.

She hugged him warmly and kissed his damp cheek. Patrick Murphy had been the closest thing in her life to a father figure over the past three years. He was a middle-aged overweight copper, a workaholic who was unaccustomed to daylight and prone to bouts of melancholy and fits of rage. But Summer loved him. Murphy did not look well. The recent hot weather had played havoc with the broken veins on his cheeks and his face was even ruddier than Summer remembered.

'Hello, Tabby,' he said fondly to the girl as she reached up for a cuddle. 'Funky hair.'

'So,' asked Murphy as he collapsed onto the couch in a sweaty heap. 'What's the plan?'

Jack threw three plane tickets onto the coffee table and explained. 'We're booked on a flight to New York first thing in the morning. I've got an apartment in Midtown Manhattan. We'll be quite comfortable there. And safe. They won't follow her to the States, will they?'

Murphy shook his head.

'For one thing, they won't know she's there,' he replied. 'And for another thing, I'd bet my golf-club membership that Mr Big will be locked up by the end of the month.'

'No way,' said Summer. 'You've got something on him.'

Murphy nodded solemnly. 'Something big. Something that'll stick this time.'

'I can't believe he wasn't put away after my evidence,' said Summer, remembering the horror of the trial, when she'd been the star witness for the prosecution, giving evidence against the villain who was her ex boss.

'He got to the jury, I'm sure of it,' muttered Murphy darkly. 'Your evidence was as damning as I've ever heard. He was bringing in those girls from Eastern Europe, stealing their passports, forcing

402

them into prostitution. Not to mention the drug dealing. Oh, while I remember.'

Murphy reached into his jacket pocket.

'Two passports. One for you.' He handed Summer her freedom.

'And one for you, little lady.' Tabby grinned.

'We rushed that through specially,' he told her. 'I had to have a word with the Home Secretary himself.'

Tabitha fingered her new passport proudly. She had never had one before. She'd never been abroad. Murphy turned to Summer and smiled.

'You're Sharon Ashton again now,' he said, pointing at the name on the passport. 'If you can remember who she is.'

'I'll remind her,' said Jack.

'So, it's over?' asked Summer.

'Almost,' Murphy reminded her. 'It's not over until you get on that plane tomorrow. Mr Big won't let you go without a fight, and he knows where you are. At least, he knows where your cottage is. As far as we know, he doesn't know about Jack, or this place, so let's just pray it stays that way until tomorrow. In the meantime, we'll be watching you. We'll keep it low-key, but you can rest assured we won't be far away. I haven't kept you alive this long to lose you now.'

'So as of tomorrow,' asked Tabby, 'we're no longer part of the witness protection programme? We're back to being normal people who can do normal things?'

'That's right,' said Murphy, ruffling her cropped hair. 'When you get to New York, you can be a regular American gal.'

'Cool,' said Tabitha. 'I'm going to visit Scarlett in Beverly Hills and she's going to make me a Hollywood actress.'

'That sounds like a great plan,' said Murphy. 'Just remember to thank your old Uncle Murphy when you collect your first Oscar.'

He stood up with a breathless grunt and cracked the bones in his neck with an abrupt jolt.

'Right, I'll be off then,' he said a little sadly. 'You take care now.'

'We will,' promised Summer, walking him to the door. 'And Murphy?'

Murphy turned round. There was a hint of a tear in his watery grey eyes.

'Thank you,' she whispered. 'For keeping us safe.'

Murphy hugged Summer to him as if she were the daughter he'd never had. Keeping this broken little family alive had been the most important job of his life, and their departure would leave a gaping hole.

'Give me a call from time to time,' he said. 'Just to let me know you're OK.'

'I will,' said Summer. 'I promise.'

Simon and Harriet sat side by side on the study floor, wearing matching expressions of con-centration, surrounded by piles of paper and sleeping dogs.

'We're getting there,' said Simon, scratching his head. 'We've paid off the loan shark, the under-takers, the Inland Revenue and the credit-card companies.'

'And we've sold all the furniture, cars, jewellery and two fields,' huffed Harriet. 'Not a lot left, is there?'

Simon shrugged. 'Oh, I don't know,' he said. 'Not many women your age have a stately home and several acres of land. OK, so they might have a few little luxuries like a sofa and a TV, but it's not all bad.'

Harriet smiled weakly at Simon. He was a great guy, she'd discovered over the last few days, as he'd patiently waded through the chaos of her father's financial affairs. She could see why Rachel had loved him so much.

'At least TJ bought the land, not some greedy property developer who would have filled the village with executive homes.'

'You never know,' teased Simon. 'He might be planning to build a dozen mini Millsboroughs right on your doorstep.'

'Don't put ideas like that into my head,' warned Hattie. 'That's a really scary thought.'

Simon shook his head. 'I'm teasing. I was talking to him in the pub last night and he's bought the twins a pony each. He's going to use one field for them and then he wants to build a state-of-the-art stable in the other. Then his plan is to have jumps and that sort of thing, for when the girls are representing Great Britain in the Olympic equestrian team.'

Harriet rolled her eyes. 'They're only two and a half. He's getting a bit ahead of himself, isn't he?'

'Oh, and he wants you to teach them to ride. Says he'll pay you, of course.' Simon gave Harriet a sideways glance to see her reaction. He had a suggestion for her, but didn't know if now was the time.

'I suppose I could do with the money.' She sighed. 'So what's the bottom line, Simon? Will I manage to keep the house?'

'Well that depends on you,' explained Simon. 'The debts are gone, but there's nothing left in the pot. Obviously you need money to live, to keep this place ticking and you're going to need to eat.'

'So, what are you saying?' Harriet looked thin, drawn and scared.

'I'm saying that you're going to have to get a job. That's what most people do to pay the bills.'

'You don't,' retorted Harriet.

'Touché,' said Simon. 'But I'm temporarily "between" careers rather than bone idle.'

'I'm not lazy.' Harriet pouted, slapping Simon playfully on the arm. 'I used to work. Modelling is much more exhausting than most people realize. There's the travelling, the late nights, the early mornings . . .'

'The champagne, the cocaine, the parties . . .'

'Anyway, that's irrelevant. I'm too old to make a living from modelling these days, unless I want to do TV ads for stair lifts and walk-in baths. And I'm not qualified to do anything else. I'm completely unemployable.'

'You could work for yourself,' suggested Simon.

'Oh God, no. I'd be a terrible boss. Anyway, what would I do?' demanded Harriet.

'What about a riding school? You've got the horses, the land, the stables, the skills.'

'No, I couldn't,' interrupted Harriet. 'I'm rubbish

with children. They hate me at first sight.'

'Nonsense,' scoffed Simon. 'Alfie loves you, so do the twins and TJ was saying last night that Scarlett hasn't stopped singing your praises since you saved Bianca's life.'

Harriet smiled shyly. 'Really?'

Simon nodded. 'You're great with kids once you get to know them and anyway, I think you'd make a rather good teacher – a bit scary maybe, especially with a whip in your hand, but good.'

'There's a major flaw in the plan, though, Simon. I'd need money to set it up.' Hattie frowned.

'You have rich friends,' he reminded her.

'I won't take charity.' She sulked.

'It wouldn't be charity. It would be investing in a local business. I'm sure TJ would jump at the chance to extend his business portfolio. Think about it,' suggested Simon.

Harriet's thoughts were interrupted by a knock on the front door and a voice shouting, 'Hello? The dinner lady's here.'

It was Rachel. She had Alfie strapped to her stomach in a papoose and was carrying a basket full of goodies.

'Chicken and avocado sandwiches, tuna mayonnaise rolls, bananas, a couple of melted Kit-Kats and a chilled bottle of Pinot Grigio, straight from the fridge,' she announced, emptying the contents of the basket onto the study floor. The dogs sniffed around excitedly at the prospect of lunch.

'Harriet's going to open a riding school,' announced Simon as they tucked into their sandwiches.

'What a brilliant idea.' Rachel nodded enthusiastically.

'No, I'm not,' said Harriet. 'I'd never manage. It would go bust in about three weeks and, anyway, who would come here? No one even knows we exist.'

'I could help there.' Rachel smiled. 'I can write press releases, organize stories in the local press, put up leaflets in shops and community centres. It's easy, it's called PR. I could "spin" you, "sex you up" a bit.'

'Oh, hark at Alastair Campbell over there.' Simon laughed.

Harriet rolled her eyes, but the seeds of a dream had been planted in her mind.

Once Rachel had left, Simon and Harriet got back to their bills, but Simon's mind was not on the job.

'Hattie, you know Rachel better than anyone these days,' he started nervously. 'And I was wondering . . .'

'Yes?' She knew what was coming, but thought she'd make him crawl.

'I was wondering how I could get her back,' he explained, blushing.

'It's not going to be easy,' said Harriet, cruelly playing with her prey. 'What you did was pretty bloody awful. If you were my husband I'd have chopped your balls off with a blunt knife.'

Simon winced at the thought.

'But she does seem to have thawed slightly. I mean, you're getting on quite well, aren't you?'

Simon shrugged. 'Yes, but she won't even let me sleep in the spare room. She's got me staying at the pub.'

Harriet giggled. 'I know. She's great, isn't she?'

Simon nodded in agreement.

'There might be something,' said Harriet with a twinkle in her eye, 'that would make her see how much you love her.'

'I'd do anything,' said Simon with certainty.

Despite the best efforts of the gardener and his elaborate sprinkling system, the lawn at High House was looking thirsty and dry. The summer had been the longest and hottest on record, and even now, in early September, the air was so humid and close that it was difficult to breathe. But the sky was no longer clear. It was hazy and tinged with grey, and the view of the valley was fuzzy and out of focus. Somewhere on the horizon a storm was brewing, bubbling and boiling in the steamy atmosphere.

The book club took their places on the terrace and clinked glasses of champagne.

'What's with the bubbly?' asked Bianca, sipping her cool drink gratefully.

Summer squeezed Jack's hand reassuringly as he stood up to make a toast.

'To the Combe Village Book Club,' he said rather formally. 'And the best summer I've ever had.'

'You make it sound like it's over,' said Bianca.

Jack took a deep breath and said, 'Well, the thing is, it is. I'm afraid this will be the last book club meeting . . .'

He watched the women's faces drop.

'. . . for a while,' he added, hoping that somehow that could be true.

'Why?' demanded Harriet.

'I'm going away for a while,' he explained. 'On business.'

'Oh,' said Rachel forlornly. 'What a shame.'

'What are we going to do without you?' asked Bianca, looking grief-stricken.

'You'll be OK,' Jack said. 'You've got each other. And I plan to leave in style. I've organized a party here tonight in honour of my girls. It's a kind of final fling, and a thirtieth birthday bash for you all.'

'What? Tonight?' asked Harriet incredulously. 'That's short notice.'

Bianca looked shell shocked. 'How on earth am I going to find something to wear by this evening?' she asked.

'Oh, I'm sure your wardrobe will survive,' grinned Jack.

'I'm not sure mine will,' muttered Harriet. 'Unless the dress code is jeans and wellies.'

'You can borrow something of mine,' offered Rachel. 'A party is a brilliant idea. We'll see the summer off in style.'

'Well I suppose I might be able to find something lingering at the back of a cupboard,' Bianca mused.

Summer laughed and shook her head. She was going to miss these girls.

'In the meantime, let's get on with today's book-club business. Who's going first? Bianca?'

Bianca stood up nervously and unfolded her paper. Their homework that week had been to prepare something they'd written to read to the group. Bianca had decided to go public with her poem. She read the words nervously without meeting the others' eyes. When she'd finished, she sat back down and stared at her lap.

'Bianca, that was beautiful,' enthused Rachel. 'Really lovely. Has TJ heard it?'

Bianca shook her head. 'I'm a bit embarrassed,' she admitted. 'He might think it's really cheesy.'

'It's not cheesy,' said Summer honestly. 'It's heartfelt and honest and true. He'd be flattered that you'd written it for him.'

'You have hidden depths,' teased Harriet. 'You're not all boobs after all.' Of course, Harriet had known that about Bianca for a long time.

'Thanks guys.' Bianca smiled gratefully. 'I was really worried about sharing that with you.'

'I'll go next,' offered Rachel. 'Mine's something completely different. It's a press release for a riding school that will shortly be opening in the village.'

'Rachel, you're naughty,' said Harriet, laughing, after Rachel had read her spiel. 'I haven't even decided to open the school yet.'

'Well you'd better hurry up and get on with it,' warned Rachel, 'because I sent this off to the local papers earlier.'

'Who's next?' asked Jack.

Harriet stood up and explained. 'This is the epitaph for Daddy's gravestone. The vicar's getting a bit impatient, so I thought I'd just bite the bullet and write something. As you all know, I'm not great with words, so it's short and to the point, but I thought this would be fitting and I hope it's what Daddy would have wanted.'

She cleared her throat and read from the notes on the back of her cigarette packet: 'Here lies Larry, the

411

last of the Lilywhite Smythes, sorely missed by his daughter Harriet and his menagerie of dogs.'

'But you're a Lilywhite Smythe too,' Jack pointed out. 'And you're very much still with us.'

'No,' Harriet waved her hand impatiently. 'Only men count in families like mine. One day, hopefully, I'll get married and then I won't be a Lilywhite Smythe any more and neither will my children.'

'I thought you weren't having any children,' Bianca reminded her.

'Well I might. One day,' mused Harriet.

'Well, I'm sure that epitaph is exactly what Larry would have wanted,' said Rachel kindly.

'I do hope so,' said Harriet sadly. 'But I'm not sure the vicar will approve.'

Finally, it was Summer's turn to speak.

'Are you sure you want to do this?' asked Jack, stroking her back tenderly.

The others looked at each other, sensing that something important was about to happen, feeling the tension in the stuffy air. Summer nodded with certainty, held her chin up high and said, 'I'm going to tell you something that you deserve to hear. You've been good friends to me and I know that can't have been easy because I'm secretive and a bit difficult to know. But now I want to explain why I am the way I am, and what led me to be this way. Perhaps if I'd had friends like you when I was younger, none of this would have happened, but it did happen and this is my story. It's a story about a girl called Sharon Ashton – that's me.'

Rachel, Harriet and Bianca listened silently as

Summer spoke softly in her Bristol lilt. They listened to the details of her gruesome upbringing, about her mother's job as a prostitute, the beatings she got from a string of 'uncles' who came and went, the poverty, the deprivation, the drugs and the violence she had witnessed first hand. They listened to the love story that unfolded in the chaos, about the boy from her neighbourhood who was destined for great things but who loved her, Sharon Ashton, more than anybody else ever would. They listened to her as her voice broke and the tears came, as she talked about the unplanned pregnancy, about ending the relationship for Jack's sake, about how she'd missed him desperately and yearned for him as her mum died and the baby was born. They heard about the brave attempts the teenage mum had made to scrape a living and keep her child safe, about the jobs in massage parlours and brothels and the homes in rat-infested squats. They listened to the sick details of Mr Big's business, about young girls from Eastern Europe being smuggled into Bristol, squashed into airless lorries and then forced into prostitution. They heard how Sharon had gone to the police and given evidence against the gangland boss. They learned about Inspector Murphy and the witness protection programme and how Summer had been born from a plan to keep Sharon Ashton alive. By the time Summer came to details of Jack finding her and keeping his promise about putting a light at the end of his garden, there wasn't a dry eye in the house.

'That is the most romantic thing I have ever heard.' Harriet sniffed, dabbing her eyes.

Rachel couldn't speak. She was too shocked by the details of what Summer had been through.

Bianca sighed deeply and turned to Jack. '*The Great Gatsby*,' she whispered in awe. 'You got the idea for the light from F. Scott Fitzgerald. It's the most beautiful thing I've ever heard.'

Jack nodded and smiled. 'I've certainly taught you something. You're quite the literary scholar now.'

High House lit up the angry sky with its twinkling lights. The hot air was filled with the sounds of chattering voices and tinkling glasses. High heels sank into the lawn as hips swayed to the sound of the steel band. Mack looked up from his equipment just in time to see Harriet arrive. She was hard to miss, as she stood head and shoulders above the crowds. Harriet looked even more startlingly beautiful than he remembered in a tight, emerald-green gown. Her fine blond hair fell loosely over her delicate collarbone as she talked to her friends, tossing her head back and laughing at what her companions had to say. She was smiling, but Mack thought she looked as if she'd been knocked down a peg or two since he'd last seen her. Some of the haughtiness had gone, perhaps it had evaporated into the summer sky. Mack wished he could pick her up and place her back on the pedestal where she belonged. But Harriet would have to wait. The steel band were almost finished and he had work to do.

Down the lane, away from the celebrations, Murphy and his partner Smith sipped lukewarm

414

tea from plastic cups and watched Mr Big's men watch Summer's house. She wasn't there, of course, she hadn't been back for days.

Only Murphy had been inside the place and that was just to feed the cats as Tabitha had instructed.

'They're ready to do something,' said Murphy as he huddled behind a bush. 'Let's just hope they're too late.'

'It's all a bit too close for comfort,' agreed Smith. 'The target's only a few hundred metres up the road. I don't like it, Governor. I don't like it one bit.'

The lawn had disappeared under a throng of dancing bodies. Mack expertly spun his records, but his eyes never left Harriet as she swayed sexily to the beat. She had a taut athletic body, and he knew already that she'd be an animal in bed. Every now and then she would glance in his direction and give him a hint of a smile.

'Are you flirting with the DJ?' asked Bianca.

'Oh yes,' replied Harriet. 'That's Clinton MacDonald and we have unfinished business.'

'What kind of unfinished business?' asked Bianca blankly.

'The kind that leads to the bedroom, of course.'

Summer and Rachel laughed as Bianca blushed and wished she'd never asked.

'I love your dress,' said Summer to Harriet. 'Where's that from?'

'It's Rachel's,' replied Hattie. 'I've sold all mine to a second-hand designer shop in Bath, so I had absolutely nothing to wear. Fortunately for me,

415

Rachel just happened to have this fabulous little Chanel number in her wardrobe.'

'It's vintage couture,' explained Rachel. 'She's been eyeing it up for months and tonight I gave in. It was obviously made for some skinny model anyway because it looks much better on her than it does on me.'

Jack stood on the terrace and watched his garden as it heaved with guests. There in the middle were his girls boogying on down to Mack's tunes. He noticed how they shone and stood out from the crowd. He would miss them when he was gone.

As soon as he'd finished his set, Mack made his way purposefully towards Harriet. He had almost reached her when an overenthusiastic little American threw herself at him.

'Hi,' said the American. 'I'm Scarlett. Do you wanna hang out?'

Mack grinned at the girl in a friendly manner and gently removed her hand from his bum.

'Go and find some friends of your own age to play with,' he replied. 'There's a lady over there I need to talk to.'

Scarlett watched as Mack approached the tall blonde from behind and slipped his arm around her long neck.

'When I'm older,' she decided. 'I wanna be just like Harriet Lilywhite Smythe.'

Rachel was wondering where Simon had got to. He'd promised he'd pop in and say hello. She'd organized a babysitter so that they could both be there, and when she'd dressed earlier in the evening it had been for him. She was wearing his favourite blue dress and the diamond choker he'd given her as a wedding present. It suddenly dawned on Rachel that she'd subconsciously been thinking of the party as a date with her husband. She felt gutted that he wasn't there.

Suddenly Rachel became aware of a commotion on the terrace. People were laughing and pointing to the driveway at the side of the house. She could see the crowds part and gradually became aware of a ridiculous scene. A man, dressed as a knight in a full suit of armour, was riding unsteadily on a huge black horse.

'That idiot must have thought it was fancy dress,' she declared to her friends. 'He must be boiling in that outfit.'

The horse and its wobbly rider approached Rachel at speed.

'That's Monty,' she said, confused.

Harriet was too busy laughing to explain. Monty gathered pace as the man struggled to open his helmet and reveal his identity.

'Simon?' said Rachel. 'Is that you?'

Simon pulled on Monty's reins and tried to come to a halt beside Rachel, but the stallion was getting irritated by the novice on his back and decided to gallop full speed ahead. As Simon whizzed past her, Rachel could almost make out the words, 'I love you, Rachel!' before he disappeared down the garden, knocking startled guests onto their back-sides as he went. Rachel ran after the horse and eventually found her husband in a crumpled heap at the edge of the garden, inches away from the sheer drop into the valley below, while Monty nonchalantly tucked into a pint of lager that had been abandoned on the lawn.

'Sorry,' said Simon, struggling to get to his feet in the heavy armour. 'That was supposed to be a grand romantic gesture of love, but it didn't go according to plan.'

Rachel giggled and offered Simon her hand.

'You idiot,' she said. 'You lovely, great big buffoon of an idiot. What were you trying to prove?'

'That I love you,' he said.

Rachel looked at Simon for a long time. She took in the worry lines that had appeared recently and the sorrow in his eyes and it dawned on her that she had no hate left for him. The anger she had felt over Zoe had cooled and turned into a hard ball of pain that had settled into her heart. It would always be there, as a reminder of how things could go wrong, but it was no match for the love that she felt for her husband, even now, as he stood before her, dressed as a comedy knight.

'I love you too,' she replied softly.

'You do?' Simon's worried face broke into a beaming grin.

Rachel giggled. 'I do,' she repeated.

Simon held his armour clad arms in the air and shouted, 'Did you hear that? She bloody loves me!'

And then he wobbled slightly, tripped over his metal shoes and fell flat on his back.

'I can't move,' he guffawed as he rolled around on the grass.

'Neither can I,' spluttered Rachel, clutching her stomach as she laughed. 'You look ridiculous.'

'Help me up,' pleaded Simon.

Rachel shook her head. 'I can't. I can't stop laughing.'

Monty wandered over to see what the fuss was about. The idiot who'd been attempting to ride him had now collapsed onto the ground. The horse licked the man's face compassionately.

'Rachel,' spluttered Simon. 'Get this beast off me. He's got his tongue down my throat.'

But Rachel was no help. She was laughing so much that she'd collapsed onto the grass too. Monty looked at the silly humans, rolling about on their backs, snorted and wandered off to find something more interesting to do.

Simon managed to hook a heavy armoured arm around Rachel's shoulder and he rolled her towards him. Her shoulders were still shaking with laughter. She pulled herself up and sat astride his metal chest. They grinned at each other idiotically.

'Kiss me,' said Simon.

Rachel shook her head. 'I can't.'

Simon's face fell.

'I mean I can't kiss you until you take that stupid helmet off,' she giggled.

'Oh right.' Simon struggled with his head gear, threw it across the grass and held his wife's face gently in both his hands. Then he kissed her with such passion that she could taste the relief, the remorse and the repentance on offer.

Over on the stage, TJ took the mike and spoke to the crowds. 'This is a song that's very dear to my heart,' he began, searching the sea of faces for his wife. 'And I'd like to perform it for you tonight as a celebration of the love I have for my wife, Bianca. Babes, this one's for you.'

Bianca spun round from her conversation with Summer and said, 'TJ? What's TJ doing up there?'

Bianca didn't recognize the tune, but as TJ began to sing, the words were more than familiar.

'I gave my love flowers and said she was fine
I wooed her with words and expensive wine
She got into my head and my heart and my bed
And in the morning I said, "Now you're mine"

She taught me to fly, showed me how to be free
My love was so much smarter than me
She said it was love and that was enough
For a good Catholic boy like me'

'That's my poem,' she said to Summer, but Summer had gone.

Bianca stood glued to the spot, watching her husband sing her words. He stared right at her as he sang and Bianca stared right back in a daze. 'Thank you,' she mouthed across the crowd. He nodded and smiled and then kept on singing his heart out. There was a spark about him that Bianca had never seen before. TJ was on fire and she was the reason. Bianca thought she would faint with the sheer perfection of the moment.

'Are you ready?' whispered Jack to Summer.

She nodded nervously.

'And Tabby?'

Summer nodded again. 'She's in your room, changing out of her party dress.'

'OK, let's go.'

And so Jack, Summer and Tabitha stole away from the party and, like the Von Trapp family, changed into their travelling clothes, got into their car and disappeared silently into the black night.

Rachel lay comfortably in the crook of Simon's arm and traced the line from his chin to belly button with her finger.

'This feels right.' She smiled up at him.

'It feels very right,' he agreed. 'And that, that just then, that was better than right. That was amazing, out of this world, mind-blowing. It's never been like that before, has it? Perhaps we should split up more often if the making up is going to be that good.'

Rachel smacked him playfully on the arm. He was right, of course. They had just made love like they'd never made love before, but Rachel wasn't surprised. She knew exactly what the difference was: for the first time in their marriage, she hadn't had to fake an orgasm. She closed her eyes and silently thanked Ben for teaching her to let go. Rachel drifted off into a delicious, warm sleep, feeling cosy and loved in her husband's arms.

She woke up with a start.

'What was that?' she asked Simon. 'There was a bang.'

'It's just thunder,' replied Simon sleepily. 'The weather's breaking. It's a storm.'

Rachel lay awake and listened to the thunder overhead.

'It's not far away,' she said. 'But I don't think

421

there's any lightning yet. I'm going to have a look.'

She got out of bed and pulled open the curtains. A strange glow hit her face and as she peered out of the window, it appeared that the whole world was ablaze with fire.

'Quick! Simon!' she shouted. 'Call the fire brigade. Summer's house is on fire.'

Rachel ran out into the lane and tried to reach Summer's door, but the searing heat of the flames knocked her back. The entire thatched roof was alight and Rachel could see flames dancing behind every window of the cottage. The noise was deafening as timbers creaked and burning pieces of thatch fell to the ground. Rachel collapsed onto her knees and shouted desperately, 'Summer? Tabitha? Are you there?' A cat appeared from the flames, followed by another and another. Rachel picked them up, one by one, and took them to the safety of her house. They thrashed wildly in her arms, terrified by the flames, tearing Rachel's skin to shreds. By the time the fire brigade arrived, Rose Cottage looked like a burning meteor that had crash-landed in Wiltshire. It was barely recognizable as a home.

'I think my friend is in there.' Rachel sobbed. 'And her daughter. They said they were going home tonight.'

She turned to Simon and said, 'They didn't stay at Jack's. I saw them leave.'

Simon held Rachel to him, but there was nothing he could say. Above their heads, thunder roared and lightning crashed against the black sky. As the fire-fighters struggled to put out the flames, mother nature gave them a helping hand. The heavens opened, and for the first time in weeks Rachel felt the rain on her face. It splashed onto her cheeks and merged with her tears.

Simon and Rachel sat huddled together on the curb, watching the fire die and waiting for news. A fireman appeared in the scorched doorway of the cottage carrying something in his arms.

'Oh no,' said Rachel with her hand over her mouth.

'There's two of them,' said the fireman, sadly. 'I'm afraid they didn't make it.'

Rachel looked up with wide eyes and watched as the fireman gently laid the bodies of the two cats on the grass at the side of the road.

'Poor little mites,' he said, wiping his eyes. 'I've been doing this job for seventeen years, but it always gets to me when the pets die.'

'What about my friend and her daughter?' asked Rachel desperately.

'Oh, there's no one in there,' said the fireman. 'The place was empty apart from the cats. They were curled up in their basket fast asleep. They won't have felt a thing. The fumes will have got to them and they just never woke up.'

'There are definitely no people in the cottage?' asked Rachel, just to be absolutely sure.

The fireman shook his head. 'As I said, the place was empty. Looks like arson, though, so somebody thought your friend was at home.'

'Mr Big,' muttered Rachel to herself.

In the cold light of day, Rachel could see that Rose Cottage was gone for good. The rain drizzled on its charred remains and rivers of black soot ran down Chillyhill Lane. Rachel shivered. There was a cool nip in the air. The storm had broken and now summer was gone for another year. Rachel sighed deeply and made her way up the lane towards High House. The police had said there was no reply in the middle of the night, but Rachel was convinced that Jack, Summer and Tabitha must be there. Where else would they be? She had to find them, to let them know about the cottage. That would be hard enough, but telling Tabitha about the cats would be almost impossible. The poor girl would be heartbroken.

High House was eerily silent and seemed somehow less elegant in the rain. Rachel tried the bell several times, but there was no reply. Jack's Jeep wasn't in the drive. She wandered round the house, peering through windows, trying to see whether anybody was there. The debris from the party was strewn across the garden and the lawn had turned to mud. Rachel knocked on Jack's office window, but there was no reply. She noticed that his laptop had gone from his desk, but other than that, everything looked exactly as it had done the day before. Rachel sat down on a sun lounger on the terrace, stared across the valley and let the rain drench her thin summer clothes.

'They're not coming back, if that's what you're wondering,' said a deep Irish voice out of the blue.

Rachel spun her head round and came face to face with a stout man in a mac.

'Murphy,' he said, with a polite nod. 'DI Murphy.'

'I'm Rachel. I'm their friend.'

'Well, I'm afraid, Rachel, that you won't be seeing them for a while.'

'Where have they gone?' asked Rachel.

'I'm afraid I can't tell you that. But they're safe and that's the main thing. At least nobody got hurt.'

'Try telling that to my husband,' smiled Rachel weakly. 'He's just had to bury a couple of cats.'

As Rachel wandered back down the lane, she noticed a chink of sunshine between the clouds. Gradually, a rainbow appeared. It began at High House, and at the end of the rainbow lay the burned remains of Rose Cottage.

Chapter Eighteen

The Following Spring

Much had changed in Combe over the winter months. Ivy Cottage had turned into a bustling cottage industry, with Rachel and Simon running their small but successful PR and advertising agency from the front room. Most of their income came from representing the new and improved brand that was TJ Mills.

Rose Cottage had been razed to the ground. TJ had bought the land, but was struggling to get planning permission for the new cottage he wanted to build on the plot.

The Beeches had had a much-needed overhaul, paid for by Mack, who'd been the DJ responsible for the funky remixes on TJ's latest number-one album, 'A Good Catholic Boy'. The paddocks and fields around the house were full of ponies and horses belonging to Harriet's riding school. One of the old barns had been turned into a high-tech recording studio, where Clinton MacDonald and TJ Mills spent much of their time. The house itself had recently appeared in *Elle Decoration* magazine as an example of a thoroughly modern stately home.

Millsborough was as fantastically tasteless as always – and had little chance of ever appearing in *Elle Deco* – but its rooms were once again filled with love and laughter. Scarlett had returned to Hollywood to take a supporting role in her step-father's latest movie, but promised to come back in August. Bianca found, to her surprise, that she was quite looking forward to her stepdaughter's visit. The marble mantelpiece in the drawing room of Millsborough was now decorated with three gleaming Brit Awards. Two – for best single and best album – belonged to TJ, the third was Bianca's. She was now officially songwriter of the year.

It was the first warm day of the year and the remaining members of Combe Village Book Club were reclining gracefully on wooden sun loungers on the neatly mown lawn of The Beeches. They lay motionless in the mild April air, drinking in the delicious warmth of the pale spring sun. A fresh breeze rustled the soft young leaves on the trees and turned the pages of the books that lay on the grass. As self-appointed chairwoman, Bianca Mills had decided on that week's reading material.

'We have two books this week,' she said in her cheerful sing-song voice. 'The first,' she continued, sitting up with a grunt. 'Is an Australian child-rearing book which has had fantastic reviews in the papers. It's quite revolutionary in its thinking and has a particularly strong section on coping with your first baby.'

She struggled to sit up under the weight of her

belly and nearly fell off her sun lounger trying to reach the pile of books. She tossed a copy onto Harriet's swollen tummy. Harriet picked up the book with a yawn, turned it over disinterestedly, briefly read the blurb on the cover and then threw it back onto the ground.

'Clinton and I are going to raise Junior in our own unique way,' she announced, patting her stomach.

'Heaven help the poor child.' Bianca sighed.

'I think your selection is slightly biased,' said Rachel, turning onto her flat stomach and feeling delightfully svelte in comparison to her rotund friends. 'You two are both pregnant, but what about me?'

'There's a section on nightmare toddlers too,' said Bianca gravely. 'And in a couple of months time, you'll need all the help you can get to stop Alfie from destroying your house.'

Rachel shrugged. 'OK, I'll read it, but it's a bit like having homework. What's the other book? Something a little more entertaining, I hope.'

Bianca propped herself up on her elbows and grinned excitedly at the others. 'This,' she announced, waving a brightly illustrated paperback in the air. 'Is Judy Jones's new novel.'

'How did you get your paws on that?' asked Harriet. 'I thought it wasn't out for months yet.'

'Jack sent me three proof copies. They arrived from New York this morning.' Bianca smiled proudly and then added, 'With a letter.'

'What did the letter say?' demanded Hattie.

'It was a bit odd really.' Bianca wrinkled her nose.

'It said, "Please forgive me." And it was addressed to us all.'

'How the hell did Gatley get his hands on a book that's not out until the summer?' Harriet asked thoughtfully. 'I swear he's doing this to punish me. He knows I can't stand that Jones woman.'

Rachel was reading the back of her copy with a studious frown of concentration. She scratched her head and bit her lip with a worried expression.

'Have you read any of it yet?' she asked Bianca.

'No, the parcel arrived literally two minutes before I came over here. Why? What's up?'

'There's something seriously weird about this.'

'Let me see,' snapped Harriet, grabbing a copy. '"The Last Days of Summer",' she read. '"A heart-warming tale of friendship, love and long summer days in the country." Oh yawn. Sounds deathly dull to me.'

She turned over the book and read the back. Rachel watched as the colour drained from her face. Bianca did the same.

'Now read the dedication,' ordered Rachel.

'For my friends at the Combe Village Book Club, with all my love,' read Bianca. 'I don't get it. We don't even know this Judy Jones woman. Why has she dedicated her book to us?'

'Because this book is the story of our lives,' snapped Harriet. 'I'm going to fucking kill him. I'm going to go to New York and strangle him. How could Summer let him do this?'

'Sharon,' said Rachel quietly. 'She's Sharon again now.'

'What are you talking about?' asked Bianca,

perplexed. 'Has Jack told Judy Jones all about us or something?'

'Oh shit,' said Rachel, cringing into her lounger. 'There's a whole chapter about teenage surfers in Cornwall.'

'Really? Where?' asked Harriet. 'Are there rude bits?'

'I don't understand!' screamed Bianca. 'Will somebody tell me what's going on!'

Rachel sighed and turned to face Bianca. 'Jack is Judy Jones,' she said flatly. 'It explains everything – his money, the book club, his interest in us.'

'No.' Bianca pouted. 'Jack's a bloke. He couldn't write chick lit. And anyway, he wouldn't do that to us; he's our friend.'

'Don't be naïve, Bianca,' spat Harriet. 'He was using us. That's what last summer was all about. We were his research. Bastard!'

'Wait a minute,' said Rachel. 'Listen to this. It's in the acknowledgements. "This book would never have happened if it weren't for my great friends, Rachel, Bianca and Harriet. They are the most wonderful, warm, inspiring and entertaining women I have ever had the pleasure of meeting and their friendship means more to me than they will ever know. I have spent the best days of my life so far with them and I look forward to spending many more days in their delightful company. I pray they can forgive my intrusion into their lives and hope they can see this novel for what it is – a celebration of their world. I would also like to thank Sharon and Tabitha, for their unflinching love and support, and my agent Gerry Delaney . . .'

Blah, blah, blah. Then he goes on to thank his publisher and all that stuff.'

'I'm going to sue him,' announced Harriet crossly.

'I'm going to have to hide the book from Simon. If he reads that scene about the surfers we'll be separating again,' said Rachel.

'I wonder who'll play me in the film of the book,' wondered Bianca. 'Jennifer Lopez maybe.'

Harriet sat up suddenly. 'I bet my bloody boyfriend knew about this all the time. Mack and Jack have no secrets. I'm going to kill him.'

She struggled off her lounger and half ran, half waddled towards the barn, shrieking, 'Clinton! Clinton! Clinton MacDonald, prepare to die!'

'I suppose it's quite flattering really, isn't it?' mused Bianca. 'He must have thought we were something pretty special to write a whole book about us.'

Rachel smiled affectionately at Bianca and nodded her head.

'At least he's changed our names. Nobody will know it's about us,' she reminded her friend. 'It'll be our secret.'

'He's changed the characters' names but we're in the acknowledgements. Everyone in Coombe will know it's about us . . . Oh well, perhaps there have been too many secrets already,' mused Bianca.

The women lay in silence for a while, each lost in their own thoughts, both remembering the summer before.

'I miss them, you know,' announced Bianca suddenly.

'Me too,' murmured Rachel.

'I wonder who'll move into Jack's house,' mused Bianca.

'It's a mystery,' replied Rachel sleepily.

High House had remained empty all winter, but rumours were surfacing that it was soon to be inhabited again. Some said the new owner was an international pop star, others swore it had been bought by a mysterious drug baron, or a Middle Eastern arms dealer, or a human trafficker. Much had changed in Combe, but some things remained the same.

Rachel could hear her family playing on the other side of the hedge. Alfie was squealing with delight, Delilah was yapping excitedly and Simon was singing 'Bob the Builder' woefully out of tune. The sound of Harriet ranting at Mack could be heard quite clearly across the garden and Rachel could hear Mack replying, 'Hattie, you've got to control that temper of yours. You're eight months pregnant, for Christ's sake!' Rachel lay back on her lounger, listening to the sounds of village life, watching the birds circle above in the watery blue sky and thinking that there was nowhere on earth she would rather be. She was very definitely home.

THE END